Suzanna Eibuszyc

Memory is our Home

Loss and Remembering:
Three Generations in Poland and Russia 1917–1960s

Suzanna Eibuszyc

MEMORY IS OUR HOME

Loss and Remembering:
Three Generations in Poland and Russia
1917–1960s

Edition Noëma

Bibliografische Information der Deutschen Nationalbibliothek

Die Deutsche Nationalbibliothek verzeichnet diese Publikation in der Deutschen Nationalbibliografie; detaillierte bibliografische Daten sind im Internet über http://dnb.d-nb.de abrufbar.

Bibliographic information published by the Deutsche Nationalbibliothek

Die Deutsche Nationalbibliothek lists this publication in the Deutsche Nationalbibliografie; detailed bibliographic data are available in the Internet at http://dnb.d-nb.de.

Cover images:
Kesu01/Bigstock.com; josefkubes/Bigstock.com; Elena Odareeva/Bigstock.com; Aleksei Zakirov/ Bigstock.com; Viselchak/Bigstock.com

ISBN-13: 978-3-8382-1482-5
Second, expanded and revised edition
© Edition Noëma, 2021
Alle Rechte vorbehalten

Printed in the EU

The past is never dead. It's not even past.

William Faulkner

This book is based on my mother Roma Talasiewicz-Eibuszyc's diary, her writings about Warsaw, Poland during the years following World War I and the six long years of World War II, and how she was able to survive in Soviet Russia and Uzbekistan. Interwoven with her journals are stories she told to me throughout my life, as well as my own recollections as my family made a new life in the shadows of the Holocaust in Communist Poland after the war and into the late 1960s. By retelling this story I try to shed light on how the Holocaust trauma is transmitted to the next generation, the price my family paid when we said good-bye to the old world, and the challenges we faced in America.

For my daughters:
You possess the voice that Roma's generation was forced to silence.
S.E.

In loving memory:
Bina Symengauz and Pinkus Talasowicz,
Adek, Pola, Sala, Anja, and Sevek
Their five young children
Icek Dawid Ejbuszyc and Ita Mariem Grinszpanholc,
Sura-Blima and Dwojra and Jakub-Szaya

Dedicated to:
Mother and Father and the memory of
their generation that perished in the
Holocaust

"Seen and Unseen"
A foreword to *Memory Is Our Home*

There are many reasons why survivors decide to record their memoirs. In cases recounting the pre-Holocaust and Holocaust periods, memoirists are often explicit: to bear witness to human cruelty; to speak on behalf of those who were killed; to help successive generations understand what happened to families and a people; to describe how they survived; or to warn about the possibilities of injustice and therefore to seek justice. All these reasons are represented in this memoir, but I am particularly interested in one apparent reason that memoirists, as a rule, don't mention: memoirs give victims a "voice." Memoirs are expressive as well as instrumental. They play a key role in memoirists' transition from victims to survivors. They achieve standing by reconstituting their self-respect after periods of profound humiliation, helplessness, and traumatic fear. As such, survivors' memoirs are important for deliberating on life after ambient death. No other genre is dedicated to exploring this surprising reversal of the natural order.

This memoir, however, is unusual. It is not only the result of a conversation between mother and daughter; it is also constructed in two voices. We learn about the past and the present, or more technically, about intergenerational transmission. I am drawn to the mother's direct account of her experience in Poland between the two world wars, the new realities she encountered, and her life-changing disillusionment that resulted from an exposure to aggressive behavior that came as a complete shock to her and her generation of Jews who were looking forward to an affirmative life. "Home," as in the title of this memoir, would have to materialize where it could: in survivors' memories.

This story takes place after Poland gained its independence in 1918. Roma was born the year before. We overhear Roma telling Suzanna about her family and its Jewish traditions, her romances, and her Jewish and Catholic neighbors. We learn about the family's economic hardships and struggles for its livelihood. These stories matter to Roma, but she concerns herself with the deterioration of life for Jews in the 1930s as a result of popular and organized anti-Jewish hostilities. She reflects on the destruction of Polish Jewry during her and her sister's relocation to Russia during World War II. As acute as her observations are, they are deeply emotional. Suzanna tells us that her mother suffered irreparably: "She was forever haunted by horrific memories....She never stopped mourning." Roma, herself, recalled the "unrest" she felt each day. Virulent anti-Semitism would surely explain that, but it didn't help that she played an active part in the political opposition to the ascendant fascist National Democratic Party: "The mailman looked at me suspiciously. I was sure that police inspection would follow. Being guilty by association was one of the biggest fears in those days."

Suzanna writes about inheriting the emotional burden. One of the significant narratives in this double memoir is the urge for both mother and daughter to remain invisible, to live in psychological hiding, or, as Suzanna commented about her own life, "to be unseen and to be afraid, lest be subject to some kind of harassment." Being invisible was, indeed, the price Roma paid for self-protection from political reprisal and anti-Semitic attack. The fatal paradox of Roma's predicament – indeed, for all members of a vulnerable minority, whether by political choice or by dint of pedigree – was the exigent condition of secrecy, for a furtive existence fuels a vicious cycle of suspicion and further self-concealment.

Roma's story provides testimonial confirmation of a landmark scholarly argument for local culpability in the destruction process during the Nazi era. Launched in 2000 by the Polish-Jewish émigré intellectual Jan Gross, the case for villagers turning against their Jewish neighbors has revised the standard view, which is still salient among students of the subject, that the central Nazi state was exclusively responsible. As she reminds us, Jews felt vulnerable before the Nazi invasion of Poland in 1939. She tells us about her neighbors' dedicated hostility. Indeed, Roma observed that Poles did not see Jews as true Poles, a reality reflected in the distinction she made – significantly, in passing – between a Pole and a Jew. She referred to her childhood's building's courtyard as a self-imposed "prison" where she felt safe. It's surely not by chance that she devoted considerable space to actual prisons where local officials detained her political comrades. Life before the Holocaust became progressively restricted for Polish Jews. Suzanna ratified the account: "Poland, as a nation, has to face its demons."

Importantly, Roma also recalled feeling hopeful. We often read survivors' memoirs as testaments to human degradation, and, indeed, Roma felt "an obligation to bear witness." As Suzanna rightly states, her mother's memoir is a story of tragedy and triumph. But for Roma triumph was not something to declare. Her decisive inclination to look forward, even as anguish darkened her daily existence, was evidently important enough for her to recall that she did so in great detail. Congruent with her time, Roma was a true believer. Her cause was the achievement of human and common national fellowship. We get hints of this early on in these pages: her youthful zeal for learning the Polish language, or her love for the movies and Polish (not Polish-Jewish) literature that opened her eyes "to [the] world outside my immediate surroundings." Her description of Warsaw's streets was particularly evocative – the magic of its beautiful boulevards and elegant store windows. After returning from Russia, she reminisced about "my once beloved city" and her "beloved Poland," a disposition that Suzanna confirmed, for herself as much as for her mother.

Roma joined organizations before World War II that promised a future when Jews and Poles could "coexist." The Socialist Bund movement represented her commitment to making Poland a great country "for all workers." She also joined a workers Esperanto movement to help promote communication across social factions. She participated in the currents of the Jewish Haskalah, or Jewish enlightenment, that, from the 18th century on, redefined Jewish tradition in terms that could ease modern Jewry's integration into secular society. For Roma, this meant affirming her Polish patrimony, but also following a Jewish way of life that, for example, permitted her to venture out to the movies on a Friday night, the Jewish Sabbath that traditionally proscribed such activities, or to regard romance and marriage as a matter of love and not as a means of preserving religious or ethnic boundaries (though she respected those boundaries for herself). A member of her family elected to live in a Polish (Christian) neighborhood. As Suzanna remarked, "My mother's homeland never stopped being part of her very essence."

The real story we can glean from Roma and Suzanna's tandem memoir is what Holocaust survivor Primo Levi called inner "unseen realities." From the outside, the historical narrative about modern Jewry is a delineated story of Jewish attempts at social integration and anti-Jewish persecution. But from the inside, as Roma made amply clear, life for Jews was a "riddle." On the one hand, Jews, like Roma, understood that they did not belong in Polish society. They could see, and feel, that they were disfranchised. On the other hand, many, including Roma, were committed to the prospect of their social acceptance. Did they delude themselves, preferring an illusion to reality and believing, contrary to evidence, that, as critic Jan Błoński noted "the future [for Polish Jews] would gradually become brighter, [when] what actually happened was exactly the opposite"? Perhaps. But I would rather address the riddle from the perspective of those who lived out history from within rather than from hindsight. Roma's recollections help us.

Roma's attachment to Poland and Polish culture; her preference for secular values and a humanitarian ethos was, above all, emotional and beyond anything that she could or, just as important, wanted to calculate. Notwithstanding the evidence, her love for her homeland was paramount. This surely led to some confusion: at one point she refers to the police as a symbol of protection; elsewhere, she describes its wanton brutality. What actually helps us to achieve some clarity is Roma's expression of "rage and sadness": She expected more from her beloved homeland. She commented on the complexity of romance after having previously been betrayed, but I feel that betrayal is the conceit of her story overall. Her commitment to the future was not a matter of self-delusion, something pathological. Even, if not especially, against the background of deterioration, it is the human condition, often with unexpected and sometimes with tragic consequences.

Roma survived. Her life after death granted life to Suzanna and her second generation. Suzanna talks about the third generation. We know that Roma, by writing this memoir, was thinking about posterity. We cannot know for sure, however, what the future looked like for her. Suzanna tells us that her mother died of a "broken heart." This memoir looks forward but is simultaneously burdened with heightened caution. For her, exceptional cruelty was the rule, not an exception. Aggressiveness, she believed, was endemic. She remembered when one of her boyfriends carried a gun "just in case he needed it." Incarceration by the authorities had nothing to do with the law or any other rational standard. It was plainly and crudely an instrument of power. The new order exalted might, not right. Suzanna, like the rest of us, inhabit this new order, knowing "what people are still capable of doing."

The future for Roma and other survivors of extreme violations was surely not as hopeful as she believed it was before the Holocaust. After the catastrophe, fellowship among former enemies, or what we sometimes refer to as meaningful reconciliation, would be an idle dream for her, if not impossible to imagine. Our world is post-rational. We need to understand Roma's unseen realities. After reading her memoir, we can now see that coexistence is a matter of power relations, not comity. Conflict is a normative state of human existence. We should enter unstable circumstances with this significant awareness so that, in defeating impracticable expectations, we are not surprised by and helpless before the relentless evidence. We should recognize human fellowship as a protean negotiation among insiders and outsiders. In light of this memoir, how can we regard human rights without acknowledging the reality of tribal intransigence? Yes, we now should know that, at heart, Jews are Jews and Poles are Poles. Common ground, as crucial as it is for civilization, is brittle. I believe we would be in a stronger position to achieve a more stable world once we fight for it with our eyes open.

＊

Dennis B. Klein
Professor of History
Director of Jewish Studies Program
Kean University, NJ, USA.

Introduction: Suzanna's Story

When the train started to pull away from the platform from Ziebice, my mother became hysterical. I heard a cry that was not human. To this day I have not heard a sound like it, but I understand now. My mother saw herself a deserter, leaving from her country for good; she knew she would never be returning to Poland.

After having lost so much, she was once again going to lose everything—including her identity. In her years in America, my mother's homeland never stopped being part of her very essence. Her upbringing and heritage, her husband's grave, and the ghosts of her murdered family—these things were always at the forefront of her mind, a piece of her forever left to linger in Poland.

Technically, our family left Poland by choice. In 1968-1969, two years after our departure, most of the remaining Jews were forced out of Poland during an anti-Zionist campaign sponsored by the government and its Communist leader Wladyslaw Gomulka. With a political crisis and a bad economy threatening the Communist system, history once again repeated itself and minorities became the scapegoats. The Jews before the war were viewed as left-wing Socialists and Communists; they were seen as responsible for bringing Communism to Poland and therefore blamed for its failure.

When Israel won the six-day war in 1967 and the young Jews of Poland openly celebrated for the first time, the Communist Party was infuriated. Poland was ruled by Russia and Soviet tanks were found in the desert. Israel defeated not only Egypt but also Russia. The Polish party took 'this Jewish pride' and made up a theory that in Poland, a 'Zionist conspiracy' was growing against the government. Mass media and the secret police went on the offensive. Civil rights demonstrations held by students and 'intellectuals' the government, turned into propaganda. An unmistakable anti-Semitic undertone followed, and 'intellectual' and 'Jew' were words used interchangeably to degrade those who criticized the government. Thus began the targeting of Jewish students, professors, and professionals. The result was that most Polish Jews lost their jobs and about 40,000 were forced out of Poland. Of the over 3 million Jews who lived in Poland before the war, about 100,000 Jews remained at the end of World War II. By 1958, 50,000 emigrated to Israel and other parts of the world, the rest chose to stay, and ten years later they were being forced to leave once again. By the time Communism fell in Poland in 1989, only 5,000–10,000 Jews remained in the country, most chose to conceal their Jewish identity.

While traveling through Europe and Israel, I met so many Jewish Polish friends who never intended to leave Poland. They all told me the same story: They had no choice but to flee. They now were living abroad without their elderly parents, who chose to stay behind. Some were in mixed marriages, many had been able to hide their Jewish identity, or were hard-core Communists.

Communism, in theory, was incompatible with religion. The government in postwar Poland saw the church as a counter-revolutionary organization, using its religious influence over the masses, against the dictatorship of the Communists. The Communist government's strategy of condemning the church, however, backfired and instead it drove the Polish people into the church. In 1978, Karol Wojtyła, the elected Polish Pope John Paul II, became an important supporter of Solidarnosc—the union that brought down Communism in Poland in the late 1980s. Lech Walesa, the founder of Solidarnosc, credits John Paul II with giving Poles the courage to demand change. The pontiff told his countrymen: "Do not be afraid, let your spirit descend and change the image of the land, this land."

The climate of anti-Semitism in Poland, of course, was present long before the spring of 1968. My mother lived through the Great Depression of the early 1930s; she witnessed the tension between the working class and the capitalists, as well as the deterioration between Polish nationals and Jews. The state of affairs between Jews and Poles began its sharp decline after the death of General Jozef Piłsudski in 1935 and it continued until the German invasion on September 1, 1939.

My parents, and many other Jewish survivors who had remained in Russian territories through the war, chose to return to Poland and raise families. But life in Poland for Jewish families proved to be challenging. In the summer of 1946, after living with Russia's Communism during the six years of war, my parents refused to join the Communist Party. Our family was Jewish in an overwhelmingly Christian country and by refusing to join the Communist Party, we paid a heavy price. We were excluded from the social structure reserved for party members. My mother could not find a job. My father, after battling frequent bouts of pneumonia in Russia during the war, without any medical treatment, was declared terminally ill with tuberculosis in 1951. He was given a small disability pension. In order to sustain us, my parents were forced to operate a small private business that was strictly regulated by the Communists. This small business, however, could not support a family of four; they had to find other creative ways to trade and break the restrictive rules. My parents and the surviving Jewish community not only were persecuted by the government that controlled the freedom to speak, to think, and to express ones ideas, but they were also encircled by the Polish Catholic Church with their unchanged-for-centuries attitudes toward Judaism. Anti-Semitism in Poland, sanctioned by the Church, never went away. After the war the Church continued its harmful and hostile position toward Judaism and Jews that it had for centuries. The position of the Polish Church was not atypical; it was the same as the viewpoint held by the Vatican and other national churches. Starting in 1978, Pope John Paul II went on a mission to significantly improve the Catholic Church's relations with Judaism. He was the first pope to visit the Auschwitz concentration camp in Poland, where Polish Jews had perished during the Nazi occupation in World War II. He issued "*We Remember: A Reflection on the Shoah*," his thoughts on the Holocaust. He became the first pope known to visit the Great Synagogue of Rome and he established formal diplomatic relations with the State of Israel. He hosted a Concert to Commemorate the Holocaust, first-ever Vatican event dedicated to the memory of the 6 million Jews murdered in World War II. John Paul II visited Yad Vashem, the national Holocaust memorial in Israel, and he made history by touching the holiest of sites in Judaism, the Western Wall in Jerusalem where he placed a letter with a prayer asking for forgiveness for the actions against Jews.

* * *

My father died fifteen years after returning home from the Russian territories. When he died, my mother went into despair. They had been together for twenty years. My mother suffered a severe attack of eczema that covered her face with sores. Even in those days it was known that her ailment was stress related. My mother, my sister, and I had no other family in Poland; my mother had one sister who survived the war, who ended up in America by a lucky chain of events. Together they survived six arduous years in Russia only to be separated on their trip back to Poland after the war. Twenty years would go by before they would see each other again.

When my father died, my mother chose to be reunited with her sister Pola. With a strict quota system in place, it would take another four years before my mother, my seventeen-year-old sister Bluma, and I would leave Poland. I was thirteen years old. Till the last day my mother was uncertain about emigrating. She knew she was going an ocean away, never to return. Educated in the Polish public school she learned at an early age to be a patriot. She would be abandoning Bund's ideology, the duty of keeping watch over Jewish heritage on Polish soil. Bund's ideology taught her that Jews could coexist with other nationals anywhere in Europe while preserving their Jewish identity and heritage. Poland was her homeland and that of her ancestors. Poland was where she felt at home, and where she felt she belonged; she survived Russia with only one hope, to return to Warsaw. In leaving, she would be forsaking the ghosts of her murdered family and abandoning the promise she made to her husband that she would fight for his dream of reclaiming his ancestors' property.

After the war, too, my mother forever lived with the hope that a member of her extended family would be found and walk through the door of our home.

When my sister and I tried to console her on that train leaving Poland, she did not hear us, and it was only later in my life that I understood how my mother felt back then.

* * *

When I first read Elie Wiesel's writings, I realized that the psychological impact of the Holocaust on survivors was real and it was enormous. For the first time, I understood the importance of my mother's stories that she passed on to me when I was a child, and I persuaded her to write about her tragic and triumphant life. My mother hesitated at first, but as I persevered, she agreed. I understand now that for my mother to reenter the world she suppressed for so long was a great risk to her safety and sanity. But for the sake of truth, she relived terror, hunger, and pain. She bravely remembered the family she abandoned in Warsaw and brought them back to life. She confronted the memory of impossible hardship, surviving in Russia, and added her voice to a generation that was silenced by Hitler.

In writing down her story, my mother restored herself and left me with a better understanding of the second generation. With her heartbreaking childhood, her will to survive in Russia, a resolve to pick up the pieces after the war, and the courage to start a new life in America, she leaves behind a legacy of extraordinary spirit, perseverance, and hope for future generations—for my daughters and for me. Until the very end of her life, she tried to make sense of the horrific time she endured. All she could do was to write down her personal account of what happened. It was how my mother was finally able to emerge from her exile and give herself permission to heal.

My mother understood the importance of history and of remembering, not just in regard to the Holocaust, but also commemorating the vibrant Jewish culture in Poland she had been part of, and the legacy they left behind in Eastern Europe. She wrote her story in Polish. My huge regret is that I did not get to work on her memoir while she was still alive. As adults, we never had the chance to take this journey together and emerge from her trauma.

* * *

In the early hours of my fifty-fifth birthday, I received a call that my eighty-nine-year-old mother had died. She was not well for the last months of her life. For the past couple of years my mother lived at the Jewish Home for the Aging, fifteen minutes away from me, and I had gone to see her almost every day. We had made plans to spend that morning together.

In the Jewish tradition, it is customary to mourn the loss of a parent by staying home for a period of a week. I sat *Shiva*[1] for a full month, flooded with memories of my childhood in Poland, a time when I lived in constant fear of losing my mother. Survivors of the Holocaust, my parents had transmitted this fear of abandonment to my sister and me at birth. Now, my childhood fear had been realized. In losing my mother, I lost my only link to my roots and to the family I never knew. In Poland our tiny family of four was alone, but with my mother's death, in an instant, all connections to our ancestors were severed forever; my sister and I had become orphans.

Six years before she died, my mother made her very last trip to be close to me, moving from New York to Los Angeles where I lived at the time. In 2006, the last year of her life, I had a daughter away in college and another still in high school; I felt fortunate that I was able to see my mother every day. We would pass the time talking about her life. Her memory was sound and her blue eyes came always alive with the recollections. Going back in time brought my mother both comfort and torment.

It was obvious to me that there had never been any closure for my mother. She seemed forever bewildered by the events she was forced to live through. Robbed of a life and a family, her anguish increased as she aged. She died of a broken heart, of never knowing what happened to the family she loved. The suffering she endured during the six years she was in Russia became meaningless once she discovered what had happened to the Jewish community of Warsaw.

She was forever haunted by horrific memories. At night, in her dreams, she was always running away from the Germans and from the bombs falling over Warsaw. Her reoccurring nightmares and screaming left me feeling helpless and frightened. During the waking hours she tormented herself with recollections of the family she left behind in Warsaw. And of the horrible fate that awaited them. She saw her brother Adek, sisters Sala and Anja, their wife, husbands, and their five young children starved and frozen to death in the streets of the Warsaw Ghetto. She recalled her large extended family on her mother's side, her uncle Motel and aunt Hadassa with all their children, her cousins. She saw them in the cattle cars that took them to the Treblinka death camp. She saw her brother Sevek, sent to

---

[1] Literally, "seven." According to the Jewish tradition, mourners stay at home and receive visitors during the initial period of bereavement, which lasts seven days following the burial.

the front lines, a soldier without a gun, to serve as a human shield, cold and barefoot, to be killed by either Russian or German bullets in the city of Astrakhan.

My mother never forgave herself for leaving Poland to save her own life and abandoning her loved ones to the horrible deaths that followed. She never stopped mourning. Fixed in my memory are the words she repeated: "My life was spared in Russia but my family died in Poland because of Hitler."

My mother suffered unfathomable losses. My father suffered too. Over time, I came to realize that it is impossible to recover from such a tragedy. After the war, my parents did their best to carry on with their lives and raise their family, but the Holocaust's inevitable aftermath played out on daily basis.

My mother was never able to understand or accept how the Holocaust was allowed to happen. How could the civilized world stand by and watch 6 million of her brothers and sisters being murdered? The years of war changed her; she emerged as a hardened woman no longer able to believe in God. But surviving the poverty of her childhood and teenage years also made her strong, and with this strength she somehow managed to survive the war. She made it through the Holocaust scarred and shattered, refusing to permit herself to experience happiness or joy. I believe this is how my mother paid respect and honored the dead in her family. She trusted no one, never let her guard down, and chose seclusion in place of connecting to others. Consciously and unconsciously, her trauma was transmitted to the next generation, her daughters. The trauma of loss, the disconnection from family and community has influenced how we the children of survivors live our lives. We, too, have built a wall to protect us from the traumatic home lives we grew up in. Even as a small child I found a way to protect myself when I imagined my life was in danger by withdrawing and retreating into my world. I would exile myself and build walls of protection around me. I found this protection under our large kitchen table, covered by a crisp, white tablecloth that reached to the floor. I remember having an abnormal fear of people who came to our home often. I hid in my sanctuary and would not come out until they departed and the world was safe again. Under the table I felt safe and protected; no harm could come to me there. As a child in postwar Poland, countless times I had to watch our friends and neighbors pack their belongings and leave. From those early experiences, I learned that friendships were short-lived and that nothing around us was permanent. In that respect our life after the war was oddly similar to my mother's description of life during the war.

As an adult I was forever torn between letting go and staying connected. Often my mother's gloom was too intense for me, but I continually found myself being pulled back into her world despite myself. My conscience would not allow anything else. And with my mother's death, memories became sacred.

* * *

On the day my mother died, I opened the small white box containing aged pages torn from various notebooks she had kept over the years. Tears stained some of the pages. This was a memoir she had first brought to me six years earlier. In thin, shaky handwriting she recalled heart-searing memories that began with being born Jewish in Warsaw in 1917.

Her rushed handwriting looked as if she was afraid she might forget something or run out of time. Reading my mother's pages took me back to the often-told stories I heard as a child. These stories had haunted my childhood, giving me nightmares of my own, but now I understood their purpose; it was her way to insure that her doomed generation be remembered for generations to come. She guarded this box as if it was a prized possession. She handed it to me right after we got home from the airport, the day she arrived in Los Angeles. On two separate occasions my mother and I sat down to work on the pages together, but other things got in the way. We became fluent in English but never abandoned our native tongue. Now, as I sat alone, looking down at my mother's handwriting, so familiar to me, absorbing her haunting words, I found myself being transported back to my childhood in Poland. I was inundated with flashbacks of the times she and I sat together, my mother describing the life she once had that was forever destroyed.

Theodor Adorno, a twentieth century critical theorist, once wrote that after Auschwitz poetry could no longer be written. He revised this comment in his later work. More recently, I read a comment that determined after such thing as Auschwitz, poetry should only be written about the Holocaust.

* * *

My daughter has convinced me to write about my life. Painful though it will be, I have decided to do this; not so much to preserve my story, but so that my brothers and sisters—and my entire lost generation—will not have perished with their stories untold.

I risk feeling again my stomach gnawed by constant hunger, the clutch of terror in my chest at seeing German planes over Warsaw, and hearing the explosions of bombs, the tormented sleep on an open field with one thin blanket between me and the sky. How can I describe the despair and loss of an entire family, the nonstop guilt, the haunting nightmares, and the chill that seeped into my bones and never quite left?

Still, I know that I have an obligation to bear witness. It was beshert—meant to be—that I survived to write what I remember.

Roma

* * *

My mother's handwriting, her words made me feel close to her. As I started to read her story she came to life on the pages—I knew instantly that I had a responsibility to translate and retell her story.

> I thought of the Campo dei Fiori
> In Warsaw by the sky-carousel
> One clear spring evening
> To the strains of a carnival tune.
> The bright melody drowned
> The salvos from the ghetto wall,
> And couples were flying
> High in the cloudless sky.
>
> —Czesław Miłosz

Part I

Warsaw, Poland, April 1917–November 1939

CHAPTER ONE

In Warsaw, the only running water in our apartment came from a small kitchen sink. In order to wash or relieve myself, I had to use a public bathhouse in the courtyard of our building. I tried not to go there any more than necessary; the bathroom was dirty, dark, and scary. Next to the bathhouse, garbage was dumped into open containers.

The lack of sanitation contributed to the spread of tuberculosis, typhus, and dysentery, but by some miracle our family was spared these illnesses. Still, there were many times in later years—as I slept in the cold of an open field, or when I saw my brother the day he came back from Stalin's labor camps—that I wondered if it might have been better to have succumbed to these diseases than endure what we suffered in our lives.

I was born on April 16, 1917. World War I was raging, and Poland would regain its independence with the conclusion of the war. The casualties were horrendous and the Polish people were impoverish, starving, and frequently dying, but even people living in poverty continued to bear children.

We lived in a tiny, fourth-floor apartment in an old tenement building at 54 Nowolipki Street. I was the sixth and the last child born to Bina Symengauz and Pinkus Talasowicz. My parents named me Rajzla, although on the streets of my neighborhood I was called by my Polish name, Roma.

Mother came from a poor, religious family. Her mother had stayed home and raised eight children. It was expected that our mother would likewise take on the difficult job of raising her six children. But her circumstances would become dire before the end of the war, when my thirty-six-year-old father died suddenly from a simple ear infection. Like most men of his class at that time, he had worked two jobs to support us. Now the burden was on my mother. I don't remember anything from this time because I was only a baby. I can't imagine how Mother managed, with no husband and six young children in a city ravaged by war, where almost everyone was struggling to survive.

My oldest brother, Adek, was twelve years old when Father died. It was considered a blessing by all that the owner of the textile factory where Father worked let Adek take Father's job. I am convinced that we were able to survive that first year due to this generosity.

My twin sisters Pola and Sala were both eleven years old. Hungry as we were, Mother did not have the heart to send them off to work, too. My sister, Anja, and my brother, Sevek, were only seven and four years old, respectively, at the time of Father's death.

My earliest memories are hauntingly painful; they take me back to a day when Mother came home with just a piece of bread. I don't know how old I was, but I can see myself sitting with my brothers and sisters—hungry, cold, and alone in our room, waiting for Mother to return. I sat on the edge of the narrow bed that I shared with Mother and watched the door for hours, just waiting for her. We didn't know where she had gone, but she had been gone all day, and my fear that she was never coming home grew stronger as darkness descended. We were forbidden to light the kerosene lamp when we were alone.

I remember how Mother looked when she opened the door, disheveled and out of breath, as though she had been chased. She paused for a few seconds, walked over to me, and gave me the small piece of bread she clutched to her chest. Turning away from my starving brothers and sisters, I devoured it. Rationally, I know in hindsight that there was no reason to feel guilty; I was too young then to be accountable. But in my heart, I ask myself over and over, "How could I have not shared even a bite?"

* * *

In 1919, when Pola and Sala turned twelve, Mother relented and sent them off to work. Despite working long hours, the low wages they earned did not help much at home. It seems that when Father was alive, the family had managed in the tiny, two-room apartment. However, when Mother could no longer afford to pay the rent, she felt compelled to rent out our kitchen to a couple and their son. But their family grew and eventually there were five people living in our kitchen.

As a family of seven, we had to make do with two beds, three chairs, a large table and a dresser. Finding a place to sleep for everyone was a challenge. We slept two to a bed. At night, Mother unfolded an additional cot and my older siblings took turns sleeping on a hay-stuffed mattress that we placed on top of the table. This was the least comfortable place to sleep, but every spring before Passover we stuffed this mattress with fresh hay, which infused the room with its sweet smell.

Regardless of how little money she had to feed us, Mother secretly saved to make sure we had a proper Passover. She made sure we understood the importance of this holiday: the celebration of the Exodus of our people from slavery in Egypt. We barely saw her for six weeks leading up to the holiday. Mother, along with the other Jewish women in our neighborhood, worked through the night in a bakery to earn extra money making *matzah*. I remember how we tiptoed in the day so that she could sleep. Today, when I contemplate Mother's preparations for Passover—realizing that most days we had practically nothing to eat—I am struck by her devotion to her faith.

Our room was always dark, even in the daytime, since the sun never reached our small window. But the night before the holiday, in the light cast by the kerosene lamp, Mother washed all the dishes, shook out the linens, and cleaned the entire apartment.

Passover began at sunset with a traditional *Seder* that progressed late into the night. Mother always forced me to nap in the late afternoon so that I could stay up late with the rest of the family. I looked forward to Passover, not just because of the religious ceremony and the extra food, but because it meant spring was coming and I wouldn't be cold all the time. It also meant I would be allowed to leave our dark apartment to play with the other children in our courtyard. How I'd run down those stairs! I'd step out into the courtyard and take a long, deep breath, fill my lungs with spring air and turn my white face toward the sun, welcoming its warm rays.

As a young child, I was small for my age and quiet. I was also frail and often sick. I lived in a state of almost constant hunger, but I had no idea that my back was growing round from malnutrition. There were times when, due to my poor diet, my leg bones would pop out of their joints. At first I would cry for Mother to help me, but there was nothing much she could do. Seeing the pain in her face hurt me more than the physical pain in my legs. Medical care was primitive, and most of the families in our neighborhood could not afford to pay a doctor. Instead there were home remedies, like using young onion shoots for skin infections. I don't know how effective they were, but even now, when I smell an onion I find myself feeling better.

When I was six years old, my tongue erupted with an infection that no home remedy could cure. Mother used the last of her money to take me to a doctor's assistant, which was a slightly less expensive way to get medical help. We came home with an awful-tasting liquid medicine, which my brother Adek administered once per day by wrapping a stick in cotton and applying it over my tongue. The tonic stung and I cried bitterly from the pain, but after two weeks my tongue was healed and Adek was proud to have played such an important role in my recovery.

* * *

I was too young to remember when the war ended in 1918, but Mother described to me many times how the other wives, with eyes and arms raised toward the sky, begged God for the safe return of their husbands. Their children danced happily around them, waiting to be reunited with their fathers. I remember sitting on mother's lap as she would put her hands over her face to finish our sad story: "Of course, my husband was not coming home," she would say with a stifled sob. "I had only the black earth that covered his body."

I often wonder what it would have been like to grow up with a father. I never saw a photograph of him, so I don't even know what he looked like. I am told that he was a tall, thin man who had dark hair and eyes. He was a good husband and devoted father. One of nine children from an observant and financially well-off family, Father worked as a supervisor in a textile factory. His other job was in the back room of a pharmacy, which in those days was considered an important job.

My father, Pinkus Talasowicz, was born in 1882, and he married my mother, Bina Symengauz, in 1901, in Warsaw. A Warsaw telephone directory from 1908 lists Pinkus Talasowicz as a weaver, living on 10 Stawki Street. This meant that, for a while, my parents were probably living with the father's in-laws.

His father, my grandfather, Gerson Talasowicz, was a well-known rabbi and teacher in the Jewish community. Grandfather ran a private Jewish school known as a *cheder*, where he was feared by his students and known for his strict discipline. He wore traditional black clothes and always walked with a fashionable walking stick. I often saw people bowing to him and stopping him in the street to ask for advice. Grandfather was an intense, serious man.

To attend grandfather's *cheder*, which accommodated about forty male students, a boy had to come from an affluent family. The *cheder* was located on Stawki Street, across the street from where we lived, on a sizable piece of land surrounded by a fence. The gate was almost always locked. To the side of this property stood a small house, where my grandparents lived with their spinster daughter.

Although Mother and Father both came from religious backgrounds, they were from different socioeconomic classes. I can still remember Mother telling me, her head hanging low and her voice filled with humiliation, how our affluent grandfather never approved of his son's marriage to her. When my parents met, Mother was a motherless girl from a poor family and less educated than Father. She often described to me how she and my father noticed each other on the streets of their neighborhood; how they fell in love and got married. They did it without asking for their parents' permission. Grandfather never forgave his son for marrying beneath his class. When Father was still alive, Adek was allowed to attend grandfather's *cheder* for free. But this single act of kindness that we received from Father's family was terminated after Father's death. One summer morning, after Father had passed, Mother sent the three youngest, Anja, Sevek, and me, to visit grandfather. Upon seeing us at his front door, grandfather grabbed his walking stick and promptly chased us away. We were so startled and shocked that we tumbled down the stairs. We ran home to tell Mother, who listened to our story with tears of shame burning her eyes. After that day, Mother never sent us to see him again.

Although Father's family became strangers to us, Mother came from a warm, kind family of eight siblings who visited often. We remained close for twenty-two years—until World War II ripped us apart. My grandmother died young, but I met my maternal grandfather who lived near us before the war. Mother visited him often, but she usually went alone. I remember hearing that he never helped his daughter or grandchildren because he was stingy.

In those days, it was customary to keep saved money under a mattress instead of putting it in the bank. I often heard Mother express her worry that upon her father's death, the neighbors would be the first to get to his money. The morning that someone knocked on our door with the news that grandfather had died, I watched Mother run to his house. She was right to worry. By the time she got there, the bag of money that he kept under the mattress was gone.

Suzanna
Fear of Holidays

In the mid-1960s, Jacques Derrida, one of the most well-known twentieth century French philosophers, developed an analysis called "deconstruction". Jacques Derrida and his model of deconstruction examines ethical themes in which he describes relationship and faith. When reflecting upon Jewish tradition, Derrida asserted that a person who lacks any kind of concrete faith loses any claim to historical reality. That deconstructive 'faith' is no longer faith and when it ascends, it is something different altogether.

After the war, after such thing as the Holocaust, my mother was among the living, but she no longer believed in God. She was not alone holding such views, there were many who were left feeling as she did. She would repeat this often, if God had existed, six million of her brothers and sisters would not have been allowed to be murdered. At the same time, every Friday night my mother lit Shabbat candles and performed the ritual. She also observed all the Jewish holidays with the traditional religious rituals. Although the war left my mother as a nonbeliever, she stood steadfast and carried out the Jewish traditions she inherited and learned from her family as a child in Warsaw. My mother never stopped being a Jew. The traditions stayed with her, she held on to them, they were the same traditions as they were before the war. Her relationship to faith never became something different.

Jesus never wanted to start a new religion, he died a Jew. The early Christians visibly continued the Hebrew roots, they celebrated Shabbat, Passover, and other Jewish festivals. In 313 AD the Roman Emperor Constantine the Great officially ended the persecution of Christians, the state and church merged as one. By 321, Constantine passed a ruling that Christians and Roman Sun worshippers should unite in observing the Sun or Sunday. In 325, Constantine separated the dates for celebrating the feasts of Easter from the Jewish Passover. He blamed the Jews for the death of the Lord. Separating the customs was to make Christianity have nothing in common with Judaism. This split marks the beginning of state sponsored anti-Semitism. The Roman State and the Church separated Christianity from its original Jewish roots and the persecution of the Jews continued for century after century after.

Countless times I have reflected on my childhood in the city of Ziebice, where my parents were forced to settle after returning to Poland from six years of exile. They were among the 86,500 Jewish refugees throughout the Russian territories who had survived. With documents in their hands, they returned in the summer of 1946 and attempted to return to the places of their birth, Warsaw and Łódź, but were unable to receive permission to do so. According to J. Adelson's book[2] published in 1993, 124 transports with 86,563 Polish Jews left Russia for southwestern Poland, a region that belonged to Germany before World War II. They were made to settle in forty-two towns in the spring and summer of 1946 as part of repatriation.

Historically more Jews have lived next to their Catholic neighbors in Poland than anywhere in Europe. Jews had been expelled from Western Europe, England, France, and Germany. Societal and political discrimination toward the Jews has existed in most Christian countries. Persecution, pogroms, social hate, forced baptisms, and conversions stain European history. Jews were blamed for the Black Death (1347–1351). Black Death, the bubonic plague, was spread by rats that came on trading ships from Asia. In the warmer weather, the plague grew with greater fierceness giving the infection a mysterious quality in the medieval times. It spread through human contact and through the air; one could be infected by simply inhaling. The European Christian masses subscribed to the notion that the Black Death was ravaging their land because they allowed the Jews to live in their midst as Jews. From 1349 until about 1390, the Jewish communities of France, Germany, and England almost completely disappeared. If Jews died at a lesser rate, this can be attributed to the sanitary practices of Jewish law, like washing hands many times throughout the day. Jewish law also has strict sanitary conditions in burying of the dead. Leaving corpses unburied helped the conditions that spread the bubonic plague, typhus, and other diseases.

The Spanish Inquisition followed. Pogroms of 1391 were especially brutal, Jewish communities in Seville, Castile and Aragon were massacred, their homes plundered, in the end they were faced with the choice between baptism and death. In addition, there remained a significant population of Jews who had professed conversion but continued to practice their faith in secret. Known as Marranos, the Marranos were denounced as a danger to the existence of Christian Spain. In 1478 inquisitors were named to address the issue. The Inquisition remained a force in Spain and its colonies for hundreds of years (about five hundred) and was finally suppressed permanently in 1834. The Portuguese Inquisition was suppressed in 1821. The Holocaust came next.

Jews flourished in 15th century Poland; most merchants and artisans were Jewish, all under the protection of the king. By 16th century, elders were elected, as a rule, from among the local wealthiest (kahal) and governed the Jewish community. By 1550 the Polish King recognized that

---

[2]   Adelson J., *W Polsce zwanej Ludową.* [w:] *Najnowsze dzieje Żydów w Polsce w zarysie (do 1950 roku)*, red. J. Tomaszewski, Warszawa (1993).

Jews could select their own leaders. Jewish Nobility (szlachta) was represented to the parliament (sejm).

The establishment of Poland is traced back to 966 when the pagan state converted to Christianity. Within several decades Poland was recognized by the papacy and the Holy Roman Empire. In Poland, the Church supported the state, and in return received key government titles. To safeguard Christianity, Polish Church remained acutely anti-Judaism.

The Blood Libels have their origins in England, as far back as 1144, and France since 1171. As Jews moved east, by the middle of the 16th century, ¾ of all Europe's Jews lived in Eastern Europe. Anti-Semitism and the societal hate followed Jews to Eastern Europe. In Western Europe those superstitions mostly disappeared, never to return. In the 17th century, blood-libel increasingly spread to Eastern Europe, to Poland and Lithuania. Blood Libels never disappeared from Eastern Europe as they did in the West, and were propagated by the church.

Blood libel, also known as blood accusation, the superstitious claim that Jews ritually sacrificed Christian children at Passover to obtain blood for unleavened bread, first emerged in medieval Europe in the 12th century and was revived sporadically in eastern and central Europe throughout the medieval and modern periods, lead to the persecution of Jews. During the sixteenth century, while Poland became a haven to different religious groups, the Catholic Church continued its harmful and hostile beliefs toward Judaism and Jews. This negative preaching lasted for centuries, reinforcing the social attitudes of contempt toward the Jews. The Polish hierarchy and clergy were determined to create and preserve what they conceived of as a 'Catholic Poland'.[3] It was 1978, when Pope John Paul II went on a mission to greatly improve Catholic Church's relations with Judaism.

As a child, I never quite understood Mother's anxious behavior during the Jewish and Christian holidays. She seemed to want to make us invisible. Holidays were times to stay indoors, to be unseen and to be afraid, lest be subject to some kind of harassment. This behavior on her part only intensified the fear in my imagination.

In Ziebice, with a dwindling Jewish population, we did not go to a temple to pray or celebrate our own religious holidays. The temple was turned into a warehouse by the late 1950s. Every Friday night, my mother lit a Shabbat candle behind closed doors. She covered her face with the palms of her hands and recited a short and emotional prayer. She would never explain to her young daughters the Hebrew words of the prayer or what it meant. This unexplained act brought its own kind of discomfort. Although the war had left my mother a nonbeliever, she stood steadfast and on the Sabbath she would carry out her family tradition she had learned as a child in Warsaw. Surrounded by the hostile environment of

---

[3]   Edward Flannery, *The Anguish of the Jews* (1985).

the Catholic Church, the Communist Polish government, and her own post-traumatic stress, she found some degree of comfort in the rituals from her childhood; that was the only thing she had left of her murdered family.

I never realized how deep-rooted my mother's fears were. I always imagined those were her fears alone, but they were not. Her fears and suspicions have century's long tradition. In the Middle Ages under Christianity, Jews were often forbidden from appearing in public during the Christmas holidays and Christmas Eve frequently marked the beginning of attacks on Jews. Many Jews observed Nittel Nacht by avoiding to leave their homes. Many also sought to avoid experiencing any pleasure or joy on Christmas, to ensure that no glory would be given to the day. Another belief during this time was that Jews feared Jesus for spreading false teachings and abstained from reading the Torah. Nittel Nacht was derived from the Medieval Latin name for Christmas, natalis, although it is also often associated with the Hebrew nitleh ('the hanged one'), which was used in medieval times to refer to Jesus.

Throughout my childhood, I was aware of the Church's anti-Semitic attitudes and this was especially rampant during Christian holidays: the annual celebration of the birth of Jesus at Christmas and his resurrection at Easter. Jesus and his mother Mary were Jews from the Galilee. Beneath the Church of the Nativity in today's Bethlehem is where Jesus is believed to have been born. I never knew about any of this while growing up; instead the rumors I heard in postwar Poland was that Jews were responsible for killing Christ. This folklore had its origins in the Church and was widespread, accepted by Christian Poles and passed from one generation to the next. The fact that the Middle East region at the time when Jesus lived was under Roman authority and that crucifixion was a means to terrorize and punish the subjugated people never came up. While in Poland, I was never exposed to historical information that Jesus preached and campaigned for social justice, that his popularity grew during Pontius Pilate's power in Judaea, and that he was condemned to death as a political agitator. It was when I came to the United States that I heard for the first time that Jesus was actually a Jew who lived at the time when the Middle East region was under Roman control and was crucified by the Romans.

Celebrating Passover and eating *matzah* in Poland also brought with it another kind of shame. Rumors still circulated that *matzah* was made with the blood of Christian children. Still, I remember the holiday of Hanukkah with joy. I was able to merge this holiday with snow and Christmas trees. And with candy, chocolates, and the oranges that made their way to us all the way from Israel, which we hanged on our Christmas tree as decorations.

To this day, I do not hold an emotional attachment to holidays. I welcome those days with a nagging sense of trepidation. It is only in my adulthood that I finally understood how this disconnection came about.

CHAPTER TWO

The American allies established soup kitchens to feed the hungry and impoverished Polish people, as the country slowly recovered from World War I. Every day, before going to work, my brother Adek took me there, and I would get a cup of milk and a piece of bread. America also helped open orphanages, and many children who weren't orphans lived there because their parents couldn't care for them. Thankfully, Mother never considered sending us there.

Winters were hard on everyone, and in Warsaw the winters were especially severe. I wanted so much to go out and play despite the cold, but I didn't have shoes. I stayed inside and all I could do was work on defrosting the one small window of our room so that I could look outside. But as winter progressed Mother had to cover the window and seal the frame with rags to keep out the freezing draft.

Coal was expensive and Mother could not afford to burn it every day. Twice a week—usually on Tuesdays and always on Fridays before the Sabbath began at sundown—Mother managed to burn a little coal in our oven. By Saturday morning much of its warmth was gone, but since we were all home together we had another kind of warmth.

One Friday night, as we sat around the table in the warm glow of the Sabbath candle, Mother looked down at the potato soup and then up at us. "Poor but always together, like a mother bird with her newborn chicks in a nest," she said. After dinner, Adek would bring out a book of Jewish songs and we would all gather around Mother and sing. In our limited way, we created a loving and joyous atmosphere for the mother we loved beyond words. My mother worked hard, she was always busy with chores, but on Sabbath night she appeared to be carefree and even happy. In the flickering light of the candle Mother looked content.

For us children, the Sabbath was also hard. Mother insisted that we strictly observe the Sabbath rules, so from the Friday evening meal until the concluding *Havdallah*[4] prayers on Saturday night, we

---

[4]   *Havdallah* means 'separation' and the blessings mark the distinction between the holy time of the Sabbath and the secular time of the rest of the week. The earliest time the service may be recited on Saturday is when three stars are visible in the night sky.

were not allowed to do anything, even read or write, and all foods throughout Saturday were eaten cold. Our neighborhood was Jewish and Sabbath mornings were peaceful, our courtyard as well as the street outside were quiet and the neighborhood shops were closed. As soon as we saw three stars in the sky, we quickly said the blessings and lit the kerosene lamp. Afterward, Mother always managed to prepare a warm meal.

* * *

When I was six years old, I got my first pair of shoes. My older sister Sala went with me to buy them, and we walked home from the shoemaker's store holding hands. It didn't matter that they were uncomfortable and made of wood. I walked proudly in my new shoes, my head held high. But on the way home, I saw so many children without shoes turning their heads and looking at me with envy, I felt guilty in the midst of my happiness.

I don't remember ever getting new clothes, although I did have two of everything because I wore the clothes that my sisters outgrew. Mother washed one set while I wore the clean one. When my sister Anja turned twelve, Mother arranged for her to work as a seamstress. At that time, it was customary for a young person to work as an unpaid apprentice for the first few months. I overheard Mother talking to our neighbor on Anja's first day of work: "What can I do?" Mother said. "I know Anja is being taken advantage of, but we need to eat."

"The rich capitalists have no pity," the neighbor agreed. "They take advantage of children most of all." She turned and walked away.

After a few months, Anja was bringing her wages home on Friday, along with my three other working siblings. Everything they earned was given to Mother, so life slowly started to get a little better. We were able to afford meat and *challah* for our Sabbath dinner. Daily meals now consisted of soup, bread, herring, and onions, but we still could not afford fruit. When someone was sick, Mother would buy a lemon to add to tea; otherwise, fruits were for rich people. It was common when you walked through the public gardens to see wealthy mothers loudly encouraging their children to eat their bananas and oranges. I would watch, imagining the taste of these exotic fruits.

Although Mother observed a strict Sabbath and we celebrated all of the other Jewish holidays, we dressed in Western-European fashion. Warsaw was home to many acculturated Jews who dressed and looked like Polish nationals; a large number of Jews, however, remained Orthodox and Yiddish-speaking and dressed according to traditional Jewish customs. The overwhelming majority of Jews lived separate lives from Polish Catholics and listed Yiddish or Hebrew as their native language.

In the northern part of the city, Nalewki Street, the main boulevard, was the center of Jewish life in Warsaw. Here, the stores, street peddlers, and the Jewish restaurants bustled with life. Most of the Jews who lived in the city were just like us: poor, working class. We were shopkeepers, bakers, shoemakers, painters, barbers, and tailors. We stayed together, living in certain neighborhoods and even on specific streets. Some non-Jewish Poles did live toward the end of Nowolipki Street, and we learned not to go there. To wander into this part of Nowolipki Street meant the possibility of being beaten or pelted with rocks.

Our street was long and narrow. We had a few small grocery stores, two bakeries, and a milk store, *mleczarnia*.[5] When we had money, one of us would run out to the bakery in the morning for fresh Kaiser, onion, or caraway seed rolls. In the evenings, men went from courtyard to courtyard with baskets full of fresh, hot bagels. These crisp bagels were my favorite. They were braided and baked in a special way, with a crust that crackled when I bit into them. On good days, we ate them with butter.

By law, stores in Poland had to close at seven in the evening, but every store had a back door. This setup allowed many stores to stay open longer for people who needed to shop after work. The police knew about this back door shopping and often enforced the law by giving summons to the shop owners, but a small bribe could usually keep the police away for a few weeks.

The sanitation inspectors paid visits as well. There were high penalties if businesses or apartment buildings were not clean and orderly, and with our crowded living quarters it was difficult to pass these inspections. The Jewish apartment and business owners in our neighborhood often endured the insults of the sanitation inspectors. Even as a little girl, I understood that one penalty for even the small-

---

[5] Literally, 'milk store,' where people could buy fresh milk from dairy farmers who brought it to the city.

est offense was to hear the officials in our courtyard sneer: "Jews, go to Palestine."

Much of my childhood was spent in the courtyard of our building. After a bone-chilling winter, I was able to hold my face up to the warmth of the sun, but the courtyard was a prison of sorts.

* * *

Like all the tenement buildings in our neighborhood, our building's caretaker served as both a janitor and watchman. He was the only Gentile living in the building, and some of the neighbors needed him at times to light the fires in their stoves on the Sabbath. For this, Pan Juzek would get compensated with a few groszy.

Pan Juzek was a cranky old man who walked with a limp. His face was wrinkled and his hands were always dirty. His worn-out cap covered his head, his overcoat was fastened by a thick leather belt, and his pants were tucked into rubber boots that I never saw him take off. He lived alone in a tiny room off the main entrance to our building.

Aside from taking care of the grounds, Pan Juzek was responsible for locking the front gate at exactly ten o'clock every night. At that time we were expected to extinguish all kerosene lamps, and I lived in dread of the pitch-black hallway and staircase outside our apartment. If anyone needed to go outside after ten, a candle and matches were absolute necessities.

The front gate had a bell that was connected to his room and sometimes I would hear the bell ring after ten p.m. I waited to hear the squeak of the wooden gate, and then hear Pan Juzek grumbling curse words I did not understand. At least I knew that Pan Juzek had come with the key.

There were times when I fell asleep waiting to hear the gate open, like the night when my sister was in agony from an ear infection. As I watched mother leave to get some medicine, I knew that it was after ten. She lit her candle in the doorway and disappeared into the darkness. I had no way of knowing how long it would take for mother to get back, but I did know that she did not have the few groszy to compensate Pan Juzek for getting up at that ungodly hour. That night I had a nightmare that Mother was screaming and shaking the gate to come back to me, and no one was in sight to let her back into the courtyard.

Our neighborhood streets were over-run with wild starving dogs that lived on the scraps and bones they found in the garbage. It was also not uncommon to trip on a feral cat lurking on the stairs. They, too, were starved, and their hunger overtook their gentle nature. Pouncing up in the dark, they would scratch and bite at anyone. Rats and mice lived between the walls and the floors. At night they came out looking for any crumbs they could find. I became obsessed from an early age with keeping my blankets up high on my bed as the horrible little demons scraped across our wooden floor.

Jews often went begging from house to house. Some would play the accordion and sing Yiddish songs in the courtyards, just to make five groszy to buy a piece of bread. Still, even poor people managed to give something to the beggars. I remember the pride I felt as I watched Mother search through the cupboard for something to give an especially hungry-looking beggar with a sad-eyed, little boy. She sent me downstairs with two small pieces of *matzah* left over from Passover.

* * *

Since most children had put their schooling on hold during the Great War, now there were thousands of children who needed to catch up, along with the many just starting their educations. There weren't enough public schools for even half of the school-aged children in Warsaw, and although new schools were being built, construction was slow. Private schools always had room, but only wealthy families could afford to enroll their children.

In 1924, my brother Sevek and I tried unsuccessfully to register for the third and the first grades, respectively. Mother decided to send Sevek to a private, Jewish school. He needed to start his education as soon as possible. She was fortunate to find him a school where she would pay only what she could afford. On the first morning, Mother left wearing her most determined face, marching with her son to register him.

Sevek's new school was progressive, and to Mother's surprise she discovered that Sevek would also be learning Polish. I had mixed feelings the first day I watched Sevek go to school, leaving me behind. I was happy for him but felt sorry for myself. I wanted so much to go with him, not that I would dare complain. The Jewish school he attended allowed girls, but my Mother did not have the money to send us both.

I waited in the courtyard of our building for Sevek to come home from school every afternoon, rain or shine. When he arrived I would grab his books, honored just to carry them upstairs for him. Sevek was an eager student and he enthusiastically shared at home what he was learning. Mother was elated and I vowed to be like my brother if given the opportunity. Meanwhile I copied everything he did for homework. It didn't take long for me to learn the Polish alphabet, and I soon moved on to reading from all of his Polish schoolbooks. I had plenty of time to teach myself while the rest of my siblings were at work and Sevek was at school. As the months went by, my pride at learning to read and write washed away my sorrow.

One night Sevek was looking over my shoulder as I copied his work.

"See, Roma," he said. "You are not missing out, you are learning."

One year later, the construction of a beautiful, modern elementary school was completed right in our neighborhood. It had playgrounds on each side, newly planted trees and flowers, a bathhouse for the students, and even a small house in the rear for a caretaker. It was a school straight out of a fairy tale. Staring at this breathtaking building, I made up my mind that I would be admitted to that school at the beginning of the school year, no matter what.

It was still dark the morning that Mother and I left the apartment to register me at my fairy tale school. My heart sank when I saw the long line of mothers and children already waiting there. I watched silently—tears rolling down my cheeks—as the front door of the school opened and closed, opened and closed, each time letting in only a few mothers and children. Each time I looked up at Mother, and she smiled at me and patted my shoulder in a consoling way that confirmed my fears, that they would never get to us.

We had been waiting in the line for two hours when something happened that to me could only be described as a miracle. My eyes were fixed on the window of the registration room when suddenly a well-dressed man inside walked to the window and opened it wide. I didn't hesitate. I didn't worry that a Jewish woman, a teacher saw me. I climbed through the low window and took my place in front of the big desk. I stood there for the rest of the morning.

I was asked to come back with my mother when my turn came, and I momentarily panicked, but then a Jewish teacher stepped forward, put her arm around me and said that she knew me well. She assured the school official that there was no need to bring my mother, and offered to vouch for me. Mother's face lit up with amazement and joy as I came out of the school waving a paper that showed I was registered for second grade.

The first day of school on September 1, 1925 was one of the happiest days of my childhood. I walked proudly with all the other children from my street, wearing the same uniform as the other girls—a navy blue dress with a white collar. The boys, in their dark slacks and white shirts, looked so handsome. It wasn't until I got to my assigned class that I realized that the boys and girls were together in all the classes. This was surprising to me, because boys and girls in the Jewish schools usually studied in separate classrooms.

There was a school library where I could check out any book I wanted. I loved to read and so I used this privilege more than anyone I knew. As most of our families did not have the money to buy books, the mothers in our building worked out a way to buy one book that we could all share. I studied each day with my classmates who lived in my building or on my street, and this way we all helped each other, and we all excelled in school. In the second grade I was already memorizing Polish poetry and short stories. We had a gym at one end of the school's corridor. Twice a week we went there dressed in black shorts and white tee shirts to climb ladders and to jump on a trampoline.

In spring, during recess, we would play outside in the sun, dancing in a circle and singing. In the winter, we also went outdoors for an hour, despite the cold. As a deterrent against the spread of tuberculosis, the classroom windows were opened to bring fresh air and ventilate the rooms. The school did not have a cafeteria, so we ate breakfast outdoors during the twenty-minute morning recess. In bad weather, we ate in our classrooms.

At the end of the school year, anyone with two low scores in any subject had to repeat the grade the following year. I didn't have to worry about such things. I graduated at the top of my class and marched home with a diploma in hand and a wide grin on my face. I knew that some children had not passed, because I saw them crying bitterly when they learned they had to stay another year in the same grade.

During the summer break, wealthy children went with their families to the well-known summer towns and health spas of Falenica and Otwock. They came back suntanned and rested. As Mother could not afford such things, I stayed home and played with the other kids on the street or in the courtyard. We entertained ourselves by playing with a ball or jumping hopscotch, but I lived every day with the anticipation of being back in school in September.

* * *

At home, life got easier. By 1925, four of the six siblings were working. The typical work week in Poland was six days for Jews and Gentiles. The Poles, like the Jews, were strict in their Sabbath observance. However, the Polish Sabbath is observed on Sunday, the first day of Jewish work week, and according to Polish law everything had to be closed on Sunday. Since the Jewish economy would have a hard time surviving on a five-day workweek, most Jews secretly worked on the Polish Sabbath.

Warsaw was already terribly overpopulated. People came to the city from smaller towns in search of work. Those who already lived in Warsaw would make room in their own living space for a bed and rent it for 15.00 złoty a month and this extra income helped people to survive. Many people also lived in basements or attics where rents were cheap. These people worked hard, often doing seasonal work. They worked from sunrise until midnight, so that it hardly mattered where they slept. The goal was to make as much money as possible before the season ended.

In nearly every city and town with a Jewish population, a *Kehilla* organization was established to offer social and religious support to the poorest in the community. Every Saturday, after Sabbath services concluded at the synagogue, volunteers went from courtyard to courtyard with large baskets, collecting donations to feed the sick in the Jewish hospital. People gave them cheese, bread, butter, and fruits; whatever they could spare.

When a doctor was called to a poor home, he often refused to accept any money. Our neighborhood doctor came whenever we needed him—day or night, rain or shine—always wearing a suit. Dr. Szolemski had a kind face, and his huge form filled the doorway. I thought his black bag was magical; it seemed to contain everything that was needed to treat us when we were sick. Nearly everyone was weakened from the deprivation suffered during the war. A shortage of food, coupled with our living in crowded rooms with the windows tightly closed during the winter months contributed to the tuberculosis epidemic that was raging throughout Poland. This devastating disease claimed entire families. There was no treatment, prevention was the only cure. I remembered hearing Mrs. Meir upstairs crying and begging God, to no avail, to save her son. Even Dr. Szolemski was helpless. We were spared this deadly disease although there were seven of us living in one small room with five more people living in our kitchen. Ironically, a quarter of century later, tuberculosis affected my family with devastating consequences.

At school we had to obey strict sanitary regulations. In addition to opening the windows during recess to let in fresh air, our teachers kept the classrooms clean and made us scrub our hands before eating. A hygienist would come weekly to check us for cleanliness, especially our hair, because there was also an epidemic of lice in Poland. The treatment for the unlucky child was to have his hair cut very short and the scalp saturated with kerosene. Sevek was the unlucky one in our family. As the kerosene-saturated cloth was rubbed on his scalp and burned his skin, his indignant cries reached the entire neighborhood.

One day, a classmate invited me to her home to do homework together. I went without giving it much thought, and spent a few hours working on the homework at her house. During that time, my mother became worried and went to school to look for me. The school's caretaker told her that all the children were gone, and she began combing the streets. When I finally headed home, I saw her pacing in front of our building, her arms folded across her chest as if holding on to herself. I ran toward her, as she managed to say, "Where were you?" while swallowing back her cries as tears rolled down her face. My mother had imagined that something terrible had happened to me. Of course, I heard and saw signs of anti-Semitism in our neighborhood, but it had never occurred to me that it would be ever directed toward me. I promised myself that I would never make her worry like this again.

I was never a difficult child. I loved my mother very much and helped her in whatever way I could, often going to buy wood or coal and never demanding things from her. I was the quiet child at home, as well as in school. I never complained that I had to do without so many things. Instead, I made the best of my circumstances. Mother was proud of the way her two sons and four daughters lived in harmony.

Every season brought something different to our lives, and the seasons gave meaning to our otherwise colorless existence on Nowolipki Street. Spring brought life with its green grass and budding trees, and the flowers blooming in hues that we saw nowhere else. I thought May was the most beautiful month of all, with the beautiful chirping of birds and fragrance of lilac in the air. On Saturday and sometimes on Sunday mornings in the summer, my family carried blankets and a basket of food to the nearby Praga Woods, on the east bank of the river Wisła, where we filled our lungs with fresh air after a long week of hard work.

Summers in Warsaw were as hot as the winters were cold. To keep our food from spoiling, we kept it in a large container together with a block of ice. As the days, weeks, and months after the war passed smoothly, we finally relaxed and allowed ourselves to think the sun was shining for us, even if we were still living in that small gray room on the fourth floor. The sunshine entered our lives in spirit, and we allowed ourselves to believe in a bright future.

Suzanna
My Mother in New York

My mother would awaken at six in the morning and take the one-hour subway ride from the Bronx to Manhattan. With an address scribbled on a piece of paper and directions from strangers, she managed to get to work and back home again. She was determined to make the best of her new situation. She was a survivor and she was not going to surrender to her fears. She took a job in a cosmetic factory, working for minimum wages and long hours.

In Warsaw she had studied French and Esperanto, spoke Yiddish and Polish. She had become fluent in Russian. And so, at the age of fifty, she started again, enrolling in school and attending nightly language classes after working in a factory all day long. She soon became fluent in English, and two years later she was working in a bank. I watched her navigate through her new life, never giving up and never complaining. She did not burden us with her worries and problems, she buried those deep inside.

My mother's love for reading never faded away. Instead of the stories she read as a child about Konopnicka's heroine Marysia, now the books she read were in English. She would check them out from a nearby library in the Bronx where we lived. The first English book my mother introduced me to was *A Tree Grows in Brooklyn*[6], excited that we could share it. She fully identified with Francie Nolan, the eleven-year-old girl who sees the world around her with a keen eye for detail—and who lives in a humble apartment in a run-down section of Brooklyn.

My mother never knew, but as Hitler and his enthusiastic supporters were burning millions of books that were not about the Nazi propaganda, in America, a grassroots movement developed. As Hitler attempted to strengthen fascism, American librarians and everyday civilians encouraged to read more. Librarians and ordinary people started an extraordinary program: 120 million, small, lightweight paperbacks were collected, for troops to carry and read while fighting Hitler's evil in godforsaken blistering and frozen parts of the world. The most popular book American soldiers read was *A Tree Grows in Brooklyn* by Betty Smith. The first book my mother read in English, decades later.

---

[6]   A novel written by Betty Smith, published by Harper & Brothers in 1943, New York City.

CHAPTER THREE

I loved going with Mother on Fridays to shop in the open market where food was fresh and less expensive. Many Jews and Gentiles from the surrounding villages were farmers. Early in the morning, these farmers would arrive in the streets of Warsaw with fresh milk and eggs, chickens, and fresh produce. This makeshift market was the least expensive place for people to buy food. We had to boil the milk we bought there, because many cows were sick with tuberculosis.

On Fridays the market was always crowded, dusty and loud, packed with people shopping for Sabbath. I was always astounded by the wide array of colors of the fruits, vegetables, and flowers. The farm animals made all kinds of noises, and people bargained loudly. The farmers were friendly and always put morsels of produce into shoppers' hands, especially to children. I also knew I had to stay close to Mother—it was so easy to get separated from her among the stands, goods, and the crowds of people shopping.

One time, I remember that Mother's face was pale and drawn as she waited for me to finish my afternoon snack of tea with a slice of bread and butter. When I told her that my teacher made an example of my homework in Polish class again, she nodded and looked away as though she had barely heard me. I wish that I had said something—anything—about my concerns that day, but at ten years old I could not have offered to go to the busy market alone, nor did I have the courage to suggest that we stay home.

That Friday, Mother did not rush from stall to stall, grabbing the vegetables and smelling the fresh produce, as she usually did. She walked slowly, haphazardly putting things in our baskets and showing little interest in her purchases. As soon as we got home, Mother lay down in her bed and fell asleep. At sundown, the beginning of Sabbath, we lit a candle and prepared a meal the best we could without her help.

The next morning Mother awoke to find that her both left hand and leg were paralyzed. Adek ran to bring a doctor, who later explained that a vein had burst in Mother's brain. She had suffered a stroke. She was unconscious when the ambulance arrived to take her to the Jewish Hospital at Czyste in Warsaw. The doctor was still with us as we watched the stretcher slide into the ambulance. His kindly face was serious as he spoke the awful words: "There is nothing I can do for your mother."

Every day, after the doctors made their rounds in the morning, a family member was permitted to visit. The Jewish Hospital allowed only one family member to be with Mother during the weekly visiting hours. Anja left work early to take care of Mother at the hospital. On Sundays the six of us stood around her bed helplessly while Mother lay there, unable to move or talk. During those visits I held my mother's hand and cried.

We stopped smiling, and most of the time we each sat in our own corner of our small apartment with our heads down. It was summer, but in our room I was cold all the time. Within two weeks of my mother's stroke, we had become disheveled-looking and gaunt, eating only bread and drinking tea. We were all hoping that mother's health would improve, waiting for a miracle. But Mother's condition worsened. From lying on her back, she developed open wounds. Some nights she lay in her own urine for hours. Although the hospital did not have enough staff, they were strict about not letting family members come in to help at night.

Adek made the decision to bring Mother home, believing that we could care for her better than the hospital. She was returned in an ambulance, and we all watched the staff carry Mother up the steps on a stretcher. Although her condition was the still same, her presence in our home eased my heart—at least for a while. Our immediate concern was to heal Mother's infected bedsores. Adek bought a large rubber tube that mother could lie on so that her sores would be exposed to the air, and Anja washed the sores daily and dried them with powder. After three weeks, Mother's sores healed.

Anja, who was sixteen years old, quit her job and stayed home to spoon-feed Mother three times a day and give her the medicines that kept her alive. The money that my other siblings earned was spent to keep Mother comfortable and to buy those precious pills. The doctor put Mother on a special diet because everything she ate had to be easily digested, and she was allowed to eat bread that was made with only eggs and milk. For the first time, there were fruits in our home: bananas and oranges. She also had to drink kefir, fresh milk, and herbal teas that could only be purchased at a pharmacy.

It didn't take long for my mind to register that I no longer had a mother. I was ten years old and although my mother was physically present, she could not care for me. I wanted so much to have her hug me just once, to say a few words of comfort. After school, I would sit with Mother on her bed, kiss her, and beg her to talk to me, but she did not answer.

* * *

The neighbors were always frightened when Dr. Kozlowski, looking like a soldier walked through the courtyard. He was a tall man, a Polish army doctor dressed in uniform, his long shining sword, hanging at his side. He was sent every week from the hospital at no cost. Each time he visited, he'd look at Mother in her bed, and then at the rest of us gathered at the other end of the room. "I really want to save your mother," he said gently, "but there is nothing I can do. There are no medications to reverse her condition."

Taking care of Mother left Anja totally overwhelmed and exhausted; she could do nothing else. Everything else in the apartment was neglected—cooking and washing properly were out of the question. I was dirty and hungry all the time.

Adek was the oldest of all of us and he took on the role of our father. It was Adek who made the next big decision: Pola, who was twenty years old, would now take care of Mother and the chores, and Anja, would go back to work. This was a smart decision, as it became immediately apparent that Pola was better equipped for the job of taking care of Mother, cooking for all of us, doing the washing, and keeping our room clean. My job was to help Pola after school. I washed the dishes, took out the garbage, and washed clothes; I did everything that Pola asked me to do. The chores were never ending.

The family of five that lived in our kitchen was grateful to be in our apartment and we were equally happy to have them. Their share of the monthly rent was invaluable to us. But this arrangement offered us other hardships: to prepare meals on the small stove for a total of eleven people was a daily challenge. The added washing of clothes, bedding, and towels during mother's illness, was an intensely difficult task as well; Pola and I did this all by hand. We carried buckets of water inside from the courtyard, heated the water on the stove, discarded the dirty water, and hanged the clean clothes to dry on makeshift ropes we fastened around the room or outside in the courtyard during nice weather. I don't know if our laundry was ever truly clean, but we did not have the money to pay somebody to do

this task for us. My future seemed dark and hopeless. Dinner consisted of a thin soup with an occasional piece of meat. Pola divided the
meat among my older, working siblings, and I got the bone, which I
licked during the meal, trying to feel grateful.

During school hours, I was able to escape my awful reality.
Even with Mother lying silent and paralyzed at home, I was still at
the top of my class. I learned without having my own books. I was
able to borrow what I needed from my classmates. I didn't even have
a schoolbag for my notebooks. One day, Anja came home from work
with one she made for me out of fabric she had found at the factory.
It was a wonderful surprise: a colorful bag to carry my notebooks,
and inside it a dry Kaiser roll and the five groszy I needed to buy a
sour pickle at lunch time.

Things did not change for four years. Our siblings worked from
early morning until late at night, while Pola and I took care of Mother and the household chores. Mother's brother and sisters came and
went like shadows, leaving as quickly as they could. Every day I came
home right after school so we could help Mother to sit up in her bed.
My job was to lie behind her, against her back, to support her in the
upright position. Two years into Mother's illness Adek managed to
get her a padded chair, and Pola and I carried our mother every afternoon from the bed to the chair and back to the bed. Although
there were moments when she seemed conscious, most of the time
she was like an infant, especially after she suffered a second stroke,
and then a third one. Mother never regained her speech.

The angel of death came to take my mother on a Thursday in
May when I was fourteen years old. Anticipating the end of her life
was near, my brothers and sisters did not go to work the day before
and we did not sleep that night. Adek sat at her bedside the whole
night while the rest of us sat in a corner of the room. At five o'clock
in the morning, I noticed that the kerosene lamp was casting threatening shadows on the walls behind Mother's bed. I held my breath as
a strange black cat with blue eyes slinked into the room and ran under the bed. I wanted to scream but I couldn't. My voice would not
leave my throat. At that exact moment, Mother closed her eyes and
stopped breathing. She died in Adek's arms.

I was the only one who saw the black cat, and I never told anyone what I saw because I was sure that no one would believe me. It
was not my imagination; I saw that cat clearly as it entered the room,
but in my heart I knew what it really was. It was the angel that came

for my mother. As I looked in the direction of the open door, he entered our room. The cat's eyes shined like two sapphires. He came in without ever making a sound but I saw him slip into the room and head straight for Mother's bed.

According to Jewish tradition, Mother's body was laid on the floor with her feet toward the door. Since it was Friday, Adek had only until noon to make the funeral arrangements. A woman came to our room to sew a white cotton burial shroud. During the two hours that it took her to complete her task, she talked to us about God. She said, "God gives and God takes. God comes and you have to go to a place where you forever rest."

I cried and cried, crushed by the enormity of my grief.

"Children, don't cry," she told me. "Soon a messiah will come, riding on a white horse, and all the dead will come to life." Her attempts to reassure me did not work. During the four years of Mother's illness, we had grown more secular. We listened respectfully to her words, which reflected the strong faith that most people still had back in those days, but we were not comforted by them.

* * *

Before noon, we all walked downstairs, single-file, dressed in black, clothes my older sisters borrowed from various neighbors. Mother's body, covered in the shroud, was placed in a black, wooden casket. The wagon waiting for us in the courtyard was covered in black fabric, its back propped open for the casket. The two horses pulling the wagon were also covered in black; only their eyes were visible. My two brothers walked at the front of the procession behind the wagon. After them were Sala and Anja, who were supported by their closest friends.

Our next-door neighbor walked on Pola's side and I walked on her other, holding my sister's hand. Mother's brother and sisters, and their children came to the funeral. They had come to our room from time to time when mother was sick, bringing us food and emotional support that we desperately needed, but as we walked to the cemetery, I could hardly remember those visits. The sorrow and anger I was feeling left me with no room to feel grateful, at the same time my siblings and I knew that our Mother's family did as much as they could to help us. A decade after the first war had ended most people around us still struggled to survive.

The horses pulled the wagon slowly while funeral workers dressed in black walked on each side. Everyone was praying as we moved along. Once we arrived, Mother's body was taken to a special building.

It took two hours for Mother's body to be washed and dressed for the burial. She was dressed all in white, including white stockings and white cotton shoes. Her eyes were covered with small ceramic pieces. The grave was lined with wooden planks since the body was buried, according to Jewish tradition, without a casket. Wrapped in the white shroud that had been sewn for her earlier that day, Mother was lowered into the ground.

Over her grave, we said *Kaddish*, the prayer for the dead. For the second time in my young life, black dirt covered my parent forever. I was an orphan.

On the trip home, all I could think was that I would return home and find Mother still in her bed. But after four years of caring for her, there was no longer anyone to take care of—her bed was empty.

We did not eat that day. My three sisters and I climbed into one bed and stayed there, sobbing throughout the Sabbath. Thankfully, our brothers fared a little better than we did, and they took turns taking care of us, forcing us to drink some tea.

For one week following Mother's funeral her bed stood untouched. Afterward we had no choice but to use the bed where she lingered for four long years. Pola and Sala took Mother's bed. Since we had a total of three beds and slept two to a bed, now we were able to discard the old, stuffed mattress, which we placed each night on top of the table.

On Sunday, we started to sit *Shiva*. According to the Jewish tradition we had to sit on low stools. The mirrors, even the smallest ones, were covered and the only light came from a burning candle. Family and neighbors came to pay their respects; they brought food and distracted us with conversation. Then they left us to grieve alone. After the week passed, my two brothers and two sisters went back to work. I went back to school but Pola stayed home to take care of us.

A few weeks later, I graduated from public school. My classmates came to school on that last day with their parents, but I came alone. My siblings couldn't miss any more work and risk losing their jobs, and Pola rarely ventured out to public places. At the end of the ceremony, I stood with my graduating class. We recited the poem:

> Life goes by quickly, like a stream runs the time.
> In a year, in a day, in a minute, together we'll be no more,
> And our young years went by quickly into the past.
> In our hearts will remain sadness, a void and an absence.
> This is the last day of school; we will face many different roads,
> Into the world we will go, taking our future into our hands.

At fourteen years of age, after only six years of school, I received my diploma with only a small amount of satisfaction. Graduation day was one of the saddest days in my life. Now my life would veer in a totally different direction. Throughout my childhood I had dreamed of continuing my education, but this goal was suddenly unattainable. I would have to work.

* * *

After mother's death, we were determined to stay together. Money once again was in short supply.

It was difficult to find a job in Warsaw in 1931. People got up as early as four o'clock in the morning to get the morning paper and search the classified section for employment. As many as a hundred people applied for one position. Sometimes a newly hired worker was fired after just a few days; an employer was not required to give a reason.

Adek thought it would be best if Pola and I worked at home. He bought a spindle machine for us to use. The owner of the factory where Adek and Sala had worked since they were twelve years old gave us the wool. Spinning wool to spools was seasonal work, so Pola and I carried on from early morning until late at night, sometimes until two or three o'clock in the morning. We knew the demand for these spools lasted for only the few summer months and into fall. We wanted to make as much money as possible, in order to save for a time when work was not available. Working with wool was difficult. Soon everything in our room was covered with a layer of white wool dust. When the season for wool ended, we substituted silk thread for wool to make the season last a little longer. We managed to make money, and so we persevered. I missed going to school but I knew not to complain.

Pola continued with all the cooking and the house chores. Every day, I carried lunch to the small textile factory where Adek and Sala worked. Over time, our situation at home improved. I took orders from Pola, who was very strict and demanding. She never gave me spending money for the work that I did, and for some reason I didn't dare ask Pola for money.

* * *

My father's side of the family ceased to exist after his death, but mother's side stayed close to us. Mother had eight siblings: two escaped abroad, one sister with her husband and seven children went to Russia, and one brother escaped to Paris. I often heard stories about Dovid, one of our mother's brothers. Dovid was a Socialist who took on the dangerous job of working against the Polish government right after World War I. When the police discovered Dovid hiding guns in his mother's stove— this was in the summer time, when it was not in use—Dovid went into hiding. His family dressed him as a woman and arranged for false documents to get him out of Poland. Paris became his new home. His best friend also had to leave Poland. As he, too, was a wanted man. He was married to Estera, the youngest of my mother's sisters.

Dovid married a French woman. He sent us photographs of himself and his wife; they had no children. Mother's oldest sister, who moved to Russia in the early 1920s, died right at the time mother first became sick. We were able to stay in contact with this sister's husband and their seven children through letters until the outbreak of World War II. During the war, in Russia, my cousins from this marriage saved my life, before they disappeared in 1941, when Hitler's army battled over Moscow. At the same time, another sister, younger than my mother, became sick and lost her sight. My mother's sister Hadasa had four children, two girls and two boys. Hadasa's husband became a successful merchant. He owned a large grocery store on Gesia Street. All four of her children went to school and the oldest son became a bookkeeper. Every time Hadasa came to visit, she would clean her shoes before leaving to go back home to Nalewki Street where all the rich merchants lived.

Mother's brother, Motel, lived in Warsaw. He was the youngest of the siblings. He owned a workshop and a store where he sold fashionable women's hats on 14 Zamenhofa Street. Motel lived in a Polish neighborhood; he had two sons and one daughter. His marriage fell apart when the children were still young. To his credit, he kept the children and raised them by himself. During Mother's illness and after she died, Motel visited us often. He always bragged about how well he took care of his children, how he cooked, washed, and cleaned his home all by himself.

Motel usually visited on Sunday and Pola served him the nicest lunch, while my dinner consisted of a bone. Often, I would be playing out in the courtyard when I saw my uncle running—not walking—to our building. The first time, I thought that something must be terribly wrong. I waited a few minutes and went upstairs. To my surprise nothing terrible had happened at all. There was Pola, bending over Motel to serve him an ample lunch of fish, chicken soup with noodles, fruit compote, and tea. My uncle was actually smacking his lips. Thirty minutes later he thanked Pola and said he needed to get back to his children.

This routine went on for years. I never said a word, but the resentment built inside me. How Pola could be treating Motel this way when many nights I went to bed hungry? This ritual went on when my siblings were at work; they had no idea that Pola was extending this generosity to our uncle. My unhappiness grew. On the one hand, I heard people say that Pola had a very big heart and was generous to others. On the other hand, her actions did not make sense to me, since the six of us were still struggling to survive. There was no one to talk to about it, so I resigned myself to the way things were.

The youngest of my mother's sisters, Estera was a beautiful woman with blond hair and blue eyes. She and her one son, Itzak, were constant visitors in our little room. At the time, couples were only just beginning to marry because they were in love: This was a new, revolutionary concept. In Estera's case, we all knew that she was not in love with her husband. On the other hand, her husband was in love with Estera. After Dovid and his best friend escaped to France, Estera and her baby joined them in Paris. However, Estera missed her siblings and her life in Warsaw and after a few years she came back. This is how her son Itzak grew up with us and became like a brother to me.

Estera's former husband in Paris married for a second time and had another son. Through his second marriage, he became a very wealthy man. Estera, who was not legally divorced from him, hired an attorney. Soon, the Polish and the French courts awarded her a large amount of money and a substantial monthly allowance for Itzak until he turned twenty-four. Estera came into all this money right around the Jewish New Year, while mother was still alive but already ill. I remember my disappointment when Estera came to visit bringing with her a box of oranges when we needed so much more.

Soon, she left Warsaw for the small town of Włocławka. She lived an extravagant life and forgot all about us. When the money ran out, she came back to Warsaw. By then my mother had died. Itzak was fifteen years old and very smart, yet Estera would not permit him to go to school. Instead she sent Itzak to a seamstress to learn the craft of making and sewing clothing. He was receiving his monthly allowance from his father in Paris, and with this money, they rented an apartment. They came to visit us often until Estera became ill. She moved to Otwock where she lived with a family who took care of her. Itzak stayed in Warsaw and for a time, lived with us. He took me to the movies and once made a beautiful jacket for me. I didn't feel anything for my cousin other than a profound friendship. He was a self-educated young man, intelligent, well read, and seemed to know everything on every subject.

It was only after my mother's death that I learned the true story of "Dovid". My mother's mother, Bina's brother, Herich Simenhaus, who my mother calls "Dovid". Herich was born in Warsaw May 15, 1887 to Berek and Sury, nee Skrzynia. He escaped Poland after WWI to Paris and married a French woman, whose first name was Sara. He lived at 221, rue Jean Jaurès at Bobigny (Seine-Saint-Denis). He was imprisoned by the French Police at the Drancy detention camp on August 29, 1942 and deported to Auschwitz in convoy #12. He was murdered in Auschwitz. A certificate of his death was given to his wife on October 24, 1944. "May his memory be for a blessing".

My Aunt Pola

After the war, it was rare in the Jewish community to have grandparents, parents, aunts, uncles, or siblings. Quite simply, they had all been murdered. Clinging to life for six years in Russia, my parents returned home to Poland. My mother went to Warsaw to look for her family only to find that none had survived. Her brother Adek, her sisters Sala and Anja, and all their families were gone—no one came to answer my mother's laments. In 1957, my mother discovered that her sister Pola was alive. The transports with refugees returning from Russia after the war ended were inundated and the two sisters had gotten separated. Pola's train ended up in Germany's refugee camps and from there she made her way to America while my mother remained in Poland. Pola arrived in America, on Ellis Island, January 7th, 1951, on a ship General S D Sturgis. She made her age to be 36 instead of 44, she called herself stateless and was heading to 15 Park Row, NYC. She was alone on this trip from Europe. I am assuming her husband left first and was waiting for her. It took almost ten years before my mother and Pola found each other again. This also meant that my sister and I had an aunt. But almost a decade would pass before my mother and her sister were finally reunited.

After the war, Polish Communists, answerable to Soviet Russia, took over Poland. Diehard party leaders, Bolesław Bierut, Władysław Gomułka, Edward Gierek, and Wojciech Jaruzelski assumed leadership respectively. The "State" controlled all prices, those were set arbitrarily since the concept of supply and demand did not exist. Every aspect of existence is controlled in a Marxist economy, so people are forced to find a way to subsist, including my mother. She had no choice but to make the exchanges of foreign currencies illegally, outside of government's criteria. The illegal black market was peoples' life line and an answer to government's rule of no need for a free market economy based on competition. Everything that was needed was to be produced in abundance and scarcity was supposed to be eradicated. In reality Marx's imagined utopia never happened. The opposite did. I remember my mother standing in long queues at stores for our basic food needs. Most stores and shelves were always empty. It was not any different from the way things were during wartime in Soviet Russia.

After my mother made contact with her sister, Pola came to our rescue. She frequently sent packages from America with clothing. I remember two beautiful white cotton dresses that fit my sister and me perfectly. We had photographs taken and rushed them out to Pola by mail. Pola also sent dollars through the mail, covered by carbon paper to avoid detection. Mother would take the train with my sister to the next city, over an hour away, to exchange dollars on the black market. These exchanges gave her ten times the amount of money that legal, government exchanges paid at the time. For each $20.00 bill that Pola sent inside a letter, Mother got 2,000.00 zł on the black market. This money was of an enormous help to us. My mother was always terrified when doing those transactions; she never knew if she was being set up. I stayed up on so many nights, sitting by our kitchen window, holding my breath and waiting for the first sound of my mother's and sister's footsteps.

Mother took my older sister with her to exchange the money because she said she felt more protected. "No one will suspect a mother with a child," she would say. They always returned on the last train. While I waited, I came face to face with my biggest fears: that I would be left without a mother or my sister. For years, I lived with the fear of losing my mother: I could clearly imagine her being arrested and taken to jail for participating in the black market. In those years, my father was very ill and in the hospital most of the time.

He died when I was ten, in 1961.

In 1978, Karol Wojtyła became the Polish Pope, John Paul II, strengthening the Polish opposition to the authoritarian and ineffective communist system. Pope's visit to Poland in 1979 gave rise to a new wave of strikes in early August 1980, resulting in the formation of the trade union "Solidarity" (Polish Solidarność), led by Lech Wałęsa. The growing strength and activity of the opposition caused the government to declare martial law in December 1981. During Jaruzelski's rule from 1981 to 1989, around 300,000 people fled the country; Polish Jewish citizens were forced out a decade earlier. After the war only 50,000 Polish Jews chose to stay in Poland, the next expulsion came in 1968. The Anti-Semitic assault on the Polish Jews ended with most of them losing their jobs, forcing them to flee. About 40,000 fled, long before Communism fell.

CHAPTER FOUR

My brother Sevek was content with his job as a tanner in a leather workshop, but because it was physically demanding, he had to stop working. He was only eighteen years old when he started showing signs of a weak heart. About a year after my mother died, a doctor was again visiting 54 Nowolipki Street I believed then, and I still do today, that anything good that happened to my family was because of the generosity shown by Mr. and Mrs. Grunblatt.[7] They owned the factory where Adek worked and would later welcome our eldest brother into their family through marriage. Looking back now, I realize it was Dr. Pupko who had brought light and hope into our home. I knew, without being told, that it was the Grunblatt who arranged for Dr. Pupko to see Sevek. Many years later, in September of 1939, the thirteen of us would huddle together in their apartment during the never-ending bombings in Warsaw. But this story will have to wait.

Dr. Pupko, an older Jewish physician, normally saw patients either at his home 12 Nowolipki Street, or at a hospital, but he paid special visits to my brother. I remember the day when the short, thin man stepped gingerly out of a horse-drawn carriage. He tipped his hat to me. As we both rushed into the building, I asked him if he was the doctor we were expecting.

Dr. Pupko was a religious man who came from a poor family. We tried many times but he would not accept any payment from us. He seemed happy enough to drink the tea Pola served him and would spend a few minutes sitting and talking. We learned he had been the only Jewish student in a Polish Medical School and had to make enormous sacrifice to study medicine. Now a famous doctor in Warsaw, revered even by his Polish colleagues, Dr. Pupko lived a very simple life. Once, I asked the aging doctor if it was true that he had

---

[7] The Grünblatt family who owned the factory on Bonifraterska Street and lived on Mylnej Street. Adek, my mother's oldest brother married their daughter and became a partner in their small clothing factory. My mother was not sure if she remembered the last name correctly but the description of the factory on Bonifraterska 11-13 Street, producing haberdashery and knitter fits in with my mother's description of the clothing the factory produced.

never married. "It wouldn't be fair," Dr. Pupko said, "the way I live, to have a wife or children."

He spoke with such passion and honesty that I would inevitably be filled with hope when he left. Dr. Pupko tried to convince us that we should not worry about our brother. He promised that in time, Sevek would get better. After a few visits, he confided that he had suffered from the same heart condition as Sevek.

Our brother was confined to bed that whole winter, and Pola and I took care of him. Pola cooked his meals, and I brought them to him. While Pola and I worked, Sevek entertained us. He liked to draw funny pictures; in fact Sevek was the one with a good sense of humor. At the same time it was Sevek in my family who worried the most; he started to show signs of panic attacks. The guilt and anguish he was feeling from not working began to affect his rational thinking. On Saturdays his friends came by for short visits. It was important, we were told, to keep him calm.

Sevek loved to read. We explored all the Polish literature that I could get my hands on, and read to each other under the one lamp deep into the night. Books by famous writers like Boleslaw Prus, Henryk Sienkiewicz, and Stefan Zeromski. We read about wars, battles, struggles for Poland, and also about love and passion. Each book painted a beautiful landscape with a different cast of interesting and vibrant characters. It was at that time that Sevek made up his mind that one day he would leave Poland and travel. I had always been told that it was Sevek who resembled our father the most, tall and slender with dark hair which fell in loose curls over his forehead. Sevek and I shared a passion for learning; I secretly hoped my brother would never leave us.

When summer came, we managed to send Sevek to a sanatorium in the town of Otwock. This was only possible because Dr. Pupko wrote a formal doctor's order, and this also meant that we paid very little.

Otwock was a rural town with a peaceful atmosphere that helped those like our brother to heal. In the late 1800s a sanatorium for those with tuberculosis opened there, but soon it became a fashionable health resort for middle-class Jews from Warsaw and central Poland. The evergreen trees in the thick forest made this region and its air famous for healing.

We put Sevek on the train and stood on the platform waving as the train pulled out of the station. The railroad cars full of excited travelers, with our brother waving back through the open window and the white plums of steam soon disappeared in the distance. When I was sure he could not see I let the tears escape from my eyes. I had the irrational thought that I would never see my brother again.

The trip to the sanatorium did exactly what it was supposed to do. Sevek returned to Warsaw three months later looking and feeling better, however, Dr. Pupko insisted that for two years he would not allow him to go back to a regular job. Working again as a tanner would be too physically demanding, so Sevek made a decision to start his own business. He learned how to make women's purses. To his delight and ours, he made beautiful samples which he then took to shops, where the owners were quick to place orders. Sevek even found time to make some purses for all of us sisters.

Sevek was not the only one of us with health problems. When I was sixteen years old, I started to cough up phlegm mixed with blood. A doctor prescribed syrup for my hacking cough. He said I had pneumonia and recommended I leave for the countryside to rest as soon as possible. I remember insisting that I could just be at home, but the doctor was too smart for me. He seemed to know about all my responsibilities and insisted that I leave the city to get better.

* * *

My sister Sala had met a nice Jewish family in our local bakery. Mrs. Gelerowicz was going away with her children to Michalin. It was a small town, near the sanatorium in Otwock. I was permitted to go with them, although it was understood we had to pay for my stay with their family

I packed the few things I had: some undergarments, a dress, a blouse, a skirt, and a sweater. I was shaking from the fever as I picked up my mother's blue blanket and held it to my chest. I also took some of the books I had not yet had time to read.

Sala took the train with me to Michalin and left on the next train back to Warsaw. I had wanted to go alone, but Adek refused. I really didn't argue too much. Up until that point, I had not been out of the city alone at all.

I was not comfortable with the family I was staying with. Most of the time, they treated me as if I wasn't there. The books I brought with me were my only companions, and I spent my days reading. The more I read, the more my eyes were opened to world outside my immediate surroundings. I read Julian Tuwim, a famous Jewish Polish writer and poet, who became an inspiration. His poems were optimistic, paid homage to urban life, and were full of positive energy. I quickly moved on to Adam Mickiewicz, another famous writer in Poland who was a great champion of Jewish rights. However, it was Maria Konopnicka's fairy tales and short stories that made the greatest impression on me. How easily I associated with that poor little orphan named Marysia! I knew the pain she carried through her motherless life.

I was just finishing Konopnicka's stories about Marysia when I was interrupted. Although Tomek Gelerowicz was about my age and also healthy, his mother would send me alone to the well to get pails of water. Once again, I was being told to go to the well. It was a long walk from the house. Konopnicka's story stayed with me as I turned the wheel to bring up the pail of water. The buckets were heavy, so heavy that I could barely pick them up. I had to pause frequently due to my shortness of breath and because of coughing spells. Like Marysia, the heroine in Konopnicka's story, I felt like I, too, needed to be strong.

A sudden wave of anger and rebellion swept through me. I saw a clear difference between compassion and being taken advantage of. My host family was forcing me to perform work that was too difficult for the condition that I was in. It was unfair. A voice in my head said that no one had a right to exploit me like this. I knew I had been avoiding the truth. There was one thing I had to do; I needed to go home as quickly as possible.

As I kept walking back to the house, I wondered about that author I loved so much. While I read everything by her that I could, I knew little about her. I vowed to find out more. I staggered into the parlor and placed the two pails on the floor. I asked for them to take me to the train station and help me buy a ticket back to Warsaw. Mrs. Gelerowicz looked down at the pails of water, shrugged, and said okay. I was amazed then, and I still am. She did not even try to stop me. She did not apologize. My siblings were shocked when I walked into the crowded room of our apartment. I told them quickly what had brought me back.

As I rested for the next few weeks at home, I was able to see more clearly what my life had been like.

* * *

Purim, depending on the year, falls between four and six weeks before Passover. In Poland it was still cold in March. The slippery and hazardous snow and sleet covered the streets and sidewalks. During the Purim Holiday it was a tradition for a young man to take cake and wine to a young lady to signify he was sincerely interested in her. Every year, there was always an article in the newspapers about some unfortunate young man falling and hurting himself while bringing cake and wine to an unidentified young woman. Around this time Sala, now twenty-six years old, fell in love.

Sala made it known that she was not happy with Moniek being a house painter. They decided, or perhaps she did, that Moniek pay a barber to teach him the skills he needed to become one himself. Sala and Moniek were married by a rabbi, but there was no celebration. Neither family had money for a party. The day Sala moved out of our room was bittersweet. I was happy for my sister, but I also felt it was the beginning of the end of what was left of our family. I helped Sala move into her new home. She would live with Moniek and his mother, the three of them sleeping in one tiny room which had only one small window and just enough room for one bed and a table. Moniek's mother was to sleep on a mattress on the floor. Although Moniek learned to be a barber, he could not find a job. Sala continued working in the same factory as Adek. She sewed clothes for ten hours a day. Their financial situation was so fragile that when she realized she was pregnant, Sala and Moniek decided not to have the baby. I was amazed. I could not figure out how Sala conceived a child with Moniek's mother sleeping right there on the floor next to the newlyweds.

Sala tried everything she could to end her pregnancy, from running and jumping to taking pills to induce a miscarriage. Nothing worked. The search began to find a doctor who could help her. I was chosen to help because I spoke Polish the best of all of us. Doctors were closely monitored by the government although there were still some who did perform illegal abortions, partly for the money and partly to help a girl in trouble. Once we found a doctor, through a friend of a friend, I made all the arrangements in Polish and I wrote down details of the appointment and the directions to his office.

As much as I thought I knew about pregnancy and babies, I really didn't know very much at all. I was not ready for what was about to happen, although I tried to appear calm, to comfort poor Sala who trembled uncontrollably. I made up my mind right then and there that I would never, ever put myself through what my sweet sister was going through. Though in Russia, years later, finding myself pregnant during World War II, I broke this promise I made to myself.

The waiting room was poorly lit, but it was clean. Our appointment was after regular office hours which made Sala even more nervous. My sister reached out to hold my hand. Our eyes met; I saw in them fear and humiliation. "Do you think I am doing something wrong?" she asked me.

"It's a nice, clean doctor's office," I answered. "Everything will be fine."

I don't know that I believed it, especially when the doctor nervously asked us, again and again: "How did you get my name?" "Who gave you my name?" Finally he seemed to accept my answer, "We will wait a while longer," he said. "To make sure you haven't been followed." Only then did I understand the risk we were all taking.

About fifteen minutes later, the doctor was ready and very little was said. I handed him 30.00 Polish złoty and Sala was ushered into the next room. I followed. There were tears in Sala's eyes but the doctor said that time was precious. It was obvious that we should proceed and leave as quickly as possible.

I held my sister's hand as she lay on the doctor's table. She never made a sound. After about thirty minutes, Sala got up, straightened her clothes, and thanked the doctor. Sala and Pola were fraternal twins, but to me Sala always bore a resemblance to Pola; now as if overnight she looked fragile and small.

Two days later, Sala woke with a high fever. She had always been thin and anemic, with frequent bouts of tonsillitis. After the abortion, Sala stayed in bed for two weeks and hardly spoke to anyone, not even her husband. Although she recovered enough to go back to work, she was not the same for a long time.

Moniek still couldn't find a job. He and Sala decided that he would go to his uncle in Luxembourg and try his luck there. Sala stayed behind with Moniek's mother. After a few months with no success, Moniek returned to Warsaw. Now he decided to join a group of young men, called Halutzim, pioneers who were embarking on a trip to Palestine by foot. Some groups of young pioneers, after a month or two traveling on foot, made their way toward port city destinations. They embarked on steamers and six days later they would reach their new homeland. The HeHalutz movement[8] blossomed across Europe and Russia at the turn of the twentieth century. Their aim was to settle in the land of Israel. Before the start of World War II, approximately 60,000 had already made aliyah.[9]

Nothing Sala said could stop him. I remember the sadness in her eyes that day as he kissed her lightly on the cheek and left. Sala stayed with Moniek's mother, although I suggested that she move back with us.

At the beginning, the local Jewish newspaper wrote about the travelers' whereabouts. During the day they walked and at night they slept in small towns. After three weeks, there was no longer any news. Sala was frantic. She decided to go to the town from where the last news had come. She traveled by train, arriving to find Moniek parading around town with a young woman on his arm. Moniek stayed behind while the other young men continued with their journey. Sala told me that he did not make a fuss when she insisted he return immediately with her to Warsaw. He told her that he never really wanted to go away but was embarrassed about being without a job and not unable to support his family. I was so angry with Moniek; I couldn't look at him.

Soon after their return, our cousin Itzak came to rescue. Like a gallant knight, Itzak knew about Sala's misfortune and he made Moniek an offer. Itzak was receiving a monthly allowance from his father in Paris; he offered Sala and Moniek a loan to acquire a barbershop on 36 Nowolipki Street. Life for Sala and Moniek slowly fell into place. My sister was smiling again.

Sala soon became pregnant again, but when it was time to give birth she was afraid to go to the hospital. In Sala's mind, hospitals were a place where people went to die. She decided to have her baby at home with me, Pola, Anja, and a midwife. Moniek, like all men, was not allowed in the room while his wife was giving birth. He was in charge of boiling water. Sala's agonized screams filled the room. I am sure all the neighbors in the building heard her as well. The midwife looked on and did nothing. I didn't understand what was happening, but I had to assume that the midwife knew what she was do-

---

[8]   The HeHalutz (Pioneering) movement was motivated by the belief that immigrants to Palestine should be trained and prepared in their home countries prior to their transplantation to Palestine. It was first propounded by Joseph Trumpeldor in 1908.

[9]   Aliyah is the immigration of Jews from the diaspora to the land of Israel. http://www.jewishvirtuallibrary.org/jsource/Immigration/immigration.html

ing. Suddenly, Sala's pain seemed to subside. The midwife reported that the baby's movements had stopped.

As always, in a case of emergency, Anja and I ran to Adek for help. At that time he already was married and lived ten blocks away. Adek had married his boss's daughter, and his wealthy wife was also pregnant with their first child. He called for an ambulance using the precious telephone that they had just installed weeks before, and then the three of us rushed back to be with Sala. A doctor was dispatched, and after examining Sala, he ordered her to the hospital. The two ambulance workers had to carry Sala down the steps of the four-story walk-up.

We had to wait until the next morning until we would be allowed to visit. We counted the hours and then the minutes until we could go to the hospital to see if Sala and her baby were still alive. Anja and I went to the hospital information window on Elektoralna Street, at eight o'clock in the morning, and dozens of people were already waiting in line. When the window finally opened and our turn came, we looked at each other and froze. Anja pushed me in front of the window where I managed to ask how my sister was. Anja and I started to cry when we heard the words: "Your sister gave birth to a beautiful baby boy at four o'clock this morning."

We were not allowed to see Sala that day as only husbands were allowed to visit, and even then for just a few minutes, but we were allowed to bring food and leave it at the window.

In those days, women stayed in the hospital for eight days after giving birth. Sala was weak but happy when she walked out of the hospital carrying Pinkus, who was named after our father. We affectionately called him Piniek.

Like Sala, Adek had also gotten married in 1933. His bride's parents were both alive, and they had two younger sons. The Grunblatt family had helped to pay for Sevak's recovery and would continue through the years, to be good to our family. Not long after Piniek's birth, Adek's wife gave birth to a girl who they named Bluma, after our mother.

Adek's father-in-law owned the textile factory on Bonifraterska Street, where Adek and Sala still worked. Adek had begun working there when he was twelve, after our father died. The bride's parents, Mr. and Mrs. Grunblatt, made a gala wedding and then made our brother a business partner in the factory. The newly married couple moved in with their in-laws where Adek quickly became, as he said, 'their third son.'

* * *

Now there were only four of us left in our one room apartment. The family of five was still living in the kitchen.

Pola was different from the rest of us. She would not marry. She was firm. She demanded that her working siblings give her all of their earnings. Pola seemed to be happy with her life. She was indifferent to the outside world and only wanted to stay home, take care of us, and do the chores. She didn't pay too much attention to how she dressed or looked. Her blond hair, inherited from Mother, was always cut short and pushed back revealing her high forehead and cheekbones. Pola was close to our neighbors. She knew the latest gossip: who among the neighbors was struck by fortune or tragedy.

There was a constant battle between Pola and Anja. Anja was a smart young woman, who by 1933, was fully participating in the workers movement. Anja's rebellion brought about vicious fighting between the two of them. One Friday night, just before the Sabbath, their arguing was especially fierce. Pola stood there with her arms crossed over her chest, waiting to receive all of Anja's earnings. Anja, exhausted, rushed in only minutes before sundown. Perhaps it was because she was so tired that she responded the way she did, but she refused to hand over any of her money.

"I cook, I clean, and I take care of all of you." Pola's voice was getting louder and louder. "What am I supposed to use for money?"

"We don't need you to do this," Anja yelled. Her voice had an unfamiliar anger to it. "You don't seem to see our lives have not stood still." "It's three years since mother died and you still don't realize it. The world has changed, and we have changed, too."

Pola's mouth fell open. Her cheeks were red.

"We can all do your job equally." Anja's voice was strong and clear. "Pola, you have to get a job. And I have to start thinking about my future."

Pola stepped up to Anja and put her face close to hers. "You don't appreciate anything I do for you! I cannot believe you are my sister."

"I am not your little sister anymore, Pola." Anja took a step back. "See, I am all grown up. We all are. Look at Roma. She is all grown up, too. You can hide in this room forever but the truth is that there is no one to take care of anymore."

I stood in the corner with my hands over my ears. I shut my eyes tight. My family was falling apart.

Pola and Anja kept fighting. At the same time, our family matured and changed. Anja joined the growing workers' movement and became a guiding voice among her peers. Her courage inspired me. Unafraid to stand up for social justice, she believed that a better future for working-class people was possible. I would soon follow in her footsteps.

The Missing Photographs

What I remember most vividly from my childhood years after the war in Poland is how my mother always watched the door, always hopeful, never giving up that a loved one would enter, come back from the dead. Later, when
I grasped the magnitude of the crimes committed against Europe's Jews, I
questioned why my parents thought it was essential to stay in Poland. For
my parents it was important to restore their roots in the place where their
ancestors had lived for centuries. They needed to be among the ghosts of
their murdered family, to keep their memory alive and insure that they did
not perish in vein. In the words of Elie Wiesel, "to forget the dead would be
akin to killing them a second time." My mother found courage and strength
among the ashes of her family; she brought them back to life, daily. Twenty
years after the war, Jews were targeted again in an anti-Semitic campaign,
sponsored by the communist government. In the years 1968-1969 the
words Polish Jews and Zionists became identical. Those were Stalin's tactics after he understood Israel was lost to the Soviet sphere of influence
when Israel aligned herself economically and politically with the West and
in particular with the USA.

It is said that in every survivor's family, one child is unconsciously
chosen to be a 'memorial candle,' to carry on the mourning and dedicate
his or her life to the memory of the Shah. That child takes part in the parents' emotional world, assumes the family burden, and becomes the link
between the past and the future. I realize now that my mother chose me,
and that in turn, I chose my daughter to be that memorial candle.

As far back as I can remember, my mother shared her stories with
me. The tales she told filled me with overwhelming sadness, but also
brought color to my drab existence in southwestern Communist Poland.

My mother's childhood in Poland, her survival during the war, and
her life after the Holocaust became part of me. I grew up in a home where
my sister and I lived, day by day, haunted by my parents' experiences. Their
psychic injuries, their traumas were transmitted to us, the second generation. I absorbed my mother's abandonment and helplessness and I felt her
fears and resignation. I lived with her habits, where every crumb of bread
was precious, where fear of being cold was magnified, and where suspicion of others, and secretiveness and mistrust watched over how she in-
teracted with the outside world. Her scars became my scars.

I have never seen any photographs that connected my mother to the
extended family she so often talked about. I was frightened, confused, and

also ashamed that I did not believe her. In order for my child's mind to reconcile something I could not comprehend, I had decided that my mother had made this family up, that those people had never existed.

As a child I remember my mother, mourning her five nieces and nephews. "So young and innocent, they should be among the living," is what she repeated. Growing up in these shadows made me a witness to what had happened. For my first twenty years, I went from feeling sympathetic to being filled with contempt. I was angry and also overwhelmed for being connected to my mother's ongoing grief.

My mother was living with the ghosts of her vanished family. Her decision to run away from Warsaw after the German invasion haunted her all her life. A young woman of twenty-two, she said good-bye to her entire family, thinking she would be back in a few weeks. To stay alive, she had to keep going east into the unknown on trains crammed with other refugees. She found herself deep in Stalinist Russia, far from home and family, full of remorse and regret. But it was a decision that saved her life. Freud[10] observed that to grieve and to move on you have to know what you have lost or mourning can turn into a permanent melancholy.

From my viewpoint, there was never any evidence that my mother's family actually existed. I tried to understand how they could have vanished, Adek, Sala, and Anja, their children. Throughout my childhood, I grieved with my mother, although in truth, I could not comprehend how her family could have just disappeared. I had never seen any photographs to prove they had existed. I was ashamed that I did not believe her. I decided that my mother had made those people up.

My parents were constantly haunted by memories of the past and guilt for those who were murdered. To cope, Father retreated behind a wall of silence. Whereas Mother could not stay silent, constantly sharing her stories with a small child who could not begin to grasp what her mother had endured.

My mother's handwritten pages, a testament to her life, a testament to her family, a testament to the legacy of Jewish life in Poland, offer a glimpse into the social history of Jewish women and Jewish family life in Warsaw, between 1918 and 1968. It was in Wiesel's classes that I gained the courage to understand what my mother had lived through. With time, I allowed myself to confront the ghosts of my childhood.

Only in my classes at City College of New York at the Department of Jewish Studies, did my family history started to make sense. When Prof. Wiesel introduced us to his experiences in Auschwitz-Birkenau and Buchenwald concentration camps, I started to understand my parents. Reading his book *The Accident* made me realize that although my parents were

---

[10]   *On Murder, Mourning, and Melancholia* (Penguin Modern Classics Translated Texts) By Sigmund Freud, 2007.

survivors, that in losing their entire families, they could not escape their past. I was already in my twenties before I was able to I understand the importance of the stories my mother passed on to me throughout my childhood. When I told Wiesel about my mother he said, "Your mother must write her story. Future generations must know. You must help her to do it."

The twentieth century saw the collective horrors of Nazism and Communism, a stark reminder of men's inhumanity to men. Stalin refused to acknowledge into the pages of history the industrial scale killing of the Jews. The Holocaust was a systematic slaughter of the Jews, the crime itself was supposed to be expunged from history and while Europe's Jews were nearly eradicated for Stalin it was the Russian people who were the victims. He opportunely forgot that he collaborated with Hitler until Hitler decided to attack him. Before the industrial mass killings in death camps like Sobibor, Auschwitz, and Treblinka, 1.5 million Jews in the east were murdered by bullets and in gas vans, in about six months. Mass murder and extermination of Jews by poison gas is something that Hitler mentions in his book Mein Kampf. By early 1941 the special SS shooting squads with Ukrainian and other Nazi sympathizers were liquidating Jews in Bialystok, Ponary-Vilnus, Kovno-Lithuania, Babyiar-Kiev, Rumbula-Riga, and many other places.

The twenty first century is seeing Poland as embarking on a similar mission, rewriting and whitewashing history of what happened to Polish Jews during WWII. Its citizens are painted as the true Nazi victims, going as far as to blame Jews for their own fate. Some Polish historians, among them Krzysztof Jasiewicz, a professor at the Polish Academy of Sciences and a well-known expert on Polish-Jewish relations, is claiming that "Jews worked to bring the Holocaust about." Jasiewicz rationalizes this by adapting a Nazi style propaganda. "This nonsense about Jews being killed mostly by Poles was created to hide the biggest Jewish secret. The scale of the German crime was only possible because the Jews themselves participated in the murder of their own people." The Storm of War by Andrew Roberts is a meticulous account of WWII, including Poland's armed forces in exile, fighting fearlessly on the side of the Allies, against Hitler's Germany. Armia Krayowa, the underground Polish army, bravely but unsuccessfully tried to fight the German army and take control of Warsaw during the Warsaw Uprising, (August-October 1944) as the advancing Soviet army watched from across the Wisła River. Allowing the pro-Soviet Polish Armia Ludova, Polish Workers' Party, the communist partisan force to gain strength. Its aims were to fight against Nazi Germans in occupied Poland, support the Soviet military against the German forces and to help create a pro-Soviet Union communist government in Poland, rather than have the Polish government-in-exile in London, gain control of Poland. Another book, KL: A History of the Nazi Concentration Camps by Nikolaus Wachsmann, based on archival research, is an account of the Nazi regime and its grisly gas chambers and concentration camps. The sheer evil that happened there was possible with the help of Hitler's enthusiastic supporters; every occupied country had them.

To put it differently, it is important to examine and depict truthfully individual Polish citizens' behavior toward their Jewish neighbors during the war. We know mostly about the Righteous Poles who endangered their lives to save Jews but we never talk about those citizens who embraced the Nazi ideology and hunted down Jews. The Polish Blue Police officially came into being in October 1939, by 1943 its membership has been estimated at around 16,000. The Blue Police consisted primarily of Poles and Polish speaking Ukrainians from the eastern parts of the General Government. Polish-Jewish historian Emmanuel Ringelblum, chronicler of the Warsaw Ghetto, mentioned Polish policemen carrying out extortions and beatings. The Germans had intentionally allowed the policemen the right to keep for themselves 10% of all confiscated goods. It was the Nazis and Blue Police who rated the Ulma's farmhouse. The Ulma family, Jozef, Wiktoria, and their six children were given up to the Nazis by Polish policemen Wlodzimierz Les in 1944, because they were sheltering the Goldmans. Wlodzimierz Les knew they were hiding there and a total of eight Jews and the entire Ulma family were murdered on March 24, 1944.

Jews throughout Nazi occupied territories were dehumanized, including in Poland. Inside the temporary Ghettos they were entirely under Nazi control and outside raged a hostile population, hunting them down. Poles, in many cases cooperated and therefore bear some responsibility for some of the Nazi crimes committed by the Third Reich. One reason why the Polish safe houses were never safe. My mother's family from Warsaw, my father's family from Łódź, together with a million and a half Jews from Eastern Europe, to this day are unaccounted for. There exists no information for my mother's family that stayed in Warsaw as to how and where they were murdered. As if those people had never even existed. We know my father's family was deported from the Łódź Ghetto to Auschwitz in September of 1942. None survived this death camp.

Jews knew they were going to their deaths, for this reason most kept diaries. Those Ghetto journals were buried and survived the war and they expose the human tragedy. They bear witness to the human suffering of all those deported to be murdered in places like Auschwitz and Treblinka.

Emanuel Ringelblum and a handful of his closest friends created a collection, a secret archive which they buried under the Warsaw Ghetto to be excavated after the war. Over 30,000 written pages, photographs, posters, and more. The Oyneg Shabes Archive is the most important collection of eyewitness accounts from the Holocaust. It documents not only how the Jews of the ghetto died, but how they suffered.

From the beginning it was always about "They and We", the indifference of the Poles to the fate of the Jews is clear and is accounted for by some Polish chroniclers. In the summer of 1942, 300 thousand Jews were deported from the Warsaw Ghetto and murdered in Treblinka, this accounts for the greatest slaughter in a single city in human history. A loss of life greater than Hiroshima and Nagasaki combined. Polish Jews, 10% of Polish population, were marginalized in Poles accounts of Poland during Nazi occupation. Even after 300 thousand Jews were taken from the Warsaw Ghetto and murdered, the flyers in the summer of 1943 referred to the execution of 1000 Poles as the largest mass murder in the capital, the 300 thousand murdered Jews are never mentioned.

Zygmunt Klukowski, a surgeon and supervisor at Zamosc County Hospital in Szczebrzeszyn, Poland, a veteran of World War I, the Russian Civil War, and the Polish-Russian War of 1920-21, and a respected historian kept a detailed secret journal from 1939 to 1944. His is a first account of the brutality of the Nazis and of the round-ups of Jews. From 1939 until the end of the war the conditions for Jews became hopeless, Jews were left completely defenseless in a largely friendless Europe, and their lives became more and more desperate. "Dehumanizing" was not the Jewish choice, but a decisions made by their tormentors. This is how Jews had to survive in the Ghettos and the Holocaust in general. They had no choices, the Nazis ruled inside the Ghettos and outside the Ghettos they had a common enemy, the Nazis and all the anti-Semites who cooperated with the Third Reich's ideology. The lesson of the Ghetto is: the Jews were dead to the world and humanity did nothing to safe them. By October 1939, in Warsaw 'Judenrat' replaced Kehilla, a Jewish council under the leadership of Adam Czerniaków, responsible for the implementation of all Nazis' orders. When the orders came to start the liquidation of Warsaw Ghetto in July 1942, Adam Czerniakow committed suicide.

In the Łódź Ghetto, Chaim Rumkowski was forced to make choices, give up individual Jews, the young and the old, to try and save the Ghetto. The Łódź, or Litzmannstadt, Ghetto was the second-largest in all of German-occupied Europe after the Warsaw Ghetto. Rumkowski was able to save the Jews working in the ghetto, a major industrial center, manufacturing war supplies for Nazi Germany until August 1944. The law that prevailed in the temporary Ghettos was that of a jungle, the strongest prevailed. Upon the liquidation of the Łódź Ghetto, Rumkowski and his family were gassed along with thousands of others in Auschwitz-Birkenau.

Polish resistance fighters, among them Witold Pilecki, Irena Sendler, and Jan Karski, were the first to document and smuggle out detailed reports to the Polish Government-in-Exile and Allies. They disclosed the dire situation of Jews in the Warsaw Ghetto and the mass killings of Jews in the death camps like Auschwitz. Witold Pilecki, a Polish soldier, purposely got himself arrested. Imprisoned in Auschwitz, he managed to survive two and a half years until his escape. He formed an underground group inside Auschwitz. His resistance group was waiting for orders to commit acts of sabotage inside the camp which never came. Pilecki smuggled out detailed diagrams of the death camp, the brutality, and the mass gassing of Europe's Jews, thousands each day. Irena Sendler joined Żegota, the Council to Aid Jews. In 1940, the Nazis forced Warsaw's more than 400,000 Jewish residents into a small ghetto sealed off from the rest of the city. Thousands were dying every month from disease and starvation, Sendler, as a social worker, was able to enter the ghetto. She rescued some 2,500 Jewish children and placed them in convents or with non-Jewish families. Jan Karski was a member of the Polish resistance during WWII, a courier between his occupied nation and the West. He was smuggled into the Warsaw Ghetto by the Jewish underground in order to witness first-hand the brutality and to report to the outside world. He secretly entered a Nazi concentration camp in Eastern Poland to witness the mass murder of Jews. In 1942, he delivered this evidence to the top Allied officials in London. In 1943, he also reported it to President Franklin D. Roosevelt. The horrors of Nazism, the extermination of Europe's Jews, the mass murder of millions fell on deaf ears.

Many have witnessed and documented the horrors, brutality, and sadism first-hand. Among them, Chil Raichman, a survivor of Treblinka, Simon Wiesenthal, a survivor of many concentration camps including a death march to Buchenwald and the Mauthausen-Gusen concentration camp, and Primo Levi, a survivor of Auschwitz.

The burden to remember falls on all of us, we have a duty to become the memory keepers and connect what happened to our parents and grandparents with the future.

Primo Levi, Italian Auschwitz survivor, wrote in his book If This Is a Man about "unseen realities." Why the Nazis were so successful, too many nations and people turned away and did nothing when it came to the total destruction of Europe's Jews.

When my mother died, it was Prof. Wiesel that I contacted first. He encouraged me to start translating her memoir and not be afraid of the journey ahead.

"We must bear witness," Wiesel said. "Silence is not an option."

CHAPTER FIVE

My sister Anja blossomed into a strong, independent woman. I watched as she and her many friends took part in a growing worker's movement, spreading the principles of Socialism. My sister was among the small number of women who played an active role in recruiting and organizing earlier worker movements in Warsaw before the war. She was successful in winning the hearts and minds of many workers. I remember her impassioned speeches about the struggles of the working class. In return, workers gave her their full support and signed up as members of the movement—and the labor unions. Anja and her friends were driven by a common belief; there had to be a better future for working-class people.

Anja was also very beautiful. I see her at twenty-two with her long black velvet hair and dark eyes. The tallest of us four sisters, she took after our father's side of the family. She took good care of herself, paying attention to how she dressed; she would sometimes skip meals to save money in order to buy something in the latest fashion. Understandably, many young men pursued her.

Pola must have been very envious, because she fought with Anja every chance she got. She did not seem to take an interest in anything Anja did. People outside of our home had so many good things to say about Anja, but in Pola's eyes there was nothing that Anja could do right. The more Anja accomplished, the more Pola criticized her political involvement, her clothes, even what she ate. Their arguments were especially heated when Anja came home after spending a weekend with her boyfriend. Pola was shocked by such behavior.

Anja's relationship with Heniek had been ongoing for two years, and she was able to brush aside every obstacle Pola put in her way. Their outings were acceptable at that time, as they always went with friends. But we all knew they were very much in love. Anja never brought Heniek home. She never went to Heniek's house either. We didn't know why and we didn't get a chance to find out. We did know that he came from a well-off family, and both his parents were alive. I started to think that maybe his parents felt that their son should make a better choice than a poor girl whose parents were dead.

The social structure during this time was changing dramatically with the rise of a strong, upper middle class. Poles who attained education and upward economic mobility were the new *intelligentsia*. This middle-class society was a closely knit circle, and those people were often related by marriage. This applied to the Polish Jewish community as well. It was not uncommon to marry one's cousin and marriages between different social classes were discouraged. Upper and middle-class Jews were seeking partners for marriage among their own kind. These marriages were not just affairs of the heart but economic transactions as well.

Unexpectedly, Heniek told Anja he was leaving for Belgium. He promised to send for her. I remember her shocked face, her tears. It was so sudden. To make matters worse, Heniek asked her not come to the train station to say good-bye. His behavior caused much gossip amongst their circle of friends. Eventually we found out that Heniek didn't want Anja at the train station because his parents and his cousin—to whom he was engaged—were there.

In the beginning, Heniek wrote to my sister but soon his letters stopped. This was a heart-breaking time for Anja. She was so in love with him. Night after night, she stayed up crying. I could see that her spirit was broken by this terrible betrayal. She was my beautiful, older sister, and it was during this time that I became very close with her.

I also came to realize that I had to take my life into my own hands. Like Anja, I wanted to control the money I earned. At least, Pola adjusted and she also got a job. Now, we all contributed equally toward our living expenses. With my newfound freedom, I spent less money on food and started to dress in nicer clothes. I saw quickly how those around me responded to my new look. Suddenly boys were paying attention to me and started asking me out the movies, theater, and to restaurants for tea and cake, and sometimes even for a hot dog with mustard.

During this time, I started working with children. My first job was to get them ready for school. I was tutoring them in Polish. In most Jewish homes, the children spoke only Yiddish or Hebrew so I was paid well. Later on I worked as a nanny in the wealthier Jewish homes where both parents had jobs. It was easy for me, because these homes had housekeepers to take care of the cleaning and cooking. I only had to take care of the child. In addition to my salary I was offered breakfast and lunch, so I could save money. The best part of the day was in the afternoons when I would take the child to the park. Many of my friends came to visit me there.

A year went by in that manner. There was no one to care for at home, so we all had more freedom. For the first time since Mother's illness, seven years earlier, Pola left the safety of our room to work among people. She was like a mother to us, and we no longer needed her. Pola did not date. As I grew older I realized that as much as Pola sacrificed, she liked the safety of staying at home. To make matters worse, Pola had to learn new skills for factory work. She was twenty-seven years old. It took her a long time to adjust to this new life; as a matter of fact, I don't know if she ever really did.

* * *

Anja, Sevek, and I had many friends. There was a constant stream of young people coming and going in and out of our room. Our cousin Itzak started coming around more often. We were a high-spirited group, young and at the peak of life. There was always a guitar to accompany our happy songs. I was ready to take on the ever-changing world and planned to do it in a very different fashion from the generation before me.

I was now seventeen and, like my sister, aware that the working class was powerless. The rich had always exploited the poor, but suddenly this realization took on a more urgent meaning. The real problem was that poor were uneducated. Exploitation is easy when a worker cannot read or write. It was common for boys and girls from poor families to start working at a young age, and this was why illiteracy was so prevalent.

Tensions between the working class and the wealthy grew at the same time the relationship between Poles and Jews deteriorated. The Great Depression of the 1930s placed further strain on this relationship. Poland's economy was based mostly on an agricultural market, and our economic crisis lasted longer than in other industrially developed counties.

By 1931, there were 330,000 Jews in Warsaw, the largest population of Jews in Europe. Poles, however, did not see Jews as true Poles. Most Jews lived separate lives from the Polish majority and listed Yiddish or Hebrew as their native language. At the same time Polish laws virtually excluded Jews from working in government jobs, including transportation or teaching in universities. For the most part, we were generally restricted to jobs in retail and skilled trades. The overwhelming majority worked in commerce and industry; we were shopkeepers and small manufacturers. We were artisans and street peddlers. Only a small percentage worked in white-collar jobs such as education, culture, medicine, and social services. Hospital administration jobs as well as pharmacy jobs, even in Jewish neighborhoods, were considered off-limits to Jews. There was one Jewish hospital, at Czyste, in Warsaw, at the last stop of the trolley car. Here doctors, nurses, and all of the administration were Jewish, but in 1937 the Catholic trade union of Polish doctors restricted new membership to only Christian Poles. 'Aryan clauses' further expelled Jewish doctors, and lawyers from their ranks.

By 1938, Jewish university students had dropped from twenty-four percent to eight percent as a result of anti-Jewish riots and school quotas. The newspapers wrote about 'Ghetto Benches,' an official segregation, introduced in 1935 that continued until the German invasion. It forced Jewish university students, under threat of expulsion, to sit in classrooms on the left-hand side reserved exclusively for them.

* * *

Within the Jewish *kehilla*,[11] political life was thriving—though it was divided into Orthodoxy, Zionism, and Bundism. Each ideology was further subdivided. Each political movement published their own newspaper: *Opinia*, a Jewish weekly in Polish; *Nasz Przegląd*, a Jewish daily in Polish; *Haynt 'Today'* and *Der Moment* both were Yiddish daily newspapers. These newspapers cost very little, so that those who were not illiterate, regardless of language or monetary status, would read them. Anja's husband, Szymon, worked as a printer for one of the major Yiddish newspapers.

Jewish creativity flourished despite economic difficulties and religious persecution. Writers and journalists like Isaac Bashevis Singer, Shalom Aleichem, Sholem Asch, and I.L. Peretz were among the classic Jewish writers. Janusz Korczak, Bruno Schulz, and Julian Tuwim were Jewish writers at the time who were among those who made important contributions to polish literature.

---

[11]   *Kehilla*, governmental authority in Jewish communities. http://www.myjewishlearning.
    com/history/Modern_History/1700-1914/traditional-jewish-life.shtml

By 1932, unemployment was an enormous problem in Warsaw, and workers gravitated more and more toward revolutionary organizations. But labor organizations were short-lived. Their activities were always under suspicion of having connections to Communism. When these groups were shut down, their leaders were arrested in large numbers.

But Polish workers were persistent, with their sympathies growing more and more toward Communism. They read Russian literature about how to build a Bolshevik society, and it didn't take long for people to understand the Russian workers' five-year plan and to learn about its productivity and outcome. Soon, many revolutionaries were dreaming about going to Russia, even though the borders were closed. Many left Poland illegally to get into Russia.

I watched many of Anja's male friends leave Poland and their girlfriends behind. Most were never heard from again. They were hunted down by the police for their supposedly antigovernment activities. Our friends were afraid to endanger the lives of those they left behind by communicating their whereabouts. We could not ascertain if these men had ever even made it to Russia.

Many of the arrested were interrogated, even the innocent, until they admitted to antigovernment activities and named the organizations they belonged to. The police interrogators did as they saw fit to extract whatever information they were seeking. Police stuck pencils under fingernails or forced a hand on a door sash. Obviously these painful methods forced the prisoners to talk whether they were 'guilty' or not.

There was one such place on Mokotowie Street. Political prisoners ended up in the basement where the cells were barely large enough for a single person in solitary confinement. We soon heard descriptions of cells with dirt floors and no windows where prisoners could not even stand up. Prisoners were given only bread and water.

Not far away from where we lived on Pawiej Street was a jailhouse called Pawiak. The Pawiak was built in 1829, and after Poland regained its independence in 1918, it became Warsaw's main prison for male criminals. The women's jailhouse section was called Serbia. Serbia was a complex of a three-story building. It included warehouses, workshops, a kitchen, baths, and a laundry. All the windows in the women's jail were boarded up with wooden crates and sealed with iron bars. The women on the inside never saw daylight. A high wall topped with barbed wire enclosed the entire complex. The prisoners went out for one-hour walk every day. They had to walk in a straight line, one after the other. Families were allowed to deliver a package of food twice a week. At the jailhouse gate these packages were thoroughly inspected. Visiting was limited to once a month, and only the closest family members could enter. These conditions did not stop the determined and organized workers. In fact, their numbers increased. Unions, established inside the workplaces, had to deal with spies and snitches at every turn. Unions were constantly closed down by both the business owners and the government, but workers were determined and fought back even harder. If the union organizers were jailed, new leaders found their way to the vacant positions. Cultural centers for workers opened, the largest belonging to the Socialist Bund Movement. Bund played a very important role in the Jewish political and social life with the focus on political awareness. Anja joined the Bund Movement. Every night, together with her friends, they went to different social events that actually were political meetings where activities were organized and planned. The Jewish Bund Movement was founded in 1897. Bund sought to unite all Jewish workers throughout the Russian Empire. This included Lithuania, Latvia, Byelorussia, Ukraine, and most of Poland, areas where the majority of the world's Jews then lived. When Poland fell under German occupation in 1914, the Polish Bundists became a separate political party. The Polish Bund continued their activities until 1948; they strongly opposed Zionism and were progressive with regard to gender equality—women made up more than one-third of all members.

The Bund Movement concentrated on Jewish youth. They opened youth clubs where I soon became involved. As I became familiar with the principles of Socialism, I saw that Bund had the answers to the workers' complaints. Life took on a new meaning. There was hope for the future. The one magnificent, impossible dream became making Poland a great country for all workers.

On a personal level, I finally belonged somewhere. The youth club had programs I could join: a drama circle, sports, and exercise groups. I could sing in a choir. We even had our own orchestra. We saw who we were and what value we had.

Club Jutrzuia, part of the Bund Movement, was headquartered on Nalewki Street in a building called Pasaz Simonsa. I joined a choir named *Orfeush* named after the Greek God Orpheus: the 'father of song.' Our director, Shafrajski, was famous in Warsaw at that time.

On Sunday mornings we performed in movie houses. I was overjoyed with my role singing with the choir and with our own orchestra. Everything we performed had to be approved by the government, so when we called on the working classes to destroy the walls of oppression we sang in Yiddish. The general theme was to fight for a new and better tomorrow, praising the Soviet Union and the October Revolution of 1917. I still wonder how we got away with it. By performing in Yiddish and in a different movie house every Sunday, we kept one step ahead of the law.

* * *

The Jewish Socialist Bund supported assimilation. One of the many left-wing political parties, their aim was to build a better society for everyone in the countries where they were living. One of many movements that demonstrated together, and with police protection, Bund attracted young acculturated Jews. Their philosophy was that Jews did not have to leave, that they could maintain a satisfactory Jewish way of life right there in Poland. Bund became so successful that they even opened their own private schools. Their ideology was antitradition, but at the same time they worked to preserve Jewish culture, institutions, and Yiddish language.

Anja was at a cultural center called Progres Wieczorami, not far from where we lived. The police conducted a raid at a time the center was packed with young people. Those with identification papers would be allowed to go home and those who didn't would be arrested.

One of Anja's friends came running to our apartment to report that Anja was in trouble. She didn't have her papers with her. Although I was the youngest, I was the one who went with the papers to rescue my sister. Luckily, I had enough sense to take my identification papers as well.

It was ten o'clock at night. An officer stood guard in front of the closed doors. I explained that my sister was inside and that I had her identification papers. Miraculously he let me in. As I made my way upstairs I was stopped several times by undercover police and repeatedly questioned. Their questions were all the same. "Stop, show me your papers? What are you doing here?"

I rehearsed my answer on my way to rescue Anja. "My sister and I got separated. I forgot that her identification papers are here in my purse. I have to go back and give them to her." I finally got to the room where those being questioned were packed together. Most of Anja's friends were there. I saw my sister in the crowd. Her face was white against her black velvet hair. I could see she was trying to look brave and keep up a smile, but I saw her hand quickly wiping tears from her face when she thought nobody was looking. I made my way across the room and touched her. She threw her arms around my neck. When our turn came, I showed our papers to the police. They let us go home.

Anja held my hand tightly all the way home. After this terrible scare, she started taking me with her everywhere. We were six years apart but we became closer than ever.

Suzanna

Poland—the cradle to Poles of Jewish faith and Orthodox Jews

Bund, an ideology of the twentieth century, believed that "territory is a myth". Polish Jews were attached to Poland and Polish culture and to both leftist and Jewish nationalist ideals. My mother was a proud Bundist in prewar Poland. Bund was called the General Union of Jewish Workers which came to life in Lithuania, Poland, and Russia. It was a Jewish Socialist political movement, founded in Vilnius in 1897, by a small group of workers and intellectuals from the Jewish Pale of tsarists Russia. The Bundists came together to end discrimination against the Jews. It became a successful social organization, fighting for the rights of all workers. In 1920, the Russian Bund was divided into two groups: the majority merged with the Communist Party while the minority, led by Rafael Abramovich, continued until its suppression by the Bolsheviks. The Polish Bund concentrated on labor activism, and by 1910 created legal Bundist trade unions in four cities. The Polish Bund became a separate entity, and in December 1917 the split was formalized in a secret meeting in Lublin. The Bund was a legal organization.

Bund promoted the use of Yiddish as a Jewish national language and strongly opposed Zionism arguing that emigration to Palestine was a form of escape. The focus was on culture rather than on a nation or a place as the glue of "Jewish Nationalism." Borrowing from the Austro-Marxist school instantly caused a rift between Bundists and Communists. The Austro-Marxist idea was to make the nation obsolete, that "territory is a myth". Bundists believed that a nation did not have to be organized along territorial lines but could be an association of societies thus totally disconnecting a nation from a territory. In the 1930s, Bund was the most popular party among Polish Jews. During the interwar years, most Polish Jews were Bundists.

My mother wrote of her mistrust of Communist ideology and how those doubts were further solidified during the six years of war that she survived in Stalin's Russia. In the end, Bund's ideology proved itself to be flawed. It also exposed the lie about the stereotype of Polish anti-Semites that Jews were conditioned from birth to be communist and that Jews were responsible for Communism in Poland.

Before WWII Poland was the cradle to Orthodox Jews and Poles of Jewish faith. The Zionists, HeHalutz, the Pioneers, blossomed across Europe, Russia and Poland at the end of 19th and the beginning of the 20th centuries, and had its peak 1930–1935. Its aim was to train its members to settle in the land of Palestine. As many as 5 percent of Polish Jewry (about 140,000) emigrated for Palestine between 1918 and 1942.

The "father" of political Zionism, Theodore Herzl (1860-1904), was a Budapest born, Viennese, emancipated, secular journalist who covered the Dreyfus affair in 1894. Herzl had little interest in Judaism and little interest in Jewish matters until he experienced anti-Semitism first-hand. As Herzl made his way to cover the Dreyfus trial, he encountered demonstrators shouting, "Down with the Jews!" or "Death to the Jews." Dreyfus was a captain in the French Army who was falsely accused and convicted of treason, he was acquitted and completely cleared some years later. This case crystalized for Herzl the strong anti-Semitism rampant in the upper echelons of the French Army, in the French press and in Europe in general. Herzl witnessed that even emancipated Jews were not immune to anti-Semitism and that the only solution to anti-Semitism lay with a reestablishment of a Jewish Homeland.

The pogroms that Jews suffered throughout the Eastern European countries were a further reinforcement for Zionism. The persecutions, killings, and burnings were widespread because Jews were forced to live in confined areas. The worst pogroms occurred from 1881–83 and from 1903–06 in the Pale of Settlement, in the western region of Imperial Russia; Lithuania, Ukraine, Belarus, Eastern Poland, and Latvia. Here hundreds of communities were assaulted and thousands of Jews were murdered. Zionism and Bund grew out of this state-sponsored anti-Semitic attack on Jews. When the first Zionist Congress was convened in Basle in 1897, Eastern European Jewry participated with the greatest majority and they would only accept a homeland in the land of Zion.

At the end of WWI the Ottoman Empire was dissolved with the Treaty of Versailles. In 1919 the British promised that Palestine will be divided between the British, Arabs, and Jews using the Balfour Declaration, which promised to mandate the historic Jewish Homeland in Palestine. The homeland of the Jewish people was going to be reestablished, but the Balfour Declaration did not materialize the way it was supposed to because of Arab violence. Reuniting the Jews living in diaspora with the land of their forebears was put on hold. However, Jews were free to emigrate and to purchase land in Palestine. In 1939, The White Paper policy issued by the British government in response to the Arab revolt in Palestine put a limit on Jewish immigration. Between 3-5 % of Europe's Jews made Aliyah, moving to the Holy Land, until and during the outbreak of WWII. The last toast in the Passover ceremony was and is "Next year in Jerusalem".

Orthodox Jews at that time completely rejected any Jewish political movement and did not attend the congress. The socialist "Bund" organization also rejected nationalism and Zionism.

CHAPTER SIX

Aron lived in our building, and I remember that when we were children, he was often not very nice to me. He taunted me with baby names and occasionally gave me a push if no one was looking. I was somewhat afraid, although I also felt sorry for him. After all, Aron was an orphan, and I knew he had to deal with hardships that were similar to my own. Like us, Aron and his four siblings struggled to survive without a mother or father.

Most of the entertainment in my teenage years happened right in our room on 54 Nawolipki Street, when Sevek's friends came to visit. They were good-natured boys who came from all over the neighborhood. I didn't think much about Aron, but suddenly he was visiting Sevek and behaving differently toward me. One day he stopped me as I was running up the stairs and he was coming down. I was shocked when he asked me, right there, if I would go on a date with him. I didn't feel comfortable saying no, probably because I didn't even know how to reject an invitation like his. Although I was almost seventeen years old, I had never gone out with a boy before.

We took the trolley car to the Warsaw Yiddish Art Theater on Oboznej Street to see a play. Afterward Aron bought me a hot dog. At the time, Warsaw played a major role in the development of the Jewish theater, music, and art. Ida Kaminska with her husband Zygmunt Turkow had founded the Warsaw Yiddish Art Theatre in 1923-24, which presented not just classic Yiddish works but also Shakespeare, Moliere, Victor Hugo, and Eugene O'Neill, among others.

At the time Aron asked me on that date, he was a metal worker who made good money. I was impressed that he also belonged to a revolutionary group called 'Bojówki,' the Fighting Organization of the Polish Socialist Party. I worried about the gun he always carried. He tried to comfort me by repeating that he had one "just in case he needed it."

Aron tried to make my life easier. He bought me an expensive watch, one that I could only have dreamed about, but could never afford to get. Our dates became frequent, dinner followed by a stroll along the beautiful Warsaw boulevards. We were surrounded by trees that lined the wide streets. I gazed at the fancy store windows, admiring the latest fashions. It's hard to believe now, but though I was almost seventeen, those were the first times I had walked streets beyond my own neighborhood. I looked in awe at the women in their stylish clothes and the men with top hats holding sliver-handled canes.

Aron was strong and healthy but he did have a physical flaw. His yellow, crooked teeth created such an aversion for me that I could not look directly at his face. I enjoyed his company and being with him enlivened my otherwise drab existence but I knew from the beginning that I could never love Aron, that I could not even imagine a life with him as my husband. Aron was illiterate but he was not stupid. He suggested that if I agreed to marry him he would remove all his teeth and replaced them with false ones. I didn't promise him anything because I knew I could never love him, bad teeth or not.

Unfortunately for Aron, but not so unfortunate for me, he came down with typhus. I was there when the ambulance took him away. I did not go to visit him at the hospital, guilty as I felt. I knew that this would end our courtship, and it did. Aron survived typhus, but we never went out on a date again.

Meanwhile in 1935, Anja met Szymon, a young printer. Szymon had no family in Warsaw. Like other young men his age, he came to the capital in order to establish a career. He left behind his family in a small village, *shtetel*, never to see them again. Many young men who came from a conservative background who chose their own path in life were forced to sever their ties to the disapproving families left behind. After dating for only a brief period, Anja and Szymon got married. Nine months later Anja gave birth to a son whom she named Pinkus after our father, just like Sala did with her son. Unfortunately, the family Anja and Szymon rented a room from saw the newborn baby as an inconvenience; they were forced to find a new place to live and decided to leave Warsaw.

In 1936, many people were already leaving Warsaw. The first electric train line from Warsaw opened. The 'line to Otwock' went to a summer town where Jews would go on vacation. The air in Otwock was so pure that the very first sanatorium for those with consumption was built there in 1893. By 1923, it became a popular health resort destination, dotted with summer homes. Now, one could easily travel from Warsaw's Gdanski railroad station on an electric train to Otwock, and other towns along the way. Since it was such a short ride, people started to live in Otwock and the other small towns year-round, the men commuting to Warsaw for work. In this way, the mothers and children stayed away from the city and enjoyed the fresh air of the pine forest.

Anja found a small apartment; Szymon commuted to work in the city. Anja and Szymon did not have many choices. Only those from well-to-do families could raise children and focus on issues outside of the home. After giving birth to their first child, Anja could no longer participate in the workers movement. Her family needed her; she had to focus on her husband and baby, on their future, and on raising a family.

In the summer of 1936, I was without a job. Anja kept writing me letters begging me to come and spend the summer with her. She promised me a good time, and said that the landlord had three sons who were about my age. Their family also owned an upholstery shop in Warsaw on Długiej Street. The father and the three sons commuted to work every day. Anja was right—I really had nothing much to do in Warsaw, so I decided to go. On the second day, there I met the landlord's middle son. Max and I would talk for hours, go for long walks, and to soccer games in the village. When we were together people in the street would turn to look at us. His family was respected and well known, and so there was gossip about who this new girl might be. From the look on Anja's face I could tell she was very happy for me.

Everyone said my face was like a ripe apple. My eyes were sky blue and my blond hair was like wheat ready for harvest. To this day I remember how I was dressed that first day I met Max. I wore a tight gray skirt, a fashionable black silk blouse, and high-heeled white sandals. Max was tall, also with blond hair, and so handsome. His smile dazzled me. I could not look away. He was home for a month's vacation during the time that I was visiting Anja. Since there were no daughters in Max's family, the sons had to help their mother with chores.

During the day I took Anja's baby to sit in the grass so that my sister could do household chores without interruption. She lived on the first floor and Max and his family lived on the ground floor. Whenever Max saw me sitting with the baby in the grass, he rushed outside to sit next to me.

My memories of the time I spent with Max are wonderful. He was educated, intelligent, and full of life. All he wanted to do was spend time at my side. His mother, however, seemed to have other plans. She needed him urgently whenever she saw us together. She would look out the window, see us sitting in the grass, and call him to help her with something. I knew in my heart she didn't really need Max, and he seemed to know it, too. I saw the frustration and anger on his face, but Max always obeyed his mother.

During these times, memories of Anja's former lover not standing up to his parents either came flooding back to me. He claimed to be in love with Anja, but he put up no objections when his rich parents sent him to Belgium and arranged his marriage. Max was from a rich family, too, and I, like Anja, was a poor girl without a mother or father. Max's mother, I am sure, was planning an arranged marriage amongst their own kind for her precious son.

One moonlit night Max sang romantic songs to me as we walked along a country road near his house. Inside, he scooped me up in his arms and started to carry me toward his room. I knew what he wanted, and my heart melted. My knees were weak when I asked that he put me down. It would have been so easy in that moment to say yes. I was so in love with Max, it was as if I was under his spell. Somehow I found the strength to tell him that I would not have sex before marriage. He said he understood, but there was such disappointment in his eyes. After that night we still went out in the evenings and saw each other every day until his vacation ended. Max took my address and went back to work in Warsaw.

* * *

When it came down to getting married, I had no support from my older siblings. Adek, Sala, or Pola needed to step into the role of my mother or father, but none of them did; they were consumed with their own lives. I told Pola about Max, but she did not offer any help. I knew that she wanted me to stay single and keep her company; she wanted me to take part in everything she did, and of course, share in the expenses.

Anja's first failed love affair with her well-to-do boyfriend left a great impression on me. It was always on my mind: the fear that Max would do the same thing to me. The poverty I had grown accustomed to also made me cautious about reaching beyond my class.

Max did wait for me at the gate of my building in Warsaw a few times. I was in love with him and felt proud when the neighbors saw us together. Sometimes I would talk myself into believing that he would fight with his parents about dating me, but on the other hand, there was no denying that he always obeyed his mother. The sensible part of me knew there was no hope for us and that in the end, nothing would come of our relationship. One day I got up the courage to tell Max I couldn't see him anymore. He had tears in his eyes, but at the same time he looked strangely relieved.

I did have other male friends, and soon, I was being taken out to the movies and to the theater almost every night. I went on many dates, but I can honestly say that Max was the most perfect man I had ever met. No one ever came as close to my heart as Max, my first true love.

I am putting my pen down and walking around my apartment, my thoughts flooding my mind, there are so many. They come and go too quickly for me to capture them on the paper. Paper, as always, is patient and will wait.

When I look back, I see that my life was one big riddle that I was left to solve on my own. Conditioned by my immediate surroundings and experiences, I understood that taking risks could bring me luck, but also misfortune. What I remember most profoundly is that I had to constantly fight the sadness of knowing that if my parents had lived, they would have undertaken the job of talking to the boy's family about marriage. And so, in the end, Max just flew away with the wind. At the same time a greater riddle was about to envelop my generation as the political climate changed.

* * *

With Anja married, there were only three of us left at home: Pola, Sevek, and me. It was difficult to pay the rent and the electricity that had recently been installed. Yes, our neighborhood finally had electricity. The family that lived in our kitchen was getting older; they were in poor health and could no longer afford to pay us the rent. The rent collector for the owner of the building was still the same, tall Jewish man. I remembered that even when mother was alive, she and everyone in the tenement building were afraid of him, but the residents had organized and now the collector himself was afraid to come and ask for rent.

The Jewish owner of the building fired the rent collector and hired in his place a Pole. This new collector developed a different system. He set up a table in the courtyard and at a specific time of the month, we had to go to him to pay the rent. The owner of the building raised the rents; the tenants fought back, organizing a committee to boycott the increase. Most of us didn't have enough money to pay the rent to begin with, so the raise was unbearable. Meanwhile the building's owner decided to get even with us. He sent inspectors to look for people who lived in the building without being properly registered. Heavy citations were issued for these poor souls.

Then the owner decided that the resident's boycott was the result of Communist instigators. Late one night, the police came to our building and proceeded to inspect every apartment in an attempt to find anything connecting the residents to the Communist Party. We were all required to stay in our apartments as the police entered our homes and looked through our belongings. Our room was clean of any literature or anything else that would be considered suspicious or illegal, but in the morning we learned that a neighbor, a father of five children who lived in the building across the courtyard, was taken away. We never saw him again.

Since it was illegal, the Communist Party had to be self-sufficient. Members had to be capable of doing everything for the party in secrecy. Fliers, leaflets, and all other illegal literature were printed mostly at home. Finding such items in people's apartments automatically tied them to the party.

Some party members appeared dedicated but really worked for the police. One active party member, Cyw, was liked by everyone. Whenever he attended a secret Communist Party meeting, a raid would follow, forcing the meeting to come to a sudden halt. The members would scatter. The unlucky ones who didn't run away fast enough were arrested.

Eventually, Cyw was exposed as a snitch. In retaliation, two party members were chosen as enforcers and given guns. They set up a phony meeting on Stawki Street across from where we lived. Cyw did not suspect anything, but when he arrived at the designated place, one of the party members took out his gun and killed him. The two members had passports ready and left Poland immediately. An ambulance came to take the body away, and the police scoured the area for weeks in the hope of finding the killers. They never did. But after this incident we all were afraid to leave our apartments.

* * *

After Sala and Moniek acquired the barbershop, they continued to struggle for the first couple of years. After the birth of their first son Piniek, Sala was able to stay home with him for only a few months and then had to go back to work. Sala sent the baby to her husband's aunt for the whole day, with part of her wages going to pay for childcare. The aunt had four children of her own and a husband to take care of, so she took Salas's baby with her everywhere as she did her daily errands. Piniek developed pneumonia when he was only eighteen months old. He was so weak that he stopped walking. The doctor ordered my sister to take the baby away from Warsaw, and to go to Michalin to recover. Sala took time off from work, and together with Pola, went to the healing town. During the trip, they didn't think that Piniek would make it.

After just a week, Pola came back to Warsaw and I went to Michalin to help Sala with the baby. We spent the days outdoors in the fresh air among the beautiful evergreen and pine trees. Slowly he started getting better. As he regained his health, and his strength, he was able to walk again. After six weeks, we all returned to Warsaw. Sala went back to work, and the baby went back to the aunt for childcare. The poor child would get pneumonia two more times. Finally, I could not stand by and watch any longer.

I had to get up the courage to confront Sala and explain to her that she would lose her son if she didn't take care of him herself. Sala quit her job and Moniek changed the salon on Nowolipki Street to cater to both men and women. He hired two more employees, and finances started to finally look up for Sala's family.

In 1936, Sala gave birth to another son, named Gutek. He was a beautiful baby with black curly hair and dark eyes. I visited them often to take the older boy Piniek for a walk. I also went to see my brother Adek. He now had a beautiful little girl, Bluma, and I would take her out for a walk, too. I would do the same for Anja's little boy Pinkus.

Suzanna
Leaving the Old World

When I think about my parents' life after the war in Communist Poland, living in a constant state of fear, I often wonder why my mother did not choose to save herself. She could have gone to Paris. Her cousin Itzak and her best friend Ada had survived the war and lived there with their two children. Itzak and my mother shared a long, affectionate history; I just know he would have come to my mother's rescue with open arms. When my family finally did leave Poland in the late 1960s, we stayed in Paris. My sister and I met Ada, her son and daughter, and Ada's grandchildren. But by now, Itzak was no longer alive.

My mother never considered saving us by leaving Poland without my father. She said that the way her life turned out was *Beshert*—meant to be. After my father's death, my mother's grief overwhelmed her. They had been together from the time they had met in 1940 until his death in 1961. Overnight, with the responsibility of having to care for two young daughters, her fears of abandonment came rushing back. They were the same fears, she never got to experience what it's like to have a father, when she was ten and her mother had a stroke, and then again at age fourteen, when her mother died. After my father's death, my mother suffered a severe attack of eczema that covered her face with ghastly sores. The only thing visible was her blue eyes. It was known, even in those days, that her ailment was brought on by stress and difficult to treat. She suffered terribly. Months passed before she could go outside. It took many doctors and many medications, but finally my mother's face began to heal.

Just as my mother predicted, we were to pay a heavy price when we finally left Poland. My mother was a middle-aged widow who could not speak English and would be living in a strange country with a totally different way of life. When we came to America, we tried to keep a delicate balance between the old world and the new one. My mother confided in me later that she had made a mistake in leaving. She was convinced that if we had stayed in Poland, we, as a family, would have remained intact.

My mother foresaw future. She understood that her daughters would assimilate faster then she would to a new way of life. She was fearful that my sister and I would reject the old ways, and that this would create a distance between her and us. As much as we all tried to cling to the old, we desperately wanted to fit in. In America, the family that we once were in Poland ceased to exist. My mother and sister had to go to work and I went to school. My mother was also left with so much guilt and remorse.

She always felt education was the most important thing, but now in America my seventeen-year-old sister, who graduated at the top of her class, could not go to university. She had to work to help support us.

It had been twenty years since my mother and her sister had last seen each other. Pola was sixty years old. She and her husband had just retired to Florida. They were no longer involved in any business and could not help us find work. My mother decided we would not follow Pola because we would have fewer opportunities in Florida, so we stayed in New York.

I was shocked that we weren't joining aunt Pola in Florida. This was the reason we left Poland: to be reunited with family. I had envisioned our new life in America with Pola and Morris at our side. I wanted so much to be part of an extended family. I kept telling my mother that we need to live next to Pola. But my mother could think of nothing else but how she was going to support us in the new world. Memories of poverty, of suffering hunger as a child in Poland, and barely surviving hunger in Russia haunted her. When my older sister was offered a job in New York, Mother dismissed looking at other options. Mother had a friend in New York with whom she survived Uzbekistan. Her daughter, Miriam and her husband said my sister could work as a bookkeeper in their office. My sister, however, would have to attend night school and get a degree. My mother was grateful for their help, and for the next two years she, herself, worked in a factory in New York for minimum wages.

Once again, the possibility of becoming part of an extended family eluded us. The Holocaust had left not only my mother, but the second generation with tangible and emotional losses. My sister and I never got to experience the warmth and support that comes with being a part of an extended family. Pola, my mother's only surviving sister, never had children, and I never really got to know my aunt or my uncle. Pola was afraid to fly; she came to visit us in the Bronx only a few times and she always took the train.

Pola Bravstein died December 2, 1980 in Miami. My mother, my sister, and I flew to her funeral. By then, her husband, Morris, was no longer alive.

CHAPTER SEVEN

Both national and black flags hung low over the crying population of Warsaw. The year was 1935, a most memorable year for Poland. Jozef Piłsudski, also known as 'Grandfather Jozef,' was dead.

Piłsudski's sixty-eight years were filled with political turmoil. A young Socialist, he was arrested in 1887 by Tsarist authorities and accused of plotting to assassinate Tsar Alexander III. After serving a five-year sentence in Siberia, Piłsudski founded the Polish Socialist Party, edited its newspaper, *Robotnik* ('The Worker') and became the party leader.

Upon the outbreak of World War I in 1914, General Piłsudski's Polish Legion of 10,000 volunteers fought with valor against Russia at the side of the Austro-Hungarian Empire and Prussia. In Piłsudski's eyes, Russia was Poland's greatest enemy.

By 1918, Piłsudski was the head of state and leader of all Polish troops. He represented Poland at the Versailles Treaty in June of 1919. His army successfully defended Poland against the Russian Red Army in the Russo-Polish War of 1919–1920. The Red Army advanced as far East as Warsaw. Known as "The Miracle on the Vistula River," the heavily outnumbered Polish troops were able to stop the enemy. In March of 1921, Poland and Russia signed the Treaty of Riga, marking the end to aggression. This treaty granted Poland large parts of Lithuania, Western Belarus, and the Ukraine.

Piłsudski remained in charge of the Polish army until 1923. Troubled by the futility of the Polish government and the widespread corruption, he returned to power, waging a successful military coup after a three-year retirement. Piłsudski's *coup d'etat* of May 1926 ensured that the Left-wing liberal Sanacja regime would remain in power. The National Assembly elected Ignacy Moscicki, who became the president of Poland until September 1939. But it was Piłsudski who had the power for the next nine years. Piłsudski's aim was to restore the Polish nation back to a path of moral principles. His government, military in character, mixed democratic and dictatorial elements as it worked to develop a new Polish constitution. His government did permit a multiparty system. His main opposition was the Right-wing National Democratic Party.

In April 1935, adapted by Piłsudski supporters to his specifications, although too late for Piłsudski himself, the new Constitution reduced the power of the *Seym* and gave greater power to the president. The Constitution would serve Poland to the outbreak of World War II and would carry its government-in-exile until the end of the war and beyond.

Piłsudski and his government fought against the right-wing policies of nationalism and economic anti-Semitism. The right-wing National Democratic Party, called 'Endecja' for short, and their leader Roman Dmowski aligned themselves with the rising fascism of its time.

The economic disaster of the 1930s was especially severe on an agricultural country like ours. The start of the Great Depression brought with it more tension between the working class and the capitalists, at the same time, the relationship between Polish Nationals and Jews deteriorated quickly. After Piłsudski's death, Endecja successfully replaced liberal ideology and nationalism moved into the center of political, economic, and social life. With the poverty and suffering brought on by the economic catastrophe, the Endecja quickly became more radical. The anti-Semitism that was buried by Piłsudski was out in the open again. Endecja's growing popularity was fueled by a need to blame someone for the Depression.

New legislation called for Jews to emigrate. Universities established 'ghetto benches' to separate Jews from Polish students. Jewish university students started to drop out, as a result of anti-Jewish riots in schools and unofficial quotas. Jewish shops were boycotted and anti-Jewish violence increased. With the Depression Poles were already struggling to get jobs, but almost overnight, it became even harder for Jews. Most Jews in Warsaw were small business owners, factory workers, or merchants. A smaller percentage worked in education, culture, medicine, and social services. Hospitals were controlled by Polish doctors and nurses. By 1937 the Catholic trade union of Polish doctors restricted new membership to only Christian Poles. 'Aryan clauses' expelled Polish Jewish doctors, as well as lawyers.

* * *

The Depression made it difficult for us to pay the rent and electricity for our room on Nowolipki Street. We tried desperately to hold on to this meager little place because it had been not just our home but our parents'. To make matters worse, the family that lived in our kitchen stopped paying us rent. Mr. and Mrs. Ulman were without jobs. They had no money, and it was hard for them to walk up the four flights.

Their son Elek had married his cousin who was pregnant. His new bride had been going out with many men, but when she became pregnant she asked Elek to marry her. To begin with Elek wasn't very smart. To make a living, he sold hangers from courtyard to courtyard. He didn't make very much money this way and he didn't have any extra to give to his parents. Strangely enough, Elek seemed happy just to have a wife with a baby on the way. The Ulman's oldest daughter went to work as a live-in maid; she managed to send some money to her parents. It was sad and hard on everyone, when the Ulmans decided to move to the converted army barracks on Powązki Street.

When Father died, my mother told the owner of the building that her oldest sister and husband were moving in. The owner then registered the Ulmans on his books but never checked if mother and Mrs. Ulman were related. He must have felt sorry for Mother, and strangely, Mother and Mrs. Ulman did look somewhat alike. They both had fair skin, light hair, and blue eyes. I remember that they always dressed in the same manner, a long flowing skirt, and a blouse that was always tucked in neatly. There was the ever-present sweater, even in the summer that buttoned in the front and a small handkerchief that covered partially their hair that tied in the back. We always knew that renting our kitchen this way was illegal. The money we collected from the Ulmans should have gone to the owner but we maintained that they were family. After a while, we almost believed they were. We even referred to them as Aunt Zusia and Uncle Leon.

The four of us, including cousin Itzak, moved to a cheaper room in somebody else's apartment. Rooms in Warsaw were easy to find because people were always looking to make some extra money. Our new, smaller room had a window that looked out into a courtyard, and was not far from where we had lived. Our new landlords were a nice couple with two small daughters. They had a dressmaking shop right in the apartment. We only paid for the room. Electricity was included and the rent was less than at our old apartment. We hired a street peddler to haul our belongings down the few blocks.

But after a few months, the apartment was inspected by the building owner. We had no choice but to move out and find a new place to live. Eventually our moving became more and more frequent; we started to sell our meager possessions since most of the rooms we rented were already furnished.

Next we found a lovely room with a balcony on the busy Krochmalna Street. The tenants lived in one small room with a tiny kitchen next to our room. There were six people in the family with barely enough space for anyone to move around. We were not allowed to use their kitchen even to boil water for tea, so a large amount of our money went to buy ready-made food. It didn't take long for us to start looking for another place to live.

One day stands out in my mind during that time. It was about three in the afternoon, and I was hungry. I know it will be difficult for people today to understand how three people in my family could all be working and I could still be hungry. My sister Pola was a factory worker and made very little money. Sevek's work was seasonal, and he was limited because of his heart condition. Itzak was the only one who was relatively well off; he worked and also had the money his father sent him from Paris. But with this money Itzak also supported his mother. Regardless of Itzak's slightly brighter financial position, he was one of us and helped when he could. It was never enough.

I was looking for a job. I walked aimlessly up and down the streets and into shops, asking everyone if anyone knew where I could find some work. On that day, I ran into Adek coming around the corner. He knew I was looking for work and asked me if I had eaten. He wanted to give me a little money but I was too proud to take it. I lied and said I had just eaten because I knew that Adek had his own family to take care of. I was young and strong and needed to be responsible for myself.

Eventually I found a job in a library. Pola still wanted to be in charge of my earnings, but I was determined not to let her. I had not forgotten the things that Pola did in the past that made me unhappy. I remembered the constant fighting between Pola and Anja, always over the money that Pola wanted to control. With all the hopelessness throughout my childhood, it was time for me to be in control.

This newfound independence was not easy. There were times when I felt guilty and insecure. My first step was to keep the money that remained after contributing my share toward the family expenses. Pola, however, was always in need of more. She did not manage her money well; sometimes she foolishly lent it to friends who never gave it back. At times she was wasteful, buying too much food that would spoil and had to be thrown away. In any event, Pola was always borrowing money from me and she never paid it back.

Still, I was able to save a little for a time when I would need it more. I kept my extra money at home. We didn't keep money in the bank. We grew up keeping money in a jar at home, and that is how I still did it. I started to dress nicely. I realized that my childhood dreams of continuing my education could become a reality. I started taking language classes in Esperanto and then in French.

In the 1930s, Esperanto, a universal language, had become very popular. Dr. Ludwig Zamenhof created it in 1887 so that the various nationalities in his own native city of Białystok could communicate with one another, and thus (in his belief) solve many problems.

It didn't take long for me to realize that I had a natural gift for learning languages. I modestly kept the diplomas I received in a box near my bed. Every night before I went to sleep, the last thing I would do before turning down the light was to take them out and re-read them with pride.

* * *

Cousin Itzak and I joined the 'Laboro' Workers Organization Esperanto Movement on Dzikiej Street. I ran the library in the evening and acted as the secretary, accepting new members. With membership came free classes in Esperanto, French, drama, and choir and other creative workshops. We had the use of the famous Broniewski-ego Studio. Here the students created evenings of 'Political Satire/Sketches' connected to the Worker's Movement. These evenings became one of my favorite pastimes. I learned to look at politics with humor. I was also proud to be a member of an organization that drew its *intelligentsia* from the various youth groups in Warsaw.

In the beginning, everyone thought that Itzak and I were a couple. It was comical, at least to me. I don't know if Itzak believed that I was capable of only a sisterly kind of love toward him. However, by joining Laboro we both made many new friends. My closest girlfriend, Ada, also joined. We went often to her home, and I became close with her parents.

I started dating Roman, another member of the Laboro group. He was an electrician. He was born in Russia during World War I. His family came back to Poland where Roman grew up to be an active member of the illegal Leftist Party. He confided to me that his dream was to return to Russia. He believed the Communist Revolution was the only answer for the workers, and he wanted to be part of the revolution.

All this meant that there was no place for Roman in my life. Politics, and especially Communism, did not play a part in my dreams for the future, and I certainly did not want to go to Russia. My home was right here in Poland, where my family and I had always lived. Furthermore, I felt the answers for workers lay within the philosophy of the Bund Movement, where Poles and Jews could coexist peacefully. Bund's aim was to build a better society for everyone in the countries where they were presently living.

Roman and I dated for a while. Eventually he ended up in a local prison where Ada and I brought him the boxes of food and money given to us by his revolutionary organization.

The young members of the Laboro Club went out together in the evenings. On Sundays we would make our way out of the city and into the nearby woods. Sometimes we boarded a boat and sailed on the River Vistula to a place called Młociny, a small town outside Warsaw where people went for a day of rest. I had some of the best and happiest of times there. We played ball and rented bicycles. We each brought food to make a grand picnic. The boys bought us girls sodas and ice cream and took pictures with their cameras. Almost every girl had a crush on a boy. At the end of the day, a boy would take a girl to the movies, and then to a coffee house, where we stayed until midnight.

I had a lot of young men who were interested in me, but, truthfully, I lacked the confidence to get involved on a deep level. I had a recurring dream: I was in the arms of a boy. The dream, however, always ended the same way, with the boy floating away.

There were many young men in my French classes too. I soon got interested in a handsome young man named David. We started talking during recess and discovered we had gone to the same public school and were in the same classes. David was very tall; I barely reached his shoulders. The difference in our height didn't stop us from going out on a date the next day. He took me to the movies and to a coffee house, where he confessed that even in elementary school he had a crush on me. He reminded me that during gym class he had always been my partner. We dated for a short time, but I quickly realized that I was not attracted to him in a romantic way. David and I

stayed friends. He soon found a girlfriend, and I started dating someone new.

I had to admit to myself that although a year had gone by I was
still comparing every boy to Max.

Suzanna
My First Day of School

In Poland, after the war, I could never understand how others knew who the Jews in the community were. It mattered not if we practiced or not our religion, we were still seen as Jews and not as Poles. It was how others saw us, how we were seen in their eyes and not how we saw ourselves that counted.

Here, the French Philosopher Emmanuel Levinas and his notion of ethics and relation as determined by the encounter with the other comes to mind. His model of how others see us serves to understand the Jewish system of belonging and assimilation.

My mother always remembered her school days with emotion. She had always been eager to learn and felt lucky to have been accepted to the second grade in a time when so many school children were still receiving no education. School became the place where she could forget the hardship and poverty at home.

My first memory of school is very different from hers. I was seven years old when I learned that being Jewish meant I was different from my Polish schoolmates. September 1, 1958 was my first day of school. The day began with so much anticipation. I have been looking forward to this day for four years, since the day my older sister first started going to school.

On my very first day, I was taunted by classmates before I ever entered the building.

"You are Jewish, Poland is not your country, and Palestine is where you belong."

I didn't understand. This was the first time I'd heard that my home was in Palestine. It also was the first time I wondered whether being both Jewish and Polish was actually possible. I could not wait to run home. The day became a blur and what I remember clearly is that I was already crying as I opened our kitchen door.

My mother sat with me and patiently explained what it meant to be Jewish. I can still remember the sadness in her voice and the tears in her eyes. My mother's reaction was eclipsed by my amazement. Our true homeland, she told me, was in Palestine. My response was a simple one: "Let's go to where we belong."

CHAPTER EIGHT

It was a blessing that Adek's heart was so big. He was only twelve years old when our father died, but as the eldest son, it became his job to replace him. I often think that our large family was able to survive because of him.

Adek was extremely smart, and I just know he would have gone far as a student if given the opportunity to study. Whatever he saw, his hands could copy, and so could his feet. Adek was an incredible dancer. There seemed to be nothing that Adek couldn't do and for as long as I can remember, I was proud of my brother. He was the most patient and caring of us siblings.

It was easy to believe there was a divine power when Adek's many sacrifices were rewarded by the wonderful Grunblatt family. The Grunblatt's silently watched over him from age twelve until the day he joined their family through marriage to their daughter. Mr. Grunblatt even made Adek his partner in the family business. Adek was the most successful of all of us. As a business partner in his father-in-law's clothing factory he was treated with love—and as a son. Adek married Bronia when she was twenty years old and he was twenty-seven.

My sister Sala's marriage to Moniek had a much more difficult beginning. But after a rough start, Moniek turned out to be a hardworking man. He and Sala joined the middle class, and Sala received everything she ever wanted. She had a small but comfortable apartment with all the modern conveniences, and furnishings in the latest fashion. She no longer had to work; she was proud that she could stay home with her two boys.

Pola had no interests outside our home. With us, she was firm and unyielding, but when it came to the neighbors she was very accommodating, ready to help them with almost anything. I know now that she had a kind heart; she desperately needed to be loved by everyone around her and at the same time she always had to be right. I also know that her childhood came to an abrupt halt when father died. She was forced to grow up overnight. Pola had longed for our mother's approval; our poor mother, however, had been overwhelmed with the job of keeping us alive. Pola did a wonderful job taking care of Mother for four long years. After her death, it was difficult for Pola to go back out into the world.

Money has always been the biggest cause for conflict in our family: the stress of not having enough money, always being short, and never being able to save resulted in many heated arguments. Pola managed our money poorly. After going back to work, she worked hard for her paycheck but she also moved from factory to factory and never stayed long on any job. Her life was a puzzle to me because she never once went out on a date. Now I see that socializing must have been very difficult for her. She needed to feel safe, and where would be safer than her own home or her own neighborhood? Eventually I stopped paying attention to my sister and started putting all my efforts and energies into my own life.

Anja's family did not have much money. Daily life was challenging for them, but at least there was love. A loving husband and father, Szymon worked nights as a printer for one of the big Jewish newspapers so Anja could stay home with their son, and then later, a daughter. Anja suffered when Heniek, her first lover, broke her heart, but Szymon was able to mend it. My siblings and I adored Szymon, his love of work and our sister won him our sincere respect.

Sevek was only three years older than me. We had always been close. Sevek managed to stay in school until he was thirteen years old, when mother's illness interrupted his education. When Sevek became an adult, he went back to school. He enrolled in evening classes and stayed up reading late into the night from a large stock of books. Sometimes on a Friday night Sevek would take me to the local movie theater. Movies captivated Sevek: I still remember how eager he was to see Charlie Chaplin, Tarzan, and Marlene Dietrich.

Now we were constantly faced with moving from one room to the next. Sevek's screams were so loud that he woke the neighbors in the middle of the night. Doctors had no medications to give him; they told us it was his nerves. I tried to keep bad news away from Sevek. I knew that stress and anxiety were harder on him than on most people. Sevek was very handsome and the tallest of all of us. He was the artist and the dreamer. Friends gravitated to him, and many came to our room in the evening to play the guitar and sing songs

One summer evening in 1938 in Saski Garden, a group surrounded Sevek and his friends and beat them with sticks. The young attackers were members of Endecja, an anti-Semitic organization that represented the extreme right political party. Most of Sevek's friends were able to escape, but my brother was severely beaten. He came home with arms and legs that were bleeding and swollen. His face was covered with cuts and bruises. The most painful to see were Sevek's precious hands; he had used his hands to shield his head and face and they were badly cut. Sevek had to stay in bed for weeks. He was not a strong person to begin with, and Pola and I lived with the unspoken fear that he would die young from heart disease.

Sevek didn't chase after girls like the other boys. He would sometimes go out with a cousin on our mother's side but these never lasted long. Sevek's only dream was that he might someday emigrate abroad.

Sevek did date one other girl, a good friend of Pola. Sara was five years older; I always believed that Sevek dated her because she represented a very real chance for him to emigrate. Sara came from a good family who lived outside of Warsaw in a town called Wiskowie. She also had a sister who lived in Australia who promised to send for her. The relationship between Sevek and Sara became a serious one, and the plan was for Sara to leave first for Australia and then send for Sevek to join her. Sevek promised that as soon as he arrived in Australia, he would send for me and Pola. But things like this took a long time.

In the early months of 1939, Sara left Poland and started the papers to get my brother out of the country.

* * *

In 1937, Itzak was twenty-one and wanted to join the army. His mother cried uncontrollably, repeating that he was her only son. Itzak obeyed his mother's wishes. He had been supported throughout his childhood by his father who had remained in Paris. It was around this time that he realized that his mother had squandered everything that they had. Aunt Estera died suddenly in Otwock. Itzak brought his mother's body back to Warsaw. We all went to her funeral to pay our respects.

After the death of his mother, Itzak announced that he and my best friend Ada would marry. Ada's mother and stepfather supported this union. They arranged for a rabbi to marry them officially, and held a celebration in their house afterward for all of us. After their wedding, Itzak left for Paris to be reunited with the father he hadn't seen in over fifteen years. A few months later, Ada joined him there. In Paris, she first gave birth to a boy and after two years, a baby girl.

Pola, Sevek, and I moved to a yet another new room where the rent was even cheaper. Our new landlord was an older couple who had an extra room in their apartment. They were kind to us and even let us use their small kitchen. We had a couch, a table, four chairs, and a closet. We had just enough room at night to unfold two beds.

The apartment was on the ground floor of a five-story building one block away from the bustling business center. The location turned out to be a good place for Sevek. Sevek managed to have a workshop in the corner of our little room. It was here that he made women's purses, even beautiful ones for me and Pola. Sevek actually had two young men working for him. From time to time I also helped him with simple tasks like gluing little mirrors inside the purses. Sevek sold those purses to store owners and he managed to make good money during the spring and fall season.

There were many jobs Sevek could not take because of his weak heart, and there were months that he had nothing to do. Not working took a huge toll on my brother. Some nights he jumped out of bed screaming. It would take two of us to hold him down until he woke up. The elderly couple with whom we lived were very remorseful when they asked us to leave, but it was only a matter of time until Sevak's outburst would have been exposed to the owner of the building.

In Warsaw the middle class remained the working class, but they had achieved some success in small businesses. Many celebrated New Year's Eve attending dances in ballrooms. The men dressed in tuxedos or smoking jackets, and women in long gowns. Adek and his extended family belonged to this upper middle class. Sala and her family, too, rose to the middle class after three years of hard work. On New Year's Eve, Adek with his wife Bronia and Sala and Moniek all celebrated by going to a stylish ballroom.

On December 31, 1938, the Laboro Club members threw a New Year's Eve Party. We all contributed money, food, and drinks. Sevek and I danced and laughed the whole night. In the early morning hours, we descended on the banks of the Vistula River, as was the tradition. Every New Year's at sunrise, thousands of working-class people came to the banks of the river to sing and cheer.

It was very cold outside. Snow crunched under our feet, but the young faces around me were warm and joyful. People walked around singing and wishing each other, even strangers, a Happy New Year. The air was filled with a feeling of incredible happiness and hope for the future.

After Piłsudski's death Poland was under a military dictatorship ruled ineffectually by Piłsudski's men, Marshal Rydz Smigly and President Mościski, who remained in power until 1939. Meanwhile, Fascism grew stronger. The right-wing National Democratic Party, Endecja, moved to the center of political life. Anti-Semitism came out into the open again. Roman Dmowski's theories and his Endecja party came alive. In Dmowski's view, what Poland needed was 'a healthy national egoism.' Dmowski was a fierce challenger to Josef Piłsudski throughout his political career and fought against the left-wing Socialist Party liberal morals. Dmowski co-founded the National Democratic Party or *Endecja* in 1897. He was an accomplished and well-respected scientist who saw Poland as a country that needed to be purged of minorities. Dmowski was openly anti-Semitic. What made him so dangerous was that he was well respected, affluent and educated. He knew nine languages, also had a doctorate in biology. He traveled widely, visited Brazil, Japan, the United States, and Algiers and had been to all of Europe. One can safely assume that he was not a bigot, but he was an anti-Semite. He successfully tapped into centuries-old popular anti-Semitism and blamed all of Poland's problems on its Jewish citizens. He wrote: "This race (Jews) has different values, (they) are strange to our principles and harmful to our life." He and his followers felt that assimilating large number of Jews would destroy the Poles, and turn them into a degenerate element. Dmowski started his speeches with the words, "My religion came from Jesus Christ, who was murdered by the Jews." In his 1926 book, *Polityka Polska*, he accused the Jews of being Poland's worst enemy. By the 1930s, Endecja principles were becoming increasingly incorporated into the government's policies. The economic instability of the times and the Great Depression went hand in hand with anti-Jewish sentiment. Discrimination, exclusion, violence at the universities, and the appearance of 'anti-Jewish squads' were all associated with some of the right-wing principles.

The Endecja movement was anti-Semitic, anti-Communism, anti-capitalism, anti-liberal democracy, pro-nationalism, and pro-traditional right-wing conservatism. Dmowski had long advocated emigration for the entire Jewish Polish population as the solution to the 'Jewish Problem' in Poland. Although he did not advocate for the outright killing of Jews, attacks on Polish Jews escalated rapidly in post-Piłsudski Poland. On the eve of World War II, many typical Polish Christians believed that there were far too many Jews in the country and the Polish government became increasingly concerned with the 'Jewish Question.' In July 1939, the pro-government newspaper *Gazeta Polska* wrote: "The fact that our relations with the Reich are worsening does not in the least deactivate our program in the Jewish question—there is not and cannot be any common ground between our internal Jewish problem and Poland's relations with the Hitlerite Reich." Escalating hostility toward Polish Jews and the Polish government's desire to remove Jews from Poland continued until the German invasion.

* * *

The people in Poland were aware of events in Germany and the rise of the Nazi party and its leader, Adolf Hitler. When a German diplomat, Ernst vom Rath, was assassinated by Herschel Grynszpan, a German Jew, in Paris on November 7, 1938 to protest the expulsion of 12,000 Polish Jews from Germany by the Third Reich, among them Herschel Grynszpan's family, Hitler ordered a brutality of unimaginable proportion. Rath's assassination unleashed a collective punishment on all Jews throughout Germany and Austria. Violence by Germans against Jewish targets became known as *Kristallnacht*, the Night of the Broken Glass.[12] Over a period of 48 hours rioters burned or damaged over 1,000 synagogues, some 7,500 Jewish-owned businesses were ransacked and vandalized, and over 90 people died. The Nazis arrested some 30,000 Jewish men between the ages of 16 and 60 and sent them to die in concentration camps.

After Kristallnacht, we learned of Hitler's expulsion of all the Polish Jews from Germany who did not have German citizenship. Nazi ideology fit in with what was happening in Poland. As the Jews became scapegoats for the entire problem in Germany, Endecja's preaching of 'healthy national egoism' and purging the country of minorities moved Poland closer to Fascism.

Demonstrations in Warsaw intensified. Masses were arrested. Jails overflowed with demonstrating workers who took to the streets. At first, the Communist Party in Poland looked to the Communist

---

[12] Jonathan Kirsch, *The Night of the Broken Glass, The Short Strange Life Of Herschel Grynszpan.*

Party of Germany for support. But with the rise of Nazism, the Communist Party in Germany collapsed. The same fate awaited the illegal Communist Party of Poland.

One day I got a letter from my old boyfriend Roman, who had been often arrested. The mailman looked at me suspiciously. I was sure that police inspection would follow. Being guilty by association was one of the biggest fears of those days. I quickly cleaned out of our room anything that would be considered illegal. The police never came.

Roman's letter was short. He was being held in the men's Pawiak jail. He was worried that he was forgotten by his comrades and would be left there to die. He wanted me to take his letter to his friends. He needed food, clothes and, most importantly, to be rescued as soon as possible. In those days, corruption was widespread: Roman could get out of jail if someone gave enough money to the right people. Though I was frightened, I knew exactly what to do. I took the letter to the Communist revolutionary organization to which Roman belonged. I learned later through a friend that the organization was able to get Roman out of Pawiak.

Most young people had faith that a brighter future was ahead for working men and women. This hope was kept alive by antigovernment literature. I also got involved, handing out packages of these pamphlets. One day I was standing calmly in a doorway of a building on Dzielnej Street after having left a package behind the door. My job was to wait there and distribute the literature to a few group leaders. Then my friend Anka stuck her head in the entrance and whispered that undercover police were observing the building, and I'd better run. It was at just this moment that the building watchman, who lived in a little room next to the doorway, stepped out into the hall. I calmly walked out of the building as he went to pick up the package behind the door. I was young and fast, and even though it seemed he was about to come after me, I quickly found myself at the corner of Karmelickiej Street, the most busy Jewish street in Warsaw, and I got lost in the crowd. It was a miracle I didn't get caught that day. I was one step away from being hauled off to jail.

In November of 1938, we had a demonstration in celebration of the Russian October Revolution. The government sent out police on horseback to break up the crowd. I remember so clearly how people ran, panicking, and fell on top of each other. In a split second I made a decision to walk slowly, as if on a stroll, toward the policemen on horseback. At this point the street was empty. According to the new laws, every building watchman had to lock the gates so that the demonstrators wouldn't be able to hide in the buildings or the courtyards.

I will never know where I found the courage to walk toward the police officers that day. I thought my racing heart would burst right through my chest. I walked right next to a policeman on horseback. He didn't seem to notice me. I just kept walking until the police force and the demonstrators were behind me. I filled my lungs with air and exhaled. Then, I ran all the way home.

The Communist Party in Poland, although illegal, was very active. Workers were clever and creative in getting their voices heard. They glued posters on the streets demanding the resignation of the current government. On almost every street corner people gathered to listen to speakers calling for workers to unite. Again, police came riding on horseback. Those who could get away quickly did so, but many were arrested, booked, and held in jail for at least forty-eight hours. It was customary for secret police to beat the detainees to get more information. Arrested men and women always claimed that they were only passing by. In many cases, the police let the arrested people go. Unrest was a daily occurrence, and often there was no room to hold all of the detainees.

The Red Ones, as the Communists were called, successfully hung red flags bearing antinational slogans on the electric wires that serviced the trolley cars. Some of these slogans demanded the release of political prisoners from jails; others demanded the resignation of government leaders. The red flags were a daily occurrence; we called them 'daily bread.' A lot of exertion resulted from the hanging of these flags. The trolley cars had to be stopped, and the fire department had to come with their long ladders to remove the banners. As soon as one trolley line was cleared another line on another street suddenly had the same problem. The havoc created was right in line with the plan to bring attention to the demands of the Party. Things got much worse when people went out into the streets with their red flags, demonstrating and singing.

Soon the police officers started pushing people back: They had orders to shoot the demonstrators. There were many deaths. The ambulances were now a familiar sight. I saw many friends die this way, among them my good friend Josef Kaszewski.

As the year 1939 approached, both rage and sadness settled over Warsaw. Jews were singled out and treated badly even before the German occupiers entered Warsaw. Promoted by right-wing Endecja, national boycott of Jewish businesses, encouragement for their confiscation and the term 'Christian shop' was introduced. A national movement was organized to prevent the Jews from the kosher slaughter of animals. Animal rights were used as a motive. At the same time harassment, including violence and looting aimed at Jewish stores was on the rise.

Hitler's book *Mein Kampf,* which I had read, haunted my thoughts. After 1933, when Hitler became the chancellor of Germany, the sales of the book soared and in my circle of friends somebody always passed around chapters from the book that were translated from German to Polish. His potent hatred of Jews displayed so openly terrified me. The mad visions, the evil racist propaganda, and the glorified significance of the pure German bloodline were all there in his book. The hatred of Jews and his use of Jews as scapegoats for Germany's problems were plain. I was the only one in my family who had read the book.

CHAPTER NINE

The year was 1939; the threat of war hung in the air. Still, in the midst of an impending catastrophe, young people continued to fall in and out of love. I was not different. Adolfo, who came from a good Romanian family, seemed interested in me. We had been going out for about a year and even his parents liked me. They were not rich people, but they were honest and hardworking. I felt Adolfo must surely be the same. He was the middle child, with two older brothers and two younger sisters. Being with his large, welcoming family was like a dream for me. None of my siblings, however, took an interest in my relationship with Adolfo. By this time, I had become more and more aware that my sister Pola did not really want me to get married at all.

My relationship with Adolfo was not to be. It ended abruptly when Stas, a mutual friend, started asking me out on dates. Although I refused his advances adamantly, poor Adolfo saw him as a threat. Adolfo must have felt insecure because suddenly he was asking other girls out on dates. Our relationship had a painful ending and I learned shortly thereafter that Adolfo was about to get married, after knowing a girl for only a few months. He had met her in the Laboro Club where I had met him the year before.

I started going out again, but my heart was not into dating. I felt betrayed, and thought I could never love again. Even though a new boy, Mietek, spent a lot of money on me, I did not think I loved him. He took me to the movies and the theater and afterward always to a coffee house for a midnight snack. I made it very clear I was not in love with him, but he would not give up. He followed me everywhere hoping I would change my mind. Later, when World War II had become a certainty, I realized what Mietek said was right: that I had been betrayed and was afraid to give love another chance. Now it would be too late for us.

As tension mounted in Poland, we started practicing for German air strikes. Soon, every apartment building had a war committee outfitted with red flashlights for emergencies. Shortly after Sevek's girlfriend had left for Australia in the early months of 1939, people started leaving Poland in massive numbers. The office of emigration was teeming with all those who wanted to leave. The process was slow with a very long waiting period. As the war moved closer, I watched helplessly as Sevek's dreams of going to Australia became unobtainable.

Prices mounted higher every day as people bought candles, matches, and soap. Basics such as flour, sugar, rice, tea, potatoes, and canned foods were in short supply and were bought up the instant they went on the shelves. Prices rose and so too did the number of the unemployed.

Anja was pregnant for the second time. From the beginning, she was so plagued with complications that her doctor recommended she terminate her pregnancy. Anja would not hear of it. Instead they moved back to Warsaw so that she could be closer to her doctor. Throughout her pregnancy Anja was nauseous. She could not keep her food down. She grew weak from lack of nourishment, and could barely take care of herself or her little boy, Pinkus. Her husband Szymon worked the night shift at one of the daily Jewish newspapers, so we took turns staying with Anja. I stayed often with my sister. My job was to make sure she and Pinkus were well taken care of until Anja's husband came home. I cleaned her small apartment after supper so that she could rest. I took Pinkus to his favorite corner to play, but most of the time I read to him. That was what he liked the most.

The city of Warsaw was mandated to buy black paper and cover all windows at night. Some people left the black paper on all the time, while others removed the paper from one window during daylight. It was illegal for even the slightest amount of light to escape through a window at night. Street lights were turned off, so it was pitch black outside at night. People bought flashlights and walked with them in the streets at night.

After his appointment as chancellor in 1933, Hitler set out to turn Germany into a single-party dictatorship based on Nazi ideology. His goal was to create and uphold a dominant, pure, Arian 'master race.' The Nazis sought to exterminate groups that they saw as subhuman. Slowly, information about Hitler's methods of control in Germany was reaching us. It was clear that his primary order of business was to eliminate Jews completely. The things Hitler wrote about in *Mein Kampf* were now becoming a reality. We walked around with our heads lowered, and people talked only about the coming war.

In the first week of August of 1939 after a difficult and long labor, Anja gave birth to a girl; she was named Bluma, after our mother. The tiny baby was beautiful. She had black hair and dark eyes and looked just like Anja. A week went by before I was finally able to see and hold her. Anja felt safer having her baby daughter in the hospital, but only her husband was allowed to visit that first week. A perfect baby was like a little miracle. I was so happy for Anja. There were no complications with the delivery, and her doctor promised that it would be a matter of time until Anja gained all her strength back.

The situation in Poland worsened. Germany was now openly threatening war. Russia wanted to negotiate and help Poland but the Polish government refused Russia's help. They had always been hostile neighbors; Poland didn't want Russian soldiers on its soil. Poland's former leader Piłsudski and his followers had always believed that if Poland was to fall under the Russian influence again "Poland would lose its soul."

It was a warm evening at the end of August 1939. I met some friends and we went for a walk. There were three boys in the group and while we walked, I sang to them:

> It is nice for us, in the deep of the night
> Wandering on a white steep road
> Looking at how stars shine our path
> And thinking about what luck will bring, let us live while there is time
> Who knows, who knows, if I will ever see you again.

After that night, I never saw them again.

* * *

On Friday, September 1, 1939 without a formal declaration of war, German planes started bombing Poland.

By September 10th, Warsaw was bombed systematically, with nonstop raids. At first people in the streets thought it was just practice maneuvers but then we heard the deafening explosion of bombs and planes flying overhead. The air raid alarms went off as our antiaircraft artillery started firing back. The siege started with over one thousand planes advancing on the city in a massive aerial attack by the Luftwaffe. The sky suddenly filled with hostile military aircraft.

I was working, then, at a club on Długiej Street, along with a group of young men and women. On Fridays, it was a tradition to start the day early. This was also about two weeks before Rosh Hashanah. The radio was on, and through an interrupted broadcast we learned that German planes were bombing Warsaw. We gathered around the radio, we could hear the explosions in the distance. I still remember how the mood changed in an instant. We sought comfort in each other's arms. Many of my friends were crying. I stood frozen with fear.

The bombing lasted two hours and then it stopped. We ran home, and we were not the only one running. Everyone in the streets was in a panic. There were sirens going off, and fire trucks and ambulances raced through the streets. In all that chaos, the police were going in all different directions. Smoke filled the sky. Little did I know that it was only the beginning.

The next day, the walls everywhere were covered with posters. Men were being called for a mass mobilization. If they owned a horse, they were to bring them.

I ran to Anja's house to be with my sister, three-year-old Pinkus, and baby Bluma. Just as I arrived at her door, German planes started bombing the city again. Anja lived on the ground floor. Everyone who lived on the higher floors ran down to the lobby, the only shelter they could find on such short warning. All of the women and children were screaming and crying hysterically. I grabbed Anja with one hand and Pinkus with the other. As I dragged them into the hallway, Anja and I realized at the same time that the baby was still asleep in the carriage in her apartment. Anja ran back inside, picked up the sleeping infant and came back with the child against her chest. Together, the four of us stayed with the other residents like this until the bombing stopped. That moment when Anja fearlessly ran back into her apartment to save her baby daughter is forever etched in my memory.

After the bombing stopped, we gratefully went back to our apartments. We were alive, but not everyone in Warsaw was.

The day of the bombing, I was supposed to meet Mietek, the boy I was dating. I was trembling after the blitz, but I went to meet him anyway at our usual place. He was already there, waiting for me. We walked together to the train station, Dworzec Gdanski, to see the soldiers being sent to the front. There were hundreds of people there, crying and shouting. One woman screamed hysterically as she threw her arms around her husband's neck before he was sent off to fight. She wouldn't let go.

It is difficult to find words to describe the horrible confusion we saw that afternoon. Every train was mobilized to bring our men to the front. Goods that normally transported to and from the city on these freight trains were now strewn onto the station platform. Every train was jammed with soldiers and horses. Huge locomotives hissed and spewed white steam. Black oil dripped as the massive wheels were ready to take the men away. Mietek and I stood on a bridge above the railroad tracks in total silence. We could not bring ourselves to speak. We looked down on the chaos and on the pale and frightened faces of young men who knew they were going to meet with death.

Mietek and I stood arm-in-arm watching this dreadful picture for some time. And then we turned toward each other at the same time. Mietek looked at me and said that he had always known in his heart that I loved him but we had run out of time. He told me he was going to try to make it to Russia. We knew we would not see each other again, so we stood there in a tight embrace, tears streaming down our faces. He had been right about my fears of loving again, but now it was too late. Mietek and I parted on the bridge, as he walked away he took with him our dreams and hopes.

German planes started bombing Warsaw every day. At night, German soldiers attacked Warsaw on the ground. It only took a week for the Germans to surround the city. The Polish army defended Warsaw for the next three weeks, determined not to give up their capital.

A firebomb fell in Sala's neighborhood. It hit the roof and her apartment building caught on fire. Sala lived on the top floor. Pola and I were on the street making our way home. There was panic in the street. The sirens were going off. We looked up and saw the fighters and bombers flying low. We could hear the roar of the engines. The only thing on my mind was to save my life. It was a miracle that we made it to safety.

We ran inside a little grocery store on Dzikiej Street, but as we ran, I thought I heard someone call out—"Pola, Roma"—but the blasts from the bombs were deafening. I hesitated to see who was calling me but Pola grabbed my arm and pulled me inside the shop. We spent the whole night there waiting for things to quiet down. In the morning, we rushed toward Sala's street. The fire had died out but the building was destroyed. There was no trace of Sala, her two boys, or her husband. We stood there in disbelief. We were frozen to the spot; around us was nothing but devastation. The rubble might very well have been their graves. Pola and I stood there crying, helpless to do anything. Pola was soon able to control herself, but I cried hysterically. Sala was the first one of us to suffer from the German bombardment. Only the day before, a six-story apartment building stood there. Over two hundred people lived in that building. Now Sala and her family were missing. I could not bear to think that they were gone forever. In the devastation and panic that surrounded us we did not know where to go and look for them, the only thing we could do was to make our way to Adek and Anja. In the midst of the nonstop air raids, Warsaw's citizens were barely surviving. I, too, could think of nothing but to stay alive. Fear and terror overtook my rational thinking. When it got quiet, I cried for Sala and her boys.

* * *

Various sicknesses had ravaged Poland during and after World War I. Now there was a growing resentment toward men who did not join the army, regardless of their reasons. As the German army surrounded Warsaw, it became more and more dangerous for men like Sevek to go outside.

Sevek spent most of the time inside our rented room. But the morning of the bombings, Sevek left our room to look for us. Pola and I frequently stayed with Adek as it became more and more difficult to get back to where we lived. When we returned to our room, he was gone. Days passed, without Sevek coming home. We thought he must surely be dead. We counted our losses: Sala, her family, and Sevek were gone.

I lived in constant fear, from one air raid to the next. Pola and I stayed together, checking the shelters for our family or going to Adek. The bombings took place every day and the sheer mass of debris in the streets made it difficult to get from one place to another.

Even in the daytime the sky was black. Streets were blocked with rubble several stories high. For weeks, we watched as one house after another caught fire, crumbled, and fell. There was no electricity, no water, and no food. The Germans had destroyed everything. Their plan was obvious: They wanted to starve the people of Warsaw.

During the bombings, we ran to the basements. If we couldn't make it, we would stand in the doorway of whatever large building we were closest to. I remember a police officer taking cover with us once. Everyone in the group looked to him for help but he was paralyzed with fear himself.

"I am just a poor man like you," he said.

A police officer, a symbol of authority and protection, was now as powerless as everyone else.

For a month, we wore the same clothes. We didn't wash. As each house caught on fire from the bombs, we would run to the nearest house that was still standing. At one point, the whole Jewish neighborhood was on fire. We listened helplessly to cries for help. Dead and wounded lay strewn in the streets. There was no place to run; what we needed now was a miracle. Pola and I jumped over dead bodies to get to the safety of next building.

The scenes from the attack on Warsaw are so vivid. I will remember them always. I saw a dead man on the street still clutching a sack of his belongings. A few steps further, a young woman lay on the pavement calling out for help. Blood gushed from her legs. We had to jump over dead bodies as we were running for cover. It took all my strength to keep going, I was terrified. The black sky, the smell of smoke, and the deafening sounds penetrated everything. I had never known such fear. I tried not to look at the corpses around me. I let Pola take over. She would tell me when to run and when it was safe to stop. I was no longer rational. All I wanted was for the bombing to stop.

Finally, during a lull, we went back to Mylnej Street to see if Adek was all right. We got to the end of his street and tried to look away. A large hotel for Jewish immigrants had stood there only days before. People had come to Warsaw from all over Poland, before traveling abroad. Only in Warsaw could people board trains that would then take them to other countries. This hotel full of immigrants was bombed. Everyone had been killed.

Adek, his wife, their five-year-old daughter Bluma and his wife's extended family lived on a street that was known as the wealthy Jewish neighborhood. Close by on Przejazd Street, the Army Archives were stored in a brick building. I suspect that the Germans had spies among us because Przejazd Street was somehow untouched. The Germans wanted to capture this building intact, with all its military secrets.

Adek and Bluma were buried in the rubble of a falling building. They had run inside an apartment building when the bombs started falling, but the building was reduced to a pile of rubble. Debris covered them, and yet somehow they were able to crawl out.

Adek took his five-year-old daughter with him when he searched the neighborhood for food. People were more generous when they saw a child. Toward the end of the bombardment, Pola and I stayed with Adek and his family. Adek's mother-in-law cooked potato soup for all of us. We ate it with sliced onions dipped in oil. There were seven family members but they shared whatever food they had with all of us.

We had been at Adek's apartment for a week, when Sala appeared with both of her boys. Their clothes were torn, their faces were dirty, and their hair was matted. A day later, and to everyone's amazement, her husband appeared, too. Moniek told us how he had been sleeping in the basement under his barbershop, trying to save whatever he could of his business. We were so happy to see them all alive. Anja and her children were safe, too; her apartment building was still standing. However, Sevek remained missing and we were slowly losing hope of seeing him again.

We decided to stay together. There was no sense in trying to get to our old room. Even when the bombing stopped, the civilian population was not allowed to go out after six o'clock in the evening. Soldiers and policemen took over the streets. Ambulances transported the wounded. Fire trucks attempted to put out the fires burning in the buildings.

As the Germans advanced, the Polish government ordered its citizens to build barricades in the streets of the capital. Watching people drag everything they had from their apartments was like seeing a nightmare enacted right before our eyes. Streets were barricaded with beds, mattresses, tables, chairs, bookcases, and sofas. Some barricades were so tall they reached to the first floor of an apartment building. But the Germans were smarter than we were. These barricades were extremely flammable. Once the bombs dropped, we were trapped by our own burning barricades. We had built our own inferno.

Dedicated to Father Karol Wojtyla, the Polish Pope John Paul II, Father Wojciech Lemanski, and to all those who walked in their path before them and to those who will walk in their path after them, for their efforts to change the Catholic Church's relations with Judaism.

Suzanna
A Young Priest

In the late 1950s, before the Communist government imposed the separation between state and religion, priests and nuns came to teach catechism in the public schools. When the priest came in to teach, a teacher would come to take me out of the classroom. I was already the only Jewish student in my class and getting up from my seat was excruciating as I was being watched by thirty pairs of eyes. I looked forward to the moment when my teacher would place her arm around me. It gave me a sense of protection from the resenting classmates and the unfriendly stare of the priest. But as much as I was being resented for being allowed to leave because of my Jewish religion, my peers also feared and disliked those mandatory religious classes. It was obvious to me that they dreaded this time of day.

Wishing to be invisible, with my eyes focused on the floor, my aim, as always, was to walk slowly out of the room without drawing any attention to myself. Most of the priests and nuns who came to teach catechism were older and very stern. One time, in the first grade, a young priest came to teach. His presence created an atmosphere of excitement in the classroom. I remember that he caught my attention as well since I had never seen him before and he was young. As I made my way past the desk where he was standing, with my head hanging low, hoping he would not notice me, he stopped me and gently held both my hands. He spoke to me in a determined voice. "You should not be afraid." "You are a special child." I remember looking up at him with the eyes of a seven-year old, frightened and bewildered. It took a long time for me to understand what the young priest meant, but his words stayed forever with me. Even as a child, I understood that he was referring to me being Jewish. While living in Poland, I had never experienced from a priest this kind of humanity, a compassionate embrace of Judaism, as I did that day in the first grade.

The Catholic Church was still anti-Semitic in its teachings—from holding Jews responsible for killing Jesus to circulating rumors that *matzah* was made with the blood of Christian children. The Church was not just a bystander to intolerance, but a leading and enthusiastic proponent. The anti-Semitism of the Polish Church, customary throughout its long history, was not unique; it represented the viewpoint of the Vatican and other national churches at that time.

In the early 300 AD, Christian Church and the Roman Emperor Constantine the Great placed the blame on the Jews for the death of the Lord and separated early Christianity from its original Jewish roots. This split marks the beginning of official anti-Semitism. Subsequently throughout history Jews suffered at the hands of Christianity and also at the hands of Islam, a religion which came into being 600 years after the birth of Christianity. The First Muslim, Muhammad, rose to power, from irrelevance to importance in Medina. To gain prominence, the First Muslim went after the weakest and smallest of the tribes, the People of the Book, the Jews. When they refused to recognize Muhammad as a prophet he gave them two choices—conversion or expulsion. Some converted and some lived as crypto-Jews. Most tribes left Medina to save themselves. The strongest and largest of the tribes, the Banu Nadir tribe, was evicted from Medina. In the 7th century the Banu Qurayza tribe was massacred by Muhammad and his followers. Islamic history is tarnished with cruelty against the Jews. It is best described in a book, The Myth of the Andalusian Paradise: Muslims, Christians and Jews under the Islamic Rule in Medieval Spain by Dario Fernandez. The Islamic conquest of Spain was a jihad. It brought with it the destruction of churches, synagogues and its Christian and Jewish subjects. The tax forced on persons of other religions, the jizya, was imposed to permit the conquerors to live off the subservient population and to intentionally humiliate the non-Muslims. The status of non-Muslims was inferior to that of Muslims. Christians and Jews had to wear identifying marks on their clothing, symbolic of the 1930s Nazi ideology. Under the Islamic Rule in Medieval Spain, non-Muslims were discriminated against, especially Jews who were equated to dogs. Any periods of calm and tolerance always ended in horrendous brutality against the Jews.

Chapter Ten

It was during the siege of Warsaw that Poland was left without leadership. The government fled into exile. The Polish army remained on the battlefield and tried to defend the city, but after a month they had no choice but to surrender. By the end of September, Poland had suffered huge losses. Warsaw was ready for the German occupation, for anything that would put an end to the bombing and artillery fire. Poland surrendered.

Everything went quiet. Warsaw, a city of 1.3 million inhabitants and a major center of Jewish life and culture, lay in ruin. Warsaw's Jewish population of 350,000 was the largest in both Poland and Europe, and second largest in the world only to New York City.

Prior to the war, the *Kehilla* organization served the Jewish people. It existed in every city and town. In Warsaw, it managed to stay in operation until October 4, 1939 when it was replaced by the 'Judenrat.' German officials ordered the establishment of a Jewish council under the leadership of Adam Czerniaków. The Judenrat was responsible for implementing the Nazis' orders in the Jewish community overseeing the soon-to-be established. Warsaw Jews were soon made to identify themselves by wearing a blue Star of David on a white armband. Jewish schools were closed. Jewish-owned property was confiscated, and Jewish men were taken to perform forced labor. Prewar Jewish organizations were dissolved. By October 1940, all Jewish residents of Warsaw were forced to move into a designated area, sealed off by the Nazis from the rest of the city.

The Warsaw Ghetto was enclosed by a wall that was over ten-feet high and topped with barbed wire. It was closely guarded to prevent movement between the ghetto and the outside world. The population of the ghetto increased as Jews from nearby towns were also forced to leave their homes. The population was estimated to be over 400,000. During the next year, thousands more were forced to move there. Typhus and starvation, along with random killings, claimed 100,000 people—this even before the Nazis began massive deportations from the Ghetto's Umschlagplatz to the Treblinka extermination camp.

It took three days for the entire German army to drive into Warsaw. They came on trucks, in cars and on motorbikes, all in black uniforms—the color of death. As they drove through the streets, they threw bread to onlookers. In no time, we were completely under German control.

The Germans imposed many of the same laws we had during the war. After six o'clock, civilians were not allowed to go outside their homes. Windows had to be covered so that light did not escape into the street. People had to give up all weapons. The surrender of weapons took place on *Placu Piłsudskiego*. The punishment for concealing weapons was death.

During the German occupation, orders were also given to bakeries still intact to bake bread at night exclusively for the German army. The Germans supplied the ingredients. Every morning, soldiers came with their own horse-drawn carriages and collected the fresh bread. Two houses down from where we lived with Adek was one of these working bakeries. We tried not to watch when these German soldiers came with a closed carriage to collect this fresh-smelling bread. As soon as the carriage was full and the bakery empty, they drove away to their barracks.

The Germans passed another new law: death on the spot for the smallest theft. I will never forget how one morning, Adek got up early and went downstairs. He waited for the moment when German soldiers placed the bread inside the carriage and went back to get more. At the end of this carriage was a small door. After having observed the soldiers' routine, Adek ran to the carriage, opened the door and grabbed a loaf of bread. We were shocked when Adek rushed in carrying a loaf of bread that weighed at least six kilograms. If he had been caught, not only would the Germans have shot Adek, but we all might have died that day as well.

We were a total of thirteen people living with Adek. The three children, Adek's daughter and Sala's two boys cried all day long from hunger. Adek told me later that even though it seemed foolish, he was compelled to do something. He was so used to being the one to take care of everyone that he felt he had no choice but to go out and steal the bread.

We all begged Adek to never do this again. I would have rather gone hungry then have him risk his life.

* * *

We decided it might be best to break into smaller groups. Sala and Moniek thought they and their two boys could manage in the storage room in the basement of the building where their salon was located. Sala argued with Moniek that people were not going to spend money for haircuts when they had no food, but Moniek insisted that he had loyal customers. He said they would come back to him now that the city, under occupation, was getting back to normal.

Pola and I made our way back to the room we lived in before the start of the war. We had stored some food there, but the room was empty. Nothing was left of our provisions. Although the room was locked, the family from whom we were renting was able to open the door and take everything. I remember that I was not surprised.

We were sure that Sevek was dead. But on the second week of his disappearance, the door opened slowly to our room. We could not believe our eyes! There stood Sevek: dirty, unshaven, carrying a sack on his back. In the sack was a loaf of bread. Pola and I ran into his open arms. The three of us stood in the middle of our room, kissing and crying out of joy. He told us that, just as the Germans surrounded the city, he decided to leave our room to look for us. He got caught in an exodus of men who were fleeing Warsaw. The men were all going in one direction, and Sevek became engulfed in this huge sea of men. They stayed in small villages and on farms, sleeping wherever they could. Sevek said that along the road people helped them and fed them. He told us how all this time he never stopped worrying about us. When Sevek heard that the fighting had ended in the city, he turned around and made his way back.

Before leaving, Sevek had the good sense to hide women's handbags he had already made. Now we decided to try to sell them. We needed money desperately, although even with money it was still hard to find food. There were severe shortages on everything. People gathered on Nalewki Street, still the center of the Jewish marketplace. Slowly people started to buy and sell again.

German soldiers also came here to buy. Sometimes they would pay, and sometimes not. When a German soldier came with a Polish Endecja, who were the worst anti-Semites even before the war, they would point to us and say "Jude, a Jew" as though that was enough reason not to pay for something. On one occasion when I was selling Sevek's handbags, an older German soldier and an Endecja came up to me. The German soldier was looking at the handbags and started flirting with me, stroking my face with his hand. In German he said,

"Beautiful girl." When the young Endecja heard this he said to the soldier, "She is a Jude, a Jew." It was October of 1939, the beginning of the occupation, we had no idea of what was to come. The women standing nearby gathered around me and together we declared, "Yes, we are all Jewish." The soldier left without buying anything.

On another occasion, Adek had given me scarves to sell that had been made in his textile factory. His factory produced all kinds of clothing depending on the season. It was already fall, and the weather was noticeably colder. Suddenly, three soldiers came up to me. They took all the scarves without a word and left. I cried all the way home. I had no scarves and no money.

I remember a time I was standing in line to buy sugar on Zelaznej Street, an area where Poles and Jews lived together. A German solder came over to me and pulled me out of the line. My heart raced with fear, although I tried not to show it. There was nothing I could do. I left.

During the daytime, most Jewish men stayed indoors—the risk of being picked up and deported was particularly high. An increased burden was placed on us women. We had to deal with many more chores, selling goods and standing in long line to buy food. It was getting worse and worse. German soldiers started coming to the Jewish neighborhoods daily in their trucks. They started in the wealthier neighborhoods. Gesia, Nalewki, Franciszkanska, and Bonifraterska were the first streets where the Germans started taking Jewish men off the streets, arresting and sending them to labor camps.

All operations at the factory on Bonifraterska Street came to a halt. Adek and his father-in-law closed it and told the employees to stay home. It was known by then that men who were caught working were among the first to be deported to camps. The German soldiers came anyway. They broke down the doors of the factory and took everything: machines, equipment, fabrics and loaded the material onto trucks to send to Germany. This attack, on Jewish-owned businesses would continue.

All this was happening right in front of our eyes. A week after the Germans entered Warsaw, men stopped going out altogether. Soon the Germans set forth a new ordinance that every apartment building had to provide a certain number of men daily. This became the responsibility of the landlord. The landlord where we lived wanted Sevek to go, but Pola and I stood up to him, insisting that Sevek was a sick man and would not be going anywhere.

We were aware of what was really going on. The men that were taken away were not coming back. We learned that they were beaten, starved, and forced to work under unimaginable conditions. More and more people started running away from Warsaw. At first it was mostly men. At this time, there still existed the notion that the great German civilization would never hurt women and children. The fleeing men never imagined what cruel fate awaited the family they were leaving behind. Young people became preoccupied with running east, to the Polish region occupied by Russia.

* * *

The Molotov-Ribbentrop Pact, otherwise known as the 'Treaty of Non-Aggression' between Germany and the Soviet Russia, was signed in Moscow in the early hours of August 24, 1939. It rejected warfare between the two countries, both pledging neutrality if attacked by a third party. It would remain in effect until Nazi Germany invaded Russia on June, 1941. In addition, the Treaty of Non-Aggression included a secret protocol dividing the independent country of Poland into Nazi and Soviet territories. In the south, the demarcation line between the two forces would run along the River San. Hitler attacked Poland from the north, south, and west on September 1, 1939. The first Germans to enter Poland were regular Army units, but they were followed by an SS[13] task force whose job was to terrorize and murder civilians, especially Jews.

The German invasion of Poland was almost immediately followed by a Russian invasion of eastern Poland on September 17, 1939. Soviet Russia occupied all territory east of the Rivers Pisa, Narew, Western Bug, and San. After annexation of eastern Poland, an estimated 13.5 million Polish citizens of mixed ethnic groups were now under Soviet control, and by November, the Russian government declared that those who lived there were now Soviet citizens. Russia took back Lithuania, Belorussia, and Ukraine, territories granted to Poland in the Peace Treaty of Riga of 1921. In this region the Polish nationals accounted for over 5 million, Jews for over 1 million people,

---

[13] The SS (German for "Schutzstaffel" ["Protection Squadron"]) was a major paramilitary organization under Adolf Hitler and the Nazi Party (NSDAP). Under Heinrich Himmler's leadership (1929–45), it grew from a small paramilitary formation to one of the largest and most powerful organizations in the Third Reich. Built upon the Nazi ideology, the SS under Himmler's command was responsible for many of the crimes against humanity during World War II.

and the rest were of mixed ethnic group. When the war broke out an additional 138,000 Poles and 198,000 Jews fled the German-occupied zone and became refugees in the Soviet-occupied region. However, the Russians brought fear, destruction, and death as well. Soviet authorities exercised harsh punishments. They executed, arrested, or deported to labor camps anyone who opposed them. Hundreds of thousands were deported to Siberia labor camps and other remote regions in four major waves between 1939 and 1941. Under the Soviet rule, if one was accused as an "enemy of the People" the punishment was swift. There were no appeals. The Polish lands occupied by Russia had mixed populations of Byelorussian and Polish peasants in the north, Ukrainian and Polish peasants in the south, Polish élite and Jews in town and cities throughout. After Russia occupied eastern territories, it proceeded to eliminate its Polish identity. They started by purging the élite and ruling class; thousands of Poles were murdered, hundreds of thousands more deported in two massive deportations in February and April of 1940.

Local Jews were now Soviet citizens. The Russians were suspicious of Jews and their political allegiance and for that reason many ended up in Siberia. In June of 1940, close to one hundred thousand Jews who had fled the Nazis were arrested for refusing Soviet citizenship. They were shipped off to Central Asia and Siberia.

Russia's official reason for invading Poland was protection of the Ukrainians and Byelorussians. The basis for this excuse was that the Polish state had capitulated to Germany and could no longer guarantee the safety of its own citizens. In the eastern region, Ukrainians, Byelorussians, and Jews welcomed the invading Russian Troops as liberators. The Polish nationals did not; they hated the Russians as much as they hated the Germans. After all, Russia and Germany were the aggressors who partitioned and occupied the Independent Polish Republic three times in recent Polish history. But because of the Nazis' hatred of the Jewish race, Polish Jews saw the Russians as their only chance for survival.

As the Russian army spread out, occupying the eastern territories of Poland, we heard rumors that a pact had been drawn between Hitler and Stalin. We heard that both aggressors celebrated their successes and they agreed on a new border. We also heard rumors that the Red Army was going to take over Warsaw. We reasoned that the Germans would soon be gone and this was why they were stealing all of our property. On the streets everyone was talking about escaping to Russia. The day came when I too had to run.

* * *

I watched as my friends and neighbors made small backpacks out of industrial fabric to carry what they could, leaving everything else behind. It was usually only a few pieces of clothing, a towel, a piece of soap, and any food still left. People wore as many layers of clothing as they could. Money was hidden inside shoes, underneath the soles. We knew that if a German soldier found a Pole hiding money, he had orders to shoot.

To get through the German lines was especially frightening. Soldiers killed people for no reason at all. Depending on the guards on duty at the time, sometimes possessions were taken, but people were allowed to go into the neutral zone. Sometimes they would kill the men and let the women go. Sometimes they took the men as prisoners. Part of the trip was spent riding on a freight train; passenger trains seldom ran and were always patrolled. One way to get out of Poland was on a horse-drawn carriage. Thousands of people left Warsaw any way they could. They already knew there would be peasants along the way who would transport them, for a lot of money, across the River Bug.

Every time I ventured from my room, I found that more and more of my friends had left. One of my closest girlfriends lived in a Polish neighborhood. She sold cigarettes that she made at home. Dora lived far away, and though it was dangerous to be out in the streets, she came to see me. Her father was a rabbi. He wore a long beard and *peas*. Dora's family was always nice to me and I frequently visited their house. Now, we got together and made plans for the future. We decided that we would leave Warsaw on the November 7, the anniversary of the Russian Revolution and the overthrow of Tsarist Russia. We also chose this day because of a widespread rumor that on November 7 the Russian Army was supposed to enter Warsaw. We both prayed that they would. This way we would not have to run east toward Russia and leave our families behind. Mostly young, unmarried people like us fled east to avoid arrests and deportations to labor camps in Germany. We hugged and parted with a handshake to solidify our promise. We would not leave without each other.

Suzanna
Restoring Our Roots

For my daughters, the third generation, Jewish and Polish legacy and history will forever be intertwined with each other.

In order to fully appreciate our family's history, I took my two daughters, Alex and Isabel to Poland in the summer of 2008. They were twenty-one and eighteen. I wanted to show them the place that they can trace their roots to; to show them the city of my birth, and where I spent my childhood and teenage years. We went to Warsaw and walked the streets that my mother and my grandmother and the generations before them called home. Some of the streets my mother wrote in her diary still bore the same name. We also walked on streets in Warsaw that had become the ghetto. We viewed plaques commemorating the horrendous atrocities that took place. We lit candles at Umschlagplatz, the site where Warsaw's Jews were deported to Treblinka. At Umschlagplatz, we talked to the ghosts of my Mother's murdered family. To this day we don't know how they died, were they murdered in the Warsaw Ghetto or were they forced to board the trains to the extermination camp of Treblinka. We could not find any trace of Mother's family as if her loved ones had never existed. The mass deportation of Jews from the Warsaw Ghetto began on July 22, 1942. Between late July and September 1942, the Germans succeeded in deporting around 265,000 Jews from Warsaw to Treblinka.

We went to the concentration camp Auschwitz-Birkenau. My mother and father had escaped this fate by escaping to Russia. In the Auschwitz museum, we learned what happened to the vast majority of the Polish Jews. But Birkenau is the place where my daughters and I both went into shock. The vastness of the place, the train tracks running through the middle, made us gasp for air. Standing there, where it actually happened, the realization fully hits you: the Nazis intended to annihilate the entire Jewish people of Europe. They almost succeeded. I could see the trains coming and going, bringing in more and more Jews, the selections that decided who would work and who would die. I could imagine the gas chambers and the ovens working. I heard the cries that went unheard. I saw the guns pointing and firing, the dogs barking without mercy, and the killing machine working at full speed as the whole world stood by in silence. In Auschwitz-Birkenau alone millions died, ninety percent of them were Jews, among them my father's Father, Mother, Sister and his entire extended family.

I took my daughters to my father's city of Łódź. Before World War II, it had the second largest Jewish population in Poland, second to Warsaw. Łódź fell a week after the German invasion, and by November 7, 1939, the city was also incorporated into the Third Reich. Its name became Litzmannstadt. Daily round-ups of Jewish men for forced labor and random beatings and killings on the streets followed. My father had run east sometime in December of 1939. My mother was to see my father for the first time on January 20, 1940, on a train that took them from Białystok deep into Russia's interior, but it was months later, in Saratov, that they became a couple.

We went to the city of Kłodzko to see my father's grave. In 1946, the southwestern part of Poland became the largest resettlement region for Jewish refugees returning from Russia. The Jewish cemetery, which dates back to when this part of Poland was part of Germany before World War II, had been vandalized after Solidarnosc came to power in the 1990s. Now, not one single monument was left standing intact. All the graves revealed the same hateful damage, and my father's monument was left broken in so many pieces that it was impossible to count them. Not one Polish newspaper was willing to report on such hate crimes, choosing to pretend they did not exist. My two daughters, the third generation, bore witness to the shameful condition of the Jewish cemetery and their grandfather's grave in Kłodzko.

My daughters' father, my husband, is also a child of Holocaust survivors. His parents, like mine, survived the war in Russia. He, too, was born in Poland under Communism and came to the United States as a teenager in the 1960s. His parents had to leave everything behind in Poland and start a new life in America in their middle age. My husband's father, Aron Lederman, like my father, was the only one from his entire family to survive. Aron Lederman came from Kovel, Lithuania, a region where Jewish history can be traced to as early as the eighth century. Some came here from southern Russia and in the 12th century, German Jews came because of persecution by the Crusaders. From July 1941 till October 1942 nearly all of the 17,000 Jews of Kovel were liquidated. Like my father, he retreated behind a wall of impenetrable silence. My husband's mother, Berta Bryj, lost a baby daughter, a husband, and a brother. Berta Bryj came from Zamość, a city in eastern Poland, established at the end of the 16th century. She, her parents, and three sisters survived the war throughout the Soviet territories.

We went to Poland to pay homage, to remember what we had lost and to mourn. It was only with my mother's death in Los Angeles, fifty years after the Holocaust, that I finally understood the magnitude of loss and suffering she and her generation endured, and the importance of never forgetting.

CHAPTER ELEVEN

My friend Szymek came by to tell me he was traveling to the village of Tarczyn twice a week by train. His grandmother lived there, just outside of Warsaw. There was a small Jewish bakery where he went to at night to buy ten loaves of bread to bring back to Warsaw and sell. In this way, he had bread for his family and also money to buy food. Szymek asked me to join him at night on these trips, but I was too afraid. The memory of Adek and the loaf of bread he had stolen from the Germans was still too fresh.

Pola, however, took this trip with my friend a few times and they brought the bread back to Warsaw. The trips back were dangerous; if stopped carrying the bread, they would have been shot on the spot. Pola and I sold the bread, but we had to be careful; selling bread was illegal, too. After only a few trips, Szymek and Pola decided to stop. The German soldiers constantly patrolled the trains.

German treatment of Jews grew worse with each day. German soldiers would walk up to people on the street and for no reason at all beat them and called them *Jude! Jude!*

One time, I'd met my old friend Roman on the street. He was the boy I dated briefly and helped get out jail. I was surprised to see him. He was supposed to be in Russia by now. His only dream had been to go to Russia and join the revolution. His face turned red, as he proceeded to tell me how he was now working for the Germans. I was shocked, but tried to stay calm. The first thing that came to mind as he spoke was the letter I took to his revolutionary organization, begging them to buy his freedom. I had been an instrument in getting him out of jail, and now Roman was collaborating with the Nazis. I quickly said good-bye, telling him I was in a hurry to meet someone. Walking away, I was dizzy with emotion. I couldn't understand how a Jewish person could turn his back on his own people and work for the Nazis. Didn't Roman see what was going on? I was both horrified and scared by his lack of decency and his cowardice. Seeing Roman's action made me realize, more than ever, how dangerous the situation around me was becoming.

* * *

By the end of October, Pola and I were not able to pay our rent. We had to leave our room. The little money I had saved was for our escape to Russia. Pola, Sevek, and I went back to live with Adek and his family of seven in their four-room apartment.

Finally, the day I had been planning and waiting for arrived. On November 7, Russia had not entered Warsaw as we expected. I felt it was time to leave. I had two friends nearby who also wanted to go east with me, but I told them I had to find my friend Dora first. By then the Polish Endecja were always walking the streets and pointing out Jews to the Nazi soldiers. Dora lived far off in a Polish neighborhood in Warsaw; the walk to her house took much longer than I expected. My heart was beating fast as I struggled to breathe. My tired legs were heavy but I kept walking. The sound of my own footsteps was terrifying. The only thing that kept me moving was our handshake, and the promise we gave to each other that we would leave together. Dora and her family lived on the first floor of a large apartment building. I went up the stairs and knocked on the door. It struck me that something was not right, the door was slightly ajar, but I did not stop and think.

I entered an empty apartment. There was no one home but their possessions were still there. A chill ran through my body. Dora and her family were always home. Dora made cigarettes in the apartment. Her father was a Rabbi. People always stopped by his study to get his advice. Dora's mother was also always busy at work; cleaning, cooking, and to make extra money, sewing. Dora had four siblings, two brothers and an older and a younger sister who were always at home helping their mother with the sewing.

I never found out what happened. Dora and her family disappeared without a trace.

I ran home, packed a few things, and went to Anja to say goodbye. Anja, once a strong voice behind the Warsaw workers, still had a fighting spark in her eyes. She was waiting for her husband Szymon and pacing the room when I came in. She held one baby in her arms while the other hung onto her skirt. I could see she was worried for her children and was doing her best not to show it. In a firm voice, she told me to stay safe and that we would see each other again soon.

It was very difficult for me to leave my family. I was one of thousands of young people who were willing to leave everything until the German occupation was over. Those with commitments, especially those with children felt it was best to stay. I tried to convince my siblings to come with me, but my efforts were in vain. They were so filled with hope that any day the English or the Russians would come to liberate Poland.

After seeing Anja, I met Sala with her children. Sala looked terrible. She was wrapped in a black satin housecoat, the same one she had been wearing when her building caught fire. She was dirty and her hair was uncombed. Her face was swollen and her eyes were red from crying. She kept repeating that she knew we would never see each other again. Her two boys, five and three years old, were practically naked and were barefoot in November.

Before the occupation, the salon had been finally thriving. Sala was even able to buy beautiful gold rings for her fingers. Her children always had extra pairs of shoes and sets of clothing. It was all destroyed when the bomb fell on her building.

Through my tears, I could only manage to say: "I promise, we will see each other again soon." This picture of my sister with her two boys, barefoot in the winter that last time is a haunting memory for me. It is still with me today.

* * *

Running away from Warsaw and from my family was the most difficult thing I have ever done. It is difficult to relay today how strong my fear of the Nazis was. I had no idea what racial genocide was, or that the Holocaust was about to be unleashed against Europe's Jews by Nazi Germany. My three older siblings had five beautiful children. I loved playing with them and I did so every chance I had. I will never know what extraordinary people they would have grown up to be and what contributions to our society they would have made. After the war, I searched for them in vain.

I often think back to how they were when I left Warsaw that November. Adek's little girl Bluma was five years old in 1939. She was a precocious little girl who was always attached to her mother. Adored by her maternal grandmother, she was always dressed in the latest style. Bluma had big dark eyes and light hair that fell in loose curls on her shoulders. A shiny, white bow was always tied to her hair right in the middle of her head. She would put her small hand in mine and let me take her for our weekly walk. On those walks I told her about my favorite *Maria Konopnicka* fairy tale but I never told her that Marysia was an orphan. Bluma was a sensitive child. I did not want to make her sad.

Though we had almost lost him from illness, Sala's son Piniek grew up to be a healthy five-year-old boy. An independent child, he reminded me so much of his father Moniek. We also had our weekly walks in the park. Piniek asked a thousand questions, and I was expected to have an answer for every one of them. Gutek took after his mother, always smiling and content. He had dark eyes and a dark head of curls.

Anja's son Pinkus was three when I left Warsaw. We were best friends. I got to spend the most time with him because of Anja's dangerous second pregnancy. He loved for me to read to him at bedtime. When I thought he was asleep and closed the book, he would open his eyes and say, "one more story *Ciocia*, aunt Roma please." I never refused. His little sister, also named Bluma, was only three months old when I said good-bye to my Anja.

* * *

My final farewell was to my Adek. I handed over to him my most precious possession, a box filled with diplomas, a few of my favorite books, and an album with photographs. I told him to take care of it. My parting words were, "I will see you in a few weeks."

At the time, England had promised to help Poland fight the Nazi invasion. We had also heard rumors about how the Russians were going to occupy more Polish territories. All of this gave me hope that Poland would soon be rid of the Nazis and I would return home to my family. Besides some clothes and food that I could carry, I left everything behind.

At the last minute, Pola decided to come with me. I told her to pack up fast. Sevek had also decided to join us. The three of us left to meet up with my girlfriends Reginka and Hanka and another last-minute friend, Janek. Our group of six left Warsaw on the morning of November 8, 1939, with a mixture of fear and optimism.

We were thankful that we had a map. Most people escaping to the east were going to Zaromb, a nearby town on the Russian side of the border. With the Germans on one side, and Russians on the other, the no-man's land known as the 'neutral zone' was our first goal. But we first had to get through the German border guards. We heard that in Zaromb, we could board trains that carried refugees to Białystok and other cities in the East.

We had heard that hundreds of thousands of Jews were able to get through the border to Zaromb, but also that thousands died while crossing to the Russian side. Thousands were stranded for weeks at a time out in the open, dying from exposure, hunger, and thirst. Many were beaten and robbed by Nazi soldiers or by Polish hooligans. Diseases and sickness spread quickly. Rumors as to what was going on in the neutral zone were circulating. I begged my group not to take this route. I was paralyzed with fear, imagining having to walk next to German soldiers in order to cross to the Russian side. At the last minute, we all agreed to travel a different road.

We chose to cross the River Bug, on the eastern border of Poland. Crossing the river was not a long trip, but very difficult to arrange and expensive. I had one hundred Polish złoty, which was a lot of money at that time. I also had the watch Aron, my first boyfriend, gave me. Sevek had six hundred złoty but Pola had no money, so we decided to pool what we had. My three friends in our group had their own money.

On our new route, our first stop would be a small town of Siedlce. From Warsaw, we needed to travel in an eastern direction in a freight train. We agreed not to call attention to ourselves by buying our own tickets. Instead, we paid a Polish train worker to get six tickets for us. We stayed on the side of the station watching for Nazi soldiers. We managed to get on the train and sit on the floor of the car with our belongings held tight against us. We knew that the Nazis were routinely stopping the trains. We heard that they pulled Jewish men off the trains and took them away to labor camps or killed them on the spot.

That day, luck was on our side. We arrived without incident in Siedlce, in eastern Poland where the Jewish population before World War II was about 15,000. The Nazis entered the town on September 11, 1939 and many Jews fled, but there were still some Jews there when we arrived in November. We only saw a few Nazi soldiers, probably because the town was so small. I will never forget the kindness of the Jewish people who were still there. They gave us potatoes with milk, and fresh hay to sleep on. That night, we lay next to each other and shared our fears about crossing the River Bug before falling into a deep, exhausted sleep.

To cross the River Bug we had to get to the next town, Losice. The Nazis had bombed Losice; many houses and the synagogue were destroyed. The town had been Nazi-occupied for a short time. By the end of the month, the Russians occupied it, also for a very short time. When the Russians left, many Jews went with them in order to get to the Soviet-occupied territories. A few days after the Russians left, the Nazis came back. Their return resulted in looting of Jewish property. The Nazis were not the only ones to loot and rob. Local Polish police and citizens did the same.

About 4,000 Jews still lived in Losice. We were helped tremendously when some of the Jews we met convinced us to shed our city clothes and dress in peasant's clothes instead. They were so kind to us, and even gave us their worn out clothes to wear on the most dangerous part of our trip.

The next day, these local Jews introduced us to a Polish peasant, who would take us on the day-long trip to a village near the River Bug with his horse and wagon. I realized how cunning our peasant was when he stopped his horse every few kilometers to ask for more money. He knew that every few kilometers a Nazi soldier would be standing guard and he took advantage of our fear. We shook each time one of these guards shouted out, "Langsam Langsam, slowly, slowly." They stopped us and looked to see if we were carrying weapons and then let us continue on our way. I believe it was our peasant clothes that saved us. We made it to our destination, a house that was essentially just a large room with a table, a bed, and an oven for baking bread. The owner gave us black bread with milk for dinner and hay to sleep on.

The next morning we were instructed to sit quietly and not make a sound. There were Nazi soldiers in the area. I realized that while the peasant was trying to get more money from us, he was risking his life by making this journey. We remained still, sitting petrified in our spot for the remainder of the day. The only time we were permitted to leave was to go into the field to relieve ourselves, and this, we had to do one at a time. At nightfall, a fisherman was supposed to come and bring us to his boat for the trip to the other side.

Night came with total darkness. A young man, Felix, came to guide us through the forest to the boat. The cost of the boat trip was one hundred złoty per person. Another small group made their way in our direction. Now there were ten of us. We walked for three hours through the forest to find the sky lit up with the bright lights

of rocket fire. Felix decided it was not safe for us to cross and we returned to the peasant's cottage. I stayed next to him the whole time.
To this day I don't know where I got my courage.

We walked through the forest to the river's edge three nights
in a row. The second night we got to the river and the fisherman and
his boat was not there. On the third morning, when Felix came to get
us he said he was curious as to who was the brave person who had
walked beside him with so much determination. He wasn't able to
see me in the dark forest, we couldn't tell each other apart from two
feet away it was that dark, and we had to walk in total silence and as
quietly as possible. I looked up at Felix and smiled, and a feeling of
pride enveloped me when he looked at me and smiled in approval.

On that night, our third trip, November 12, luck was finally
with us. The fisherman was there. We divided into two groups. Except for Sevek, who agreed to cross the river with a second group, our
original group stayed together. As soon as we were dropped off on
the other side, the fisherman was to come back for the others.

It was a cold, dark night with no moon and no stars. Pola and I
sat huddled in the middle of the little boat, silently clutching our
possessions. The boat moved slowly across the water, with the wood-
en oars making the only sound. Each splash brought us closer and
closer to safety and freedom, or so I thought.

Inherited Memories

My very first memory is the sensation of fear. I was born being afraid. I believe the Holocaust left in its path a darkness and despair that enveloped both survivors and their children. I am convinced that the fear my mother experienced was passed on to me through the sinewy strands of chemical inheritance known as genes.

The memory is vivid: I am a baby in a stroller under a big tree. I wake up from a nap. I am alone; my only companion is the canopy of leaves above me that move gently in the wind. The breeze puts me at ease, but at the same time I am afraid. I sense that my mother is not with me. I instinctually know that I need her if I am to survive.

I experienced this fear for my survival repeatedly throughout my childhood. Once when my mother became physically absent when she was ill and unexpectedly taken to the hospital. My father learned quickly that he could not substitute for Mother, and our home life went into a state of anguish as my father, sister, and I waited, desperate for her to return.

In a recent study at Emory University[14], researchers concluded that mother's fears caused genetic alterations that are passed on to her offspring, meaning fear is a heritable trait. The study showed how trauma affected the nervous system of the parent, and that this change is passed down to the next generation. This finding reinforced previous research, suggesting that fear alters our nervous system and behavior, and it can be passed on to children.

I remember vividly the trauma I experienced as a five-year old, when our town held army maneuvers in the city square, right in front of our house in the city of Ziebice. Although I understood that they were just exercises, showing off what the Polish army could do, I was inconsolable. I often wonder if my oversensitivity to the sounds of gunfire and tanks rolling through the streets that day had something to do with my mother's surviving the bombing of Warsaw fifteen years earlier. Were those sounds already familiar to me; were they part of my inherited genetic memory, passed down to me from my mother?

I remember hearing a story my mother repeated often when I was still a child. After the war, a veteran attacked my mother. The only reason he attacked her was because she was Jewish. He beat her with one of his

---

[14] Study *Parental olfactory experience influences behavior and neural structure in subsequent generations,* published in *Nature Neuroscience,* 2013, by Kerry Ressler and Brian Dias.

crutches. He ambushed her from behind. The blows landed on her back and shoulder, and thankfully, missed her head. This incident left my mother traumatized and fearful. Her fears, however, became my fears. To this day, when I walk next to someone with a cane, a walking stick, or crutches, what I experience is pure, irrational fear, and I don't take my eyes off them until there is a safe distance between us.

I was six years old when my mother took me to an art exhibit that came to our town. The exhibit was a tribute to mothers and children who suffered during the war. The art was frightening: It showed SS soldiers ripping children from mothers' arms, mothers being killed, and mothers begging for mercy. I was overwhelmed with my mother's tears as we walked through the exhibit. When I think back to that day, I realize my mother had no idea the exhibit would be as traumatic as it was. She also probably thought I was too young to understand. Her tears alone were enough to terrify me, but I also saw the horror of what the work depicted. The next morning, still lying in bed, I had a hallucination. An SS soldier was standing on each side of my bed. I was not allowed to move. If I did, they had orders to shoot me. I remained motionless, afraid to take a breath until my mother came looking for me.

That morning, my mother came to my rescue. I never burdened her with my daydream because I remembered how she cried as we walked through the exhibit.

Fragments of carefree times are also fixed in my memory, of the summer in my childhood when Max Lipszycz entered our life. He loved playing with my sister and me, and for a short time, his presence filled our home with joy and happiness. Max's cheerful disposition lured me from under my protective cover; he made me forget about being afraid. Max would chase after us as we ran from him, squealing with laughter. His visits, however, came to an abrupt end when Father returned home from the sanatorium. He forbade Max to enter our home. My mother obeyed his wishes.

Max lived in our city but we no longer had contact with him. As a child I could not understand why he stopped being our family's friend. When I was older, Mother told me that she had no choice but to respect Father's wishes. Max was a jeweler. He was a single man who had never married. My father was jealous.

A few years later he was robbed, found in his home beaten, bound, and gagged, clinging to life. After he recovered, he packed what was left of his possessions and left for Israel. My mother told me that Max pleaded with her to take us and leave with him. Once again, she stayed with my father.

What happened to our parents and grandparents, their lives forever interrupted and shattered, had an impact on us, the Second Generation.

Freud called it "shadow memories," acquired traumas. Trying to atone what can neither be undone nor ever understood, much less resolved.

Part II

Eastern Poland, Białystok, Saratov Russia, Uzbekistan, November 1939–March 1946, Poland June 1946, and Communist Poland into the late 1960s.

CHAPTER TWELVE

Our tiny fishing boat finally made it to the other side of the River Bug, the Russian side. The Bug, a tributary of the Vistula River, is not a wide river, but the darkness of the moonless night and the silence that enveloped us seemed to make the trip last forever. Just as the five of us got off the boat, four armed men jumped out from behind the bushes. Our fisherman disappeared into the dark of the river; the border patrol guards fired their guns into the air.

"Stop! You are under arrest! You have illegally crossed the river," they yelled in Russian.

They surrounded us and made us walk.

It took us the rest of the night to get to our destination, a large barn. There must have been more than a hundred men and women, sitting on the ground. They were prisoners like us. We found out that we were in the small town of Drohiczyn. Without food or water, we stayed there in the barn until the next afternoon. The Russian police officers stood guard; they would let us out only to relieve ourselves in the field. We sat and waited. We had no idea what the Russians were going to do.

The next day, Russian soldiers arrived on horseback. They threw open the barn doors and ordered everyone out. When the war broke out, the Russian Army had occupied this part of Poland. The route that we took across the River Bug was illegal, and now the soldiers told us that we had to go back to German-occupied Poland. The only legal crossing of the border was through the neutral zone. The very crossing we had evaded.

Sometimes, when the neutral zone was teeming with people, Russian soldiers allowed refugees to enter. Now the soldiers on horseback chased us out of their territory.

"Go back, go back!" they shouted in Russian.

I was terrified of the Germans. The one thing I knew for sure was that I was not going back to German-occupied Poland. I don't remember thinking about it, but I started moving away from the crowd of people in the barn. I saw a soldier on a horse galloping toward me and I threw myself to the ground. I heard the horse's hoofs circling over me. I closed my eyes tight, I was crying hysterically. Pola and my friend Reginka ran toward me and threw themselves next to me on the ground.

The sight of the three of us, sobbing and holding on to each other, must have touched the Russian soldier. He gave orders to the locals who had gathered to watch to help us. We quickly took refuge in homes of two Jewish families in the village, deciding to hide there until we knew what was to become of us. Reginka and I still had our backpacks. Pola, on the other hand, mistakenly left her belongings on the ground when she ran from the soldiers. Pola's backpack was picked up by a Russian family who later demanded money from her. This was to become the first of many encounters with locals who took advantage of us. We had no money, and Pola now had only the clothes and shoes that she was wearing.

The Jewish family who came to my rescue turned out to be good people. They took me into their home and put me to bed. I was filthy. They gently washed my face and hair. They gave me the first food I had eaten in two days, since we left Losice. They fed me chicken soup and a piece of bread. Instead of feeling better, however, I became sick. My head ached like it had never before. Irena, the woman of the house placed a cold compress on my head. I drifted off to sleep.

In the morning, I woke up and opened my eyes. Next to my bed, I saw the Russian soldier, the one who had given orders for help. Seeing him again, I entered a state of total panic but he took my hands and asked me, in Russian, how I was feeling. I did not understand, but Irena was able to translate. The soldier wanted to take me to the hospital. I insisted that I was feeling better.

I told him that I only had one wish, which was that he not send me back to the Germans. The soldier smiled and told me he would grant me my wish. He said that he would give me a few days to regain my strength, but that I could not stay at this border town. I would have to move on to Białystok, where kitchens had been set up for refugees. As night descended, Pola and Reginka who took refuge in a house with a family living next door came to see me. They said they felt safer when they were with me.

We had lost Sevek. We did not know that the fisherman succeeded in bringing the second group of people, including my brother, to the Russian side of the river. They came undetected and made their way directly to the town of Białystok.

A few days later, with Pola and Reginka holding on to me tightly, the two sons of the family got ready to take us by horse and carriage to Białystok. We stood at their door and said tearful good-byes. We apologized for not having any money to show our appreciation, but the mother and father told us they would not have taken it anyhow. Irena pointed to her sons and she said she was doing this for them, too. One day they might find themselves at the mercy of a stranger.

* * *

By the middle of November 1939, thousands of Polish Jews had arrived in Białystok. It was freezing cold, so the Jews of Białystok gave up their synagogue so that we had a roof over our heads. It was like being inside an ant farm. We met people from all over Poland. There were many other young people from Warsaw. Young husbands who left their wives and children to escape deportation to the labor camps. Not yet comprehending the Nazi 'final solution,' these men still planned to send for their families as soon as they could.

Everywhere I turned, I saw a familiar face. We were all over-joyed to be on the Russian side of occupied Poland. There were so many of us we almost felt as if we were back in Warsaw again. I met a family for whom Aron, my first boyfriend, had worked. They told me that when our courtship ended, Aron had married their daughter. They had both come from a simple uneducated background, and they made a good couple. Aron always belonged to a revolutionary group called 'Bojówki' and carried a gun. They said that when Aron heard that the Germans were entering Warsaw, he took off alone leaving his wife behind and no one had seen him since.

When the war first broke out, the refugees that descended on the synagogue were primarily family groups with women, children, and elderly people. However, after a while and as the crossing became more dangerous; the new refugees were mostly young men and women. Families became separated. Men fled in greater numbers; there was still the belief that the Germans would never harm women and children. But many wives fled, desperately searching for their husbands. The chaos was overwhelming; many refugees even changed their mind after making their way to the Soviet-occupied territories and went back to German-occupied Poland.

* * *

One of the good things about being in this part of Poland was the Russians had occupied this region without dropping a single bomb. There were no ruins or rubble. Białystok stood undamaged. The Soviet invasion of Poland differed from the Nazi because on the surface, it seemed peaceful; arrests, deportations of Polish citizens, and mass murder followed.

Poland and Russia had been hostile neighbors for centuries. Some 30,000 Red Army soldiers died in 1920 at the hands of the Poles. In 1939, Stalin finally saw his opportunity for revenge. In the Nazi-Soviet Non-Aggression Pact of 1939, Stalin sought to reclaim the eastern territories lost in the Versailles Treaty of 1919, the Byelorussian and Ukrainian republics. Over a million Soviet troops invaded Poland from the east on September 17, 1939, Russian tanks rolling into eastern Polish territories. The Russian occupiers presented themselves as friends of the people and then immediately started to eliminate the Polish nation. The NKVD[15] (KGB) arrested officials, military men, business and landowners, intelligentsia, and anyone who was regarded as a hostile element. The Polish people here were seen as nothing more than bourgeois who invoked a prewar era. Anyone who was considered as a threat was executed, arrested, or deported.

Entire families were arrested for refusing to accept Russian citizenship; they were given thirty minutes to gather their most essential possessions before being detained. Packed into cold cattle cars with little food and no sanitary facilities, they were sent to labor camps in Siberia or the remote vast farms in Kazakhstan. Conditions were brutal. Many died during deportation. Backbreaking work in the camps of Siberia and on remote collective farms in Asia continuously contributed to the wiping out of slave labor. Stalin had a plan for a new Poland; he needed its territories, he saw it as a passageway to Western Europe. The widespread abuse of Polish citizens from Soviet-occupied territories continued right up and until Germany invaded Russia in June of 1941.

Before the war, the city of Białystok belonged to Poland and then it was under Russian occupation. In June of 1941, some 50,000 Jews lived there with another 350,000 in the surrounding region. After Hitler attacked Russia, the Germans burned down the entire Jew-

---

[15]   The NKVD ("People's Commissariat for Internal Affairs") was the predecessor of the Soviet secret police KGB ("Committee for State Security")

ish quarter, including the synagogue with over 2000 Jews still locked inside. The killing of the Jewish population steadily continued until the final destruction of the Białystok Ghetto in August of 1943.

During the period when I was in Białystok, soup kitchens were open for the refugees. Twice a day, we were provided with soup and bread. For the first time since the start of the war, we did not go hungry. Polish refugees were given a refugee identification card and assigned to a specific soup kitchen. The soup kitchens became a place to meet people and even to socialize. The Russian soldiers were friendly and tried to get to know us, but none of us actually spoke Russian. We brought out whatever we had from Poland and started selling to the Russians. A soldier would pay any price for a watch.

To our surprise, the Russian soldiers were starving. Some of them were so hungry they would buy a herring and eat it whole, not even wait for the herring to be wrapped in paper. The army coats of these Russian soldiers weren't hemmed; the bottoms were a mass of hanging strands. We compared them to the well-dressed German soldiers in Warsaw. We could not understand the reason for the difference.

Some of the men among us were making good money traveling back and forth from Białystok to cities like Lvov or Wilno, buying and selling all kinds of goods. Of course, this *spekulacja*, trading on the black market, was illegal, but nobody cared. Everyone wanted to make a little money, especially enough to rent a room. People like us, Regina and Pola and I, who had no money, slept packed like sardines on the cold floor of the synagogue and were never able to change our clothes. Pola didn't even have shoes.

There was certainly more lice than people. There was no place to bathe. We had just enough water to wash our faces and hands. Conditions grew more and more desperate. I knew people who went back to the German side; I was not going back to Nazi-occupied Poland, back to Hitler.

It was freezing cold in Białystok, especially at night. A young couple with a baby remain fixed in my memory. The mother had held onto few cloth diapers which she attempted to clean in ice-cold water. She didn't have a place to dry them, so she wrapped the cold, damp, partially soiled diapers around her own body, attempting to dry the wet cloth as much as she could with the heat from her body.

After a week in Białystok, I ran into an old friend from Warsaw. He told me Sevek was looking for us, and pointed me to the soup kitchen where I could find my brother. Pola, Sevek, and I were miraculously reunited. We slept huddled together in the cold, dirty synagogue, but we knew we needed a better way to survive. I still had my watch and Reginka a diamond ring, Sevek took them to the bazaar: the plan was to sell what we had and rent a room. Sevek had friends amongst the refugees due to his business dealings in Warsaw, and immediately someone made a connection to a good buyer.

The situation, however, turned out badly. A dishonest man cheated Sevek, insisting that the diamond was only glass and gave him only a small amount of money. He even managed to cheat trusting Sevek out of the watch.

Reginka was wildly upset. She knew her ring was real and that it was a valuable ring. Her mother had bought it in Warsaw long before the war. When Sevek realized how badly he was cheated, his heart started to pound and he started to shake. He went looking for the buyer, but the man wouldn't talk to him. Sevek felt responsible for the loss of our money. He took this misfortune badly; already weak in disposition, be became lightheaded and nauseous, his heart was racing and he was experiencing severe chest pains. We all thought Sevek was dying. Eventually, his physical symptoms improved, but his guilt turned to despair. Our hopes for renting a room vanished.

Before we left Warsaw, Adek made sure that I had the address of my uncle and cousins, my mother's older sister and her family who had escaped to Russia from Poland after World War I. My aunt was no longer alive but the family of seven cousins and an uncle lived in Moscow. We stayed in contact with them through letters as Russia became their new home. I wrote to them from Białystok and got an immediate answer. Inside the envelope, my cousins had sent money.

It was the end of December and the ground was covered with snow. We used the money our cousins had sent to buy Pola a pair of boots.

* * *

In the years between 1939–1941, 300,000 Jews, that is almost 10 percent of the Polish Jewish population, fled the German-occupied areas of Poland and crossed into the Soviet-occupied zone. Soviet authorities deported tens of thousands of Jews to Siberia and remote areas of central Asia of the vast Russian territory. After Germany attacked

Russia in June 1941, more than a million Jews, now Russian citizens, fled eastward into the Asian parts of the country.

Stalin declared the people of the eastern-occupied territories to be Russian citizens. Refugees under Russian occupation were now going to be evacuated. The Russian government gave new orders for all refugees to register. They would then have to go into the Russian interior for mandatory work. As the year 1939 ended, Stalin ordered the deportation of some 200,000—perhaps as many as 300,000—Polish Jews from Russian-occupied Eastern Poland to perform forced labor. In doing this, Stalin saved Polish Jews from the death camps of the Nazi occupiers who attacked Russia in July of 1941. But while in Russia, for the next six years, Jewish refugees endured malaria, typhus, dysentery, scurvy, hunger, and exposure to both extreme cold and heat.

Russian officials started to liquidate soup kitchens. But refugees were already returning from the Russian interior with stories of total desolation. Pola, Sevek, and I looked at each other helplessly; words of wisdom that did not come. We had no idea what to do, and in the end, we shook our heads in despair. We asked ourselves repeatedly: "Is this what we fought for in Warsaw before the war?" Many of us were working-class men and women, and had been closely following the principles of the Russian Revolution. Soviet Russia and the Bolshevik Revolution had been our guiding light. Those of us who fought for Socialism and Bund's principles now saw first-hand what the Russian system was really like—where everything was scarce, where hunger and poverty was the norm.

Registration took place day and night; thousands of refugees descended on the office. In Białystok, we started to see food shortages and higher prices. As our situation became increasingly desperate, we had no choice but to register.

For Polish Jews, Soviet Russian territories were the single best chance of escaping the catastrophe of WWII

When Poland was invaded by Nazi Germany on September 1st 1939, Polish government and its military went into exile. Poland with the largest Jewish population in Europe, 3.5 mil, also had the largest number of Righteous Gentiles (a honorific name used by the State of Israel to describe non-Jews who risked their lives during the Holocaust to save Jews from extermination by the Nazis), 6,706. However, the Righteous Gentiles were terrified not only of the German occupiers but also of their Polish neighbors, too many of whom were Nazi sympathizers and gave them up for helping Jews. That is why the safe houses were never safe. Most historians agree that it took many Righteous Poles to cooperate and save one Jew or a Jewish family but it took only one Polish Nazi supporter to give them all up. After the war those who helped Jews could not talk about their heroism for decades afterwards.

Of over the 3 million Jews in prewar Poland, about 10% survived, 25,000 survived in hiding in Poland, 30,000 returned from labor camps. The largest, 245,000, my parents group, survived and repatriated back from the Soviet territories. Between 1939 and 1941 nearly 300,000 Polish Jews, almost 10%, fled Poland and crossed into the Soviet zone. After Nazi Germany attacked Russia and the eastern territories of Poland, Western Ukraine, Byelorussia, and Lithuania in June 1941, more than a million Soviet Jews fled east to the Asian parts of the country, escaping death. Despite the harsh conditions of the Soviet interior, those who escaped are the largest group of Jews to survive the Nazi onslaught. And while Soviet authorities deported tens of thousands of Jews to Siberia, central Asia, and other remote areas of Soviet Russia, most managed to survive.

Polish Jews who survived and came back to Poland left the Soviet Union in two main phases and about 100,000 Jews stayed in Poland at the end of the war. By 1958, 50,000 emigrated, some to Israel, others to Western Europe, America, Canada, and even South America. The rest chose to stay, and ten years later, in 1968, they were forced to leave once again. By the time Communism fell in Poland in 1989, only 5,000–10,000 Jews remained in the country. Most of those chose to conceal their Jewish identity.

Stalin's anti-Semitism didn't become obvious until after WWII. Stalin would not acknowledge the Holocaust, for him it was the Russian people who suffered. After the war Stalin became obsessed with Russia's Jews. Golda Meir's visit to Moscow Choral Synagogue on the first day of Rosh Hashanah in 1948 was met by a crowd of 50,000 Jews. For Stalin this represented Jewish/Israeli nationalism. Admiration for Meir was contrary to what Communism stood for. Stalin's harshest period of mass repression, the so-called Great Purge (or Great Terror), was launched in 1936–1937. It involved the execution of over a half-million Soviet citizens accused of treason, terrorism, and other anti-Soviet crimes. At that time, anyone could have been accused of anti-Soviet actions. However, Stalin's anti-Semitism was always present, in the late 1930s, 1940s, and 1950s he had few Jews appointed to positions of power in the state apparatus. Following the Soviet invasion of Poland, Stalin began a policy of relocating Jews to the Jewish Autonomous Oblast and parts of Siberia. The people here were faced with arduous work and poor living conditions but at the same time they were spared the fire that engulfed Europe occupied by Nazi Germany. The Autonomous Birobidzhan, chosen by the Soviet leadership as the site for the autonomous Jewish region, near the Chinese border, experienced its height migration in the 1940s, the Jewish population peaked at around 46,000–50,000. However, in 1948, Stalin's anti-Jewish purges made living in the Autonomous Birobidzhan unbearable.

In late 1944, Stalin adopted a pro-Zionist foreign policy, believing that Israel would become a socialist nation and would help in the decline of British influence in the Middle East. Soviet Union, together with the rest of the Soviet bloc countries voted in favor of the United Nations Partition Plan for Palestine, which paved the way for the creation of the State of Israel. On May 17, 1948, three days after Israel declared its independence, the Soviet Union officially recognized Israel. In the 1948, Arab–Israeli war, Russia was the only country who supported Israel with weaponry supplied via Czechoslovakia.

Israel did not become a socialist nation and instead chose to align itself with the West. As a result, from the late 1948 to early 1949 all Jewish cultural institutions in Russia started to shut down. In 1952, Stalin ordered the "Night of the Murdered Poets"; thirteen of the most prominent Yiddish writers of the Soviet Union were executed on his orders. Shortly before he died on March 5, 1953 Stalin accused nine doctors, six of them Jews, of plotting to poison and kill him. The innocent men were arrested and, at Stalin's personal instruction, tortured in order to obtain confessions. Stalin died days before their trial was to begin. A month later, Pravda announced that the doctors were innocent and had been released from prison. Later it became known that after their trial and conviction, Stalin intended to organize pogroms around the country, after which prominent members of the Jewish community would publicly beg him to protect the Jews by sending them all to Siberia.

CHAPTER THIRTEEN

Our destination would be a *Kolkhoz*, a collective community called Szaryk Podczypnik. We didn't know it then, but we were being sent deep into the Russian countryside. Szaryk Podczypnik was located near the city of Saratov, about one thousand kilometers south of Moscow—a fourteen-hour train ride. The Russians gave us money to buy food for the six-week trip. With money, one could always find and buy things to eat. We bought canned foods, dried fruits— anything that wouldn't spoil. In the train stations in Russia, we were able to get only boiled water, *kipiatok*. This, at least, was always available and free. We used the water mostly for drinking and to wash our hands and faces.

Reginka only talked about how she wanted to be with her mother. She had received a letter from her mother; her family was making their way to Brześć, a town some distance south from Białystok. Communication with our families in Poland was possible through letters that were carried by newly arriving refugees. There was always someone we knew who got through to Białystok. As soon as we arrived in Białystok, I also wrote letters back to our families in Warsaw to tell them of our whereabouts. I never knew if our letters, made it to them.

Reginka wept as she signed the one-year contract taking us away to Szaryk Podczypnik. As much as she wanted to find her family, she was more afraid to go to Brześć alone. The contract detailed that we were legally bound to work and live in this rural village near Saratov. We soon found out that we were being taken there to build a new Russian community.

It was the night before our journey to Szaryk Podczypnik. We were staying in a crowded room in the synagogue. We were just going to sleep, when Anja's husband, Szymon, suddenly appeared in the doorway. It was so good to see the face of a family member; we crowded around him, touching him, to be sure he was not an apparition. He had come all that way along to see how conditions were on the Russian side and to decide if he and Anja would be able to survive with a three-year old and a baby if they fled Warsaw.

Szymon told us how much worse things were since our departure only two months before. Jews were forced to give up their jobs.

There was no money. He described how the men never went out during the day anymore. He said that many Jews were making a horrible mistake when they assumed the Nazis were civilized. He felt certain that the Nazis had a secret plan, although he did not know what it was.

I also learned that my girlfriend Hanka who had left Warsaw with us and was forced by the Russian soldiers to return, made it safely back to Warsaw. She went to see Adek and his family, who were all still together at the end of December of 1939, living in the family's old apartment. They were overjoyed to see her and to learn the details of our journey. Szymon told us that now it was almost impossible to leave Warsaw, and that Hanka cried when she admitted that she wished she had joined me in the dirt that day in Drohiczyn. Szymon also told us about preparations being put into place for the implementation of the Warsaw Ghetto. As we listened to him in silence, we became overwhelmed with the realization that those who stayed in Warsaw were facing an alarming situation. Suddenly, our dream of going back home was out of reach.

The Germans established the Warsaw Ghetto on October 12, 1940. The decree required all Jewish residents to move into a designated area, which Germans sealed off from the rest of the city. A wall over ten-feet high, topped with barbed wire enclosed the ghetto. The population of the ghetto was estimated to be over 400,000 people. Adam Czerniakow, a Polish Jew appointed by the Germans to be in charge of the Warsaw Ghetto's Judenrat, government, committed suicide by swallowing a cyanide pill, on July 23, 1942, a day after the start of mass extermination of Jews.

The next morning, Anja's husband left us, deciding to get my sister and the children in Warsaw and come back to the Russian side as quickly as possible. We hugged him close, watching him walk away through our tears. We never saw or heard from him, or my sister, or their children, again.

We walked slowly to the station, where the trains were waiting for us. The cars had sliding doors that opened in the middle. Inside the cars were *prycze*, shelves, on each side of the car made of wooden planks. The cars were packed with people, and not everyone had a place on the shelves. Pola, Reginka, Sevek, and I had to lie on the filthy, black floor. In the center of each car was a small, black cast iron stove with an exhaust pipe that extended up into an opening in the roof. We had a bucket for water. From January 20 until March 6,

1940, we never washed ourselves, nor did we change our clothes. When the train stopped at a station, the men took turns jumping down first for the *kipiatok*, the boiled water. The humiliation continued, as we had no sanitary facilities and had to relieve ourselves right next to each other in the fields next to the train.

The railroad cars had small gaps in the walls which became our windows; this was our only way to see the passing landscape. The wagons were high, and the men had to help all the women climb down. There was a man named Abram who took a liking to me, and he helped me many times through that nightmare of a trip. Little did I know what a major part he would eventually play in my life. We were all so young, barely past our teens. We clung to each other for emotional support and for companionship; we were like an extended family. Also, for the first time we were no longer divided along class lines. Nobody was rich and nobody was poor. Together, we clung to the hope that we would survive our unknown future in a foreign land.

Sometimes our train was shunted to tracks no longer in use, and we were left there for days at a time. Regular passenger trains or trains carrying soldiers, equipment, or goods would pass through instead. From time to time, the locomotive was unhooked to fill the engine with coal. They would give each car a pail of coal for the stove. Most days, however, we rode in cold railroad cars as our train moved through what seemed like endless snow-covered fields. I was physically and emotionally exhausted from the monotony of the vast, frozen landscape, from the constant state of being cold and hungry, which I convinced myself would never end. My heart was heavy. I was being taken away further and further from those I loved. I could not shake my despair. I knew there was no turning back.

We traveled through western Russia, going east for six weeks before finally arriving at our destination. The train stood in what seemed like the middle of nowhere for two days and two nights. It was bitter cold. We were allowed out of the crowded cars only to relieve ourselves. Finally, Russian officials with open trucks came to take us away to the rural community they called Sharyk Podczypnik.

The harsh wind cut into our faces without mercy. Our threadbare clothes were no protection. Thankfully, after a short ride, the trucks stopped in front of a large building—a communal bathhouse. We were each handed a small towel, a piece of soap and directed toward a large, windowless room with showers in the middle. The women went first. There were wooden benches on the sides and hooks where we sat to undress and hang our clothes. After bathing, we were taken to a mess hall. By then, it was already evening. We sat on benches at long tables covered with red and white-checkered oil-cloth. We were given a bottle of beer and a quarter loaf of black, dense bread. There was also cucumber soup and a cutlet made of mysterious meat. I gave my beer to my brother, but I ate the rest of the food. Not one crumb was left on my plate!

After dinner, we went to the barracks: the rectangular building contained a long hallway with rooms on each side. The rooms were all different in size, but we managed to get a room for the four of us. Larger rooms went to the men, accommodating as many as eight to ten. The married couples got the smallest private rooms. At the end of the hallway was a tiny room with a boiler where the *kipiatok* was available morning and evening. We each had an iron bed, a covered mattress, a pillow, and a blanket. The entire building was kept warm by a large, wood-burning oven made of glazed tile.

I remembered how during the first days of the war in Warsaw most women had stopped menstruating. After a few days in the bar-racks, when we all had settled into our new home and rested our tired bodies, all the women started to menstruate again.

Finding a clean rag to use became a big problem.

* * *

The officials gave us three days to rest from our six-week journey. Russian men and women came to our barracks to dance and sing for us; we sensed something was wrong.

On the second day as we ate our dinner, we noticed children and adults crowding outside the windows, pushing each other aside to look in. It seemed to us that they were licking the windows; in fact, they were salivating, and there was a terrible, unmistakable hunger in their eyes.

On the third day, we learned the truth. Sharyk Podczypnik was a God-forsaken village with only one food distribution center. Only once, in the morning, was bread and soup sold to the local people, and always according to their individual rations, which depended on one's work situation. Nonworking adults and children received half of the ration of a working adult. Our dining hall was the only other food center, and so the local people came hoping for leftovers. Of course, there was never any food left over to spare.

We were brought to build a new settlement, and it was hard work. Our jobs fit right in with heavy industries Russia was involved with: steel production, coal mining, construction, and the manufacturing of aircraft, tanks, armaments, and trucks.

To understand Stalin's Russia, one must go back to 1919, when a brutal civil war followed the 1917 October Revolution. After three years of fighting, the Red Army of workers, peasants, and Communists triumphed over those loyal to the Tsar. After Lenin's death in 1924, Stalin was determined to make Soviet Russia a modern country with a strong army. Ten years after the civil war, Stalin put the blame for Russia's lack of progress on the workers and peasants. He embarked on a brutal and ruthless plan known as the 'Second Revolution' to turn a backward country into a modern industrial society. Stalin's plan was to eliminate millions of small, private farms and replace them with large, state-owned, collective farms run by Communist managers. Millions of farmers were moved from their small villages and into cities, forced to adapt to a different way of life. Those who refused were sent to the Gulag labor camps to build infrastructure for the new economic system. They worked as slave laborers, living on the edge of starvation and working long hours in the frigid temperatures. Hundreds of thousands suffered and died.

By mid-1930, the military was part of the new Soviet society. During Stalin's reign of terror, the forced-labor camps became concentration camps for opponents of the Second Revolution. A purge swept through the country. Anyone could be seen as a threat to the revolutionary cause. The 'guilty' one, more often than not, had no understanding what his or her crime was. Most of the victims of the 1930s were peasants whose lives were violently uprooted in the service of modernizing Soviet society.

What followed was the worst famine of the century. The peasants' resistance brought about the full fury of the Party. Stalin blamed the peasantry for waging a war against the Soviet state. The 'Terror-Famine in Ukraine' had been estimated to claim up to 5 million lives.

Under Stalin's industrialization program, the economy was focused on output for the military and heavy industry. Russia did not create a food surplus in case of a war. Until the end, Stalin refused to believe that Hitler's plans included attacking Russia. Workers on a collective farm that was successful and produced more food got the same wages as those on farms that produced little. Employees were not paid fairly for the work they did, and so naturally, everyone chose to work less. The result was empty shelves in markets and people who did not care. The Russian people relied on buying and selling on the black market, trading amongst themselves for items they needed to subsist on. At first, this bartering system was closed to us, as we could not speak the language. We lived on the government's meager supply of bread and soup.

On the fourth day after our arrival, we were called to an official meeting, where we learned that we would receive two weeks' pay. We had the choice of three different jobs: driving, painting, or molding. Most men signed up for the driving jobs, whereas the women signed up for house and room painting jobs. A handful of us, myself included, thought innocently that 'molding' would involve making things. One of the officials took our group to the place where we would learn this job. We entered a cold and dirty room. The walls were stripped and barely standing upright. The instructor was there, waiting for us. He was a young Russian man. I had seen him before when he came to our barracks, always chasing after girls. To my surprise, he told us he was a married man and had young children.

There was a big box filled with lime and sand: materials that bricklayers use. Next to the box was a long wooden tray with a leather strap. We had to take the mixture of lime and sand, and put it on the tray. Than we had to pick up the tray, which was about a meter long, and place the leather strap around our necks. With a trowel, we had to throw the mixture on the stripped walls and then smooth out the mixture. I remember the shock I felt when I realized I was learning to become a bricklayer. I had signed away a year of my life for this backbreaking work. My heart sank. I was laying bricks wearing one of the pretty dresses I had brought from Warsaw.

My legs could barely support the heavy weight of the tray. With tears in my eyes, I told the instructor I could not do it. Somehow, that day, I even found the courage to tell him that they should have provided us with some kind of apron to keep our clothes clean. The instructor listened to me politely but said nothing.

The next day, however, he brought us garments made of industrial cloth that looked almost like aprons. Pola and the other women tried unsuccessfully to smear the walls with the lime and sand mixture. When my turn came, I told him again that the work was too hard for me. I could not do the job. The instructor went to see his director. I tried to stay optimistic in his absence. I felt that they would surely come up with a solution.

After a few days, the director came in to speak to Pola, two young girls from Łódź, Hela and Bronia, our roommates, and me. He told us that he would go to a nearby city with us and help us find work there. Saratov was a big city, he said, and workers were very much in demand. The director seemed like a kind man. We laughed a lot during those trips, even though we could not understand him and he did not understand us. We were thankful that he was kind, but we also realized that he wanted to get rid of us.

On our fifth trip to the city, the director was able to find a job for the four of us in a textile factory. We now had a new problem: housing. One of the conditions of our new job was that we could not be late for work, and to commute daily from the village to the factory was out of the question. The four of us would have to move to the city of Saratov.

We moved to a room next to the factory and Boris, our new boss, allowed the four of us to take the first shift. We were to start at seven in the morning and would be finished at three in the afternoon. My job was to operate a large machine that manufactured tricot, a knit made with two sets of threads. These knitting machines required close control of the lateral bars that controlled chains made of metal links. The needles that moved in the steel plates had to be watched carefully. They broke easily, causing the threads to tangle. The material had to be kept straight. This required standing for many hours at a time. The monotony of the job was just as bad.

The 54 Lenina Street was a one-story house next to the factory in Saratov where the two main bosses, their families, and three female factory workers already lived. Our new room was large. It had four metal beds, a table, a bench and a kerosene lamp. There was no electricity. The outhouse was in the small courtyard behind the building. There was a pump next to it where we could get water for drinking and washing. To bathe, we had to go to the public bathhouse once a month. Part of our salary went to pay for the room, the rest for our food. There was nothing left over.

Still, this special treatment and our move to the city created a lot of jealousy at Sharyk Podczypnik village. I was seen by many as an instigator, whereas I saw myself as being courageous enough to talk to the people in charge. I wanted only to improve my desperate situation.

Sevek stayed behind in the collective community of Szaryk Podczypnik. He and Reginka became a couple. Soon after, Sevek was able to secure a job in his leather trade. His skill was admirable and leatherwork was in demand. The job was in the city, which meant he had to travel back to the barracks in the village every night.

My parents both grew up in a large, closely knit family. My father's loyalty and love of his family was one of the things that attracted my mother to him. The thought of going home to Poland, back to their families, was what kept them alive during their six years in Russia. Family represented a place of safety and a source of strength.

There is one story that resonates with me to this very day. My father's family had a tradition. My mother had told me how for generations, his extended family gathered in a small house, in the woods, for two months every summer outside of the city of Łódź. Adults and children came together to exchange ideas, enjoy each other's company, and share good food. To me, this was like a picture taken out of a romantic, Victorian novel. I could see them dressed in their best white linens, entertaining each other. Lounging, talking, laughing, and playing loudly among the trees and green grass.

Abram Ejbuszyc was silent about his past. He never uttered a word about what happened to him during the war or about what his life had been like before the war. From my mother's stories, I know that he did not want to die in a Russian jail after he was arrested for not wanting to give up his Polish citizenship. His only wish was to stay alive in order to come back home to Poland. He made it back only to find his entire family had been murdered. He was the sole survivor. This knowledge pushed him into a dark despair from which he never recovered. He became silent. I cannot help but wonder if his silence was a form of self-imposed punishment.

Studies have shown that there are two kinds of parents among survivors—those who cannot connect and those who cannot separate from their children. My mother could not separate herself from her two daughters. It was as if she was afraid she would lose us at any moment. To live, my father had forsaken his family and consciously or unconsciously, he chose to suffer the consequences alone. He was tormented by survivor's guilt; the terror was visible, inscribed on his stern face and in his sad eyes. The shock of finding out about the Holocaust and not knowing how his loved ones died resulted in nightmares, anxieties, and depression. My father detached himself from us, as if he was afraid to make a close connection and lose his loved ones all over again. By not talking, he contained the trauma he lived with, hoping not to pass it on to his children. He became a stranger to the new family he created after the war and we were deprived of a loving father. To this day, I know only that my father fled Łódź. The

Germans were rounding up Jewish men and deporting them to labor camps. He ran, and in so doing, he saved his own life, abandoning his mother, father and two sisters. He was never able to forgive himself.

My father's family came from Jews of Włoszczowa, a small town not far from the city of Łódź, they settled there in the second half of the nineteenth century. Father's extended large family in Łódź was religious, prosperous, and well-known in the community. He came from philanthropists who supported the arts and gave money toward education. They all died in the Łódź Ghetto and in Auschwitz.

After the war, he returned to Łódź to find that his large family was decimated. My father never learned the details: that his father, Icek Dawid Ejbuszyc, his mother, Ita Mariem Grinszpanholc, and his older sister, Sura Blima, were deported from the Łódź Ghetto, their home on Rauch-Gasse 1, Flat 18, to Auschwitz in September of 1942. A hospital record shows that his younger sister Dwojra died of *Unterernährung*, of malnutrition, in June of 1942. She was thirty years old. I was able to uncover this information about my father's family in recent years. When those records became available through documentation centers, however, this information was not accessible in the first few decades after the war when my father was still alive.

A document survived the war proving that my father's family did in fact exist and prospered in the city of Łódź. A deed to real estate made my father the owner of two homes that before the war belonged to his parents. These properties were both plundered by the Germans during the war and then taken over by Polish Communists after the war. Because survivors from Russia were forced to settle in the southwestern part of Poland as part of repatriation, my father was not allowed to return to the city of his birth. After the war, property that was not destroyed ended up in the hands of ethnic Poles. Many Poles did not expect that their Jewish neighbors survived and will be returning home. They falsified papers and claimed real estate property as theirs.

My father discovered in the courthouse records unfamiliar names on the titles of his family properties. While he was alive, he traveled regularly to the courthouse in the city of Łódź and fought to reclaim his parents' two houses. As the Communist regime took over, it took control of all private properties. People like my father lost all rights to what belonged to them. After the collapse of Communism, the Polish government estimated that the value of all the property belonging to the survivors and their descendants to be in the billions. At the same time, and to this day, Poland has not recognized property restitution or compensation for any of the survivors, Jewish or non-Jewish.

My father endured an impoverished exile with only one hope, to return to his homeland. His mind was forever haunted by memories of never saying good-bye to his family. He spent years trying to find traces to his family's summer house. There was no closure for my father; he never was able to reunite with any of the physical remnants of his family's happy past as if to tell him those happy days never took place. He survived Russia, and died alone on a very cold December day in 1961, far from his new home in a hospital in Kłodzko. My mother, my sister, and I, while very much alive, were shadows in his life after the war. It was not that he did not deserve us, but that he was unable to emerge from his despair. He simply could not recover from what he had lost.

CHAPTER FOURTEEN

I had promised my cousins I would keep writing. I was very young when my aunt, her husband, and their seven children, my cousins, left Poland after the first war and Russia became their new homeland. I didn't remember any of them. As soon as I moved into our room in Saratov, I sent a letter to Moscow. Before long, cousin Isaac arrived and he stayed for a couple of weeks. He brought food and clothing and news from the family. I felt, almost overnight, that I was no longer poor. Now, in the afternoons after our shift at work, he would take us out to eat in a restaurant and then to a movie. Sevek also started joining us after work, even though he had to make the long trip back to his barracks afterward and then return to the city early in the morning.

Cousin Isaac and I liked each other instantly. He was a famous director in a Moscow theater. He said he remembered me when I was a toddler, but I did not remember him at all. Isaac spoke perfect Polish and Yiddish; he said his parents insisted on speaking both languages at home. He was a number of years older than I was, but we had much in common. He loved the theater, and his passion for the written word brought back my own memories of the performances on the Warsaw stage. He was obsessed with Russian and Yiddish writers, and had many other interests, which included music and politics. I told him about my involvement with the Socialist Bund Party in Warsaw and in my belief in a better world for all workers. I could tell he was attracted to me. When it was time for cousin Isaac to leave, he reminded us that as soon as our year in Saratov was over, we would be free to travel. He invited me to come and visit him and the rest of the family in Moscow.

He did not forget us after he left. He came back frequently and sent money inside his letters. He also sent packages of food, carried by actors who were traveling from Moscow to perform in Saratov. We would not have survived without cousin Isaac's help. The things that he did not say to me during his visit, he was now saying in passionate letters.

During his two-week visit, we had learned from Isaac that there were no food shortages in Moscow, Leningrad, and Stalingrad. Everything was available. Stalin made sure food supplies were high in the larger cities for diplomatic reasons. Foreign dignitaries were only allowed to travel in the big cities, and so they saw only the successful and flourishing side of Russia. The Russian people wanted to move out of the smaller cities, towns, and villages where bread was rationed, but now the big cities were overcrowded and closed. To travel or move within the country, the Russian people needed a special permit. This option was closed to the refugees as well; we could not register to live in any big city. But at the highest levels of Russia's corruption, everything was possible and obtainable.

Reginka's family was living in Brześć, now under Russian occupation. They wrote that, after everything they had gone through to get there, they were well and felt safe. Soviet Russia occupied the Polish town of Brześć in September of 1939 in accordance with the secret pact between Russia and Germany dividing Poland. On June 22, 1941, Brześć was attacked by Germany in a surprise attack. Nazi Germany decimated Brześć's Jewish community, most of approximately 20,000 Jewish inhabitants of Brześć were massacred. The Red Army was able to reclaim the city in 1944.

Reginka tried to convince my brother to go back with her and join her mother. I begged them not to leave. The punishment for leaving was an automatic five-year imprisonment in Siberia. Sevek didn't want to take the risk but Reginka missed her mother terribly.

Finally after weeks of Reginka's nonstop crying, Sevek decided to take a chance and leave with her. He loved her. He told me he felt he had no other choice if they were to stay together. Once his decision was made, Sevek stopped talking to me about his plans. The last things he told me was his suspicion that secret agents were following him. At work, he had a good friend, a Russian Jew whose name was Fliker, and at the barracks he had a good friend named Ukrainski. We had traveled with him from Białystok.

I remember an incident that took place between my brother and his friend from the barracks. Sevek came to us after work. He was barefoot. His friend had wanted to go to the theater, but didn't have a pair of shoes. So my brother took off his shoes, gave them to his friend, and then waited barefoot in our room. I did not know his friend Fliker, but I did know Ukrainski. My brother's friends became his close confidants as he planned the dangerous trip to Brześć.

Without warning, my brother came to tell us he and Reginka had train tickets. Fliker helped with the purchase. They were scheduled to leave the next morning. I could see Sevek was anxious, that he had reservations about the whole thing. He kept repeating that he thought someone was following him. I tried one last time to change his mind, but he would not listen. We found ourselves crying as we said our good-byes. Sevek promised to write as soon as he got to Brześć. He left Pola and me standing in our room; my heart was heavy.

Days and then weeks went by. I didn't hear from Sevek. He and Reginka seemed to have disappeared. I interpreted this silence as a sign that they had fallen into the hands of the police. I expected that at any moment the police would come and take Pola and me away, too. In Russia, when a person was accused, the whole family was pronounced guilty. As refugees, we had even fewer rights than a Russian citizen.

At the factory where Pola and I worked, the director Boris knew about Sevek and Reginka's detention. The police already had contacted him and also questioned him about Pola and me. Boris vouched for us and gave us the highest references, which was why the police never arrested us, but at that time, I had no idea that Boris knew what had happened to our brother. He kept asking me, "Roma, why are you always so sad. Why are your eyes always tearful? Is something wrong with you? Do you want to go back to your own country? Do you not like it here?"

I was careful about what I said. One wrong word and I would be on my way to Siberia. I told Boris here in Russia life was good, but I was worried about my family who had stayed in Warsaw with the Germans. Boris persisted; he would question me about Sevek.

"But where is your brother? How come he doesn't come to visit you anymore?" After which he would say, "Maybe he is in jail in Saratov?"

I was at a loss. I did not understand why Boris insisted on talking about Sevek and why he brought up the jail. On one hand, I felt I had to be careful around Boris: maybe he was a snitch, a spy who worked with the secret police. On the other hand, I thought that maybe he was trying to help by indirectly giving me information about Sevek.

By now, Sevek and Reginka had been missing for over two weeks. Fear was taking over my rational thinking. My heart told me he had to be in jail. Finally, my love for my brother made me take action. After work, Pola and I took the trolley car and went to the jailhouse. We identified ourselves as sisters looking for a brother and his girlfriend. When I think about it now, I don't know where I got the courage to stand at the information window and insist they tell us the truth. I said our brother was not a criminal and if he had been detained, a huge mistake had been made. The administration officer did not answer any of our questions. He said we should go to the head of the NKVD, the Soviet secret police, where we could get more information. The next day, we went to the NKVD. At first, the captain would not see us without special permission. In Russia, the government and the civic administration operated at a high bureaucratic level. As refugees, we carried our special identification papers; officials looked at us with unfriendly eyes. Repeatedly, I had to explain the reason for our visit. It took many hours. We had to go through many bureaucratic steps before the head of the secret police finally agreed to see us.

The most incredible fear overcame me. Pola and I climbed winding staircases, passing through long narrow hallways. Officials sized us up as we passed, looking at us from head to toe. Out of breath, we made it to the sixth floor, where we were made to wait. Finally, the door opened and a captain called us into a tiny room barely big enough for a desk and a couple of chairs.

The captain took a seat behind the desk. He was imposing and official in his heavily decorated green uniform. He wore a pair of small, round spectacles that rested on his nose. His expression was not a friendly one. He informed us that Sevek and Reginka were arrested on the train, on the first stop after Saratov. They were both detained until deportation time in the local prison and their punishment was a five-year sentence to be served in the labor camps in Siberia.

Pola and I started to cry. We begged the captain to let Sevek go. We told him that when Sevek was eighteen he was diagnosed with a heart disease and he suffered from an anxiety disorder. We assured him that Sevek was innocent, that he didn't know what he was doing. Nothing worked. The captain's heart was made of stone. Our words did not move him. He told us that until his deportation once every week we could bring Sevek a package of food and clothes, and then he asked us to leave. I left knowing Sevek would never survive Siberia. We could do nothing for Reginka—not even bring her a box of food since we were not considered her family.

* * *

Packages were only accepted in the morning. On the day that we brought the first package, Pola and I arranged to take the second shift at work. We went to the gates of the jailhouse and handed the package over. Of course, before Sevek would get the package, the jail guards closely inspected it. We could not write any messages to Sevek and he could not write to us. I asked the guards to please find out from our brother what else he needed, and to tell Sevek that we were doing everything in our power to help him.

We waited for about half an hour until one of the guards came back. I could not believe my eyes. The officer was coming back holding the package I gave him minutes earlier. In that moment, a thousand horrible thoughts concerning Sevek ran through my head. The officer must have understood my state of panic by the look on my face because he quickly came to my rescue. "Your brother is fine," he said, "but refuses to accept the package. He says you, yourselves are hungry. He says you are bringing him your food rations."

At that moment, heaviness fell from my heart, and a cinder of hope sparked in its place. The thought that rushed through my mind was that, in this lifetime, I would see Sevek again. I didn't know what to do. It was true that we didn't have much food to eat, but I was sure it must be much worse in jail. I begged the police officer to take the food to Sevek. I reasoned with him that since only one small package was allowed once every week, we were not giving away our food rations. The officer agreed to give the package to Sevek no matter what, and he proceeded to tell us that Sevek was sick. That he was being held in the hospital part of the jail. We knew how hard it was for Sevek to manage to live under so-called normal conditions. We could not imagine how the arrest must have affected his frail physical and mental condition. The officer took the package.

Our goal became to see Sevek. After going from one office to another, we finally succeeded in obtaining permission to see him before he was sent to Siberia. I was overcome by grief. We were so close in age; he was my closest sibling. He taught me to read and write in Polish. We helped each other to survive during the four years of mother's illness and after her death. We had lived through so much suffering during the past six months—the bombs, the devastation, and the German occupation, losing him—only to discover him again in Białystok. My despair was overwhelming.

Pola and I went together to the jailhouse. Again, we took a small package with food and a few items of Sevek's clothes. Visiting took place in the administration building in a small, overcrowded room. A tall barrier divided us from the prisoners. We were made to hand over the package. At that moment before they called us in, I became hysterical. Pola kept her composure, although I knew she, too, was having a very hard time. Somehow, she was able to control herself.

A policewoman brought Sevek into the room. The sight of him made me cry even harder. I could not talk. And with my eyes full of tears, I could see that he was so pale. He hadn't shaved in weeks. He walked toward us hunched over; his always straight and graceful posture was gone. He looked as if he had aged ten years in weeks.

The visit lasted only a couple of minutes. The policewoman stood at his side, so Sevek could not talk freely. He said he had enough to eat and was in the hospital section of the jail. Before I had the chance to compose myself, the policewoman grabbed him and started to drag him away. It all happened so quickly. Pola and I were in shock. As he was being pulled away he suddenly screamed, "Fliker and Ukrainski are guilty!" and the door closed behind him. I was stunned by Sevek's words, but I believed him. I knew he would never say something like this if it weren't true.

It took two years before I found out what had really happened. Fliker, a Russian Jew, had offered to help with the purchase of the train tickets. And Ukrainski encouraged my brother to run away with Reginka. Sevek was so naïve; he thought his friend was a good man who had his best interests in mind.

Meanwhile Sevek's friends were snitches, working in cooperation with the Russian secret police. Ukrainski knew of Sevek and Reginka's arrest long before we did and he came to us a few times. Each time, he wanted to talk only about Sevek, wondering what could have happened to him. He showed so much concern, but I had come to realize this was an act. Pola always offered to make him tea and share our meager food rations. He wanted to discuss politics, and always criticized Russia—especially Stalin. There was something about him that made me uneasy and uncomfortable.

Sevek's last words about these two friends rang in my ears. I wanted to avenge Sevek's betrayal. I made the decision to go back to the NKVD, where by now my face was familiar to the officials. I was given an appointment to see the captain. I told him what Sevek had said to me, how my brother's friends had set him up, encouraging him to run from Russia. The captain listened without interruption. I was hoping that the truth would somehow help Sevek. The captain made no promises.

Meanwhile, Ukrainski was still coming around to see us. By now, we were not the only ones who suspected him of being a spy. Suddenly he started dressing in expensive clothes. No one could explain his unexplained wealth. He was spending more and more time in the city instead of in the village of Sharyk Podczypnik. He was not working. Pola and I became familiar with his routine and so we knew when he would be visiting. We would lock our room and leave in an effort to stop his visits. I had a strong feeling he wanted to do to us what he did to our brother.

When I went back to the jailhouse with food, they said Sevek had been taken away at night, and that he was already on his way to the labor camp in Siberia. They told that he would write. I didn't believe them.

My Father

While in exile in frozen Russia, my father had been often sick with pneumonia. He was overworked, undernourished, and never treated. More than ten years later, he was diagnosed with incurable tuberculosis. The illness was by then in advanced stages and he was considered contagious. When in the late 1950s, my parents discussed of leaving Poland, they learned they could not. No country would allow my father entry, and they never tried to appeal the decision.

Once, when I questioned my mother about why she didn't fight harder when we were children to immigrate to Israel, she confessed that after living through the bombing of Warsaw, she could never again live in a country where people lived with the constant threat of war.

The last time I saw my father alive was in December, 1961. He was critically ill. We were waiting for an ambulance to be dispatched to take him to a special hospital in Kłodzko, two hours away by train from where we lived. The ambulance came for my father after a one-week delay. My mother was desperate to get my father treated; she believed medical intervention would save his life. While we waited all of those days for the ambulance to arrive, we were terrified as we watched our father die a slow and painful death. After fighting illness for roughly twenty years, my father looked thin and frail, his face was sunken and he had dark circles under his eyes. The nonstop bouts of coughing, one of the symptoms of consumption, had taken its toll. My father had trouble breathing. His lungs were disintegrating and he was coughing them up with blood. That last week as my father lay critically ill, I remember the atmosphere of gloom that hanged over our home. I remember his striped pajamas, the container for spitting the blood next to his bed, and the large handkerchief he held on to for the coughing spells, the one he used to wipe the blood from his mouth.

After the ambulance took him away, I never saw him again. My mother would see him alone while he lingered in the hospital for two more weeks. She left my sister and me at home since children were not allowed inside a hospital for infectious diseases. On December 18, she saw him one last time. She came home to be with us before sundown. The night my father died, he was alone. Just as she arrived, our Post Office dispatched a clerk to tell my mother that a phone call from the hospital awaited her. We all understood the meaning of that phone call. Her husband, our father had died.

His funeral took place in a Jewish cemetery in the city of Kłodzko, where the hospital was located. On a cold winter day, fresh snow crunching under our feet, we went to the hospital's chapel to pick up his body. The small mortuary building, detached from the hospital, was surrounded by nothing but snow. My mother and my sister went inside but I could not bring myself to do this. I never said good-bye to my father. I could see his naked feet from the open doorway. My mother did not force me to go inside; years later, reflecting on that day, I wish she did. My father was buried in the Jewish tradition; his body was wrapped in white shroud, and the grave was lined with wooden planks, there was no casket. His body was covered by wooden planks and earth. Standing outside, in the snow, next to my mother and sister I cried and cried. I was overwhelmed by sadness: I was grieving for the father I never got to know.

One year later, my mother, my sister, and I unveiled a marble monument at our father's grave. The inscription read:

> Here rests Abram Ejbuszyc,
> born 22-3-1911 in Łódź died 18-12-1961
> for peace and quiet of his spirit,
> in deepest sadness asking his wife and daughters.

The Jewish cemetery in Kłodzko is located on a quiet street called Bochaterow Getta, Heroes of the Ghetto. This location happens to be right next to a large prison. Standing next to my father's grave and looking up to the heavens, you can see the faces of the guards on duty in one of the four towers, patrolling the prison.

I visited the cemetery each time I came back to Poland. The overgrown grass stood as a reminder of time passing, of the once flourishing Jewish community that has vanished. Sometime in the years after 1990, under the watchful eyes of the prison guards, citizens of Kłodzko made a deliberate choice to violently assault and destroy the Jewish monuments of those who were laid to rest there.

I was prepared for what we were about to witness at the Kłodzko cemetery when I returned so many years later with my own daughters. I had been in contact with Polish students, historians, and researchers who took upon themselves the task of preserving Jewish cemeteries. They uncovered the devastation and sent me photographs of my father's desecrated grave. But nothing could have prepared me for what we saw that day. My sister began to cry the moment we stepped through the small gates. She had begun crying ever since she landed in Warsaw's international airport. For my sister, it was her first time back since leaving Poland at seventeen. Our Polish friend Zenek was shaking, embarrassed by the acts of his fellow countrymen. Standing in the ruin, he collected the heavy granite pieces, trying to put my father's monument back together again. I made him stop.

We were not responsible for those crimes; I thought we should not be fixing the damage. I felt the world needed to see what people still did to one another. My daughters seemed hypnotized by all the devastation around them. I watched them as they took it all in, the broken granite strewn everywhere including the pieces of their grandfather's grave. In the end, they both looked at me and declared that the cemetery was beautiful just the way it was. Of course, this wasn't true. I believe it was their way to spare me the pain.

For six years, I wrote letters to the city of Kłodzko, to different Polish and Jewish organizations, trying to expose the damage done to the Kłodzko Jewish cemetery without response. In December of 2013, I finally received an email from Michael Schudrich, the Chief Rabbi of Poland, informing me that the Jewish organization in charge of safeguarding Jewish heritage in Poland will be fixing my father's grave as well as the other monuments. Today Jewish organizations are safeguarding Jewish history on Polish soil, however, I am still waiting to hear about conservation at the Kłodzko cemetery. But what I am left with is an irony of what my mother wrote on her husband's grave "for peace and quiet of his spirit" and how her simple request was violently smashed. What also can't be erased is that my daughters, the third generations of Holocaust survivors, had to witness a desecrated Jewish cemetery in today's Poland.

CHAPTER FIFTEEN

The prisoners in the Gulag built railways, roads, cut timber, and mined for coal and lead. They suffered not only the freezing climate but also had to endure living in the most intolerant of conditions, lacking food, and sleeping in overcrowded, primitive wooden barracks. Sometimes the newly arriving prisoners had to build their own shelters to protect them from the freezing temperatures. The prisoners subsisted on thin soup and stale bread. Stalin's politics of terror and the economy of slave labor were closely entangled. The Gulag system expended massively under the Bolsheviks. The Czar had his prison camps in Siberia, but they were luxury resorts compared to what the Soviets put into place, best described by a Russian political prisoner and writer, Aleksandr Solzhenitsyn.

We eventually learned that Reginka was also sent to Siberia. As we were not considered family, we were not able to see her before her departure or bring her packages of food and clothing. Still, in the midst of our misery, my cousin Isaac continued to send me passionate love letters. He wanted me to come to Moscow as soon as I was free to travel. He kept reminding me that we were a perfect match, and that he now understood why he had never married. He said, "It was destiny that our paths crossed again" and that he had been waiting for me. I must admit I loved being with Isaac. Since I met him I had stopped wondering how my life would have turned out if Max and I had a chance to be together.

As an impressionable twenty-two-year old, I found myself falling in love again. At the same time, I kept reminding myself that my destiny was to return home to Warsaw. I knew Isaac would never leave Russia. I had no choice; I had to convince myself that I could not marry Isaac. I told him that I needed time, that I was too young, and that we had just met. And that we needed to get to know each other. He was so kind, and he believed me. One thing I knew for sure, I hated Russia, and this made my determination to go back to Poland stronger. I did realize that choosing Isaac would mean not having to suffer the poverty I had known all my life. But how could I abandon Pola?

I tried my best to put Isaac out of my mind. I thought a lot about my favorite writer, Maria Konopnicka, who was not afraid to leave a controlling husband to be free. I, too, wanted to be free. I believed that the values of the Bund Movement taught me to fight for my independence. We learned that all workers had basic rights and freedoms. I deserved the same. At the same time, seeing Russia's Communism up close made me question if what we fought for before the war ever had a chance of success.

A day finally arrived when we received a letter from Sevek, written in Russian. It said he was in a camp in Karelian woods, in Archangel, Kotlas. He wrote that he was fine and he was with thousands of people from Poland. Kotlas, situated at a river-rail junction, became the labor camp for deported Poles. The prisoners there did forestry work, cut and rafted timber, built roads, and, eventually, would build a nine hundred-mile railroad.

A letter from Reginka, also written entirely in Russian, arrived shortly after Sevek's. She asked me to try to help her contact Sevek. Reginka was also sentenced to five years of hard, backbreaking work. The labor camp she was sent to was building roads. At night, guards escorted the prisoners back to the prison. The prisoners were not paid. Twice a day, they ate a piece of bread and soup. She said the soup looked and tasted like water. Reginka begged us for help, for a food package.

On my meager salary from the factory and with Isaac's help, I was able to send food to Sevek, and also send whatever I could to my brother and family in Warsaw. Abram, too, was sending whatever he could to his parents in Łódź, to the address where they last lived, to Rauch-Gasse 1, Flat 18. This street became part of the Ghetto in February of 1940 when the Germans limited Jewish residence to specific streets in the Old City of Łódź and the adjacent Baluty Quarter. If not for my family in Moscow, who were helping us, Pola and I would not have been able to help Sevek. On our own, Pola and I barely had enough money for our own room and food rations.

Sevek's second letter came, written again in Russian: this was how the government controlled what information left the Gulag camps. I wrote back that I had received a letter from Reginka and that she wanted to be in contact with him. His answer came quickly. It was short and shocking: "Together with me, you should forget about her." Sevek wrote that he didn't want to hear her name again.

Sevek never forgave Reginka. He felt that if not for her, he would never have tried to leave Russia. I didn't know what to do about Reginka. I knew she was suffering and I could not add to it by telling her what Sevek had written. I decided to tell her that although Sevek was writing to us, we did not have an address to answer him.

* * *

In Saratov, I became close to Abram, the young man who came with us from Białystok. Now he was spending his free time at my side. Eventually, we became a couple, but we did not have a place where we could be together; he lived in the Sharyk Podczypnik barracks. Abram never knew about Isaac, and Isaac never knew about Abram. Abram and I spent Sundays together, and he would come to see me during the week every chance he got. On Sundays, we went for walks. I knew that he missed his family terribly.

It was November of 1940; one year had passed since I ran from Warsaw.

On a Sunday afternoon, Abram came to see me with a small valise in his hand. He wanted me to pack quickly and come with him. After what had happened to Sevek and Reginka, I told him, "If you want to leave, go, but I am not going anywhere. The year that we are legally committed to in Saratov is almost over."

Many of Abram's friends were running away to the Polish territories that were under Russian occupation. Their destination was a city called Lvov. Somehow, they all seemed to be getting through without being caught. They wrote to Abram, asking him to come.

I remember the day I convinced Abram to stay as if it was yesterday. In my room, on a cold Sunday afternoon with all my roommates including Pola gone, Abram and I sat on my bed and pledged love for each other. This was the day that Abram and I became intimate for the very first time. Afterward we declared ourselves a couple, although we were not legally married. An official marriage ceremony would have to wait until the war was over. That day, when Abram did not leave without me and instead promised himself to me I was reassured that his love for me was real.

As it turned out, everyone who went back to the occupied Polish territories became Russian prisoners. It was the same for those who stayed behind and didn't go to live and work for Mother Russia. After the Soviet invasion of Eastern Poland on September 17, 1939, massive arrests, killings, and deportations took place. Thousands of people from this part of Poland suffered; Jews were not singled out. Stalin established a new threat: "the enemies of the people." Three major deportations of civilians took place, one in February 1940, one in April 1941, and one in June 1941. They loaded whole families into closed trucks and drove them to the train station where dirty, cold cattle trains waited to take them to Siberia or Kazakhstan, in Central Asia. From the occupied eastern territories, Stalin deported 1.7 million Poles to slave labor camps in Siberia and Kazakhstan. Around twenty percent of those deported were Jews. Of the deported, it has been estimated that around 500,000 survived. At the labor camps people died like flies, from disease, starvation, and the awful conditions.

We learned about such things from correspondence from many of our friends who ended up in Siberia's labor camps. Reginka wrote to me of how her mother, younger sister, and aunt were deported from Brześć to Siberia in April of 1941. Reginka's mother and sister were sent to one labor camp while her aunt, as it turned out, was sent to Reginka's camp where they were reunited—of course, this was not the way they had hoped.

The winter of 1941 was dangerously cold. We suffered through huge blizzards, and did not have warm clothes or boots or enough blankets at night to keep us warm. Pola and I were fortunate in that we lived only two houses away from where we worked. But Abram still lived in the collective barracks and worked far away, traveling six days a week to and from his job. He was sick through that whole winter. He came down with pneumonia-like symptoms and ran a high fever. The doctor gave him what little medicine there was available, aspirin to lower the temperature. When he could not work, the factory allowed him to stay in bed for a few days, until his fever subsided. I went to see him on those days after my own day at work and tried my best to take care of him, but all I could do was to make a hot cup of tea and keep him company.

One thing I still remember about Saratov was that it felt safe. I walked home from the trolley car through empty streets all alone, sometimes as late as eleven at night, but I was never afraid. Saratov was considered a 'closed city' during the Soviet era, because of its military factories, so I did not feel like I was in any danger while I was there.

* * *

It was January of 1941. The year of our mandatory stay would be over in a month. I was planning to visit my cousin Isaac and his family in Moscow as soon as I was free to travel. Pola and I went to the train station to have a look at the train schedule.

We walked around the large Saratov station, looking at everything. In our year in the city, we had never been there before. One of the train attendants came over to Pola and me, directing us to a small room. We went with him but had no idea what this meant. After a short wait a young man in civilian clothes entered and ordered us to follow him out into the street. A beautiful car with a driver was waiting at the curb. The young man asked us politely to step inside the car, and then he declared that we were under arrest.

For a moment everything for me stopped. It was like having a nightmare: I could not breathe, I felt I was going to be ill, I felt faint, I was panic-stricken, and in my mind, it was the end of the world. I kept thinking, "This cannot be happening." At the same time, anger was growing inside me. Somehow I managed to ask the young man why this was happening. He didn't respond.

The car trip took about twenty minutes as Pola and I rode in total silence. We stopped in front of a nondescript house that I understood was the headquarters of the secret police. We walked up some flights of stairs and entered a room where a woman dressed in civilian clothes strip-searched us. After that, Pola and I were handed over to a man who took our papers, wrote down our names and address, and proceeded to question us. He wanted to know why we were at the train station and to where we were running away to. As he questioned us I could see he was writing an order for our arrest. By now, tears were streaming down my face. I asked him to listen. I asked him how he could think we were running away when we didn't have any money to buy tickets. I reminded him that without tickets we could not board a train. I told him we both worked, and I gave him the name and address of the factory. I told him we only came to see how the train station looked since we have never been there before. I begged him to please let us go home, that all of our belongings were there and that tomorrow at seven in the morning we had to be at work. He looked us over, and then he telephoned the factory. After questioning our factory director, finally, he took our pictures and fingerprints. He told Pola and me that we were free to go.

What I remember most vividly after our release was standing outside the building, taking a deep breath of air and the relief I felt.

Neither one of us could believe what had just happened. In no time, everyone we knew found out about this incident. Abram, too, found out about our detention, and although he just got over one of his bouts with pneumonia, he came to see me after work. The intimidation tactics the Russians used worked. This was to be a lesson for all of us.

A month after this incident, the one year of our mandatory stay officially ended. Pola and I were free to travel at last. Now all we needed was money to purchase the tickets. I was just a toddler when Isaac left Poland and I did not remember my family who now lived in Moscow, but I did want to meet them. The family consisted of my mother's sister who was no longer alive, her husband and her two sons and five daughters. Abram didn't like the idea of me going, but I made it clear to him that the people in Moscow were my cousins, my family, and it was important for me to see them. Abram knew nothing about Isaac and his love letters. It was a comfort for him to know that nothing and no one in this world could make me stay in Russia. He knew we each had a dream. His was to go back to Łódź, and be reunited with his parents and sisters. Mine was to go back to Warsaw, and be reunited with my brother and sisters. Cousin Isaac would never leave Russia, Moscow was his home. He was a successful man there, and he knew the punishment that awaited those who tried to leave.

Boris, the director of the factory, was cooperative, and allowed me to take a two-week vacation. Now I was faced with the big problem of buying a train ticket to Moscow. The only tickets sold were to those traveling as part of an official delegation. Boris was always making sure no harm came to Pola and me, and I had come to realize he was a good man and not a government informant. He figured out a way for me to travel to Moscow. He told me to buy a ticket to a city called Iwanowo, which was the textile capital of Russia. To get to this city, I had to try to change trains in Moscow. This plan was not foolproof, since I still had to deal with inspectors on the train. The train conductors had the power to take me off the train and make me change trains before entering Moscow. No one was allowed to enter Moscow without a ticket, but Boris encouraged me to try. He told me that more often than not, the conductors, simple, hard-working people, were nice and "looked the other way." I had no other choice but to try Boris's plan to go to Moscow, even if it meant taking an enormous risk.

Pola and Abram took me to the train station. I bought a third-class ticket; the wagons were crowded, and I barely found room on the floor to sit. The cars were cold. There was no food service; I ate what I had brought with me from home. Boris's plan worked; the train conductor himself reminded me to change trains in Moscow. The trip took the whole night, and we arrived in the morning.

I had my cousin's address, and I took a taxi to his house. Isaac was a single man and lived in a small but beautifully furnished apartment with his father. By now, my uncle was an old man. My aunt had died a long time ago—around the time when my mother got sick and had a stroke. They were both very happy to see me, and they took care of me as if I was a beloved child. Since my mother's stroke, I had not experienced such warmth. I was tired, cold, and hungry. Isaac and my uncle hovered over me. They made sure that all my discomforts vanished.

I was fed a delicious breakfast that my uncle prepared; a table was arranged with breads, butter, jam, different meats, cheeses, and scrambled eggs. Isaac made me hot tea from an old silver samovar. My uncle, although old, was alert and wanted to know about my life in Saratov and in Warsaw. Isaac was a real gentleman. With an apology, he said I would not be staying in his apartment, that there was no room but also it was not appropriate. He wanted me to be comfortable, and he arranged for me to stay with his sister Roza. He said he would take me there later; he had to go to the theater as he was in the middle of a major production. He promised that, at the end of the day, he would be able to spend time with me.

In the late afternoon, Isaac and I took a taxi to cousin Roza's apartment. She was married and had an eight-year-old son. Most of my other cousins worked, but Roza's husband was a professor and she didn't have to. In the evening, all of the cousins came to her apartment to meet me, and we had a joyous time. I never dreamed I would be standing there being hugged and kissed by all seven of them. I remembered how my brother Adek had begged me to take their addresses when I had originally left Poland for what I had thought then would be only a few weeks.

At the time, Stalin was still an ally of Germany, and my cousins were in the dark as to what was going on outside their country. They wanted to know what had happened in Warsaw. I told them what I knew about Hitler's invasion of Poland, and how Warsaw looked when I ran East. I told them about Szymon and his last words, his fear that the Nazis had an evil secret plan for Polish Jews. There was total silence in the room. When I explained that Jewish men and women could no longer work, were being dehumanized, that their rights were being taken away, that what Hitler wrote in his book *Mein Kampf* was becoming a reality, they looked as though they didn't believe me. I remember my thoughts back then that it was just as well. For now, my cousins' lives, for the most part, were worry-free and just maybe, in Russia, things would stay this way. Maybe they will get to keep their innocence.

* * *

As promised, Isaac took me out every night. We went to the theater, to movies, and coffee houses. All over Moscow, Isaac knew everyone. Everywhere we went, we ran into his friends, so we were never alone. Isaac transported me to a time that had nothing to do with war and poverty. We ate food that we could never have afforded in Warsaw, food that was not available in Saratov. The stores were large, with signs in both Russian and French. Chicken, veal, beef: everything was available on the menu. Vegetable stores were stocked with tomatoes, cucumbers, and all kinds of fresh produce. Groceries, bakeries, meat stores were full. Ice cream was sold everywhere, even in February.

Cousin Roza took me to the Kremlin, where Lenin was laid to rest in the mausoleum. There were mirrors on each side of his open casket. He was wearing a splendid green uniform. Lenin looked very much alive. People were not allowed to hold packages as they passed the casket. Stopping was also not allowed, so we walked slowly, in single file, passing guards who stood rigidly at attention.

I have never seen another subway come even close to the Moscow metro. First opened to the public in 1935, it was the pride of Stalin's Communist Party. The stations were astounding architectural projects, with marble walls, high ceilings, and extravagant chandeliers. It was like stepping into a museum. The underground stations were large, bright, and clean—and, although it was still winter, it was warm inside. The trains were fast and quiet. It was here that I rode an escalator for the first time.

In Moscow, we had to wait for a light to cross the wide streets. The lights didn't change often, and many people would gather at a light. When we finally had the right to cross, it looked like a small demonstration was taking place.

All of my cousins had good jobs. They tried to convince me to stay. Though it was impossible to register to live in Moscow, my cousins promised they would arrange for me to stay in Moscow legally. I didn't tell anyone I was involved with Abram. I felt desperate; I did not know what to do, so I asked them to give me more time. In the end, they all said the decision was mine alone.

Isaac and I never had an opportunity to be alone together, which I know now was a blessing. Our relationship never had a chance to blossom and grow. I often wonder what would have happened if it had been Isaac instead of Abram who had spent all his free time by my side. Would I have made a decision to stay in Russia? On the other hand, I also know I would have most likely not survived the war. I believe that none of my seven cousins survived, I looked for them in vain after the war, but no one ever replied from Russia.

My vacation ended. I had to go back to Saratov. Being the gentleman he was, Isaac bought me a first-class train ticket. We were only four passengers to a compartment. I had the bottom bench. At night the conductor brought out spotless, soft white bedding; mattresses, sheets, pillows, and blankets. I was able to order whatever food my heart desired. I had never experienced such luxury and service before.

My head was spinning with so many thoughts. I lay down on my bench and closed my eyes. I was thinking about Moscow and wishing that the train ride would never end. Soon my thoughts drifted, I could picture my brother and sisters, hungry and afraid, still in Warsaw. I started to feel guilty about leaving Pola.

Then there was Sevek in Siberia. We had to keep him alive. I had never stopped sending him packages. I did not live only for myself. My conscience would not allow it. I thought of Abram, too, who was waiting for me in Saratov, and how much we loved each other. I refused to consider the reality that I would have been more helpful to those I loved if I had married Isaac.

My War Hero

In Poland, my mother always talked about her uncle who lived in America. He was my mother's father's youngest brother. Ludwig Talasiewicz had left Poland on his own when he was a young boy. He arrived in New York on January 14, 1914 on the steamship 'St Louis' from London. Under the name of Louis Tolosewitz, he joined the American army and fought what I know must be World War II where he received a head wound.

I never knew any of the details and all I know is that after being injured on the battle field my uncle spent the rest of his life in a Veteran's Hospital in Northport, Long Island. In his will, he requested that his possessions would go to any persons with the name Talasiewicz. As a child, I had always been intrigued by my mother's tales about my uncle. And I always hoped that one day I would meet him. He was the first one in our family to immigrate to America and he was a war hero. Aunt Paula was able to locate him and over the years, she kept us informed about his well-being. My wish of meeting him almost came true, but he died only a few years before we came to New York. All connections to Ludwig Talasiewicz vanished with Pola's and with my mother's death. Recently I wrote to the director of the Veteran's Hospital on Long Island to try to get information about my hero, great uncle Louis Tolosewitz, but I never got a reply.

Chapter Sixteen

I returned from my visit to Moscow loaded with clothes and food for Pola and me. My cousins wanted us to have enough sugar, jams, biscuits, fish, and canned meat to last us for a few months. Pola and Abram waited for me at the train station. I could never have carried all my parcels without them.

We still sent packages to Warsaw, even though we had no way of knowing if our families actually received them. Not one letter ever came from Warsaw. With the food from Moscow, we started sending bigger food parcels to Sevek and the rest we kept.

Sevek kept writing from Siberia, but his letters were always brief. Aside from working hard in the forest from morning till evening, he didn't say much about the life in the labor camps. Prisoners were not allowed to write anything negative about Russia. I did not like to picture Sevek doing backbreaking work from sunrise to sunset.

Because the room Pola and I shared was considered big, the factory officials decided to give us an additional roommate. Galina was Russian and new to our factory. She did not have any family. She owned one dress and one nightgown, so that when she washed her nightgown, she slept in her dress. When she washed her dress, she wore her nightgown until her dress dried. She couldn't wash her two items of clothes often, as none of us could. The rationed soap was seldom available.

Galina had the habit of combing her hair at the dining table. She would then proceed to kill the lice that fell on the table from her hair. The first time I saw her do this I became violently ill and threw up. I went to Boris, the factory director, and told him I could not live like this. He promised to talk to her. Whatever he said worked; Galina never again killed lice on our table.

Our contract had expired. We were free to leave, but we really didn't have many options. Pola and I felt that having the job at the factory and a roof over our heads, it was best to stay in Saratov until the first opportunity came to return to Warsaw. By now we were sharing our one large room with not only Galina, but also our two original roommates and factory workers, Hela and Bronia. Hela and

Bronia were married, but their husbands, like Abram, had to live in the barracks.

Soon after our mandatory stay was over, our roommate, Bronia decided to take advantage of her freedom. She left the factory with her husband and moved to the city of Krym. In her place, we got another Russian girl, Viera. We could not pick our roommates; the factory made those choices. Every night, after work, Viera went out with different men, and soon those strange men started coming to our room while we slept. She would tiptoe to the door and let them in. These men smoked cigarettes, drank alcohol, and stayed up into the morning hours while we tried to sleep and be ready for work the next day. I had a strong premonition that something terrible was going to happen to us.

As always, I went to Boris, but this time he did not try to stop Viera. It was only later, in Uzbekistan, when I was participating in the black market that I understood why Boris did nothing. The factory directors drank vodka, and these strange men gave Boris vodka to make him look the other way. This was the reason Viera was able to do as she pleased. Most of us refugees did not drink, but the Russians did, and in large quantities. The legend was that the vodka helped them forget their hunger and misery.

Cousin Isaac came from Moscow for a few days. He brought more food and clothes and once again, tried to convince me to come back to Moscow with him. All of our belongings hung on nails on the walls, or lay under our beds. No one had a closet or even a suitcase to store their belongings. Isaac saw how bad our situation was in the room, and he offered to help us move immediately to a private one. I could see he really cared about me. Even though his real goal was for me to leave with him, he couldn't see me suffer.

When it was time for him to get on the train, Isaac made me promise I would continue writing to him no matter what the circumstances. He held me tight, and begged me, one last time, to come to Moscow with him. He said I could bring Pola; that we could get on the train now. Poor Isaac kept saying he didn't understand my hesitation. I still did not have the courage to tell him how I lived for the moment when I could go home to Warsaw. I loved Isaac and telling him the truth would have broken his heart, I could not bring myself to do this. All I managed to say was that I needed more time.

When the train pulled away from the platform, I wanted desperately to run after it. I was so tired of the constant hardships. I was ready for an easier life. But it was as if my legs were glued to the pavement. I felt guilt and confusion. I was in love with two men at the same time. I was so young, only twenty-two, and a refugee in a strange country. Isaac offered me a way out, a better life but I dreamed of going back to Warsaw, of going home. Abram was just like me, a poor, hard-working refugee who talked only of returning to Poland. When we were together, we raised each other's hopes of returning to family. I remember my walk home from the train station as if it was yesterday: I was overwhelmed with a profound, tender, and passionate affection for Isaac and Abram.

Abram was full of regret. He never had a chance to say good-bye to his parents and sisters when he fled. He went east one day after work instead of going home to escape the daily round-ups of Jewish men on the street. Although I had never met them, I felt a deep connection to his mother, father, sisters, and his brother Jakub Szaya, who died in May 1930, when he was twenty-two. Abram never got a letter from Łódź and he never knew if his packages got through to his parents. He did not know if his family knew that he was among the living. I needed to be with Abram. We were both terribly homesick; we helped each other to sustain the dream of going home. What kept us alive was the hope of seeing our families again.

Thinking back to that day, the last time I saw Isaac, I think that somehow fate intervened. Hitler attacked Moscow soon after. I forever lost contact with Isaac and the rest of my wonderful Russian cousins. I would never find out what happened to them.

By now, the war was moving ever closer in the direction of our city. On June 22, 1941, under Operation Barbarossa, Germany bombed Ukraine and Byelorussia. Survivors were evacuated from those territories in cargo trains, carrying some of them to Saratov. At the train station, we saw a horrifying picture. People had left their homes in a panic. Women held children in their arms—and nothing else. They had left everything behind. Germany attacked without a warning, and Russia was not prepared. While Russia was still mobilizing, the German army took over the whole of Ukraine and Byelorussian territories. All day long, we heard nothing but Stalin's voice on the radio. He said, "The enemy is strong and the Russian country is in grave danger."

The German army reached Moscow's gates by the end of September. By October, the 'Battle for Moscow' left Germany facing their first military defeat. By early December, German troops stood less than thirty kilometers from the Kremlin; fresh Siberian troops attacked the German forces and drove them back. The direct threat to the city was over, but the Russian government ordered the evacuation of Moscow's citizens. Most men were immediately drafted; women and children were evacuated to remote parts of Russia. Soviet casualties during the battle of Moscow were estimated to be far beyond a million and a quarter. Over half a million citizens died.

Abram started working longer shifts in the factory, making weapons, and we hardly saw each other. It was the end of the summer of 1941, and the war was closing in.

* * *

We wanted to find a private room for the three of us, but even if Pola and I could come up with the money, our roommate Hela had none. We couldn't leave her behind. I realized that with German troops moving closer, perhaps moving to a private room was not even such a good idea. I felt safer next to the factory; this place, after all, was my family. When I think about it now I see how foolish this was: If the Germans were to bomb Saratov, the first thing they would have bombed was the factory.

Our plans for the future hung in mid-air. With the war so close to us, making plans had become a waste of time. Our room belonged to Viera and her influx, and fighting with her and reporting her did not help. All factory workers occupied the one-story house we lived in. Two factory directors lived there, each in a tiny apartment with their families. A windowless storage room was turned into a bedroom; two Russian girls lived there. As the fighting in our own room escalated, one of the directors decided that the three of us, refugee girls, would have to move to the small, windowless room and the four Russian girls would live together. We didn't want to move to the windowless room, but we also didn't have a choice. I knew in my heart that Viera and her friends were planning to steal our belongings. This was her plan all along and they were waiting for the right opportunity for them to be successful.

After we moved, I begged Pola and Hela that one of us would be in the room at all times. We changed our work schedule; I worked the morning shift and Pola the afternoon shift. After a week, we switched and I worked the afternoon shift and Pola the morning shift. In the end, Hela could not help us; she had begun working far away. She only came home to sleep.

We kept our watch over the room as best we could. As the war came closer to Saratov, the factory started practicing war drills and giving first aid lessons. We had to attend the classes twice a week. I remember telling my sister that she had to take her first aid lessons before her work shift, because we could not leave our room unattended. I pleaded with her that we should not go to those lessons together, but Pola was stubborn. She did whatever she wanted. Her excuse was that she didn't want to go alone and wanted to be with me.

The day we were robbed, Pola was working the morning shift and I was working the afternoon shift. Before going to work, Pola was supposed to go to first aid class, and after work she was supposed to go home. She skipped the morning first aid class and instead of going home after work, insisted on going to the lesson with me. It was my turn to go to first aid class before my shift started. Even now, I remember how I fought with her and begged her not to go with me but to go home. I was convinced that Viera and her friends were waiting for an opportunity. After the lesson was over, I went to work and Pola went home. Ten minutes later as I was standing at the fabric machine, Pola came running. She was crying so hysterically that the whole factory came to a halt. Pola was screaming incoherently. When I saw her running into the factory my first thought was that, she had received bad news about Sevek. It took a good while to get words out of her. She mumbled through her tears and screams that everything was gone.

I dropped whatever I was still holding and ran next door. Our room was empty! Everything was gone! We now had only the clothing we were wearing. I knew that Hela had saved one hundred rubles, hidden under a pillow. I lifted the pillow and the money was still there. It was only Pola and I who had been robbed. I had always helped Hela with everything. I had shared my clothes and food with her, so I felt justified when I took her money. But taking Hela's money always haunted my conscience, even when I tried to reason that a misfortune makes one grasp at any opportunity, that the instinct to survive takes over.

I called the police, they came with dogs but they did nothing. Our robbery happened on a summer day in the afternoon. To enter our room, one had to go through a tiny foyer with another door that led to a factory director's apartment. The two doors were only a few feet apart. The factory director had a twelve-year-old son who stayed home the whole day, watching over a two-year-old baby. The door to that apartment was always open, so it was logical that the boy would have seen what happened, but he denied seeing anything when questioned. Viera's plan, which I had suspected all along, was a success. Everything I envisioned and tried so hard to prevent became a reality. That night Hela came home from work, she saw the empty room, and that everything was gone—including her money. The factory did give us a loan of thirty rubles each, but we had to pay it back.

* * *

Hitler's offensive against Moscow began on September 30, 1941 and continued until January 8, 1942. In those four months, the casualties for the Red Army were estimated to be over a million men. Civilian casualties were huge as well, estimated at 650,000. Just before Hitler's attack on Moscow, I had lost contact with Isaac and the rest of his family, but I rationalized that the men were being drafted and the families evacuated.

The German army advanced, taking over more and more Russian territory. It was dangerous even in Saratov, far from the frontlines. Food went to the soldiers first, and our nourishment came solely from the daily piece of bread, soup, and boiled water that the factory gave us at work. Our new monthly rations were cut down to 400 grams of sugar, 200 grams of butter and a small piece of soap. The stores were empty. One by one, necessity items disappeared from store shelves and were not replenished. Somehow, I managed to save enough rubles to buy some black fabric. There was a Polish tailor nearby who offered to make me a coat. I still had my white beret and rubber boots; I still managed to look good.

Meanwhile, all Russians with German heritage were disappearing. They were sent in cattle cars to Siberia and Kazakhstan. The deportations were organized by the Russian secret police. The Russian German communities were taken over, their transportation and communication cut off, and their leaders killed. By the end of September 1941, 500,000 Russians of German descent were exiled and their settlements dissolved. The Russian government sent away whole families. Until then, they could have been the best of citizens, but if they were of German ancestry, they were deported. The Russian government followed this tactic in Saratov Oblast where almost two-thirds of the population was of German descent. Many of their ancestors had lived there since the seventeenth century, tracing back to Catherine the Great, the eldest daughter of an impoverished Prussian prince.

The Russian government fabricated stories that the German residents were saboteurs and spies. One such story we frequently heard was that Russian soldiers were ordered to get as much information as possible from the local German population. The government sent Russian pilots dressed as Germans. The Germans, believing the disguised Russians were fellow Germans, were happy to see them. The Russian pilots reported that the Russians with the German heritage were waiting and were ready to help the German soldiers upon their arrival.

The places where the Russian-German citizens lived became ghost towns. Our factory immediately started sending workers to those deserted towns. They sent Pola and me along with many others to dig antitank trenches. We traveled by boat, crossing the Volga River. The trip took the whole night. I didn't even have time to let Abram know that we were being sent away. For the duration of the trip, we were given a piece of bread. After the boat docked, we walked for hours to our destination. It was the end of October 1941. We walked next to a stream, where we could drink water when we became thirsty. Army personnel in cars were going in the opposite direction. The front was near.

We arrived at an abandoned German settlement. There was evidence of life abruptly interrupted. In every home, we found flour and potatoes, among other items, but we were under strict orders not to touch anything. We were told the food was poisoned. The houses were clean, so at least we had a place to sleep and plenty of wood to keep us warm. We had no food. We left Saratov in a hurry, so I had only the summer dress I had been wearing at the time. My newly made warm coat was back in my room.

After a few days, I went to see my new boss and told him I was cold, and not dressed properly for the weather. I asked to be allowed to return to the factory. He felt sorry for me and gave me a letter stating that I was not fit for digging ditches. He also gave a letter to an eighteen-year-old Russian girl named Iulia who was running a high fever. The two of us set out to go back to the factory. My sister Pola stayed behind to continue digging trenches.

To get to the river where the boat was docked, we had to walk through the forest. The Russian girl prayed continuously to God to help us, for us not to be ambushed or killed. Evening came upon us, and we realized we were lost, walking in circles. The possibilities of encountering both wild animals and robbers terrified us. It was getting dark and eerily quiet. The trees moving in the wind seemed to be talking to us. *Don't be afraid* is what I imagined they were saying. We held on to each other and kept walking. We managed to go around a swamp just as darkness descended. We knew that if a foot got stuck in the marsh, we might not be able to pull it out.

It was dark by the time we got out of the forest. We made our way quickly to the river's edge. We were shaking from the cold, but we made it to the cargo boat just as it was getting ready to depart for the other side. Some people were sitting on benches, and others were lying on the floor. We found a place in a corner and spent the night huddled together to keep warm.

In the morning, we arrived in Saratov. Hungry and frozen, I dragged myself to where I lived. All I could think about was my new warm coat. Was it still there? No one knew of its existence so I had reason to hope it hadn't been stolen. To my delight, it was just where I had left it, hidden under my mattress. I was also relieved to find that Abram was still at his job. He had not been sent away like so many others.

Although I was exhausted and hungry when I got back to Saratov, I didn't go to sleep. The factory director knew I was coming back. I went straight back to work, doing as best I could in front of the fabric machine, while anxiously watching the clock for noon to come. At exactly twelve o'clock, I got the daily roll and hot water, and my hunger subsided.

CHAPTER SEVENTEEN

Cesia was a young girl from Łódź. We had traveled together from Białystok, and here in Russia, she had married a young refugee. Before her son was born, her husband had been sent away to work in another town. In the village where she lived, she received food rations for herself and the baby. I was able to maintain contact and I never forgot any of my friends from that six-week journey from Białystok to Saratov.

Cesia came to Saratov on her way back from a visit with her husband and her three-month-old son. At the time, Hela was working at another factory in another village and Pola was still at the German settlement digging trenches. I was alone in the room. Cesia asked if she and the baby could spend the night, which of course was not a problem as I had two empty beds.

We went to sleep, but the baby cried incessantly. Cesia gave him a bottle of water, but his crying turned to screams. I jumped out of bed and lit the kerosene lamp. I could not believe what I saw with my very own eyes. Cesia was biting her own baby. She looked half asleep. I screamed for her to stop. My scream startled her and she seemed suddenly awake. All she said was, "I don't know what I was doing, I am so hungry." We all walked around always hungry; my friend's answer didn't even shock me at the time. I had to be at the factory at seven in the morning, so I made some sugar water for the baby and went back to sleep as fast as I could.

I noticed an empty shelf as soon as I woke, but I didn't say anything. During the night, while I was sleeping, Cesia must have gotten up quietly and eaten all that was left of my month's rations. What could I say? Cesia was up but she would not look at me.

Cesia came back in the late afternoon and spent another night, but it was an awkward time. We did not speak and I was very angry. The only food I had to look forward for the rest of the week was the daily bowl of soup and a piece of bread I got at the factory. Cesia surely knew that. On the other hand, I also knew what hunger was doing to all of us. Cesia probably never meant to eat all the food, only to pacify some of her hunger, but once she started eating there was no stopping. In any case, what angered me the most was that she never acknowledged what she had done, and she never apologized.

The next morning she was gone, back to her village where she had a place to stay and her own food rations.

Word finally got to Abram that I was back. He came to see me on Sunday, and we shared his bread ration. That evening, he would have to go back to his village. Monday was a workday, and being late at his factory, even fifteen minutes late, was punishable by three months in prison.

Once at my factory, an employee missed three days of work without an acceptable cause. The factory came to a complete stop while a trial took place. Two female judges came from the city. We were required to sit and watch as the trial and the sentencing took place. The worker was sentenced and sent to jail. There was no such thing as appeals.

* * *

At the end of November, Pola came back with all the other workers from across the Volga. It was no longer safe to be there. Hela, too, returned with her husband, but he had to go back to live in the village with his sister, whose husband had been missing since we crossed the eastern border, fleeing from Nazi-occupied Poland. Hela stayed with Pola and me.

After the German invasion began at the end of June, the Soviet signed an agreement with the Polish government. General Sikorski, Prime Minister of the Polish Government in Exile in England and Commander-in-Chief of the Polish Armed Forces, was among the first to realize that the nature of the war had drastically changed. On July 30, he opened negotiations with the Soviet ambassador to London to re-establish diplomatic relations between Poland and the Soviet Union. Stalin finally agreed in December to an amnesty for Poles as a gesture to the Sikorski government.

Shortly thereafter, 600,000 men were released from the prison camps of Siberia, and 175,000 of them were immediately mobilized; my brother Sevek was among them. These men were sent to the front without training, uniforms, or weapons. They formed a human shield for the Russian soldiers. They were sacrificed for Mother Russia. It is only later that I learnt of those dreadful details.

* * *

When it became apparent that Hitler did not intend to be a friend of Russia, Stalin turned to America and England for military aid. The allies planned to form a second front to weaken Germany by attacking from behind. America and England gave Stalin an ultimatum. He was to free all the refugees imprisoned in Siberia.

In London, the allies and the Polish government-in-exile finalized a pact with Russia. The result was the formation of a Polish army and an amnesty for prisoners on Soviet soil. Masses of people from the Gulag slave labor camps came down south. Men, and in some cases whole families who managed to survive, were released and given special documents. They traveled to assigned locations to join the newly formed military units. The released prisoners were desperately looking for family member, wives, husbands, brothers, and sisters.

* * *

It was right after New Year's, January 1942 when Sevek and the group of men he was traveling with changed trains in Saratov. Pola and I had just finished work and we were resting in our room after a long day's work. It was almost two years since Sevek's arrest by the Soviet Secret Police. The door to our room opened and there stood our brother. We could not believe what we saw. Pola and I threw ourselves into Sevek's open arms. All three of us cried uncontrollably. I don't think I could ever describe how happy I felt at that moment.

Our brother was alive! He was dreadfully thin; he was frail, he seemed almost half-dead. He was wearing padded cotton pants and a jacket that had been patched so many times it was impossible to tell the original color. His head was partially covered with a worn-out cap. He had no shoes; his feet were wrapped in rags and bound with string. His skin was so weather beaten, he looked like he was fifty-seven years old instead of twenty-seven. His face was covered with hair and he had a beard.

In his mind, Sevek created pictures of me living comfortably in Moscow, married to Isaac with Pola by my side. When Sevek came to Saratov looking for us, he didn't think he would actually find us. He was sure we were long gone. He had even been disappointed the trains carrying prisoners from Siberia were not permitted to go through Moscow. But as destiny would have it, the three of us were together again, right there in Saratov.

We sat huddled together on the bed. Sevek wanted to know everything he had missed. He was shocked I didn't marry Isaac. My brother had never got the chance to meet Abram. He didn't know that our relationship complicated my feelings for Isaac. And I had waited two years to finally be able to ask Sevek the most difficult question of all: what happened on the day of his arrest. He told us how two undercover agents took him and Reginka off the train, just one stop after Saratov. He heard the undercover police officers talking and laughing among themselves. "They never had a chance; they sent our comrades to buy the train tickets and told them of their plans."

My mind raced back to the day in prison I heard Sevek screaming as he was being dragged away by the policewoman. "Fliker and Ukrainski are guilty." Now I heard the story directly from Sevek. His two friends were working for the Soviet Secret Police and they turned Reginka and Sevek in.

I asked Sevek what had happened to the parcels we had brought him before he was sent away. Sevek said that, on his way to Siberia, he kept the package next to him at all times. For days, they traveled without food or water in filthy, cold cattle cars. The freight train stopped so that the men could get off and relieve themselves. When Sevek returned to his place, the men in his railway car had stolen the parcel.

Sevek also said that after his arrest, he was placed in solitary confinement for three days where he was interrogated and beaten, which was how he ended up in the jail hospital.

The guards wanted the names of everyone who encouraged Sevek to leave Russia. Among these names would have been cousin Isaac. When Isaac first came to see us, Sevek already had a suspicion that undercover agents were watching him. But Sevek never mentioned the names of our Moscow family; if he had, they all would have ended up in the Gulag. Isaac would have been accused of assisting our brother, and the rest of the family would have been automatically implicated as well.

The temperature would drop as low as −40°C. Chronic hunger and hard work was the norm. Prisoners died in unimaginable numbers. Sevek was sure that he would die. Daily food rations were almost without protein and fat. Bread rations depended on one's work output. Sevek said that the bread in Siberia was as black as mud. The rest of his nourishment came from a thin soup.

In the morning, a convoy of guards escorted them to cut lumber. At night, they marched them back again to dark, wet, and overcrowded barracks. The barracks were encircled by barbed wire. A tower stood in every corner, housing a guard with machine gun. But none of the prisoners ever attempted to escape because of the vastness and isolation of the area. They labored in the forest, cutting down trees to build roads and railroads while fighting the real enemy: cold, starvation, pneumonia, and typhoid fever.

As his recollection went on Sevek smiled to himself. He said that the prisoners who survived in Siberia were those who believed in something: those who believed that loved ones were watching over them often survived; this belief is what made them more resilient and determined. When faced with tragedy, Sevek said, people found a way to triumph. I didn't know it then, but soon it would be my turn.

My poor brother looked so worn out. Although he didn't say so, I could see how Siberia had affected Sevek's health. When we were home in Warsaw we had protected him, withholding distressing news. I could not believe he survived the intolerable conditions he was now describing, so much worse than anything Pola and I had endured.

Our reunion lasted only a few hours. I tried to give him the shoes and clothes Abram kept at my place, but Sevek refused to take anything. He had to get back to his group of men. They held one train ticket and he could not be late. I begged him to come with me to the police station. Perhaps, I pleaded, we could get a special discharge for him because of his heart condition. I wanted so much for him to stay with us, but nothing I proposed worked. When it was time to leave, Pola and Sevek said their tearful good-byes at home and I escorted my brother to the station.

On our way to the train station, everyone on the trolley stared at us. Sevek looked like a bum. He was dirty, unshaven, dressed in rags. I was wearing the black coat with the fur collar that the tailor had made for me and my stylish white beret. The contrast between the two of us must have been shocking.

At the train station, we held on to each other. I waited for a miracle but it never came. We kissed one last time. Tears streamed down our faces. We had to let go of each other again, almost more painful now after finding him again. Sevek promised he would write from wherever he found himself. I went back to my room with a broken heart. Every step took me further away from Sevek, and with every step, I asked myself if I would ever see my brother again.

Suzanna
The Past and the Present

I remember the anguish my mother suffered every time she described her brother Sevek. She would relive the discovery of his arrest by the KGB and his deportation to Siberia, their joyful but short reunion two years later, and then, his disappearance. Sevek became a nameless corpse, a barefoot soldier sent to the front lines of southern Russia, killed by the bullets of either Russian or German guns. We would never know which.

Sevek, and thousands like him, were sent from Siberia labor camps without any training, not even knowing how to hold a gun. They were a human shield for the Russian soldiers against the advancing German army. The Russians soldiers had orders to shoot on the spot anyone who attempted to flee the upheaval of the front lines. As a child, I understood none of it, but what impressed me were the words she often repeated: that her generation was resilient and determined to survive. That during a catastrophe people found ways to triumph. That their fierce need to return home to their loved ones was what kept them alive, that their human spirit rose above all suffering.

I was frightened by my mother's stories about her childhood, surrounded by poverty and death in Warsaw. Overwhelmed, I looked for ways to feel safe. I focused my attention on what I perceived to be my mother's incredible adventure in Russia. I tried to picture my mother living in exotic, interesting places: the beautiful cities of Saratov and Moscow where she even experienced romance and love. She had lived in Uzbekistan, in the desert, under a hot sun, and ate exotic food. I never allowed myself to see her hungry or sick. My mother was heroic and strong, splendid and beautiful in her tailored black coat. From those early childhood stories, I decided I wanted to be like her, to travel, to go unusual and faraway places. I decided I would walk in mother's footsteps.

My mother's accounts of Russia and Uzbekistan had a deep impact on my imagination. Her stories influenced the choices I made when I left home. Strangely, I found comfort in unfamiliar and far-off places. In college, I was drawn to subjects like anthropology and archeology. Studying ancient and present cultures was like revisiting the landscape of my childhood. I got to work under the hot sun, live in a tent, ride a camel and, like my mother did in Uzbekistan eat exotic food. I excavated in the desert at Tel Beer-Sheva. I observed the lives of Arab men and women, evoking my mother's stories of strange lands. I remembered that when I was a child all I ever wanted was to follow in my mother's footsteps. I was my mother's daughter. I inherited her spirit. We saw the world through the same set of eyes.

When I was twenty-four I went back to Poland, still haunted by my memories of our departure, my mother's inconsolable crying. I realized that I had to return. I was looking for something, a piece of me I had lost. I heard my father was calling me back to the small, overgrown Jewish cemetery where he was laid to rest. Like my mother, I too had succumbed to the notion that Poland was my homeland. The ghosts of my childhood were clamoring for attention.

My mother passed down her pessimism, her suspicion of others, the assumption that everything would turn out for the worst. However, traveling always put me in touch with my mother's strengths. Traveling temporarily wiped out the negative voices that played in my mind. While on the road, surrounded by unusual, new places, I was finally happy and at home. I was always aware of an overwhelming fear of putting down roots. Perhaps, I did not want to have them severed in the same way my mother and her generation had.

Today, we know that posttraumatic stress disorder and the symptoms associated with it are real. They are experienced not only by survivors but also the next generation. Today psychological support is available, but in the late 1960s, when I was growing up, no studies or support systems concerned themselves with Holocaust survivors and their families. Survivors and the next generation were left to deal with emotional difficulties on their own terms. After the war, survivors were simply told to forget about what had happened to them during the war and about the life they had before the war. They were told to start a new life as if their prior life had never existed. For those survivors whose entire families perished in the Holocaust the psychological distresses had no outlet. They hid behind a wall of silence; the trauma of what happened weighing heavily down on their psychic. The emotional impact of the war on survivors and their children went on without being understood for decades.

* * *

I was raised in the shadows of the Holocaust aftermath and its affect continues to burden my daughters, the third generation who grew up with the experience of decimation, defeat, and abandonment. My daughters always knew about my Jewish and Polish background, but years went by before I shared with them the horrific details of the Holocaust and what my mother, their grandmother had to do to survive. How her entire family had suffered and perished. How three decades after the war, under Communism, Jews were once again unwelcome in Poland.

We, the second generation, inherited the responsibility to remember the legacy of the vibrant Jewish culture of Poland, to never forget the horror of Holocaust, and to speak for the generation that was forced into silence.

CHAPTER EIGHTEEN

Abram was furious that I allowed Sevek to walk away with rags tied around his feet. He couldn't understand how I could let my brother leave without insisting he take some of his warmer clothes. While Abram was moved by Sevek's pride, he wished that somehow I had made it possible for them to meet.

Sevek's final letter arrived in January 1942. It was mailed from the city of Astrakhan on the lower Volga River, near the city of Stalingrad. The Southern part of Russia was a region rich in oil, of a great interest to Hitler and of even greater interest to Stalin to be protected at all cost. He was, he wrote, in a city in ruin. "We are still under heavy bombardment. My whole unit has dispersed, and everyone is running in a different direction to save his life. Every man is fending for himself." He also wrote that it was freezing cold, that a light snow was falling, and he didn't have a roof over his head or any money. He said he was walking the streets in the hopes of finding work or food.

At the end of 1941, the beginning of 1942, Hitler ordered his armies in the south to split in two and advance toward the Caucasus and the city of Stalingrad. The city of Astrakhan stood the siege but it was not occupied.

War was coming closer, and Pola and I started to think about running again. Even though Saratov was no longer safe, I had no choice but to go to work. Food was scarce, but our factory had its own store where we got our food rations.

A friend from the village came to tell me that Abram was ill. After standing on my feet all day monitoring the machines that turn out the fabric at the factory, I rushed to take the trolley car to see him. This meant traveling an hour to the last stop and then still walking to his village. Two soldiers stood next to me while I waited for the trolley. They hadn't been sent to the front; instead, their job was to keep supplies moving to the front lines. Somehow, they knew right away that I was from Poland and spoke to me in Polish. They told me they were from Lvov, which before the war, had belonged to Poland. Following the signing of the nonaggression pact between Germany and Russia, the eastern part of Second Polish Republic including the city of Lvov came under Russian domination. The local population who refused Soviet passports was deported into parts of Central Asia or gulags, the rest were considered Soviet citizens and drafted. The soldiers, Olek and Tomasz, were nice boys but bragged about never being hungry since drafted to the Russian army. They wanted me to promise them that we would meet again. Olek and Tomasz said they knew circumstances were hard for civilians. They told me that they wanted to help me, and that they would come and visit. I hesitated but in the end, I gave them my address. They got off the trolley and I continued on my way to Abram.

Abram was in bed when I arrived. I did as much as I could for him, giving him his aspirin and making tea. He needed his strength if he ever was going to get better, and I gave him my ration of bread for the day. Before I realized it, it was late and I had to take the long trip back to Saratov to be at work early in the morning. The next morning, standing before the fabric machine ready for my shift, I was already exhausted. Those long days took a toll on me, but it also never crossed my mind to stop visiting Abram. We were determined to help each other survive. We were both resolved to return to our homeland no matter what.

On Sunday, not long after seeing Abram, I opened our apartment door to find Olek and Tomasz standing there. I was surprised. I never thought they would actually come. They sensed my discomfort and apologized for the unexpected visit. They proceeded to show us the food they had brought. They even had a small amount of sugar. They had a few free hours, so Pola and I sat with them and we did what refugees in a strange land do: We talked about home. Olek and Tomasz were lonely and missed their parents. They were only twenty-three, the same as me. They described their beautiful city of Lvov and I told them about Warsaw.

A few days later, Olek and Tomasz returned with more provisions, including bread and jam. Their offerings were an enormous help to us. They came almost every week and always brought something good to eat. Pola was ten years older than us and so the soldiers showed more interest in me. They teased me in a nice way about being their girlfriend. I was grateful when they accepted that I was involved with Abram. They joked and said that if I got too lonely, they would always be around. In any case, we formed a sincere friendship that lifted our spirits as much as the food they brought.

Abram did finally get better, and I no longer went to him after my shift. I was happy to see him get well, but also relieved. The long days were taking a toll on me. Showing up for work and being on time was compulsory. I also had to be alert while in front of those large machines. I could have gotten injured if I was not careful. I was feeling exhausted and weak at work, but thankfully, I did not get sick.

The war escalated, and new Polish battalions were forming. New units traveled to Iran and the Middle East and then on to Italy and England; their goal was to attack the German army from behind. Tens of thousands of men, Jews and non-Jews, volunteered for the Polish army. While Pola and I had again started to think about leaving Saratov, everyone we knew was enlisting. We, too, concluded that the only reasonable option was to volunteer and join the army.

All Polish citizens had the right to join the Polish Army, forming on Russian soil under the command of General Władysław Anders. In the summer and autumn of 1941 many Jews were accepted in the army; by December they constituted forty percent of the soldiers. In December 1941, the Soviet government declared that only people with Polish nationality be regarded as Polish citizens. Soviet Russia declared as Soviet citizens the Ukrainians, Byelorussians, Lithuanians, and Jews, and therefore, they could not join Polish army. This decision was contested by the Polish ambassador; Russia settled and regarded Jews who came from central and western Poland to be Polish citizens. But difficulties continued for the Jews hoping to join the army. Nationalism, anti-Semitism, and limited food rations all played a role. When the Polish army was evacuated to Iran in the spring of 1942, of the 77,000 Anders Army soldiers, only 3,500 were Jews. The rest of the Jewish soldiers were demobilized and stayed behind in Russia, left to fend for themselves. During the Anders Army stay in Palestine, some 3,000 Jews deserted and joined Jewish military organizations.

* * *

When Pola and I decided to run again, we had been living in Saratov and working at the textile factory for almost two years, from May 15, 1940 until February 18, 1942. The "6th Division" of the Polish Army in Russia, that came to be known as "Ander's Army", was scheduled to pass through the city in a few weeks, and they were expected to take all the volunteers with them. The Polish army headquarters opened a registration office in Saratov. Pola and I decided to register. Our roommate Hela and her husband and his sister made the same decision. We told our boss Boris at work that we had joined the Polish army, and would be leaving in two weeks.

Abram did not want to go. He said he was tired of traveling. He still had nightmares of that six-week journey that brought us to Saratov. I tried to explain that I never wanted to hear the sound of bombs exploding again, that I would rather wander than see everything around me burn and fall into piles of rubble. I certainly didn't want to see another German soldier again ever.

I tried everything I could think of to persuade Abram to come with me, but he wouldn't agree. He hadn't lived through the Warsaw bombing; he could not understand my panic. I told him that I would not stay in Saratov to face another September 1, 1939, not even for him.

In the end, Abram gave up his job and came with me, but at the time, all he kept saying was: "We have good jobs, it's best to stay." Looking back, I know now that Abram didn't do a good job of communicating his fears. I understand those fears today, but I didn't then. Abram was concerned about his health. During the long, bitter Saratov winter he was frequently sick. This must have made him worry about qualifying as a soldier. But I was driven by my hysteria.

In the end, Abram was right. The Germans never attacked Saratov, and we should have stayed there. We would have survived in relative comfort compared to the hard life we endured in Uzbekistan. Abram and I would spend the next four years doing forced labor under increasingly depressing and deplorable conditions.

The registration lines were long. While we waited, our cousin Isaac's younger brother Lev passed us. Last we heard he was living in Moscow, but now, he told us, he had been drafted when Germany attacked and sent to the front lines. He said it all happened so quickly, he did not even have time to say good-bye to his family. He had never held a gun before. Overnight, he found himself part of a battalion, a gun in his hand, fighting off the German army south of Moscow.

Lev told us that when the Russian soldiers at the front saw how unprepared they were against the German army, whole battalions ran away into hiding. He had no option but to run with them. He ran to a nearby village and found refuge in a Jewish home. The family there gave him clothes, food, and a place to sleep. He lived amongst them and married the daughter of the family, who was now going to have his baby. They were now living in a village near Saratov, and Lev was out looking for odd jobs. It was pitiful the way Lev was constantly looking over his shoulder; he had to be careful, Russian deserters were shot on the spot.

Right before we were to leave with the "6th Division", I made a new friend, a worker at my factory. I told Salek about my sister, that she was single and available. Salek befriended Pola. They decided to leave together and would leave Saratov on the second transport, the one right after mine.

I was happy that Pola finally had a man in her life, but I was leaving Saratov with a heavy heart. Once again, I was going deeper into the Russian countryside and further away from Poland. Part of me wanted to stay in Saratov. I still lived with the hope that Sevek would come looking for us. It was only a month since we last heard from him; in my mind, Sevek was still alive.

On February 16, 1942, in the middle of the coldest of winters, we learned that the Battalion of the Polish army would be arriving in Saratov in two days. We had to be ready. I went to work: I had official papers that showed I had volunteered to join the army and was to be released from my job. When Abram heard that I was released from work, packed, and ready to leave, he went wild. He told me later that he never believed I would actually leave without him. I went with Abram when he rushed to the city to register, but the officials said that the transport was full. Abram was allowed to register only after we told the officials we were a couple and pleaded not to separate us.

When the Battalion arrived in Saratov on February 18, a winter storm was gaining in strength. Pola, who was scheduled to leave with the next transport, came with Abram and me to the train station to say good-bye. I promised to write to her from every station. As the train slowly rolled into the station, Pola and I held each other in a tight embrace. Ours was a complicated relationship; more like that of a mother and a child. For the first time in our lives, we were to be separated.

Abram and I rode with the Battalion for six weeks, from February 18 until April 6 1942. Thankfully, the conditions on the freight train were not as bad as on the trains that brought us to Saratov. The cars had *prycze*—shelves—so that everyone had a place to lie down. A portable army kitchen was traveling with our transport, so we did not go hungry. Twice a day, we had bread, soup and black coffee in warm cars, just like the regular soldiers. The train stopped a few times a day so that we could take care of our personal needs. The train carried a thousand soldiers, including generals and sergeants. Almost all of the soldiers were men. I met lawyers, judges, civic officials, and artists, all citizens. There were couples in our two cars, but mostly our group consisted of single men, and every man wished for nothing more than to have a woman of his own.

Our destination was Central Asia. The train often stood for long periods at unknown stations, where we were allowed to get off and visit the town. The stores were always empty.

Between 1941 and 1943, Uzbekistan received over a million refugees, from Russia, Ukraine, and Byelorussia. Among them 200,000 were children. More than one hundred industrial enterprises were moved to Uzbekistan. By the middle of 1942, all enterprises relocated to Uzbekistan were operated in full power for supplying military machines.

When the train entered central Asia, we got off. We stepped into old grey snow, right next to blades of green grass pushing up from the ground. The warm sun embraced me. The light breeze blowing in my face was different from anything I had ever experienced before.

Once back onboard, we pried open the wooden planks that had sealed the little windows of our train cars. The warm air rushed in. We started to unwrap ourselves from the layers of clothes. The further we traveled into Asia, the warmer it became. We opened the doors of the train cars. Even our moods changed. There was optimism in the air.

At every station stop, we were given a supply of *kipiatok*, boiled water that we saved for drinking. We filled a few buckets with snow to wash our hands and faces. On occasion, we would get hot water from the locomotive for washing.

Six weeks later we finally arrived at our destination, a village called Guzary. We got off the train and were pointed toward a bare field not far from the station. We were a small group of Jews, the rest Polish Christians. Most of the men were taken a few kilometers away where they would receive military training. A few women and old men were left. Hela with her husband and his sister rented a room from an Uzbek family. Somehow, she and her family had managed to save up enough money to do this. After sharing a room together for so long, the two of us now separated.

It quickly became apparent that we had been accepted as volunteers, part of a nationalist plan to have a Polish army on Russian

Soil. It wasn't until we got to Uzbekistan that the real selection and recruiting took place.

* * *

We lived on this open field for four months, from April 6 till August 10, 1942. Our food came from the portable army kitchen. We slept on the ground under the sky, in a desert where the days were hot and the nights were cold. I was given a single blanket and this was the only thing I had to cover myself at night.

Abram now wore a uniform. His head was shaved. He looked dreadful. He was able to come to see me a few times each week for a few hours, and sometimes he would bring me a piece of bread. Weeks passed. I lived in the middle of nowhere with no mission and no idea what I was to do.

I befriended a married couple from Łódź. I stayed close to Mrs. Eva Wygrodcki, whose husband Pawel was a recruit, like Abram. Eva ran into Max Strik, a friend of hers from Łódź, and he, too, was in the army. He had already passed his training and was accepted officially as a soldier. His group was stationed in the little town and he became interested in our well-being. He was a tall, handsome man in his late thirties, and, as I was to learn, had a huge heart. He had friends from the city of Kiev, a Jewish family who had been evacuated to this area. The family consisted of three sisters, two of them married and one a spinster. The husbands of the married sisters were drafted and went to the front.

Each of the married sisters had three children and they all lived together in one big room. Max arranged for us to live with them. After so many months on the hard ground, this small crowded space seemed like heaven. Our bit of rent money helped the extended family, and we now had a roof over our heads.

I remember how difficult it was to move from the field to the room: We had to walk two kilometers, barefoot, carrying our meager possessions in sacks slung over our backs. We looked like beggars, and the road burned my feet without mercy. I thought the trek would never end. I still remember the moment when we finally made it to our new home. I asked for a cup of water and drank it in one swallow.

It was dark when we arrived. Abram and Pawel, Eva's husband, stayed for the night. No one had a bed. Everyone slept on the floor, even the local people, the Uzbeks, although they slept on top of quilts padded with cotton. The cotton, called 'white gold' by the Communists, came from the millions of acres of cotton fields all around us.

Max came to see us every day. He brought us bread, coffee, and, from time to time, a little sugar. The floor in this room was made of clay, as was our entire *kibitka* hut. Nine family members lived in the one room, and now, with the two of us, there were eleven.

One of the children in the room, a seven-year-old girl, cried night and day from hunger. She was dying of starvation. She was too weak to even sit up. Eva and I were horrified. The girl was a living corpse and there was nothing to be done. We looked the other way as we took refuge in the corner of their hut. Without Eva's friend Max, I don't know how we would ever have survived. He brought us whatever he could get from the army kitchen. He kept us alive.

One of the oldest boys sharing this room was thirteen, and he would go among the soldiers selling cigarettes and sometimes newspapers. In exchange, the soldiers gave him bread and soup, which he brought home to his family. This, however, was not enough for them to live on. Officially, we all belonged to the army and received food rations, but those rations were so small that we were still hungry all the time.

Max's battalion, we learned, would be leaving for Iran. By now it was clear that Max was paying a lot of attention to me. He didn't have the courage to ask, but the day before his unit left, one of the sisters came to give me a message. Max wanted to sign me up as his wife; he would take me to Iran with him. I was starving, but I could not leave Abram. I found the strength to reject his proposition.

The battalion leaving for Iran created a panic. Wives were leaving their husbands, and women were signing their names next to the first available soldier. Abram and I had come here together. I could not desert him, I loved him. We were not legally married but we considered ourselves a couple. And more importantly, we vouched we would survive this new insanity together and return to Poland.

Max and his battalion left in April of 1942. Meanwhile, Abram and Eva's husband Pawel did not pass their medical evaluations, and they were dismissed from the army. Abram's earlier fears of not qualifying for the army came true. Traditional anti-Semitism was playing its role here too, and many Jewish men were dismissed. It seemed that the Polish army did not really want Jewish soldiers. They rejected them for alleged health reasons. Polish officers saw the Jews as "morally indifferent to the Polish cause," seeking an opportunity to get out of the Soviet territories. At the same time it is important to point out that it was General Władysław Anders, a general in the Polish Army, who was among the first to say that the Jewish Polish soldiers arrived at home when about 4.000 of them defected in Palestine. When there was a call for their court martial, he refused.

As our circumstances became more and more desperate, we were left to fend for ourselves. We no longer received the food rations from the army. There was no work. Guzary became another Białystok. We sold whatever we had to the Uzbeks in order to buy foods such as *lepioszki*, their flat breads. We had to walk over a kilometer to reach the river's edge in order to get water. The river was thick with clay and swarmed with mosquitoes. It took as much as twelve hours for the clay to settle to the bottom so that the water would be usable.

Suzanna
The Way We Lived

A desperate, dehumanizing survival during the war continued after the war, under Communism and within this tragedy, real people were holding on to daily life. Racism and anti-Semitism under Communism did not disappear as it was supposed to. Polish anti-Semitism did not have the homicidal aspect as Nazi Germany, however, in 1968 the appalling anti-Semitism in Poland left the country empty of its Jewish citizens.

In Poland after the war my father owned a set of tefillin, a set of small black leather boxes containing scrolls of parchment inscribed with verses from the Torah. During weekday morning prayers one is wrapped and placed on the upper arm, hand and fingers, the other is placed above the forehead. When I asked him about what they were he remained silent. He would only say "do not touch them." Those black leather boxes with leather straps usually the Orthodox Jewish men wear on their head and their arm during the weekday morning prayer. When he traveled, which he often did, to his birth city of Lodz, I pulled them out just to inspect them. My mother would shake her head in disapproval. She told me they survived the war with him. Every Shabbat, with our kitchen window secured tightly by a curtain, my mother lit two candles and did the traditional prayer, but otherwise she refused to talk about religion.

We lived at Plac 15 Grudnia 66. Today this street is called by a different name, but it is the center of the city of Ziebice. We occupied the 1st and 2nd floor of a large corner building; the ground floor housed a hairdresser's salon.

In Polish my name was Lusia or Lucyna. By the time I entered the first grade I was the only Jewish child in my class. My best friend from my class was Lilka Kupczyk. I was always a welcome visitor to her home. My sister, four years older, had many Jewish friends in her age group. They stayed together, the few of them, all the way through high school.

During the summer vacations we went to a Jewish sleepaway camp, to Gdynia Cisowa, on the Baltic Sea. Here, we met Jewish children from all over Poland. The twelve hour train trip took my sister and me far from home, but each summer for two months we got to be part of a loving community. I always looked forward to this yearly reunion with my new friends. Here I never worried about being Jewish.

Mr. Wiosna was the headmaster of public school Number 3. His daughter Dzidka and my sister were best friends. They were very kind to me and let me tag along wherever they went. Mrs. Pięta was a teacher at my school. She and I talked often. I was not even 13 years old when she told me that after leaving Poland I would remember only the good things. My answer to her was, no, I will remember everything the good and bad. Our neighbor, Wanda and my mother were good friends. She had a family in the village of Niedzwiednik. They owned a farm. Alina and Krzysiek were the brother and sister, their parents, Mr. and Mrs. Renkawik, were like a family to us. To this day I think about them.

We often went to the forest at the back of my school, for picnics, and I spent hours riding around my school on my bike. But my favorite game was in front of the bookstore with Basia Gotman. The bookstore had eight windows. We would go from one window to the next, taking turns we called out a title of a book while the other had to spot it. We spend hours playing the "I Spy" game. To this day I am in contact with Basia who lives in Canada.

For a short time a teacher came from another city to teach ballet. The classes took place at a cultural center but this did not last long. I still remember how sad I was when the lessons stopped. Not until I came to America that I started taking dance classes again, modern, ballet, and Jazz. I studied at the Martha Graham studio, where I met the famous Martha Graham and her disciple Pear Lang.

I finished primary school Number 3 and my sister finished lyceum (high school) in Ziębice. I went to a boarding school, a Jewish high school in Wroclaw, Shalom Alejchem on Pereca Street. I lived in the school's dormitory together with a dozen other Jewish students who came from other cities. We left Poland before the school year was over.

In the mid-1950s, the Jews of Ziebice still had a cultural center and a synagogue. The cultural center was a place where Jewish families congregated. I remember as a young child going with my father to this synagogue for Saturday morning services. I was very impressed that he knew what to do. I sat in the back and watched him pray with the other men next to the rabbi.

Another vivid memory from my childhood is of my father's daily hunt for news broadcasted by Radio Free Europe. I can still remember the urgency with which he listened to this station that carried information from outside of Poland. I didn't exactly understand what we were doing but I knew it had an impact on our lives. In Poland to access information from the outside we had to listen to Radio Free Europe. This was not easy, waves were always jammed and listening to this station was illegal and banned. Poland had one Radio and one TV station, those were government sponsored and controlled. We were served only state controlled information.

During the mass exodus in the mid- to late 1950s, the city officials turned our synagogue into a warehouse. The closing down of the Jewish cultural center happened suddenly; as if overnight, the sound of Yiddish and Hebrew songs came to a silence. Jewish families were leaving Poland: some for Israel, and others for America. By the end of 1950s, there was still a small Jewish community in Ziebice, but we no longer had a place to gather. The remaining Jews knew not to complain. In a Communist regime, there was no room for practicing one's religion. An adult known to be connected to Judaism was to be accused of being a Zionist and this could put one in jail for antigovernment activities.

My father died in 1961 at the age of forty-nine from tuberculosis that he contracted in Saratov, Russia, twenty years earlier. The lifesaving antibiotic, developed in 1943 by Albert Schatz to treat tuberculosis, was not available in Poland, it did however, exist in the United States. The last sanatorium for TB patients closed in December 1954. If we had lived in America, my father would have had access to the lifesaving medicine. Instead, my parents watched everyone they knew leave for America or Israel, and made plans for our family to leave for Israel, but we were denied exit because of Father's illness. Even Israel would not permit him entry because of the advanced stage of his illness. Tuberculosis is a disease that thrives in overcrowded and destitute living conditions. It attacks the undernourished whose defenses are weak. During the war and for still many years after, my father's illness went undetected and untreated. He was finally diagnosed in 1951, but by then the disease had ravaged his body and he was contagious.

In the years that followed, my parents concealed the seriousness of his condition from my sister and me. My sister, four years older, was able to figure out the reason our trip to Israel never came to pass. I never did. All I felt was anger. I saw my parents as weak, indecisive, and helpless.

I saw my parents as beaten down by the war, broken and tired, unable or unwilling to recover from their trauma. I was shocked by their passivity, the way that they were willing to live in fear under Communism. Traumatized by my mother's stories that was told to me throughout my childhood, it was only later in my life that I was able to focus on the truth, that my parents' entire families had been murdered. That recovering from such heartbreak was impossible. At the same time my parents were rebellious even if I did not understand this as a small child. They refused to join the Communist Party. This was their last shred of dignity which they were not willing to give up. They refused to be brainwashed by the dangerous communist ideology. In 1917, the Russian Revolution produced the first Communist State. Karl Marx's dream of a workers' paradise brought death to millions over two generations under its dictators. A Communist State was established and ruled by terror. The tyrants saw the root of the evil in the world in private property. Individuals had to fully submit to the group. I grew up knowing that joining the Communist Party was not an option. At a great cost to their own safety and in their small ways, they chose to reject the oppressive regime, but far too many did not follow their lead.

Up until his death, mother never explained the gravity of our father's illness; instead, my mother, my sister, and I were like the Three Musketeers. It never crossed my mind that the way we lived was strange. Mother believed that is was important not to burden children with grown-up problems. I knew my father was sick, but I did not comprehend the severity. I certainly did not understand that his illness would affect our destiny.

I can still picture him, gathering all of his energy to try to recover his family estate. I remember the never-ending trips to his city of Łódź, and my parents' hushed voices that followed his return. He was never able to recover that was handed down from his parents to him, property that was rightly his. In his humiliation and helplessness, my father's rage grew and became directed at us, the only family he had left. His love for us turned into violent rages. But my mother stood up to him. She put herself in charge.

It was years later, from reading my mother's journal and more recent conversations with her, that I learned that my parents had been very much in love during their years together in Russia. I never saw any signs of this passionate love when I was a child in Poland.

After Father died, Mother never considered marrying again. I remember—even in Poland when Father was still alive—men enjoyed her company. I was not surprised: my mother was intelligent, young, and still attractive. After she became a widow, she was adamant that no man would ever come between her and her daughters. Her eyes, the windows to her soul, always gave her away. In them, I saw that she gracefully endured a marriage that was full of hardship. Weighted down by her losses she could not hide her sadness and heartbreak. My mother was left with the regrets of what if there never had been a war, what if her life was not turned upside down and she could have married the boy of her dreams. There was a determination about her to never love again.

CHAPTER NINETEEN

There was food in the village of Guzary, but not for us. Because we didn't have jobs or money, there also was no place to wash. We had to relieve ourselves in the field. It didn't take long for those around us to succumb to typhus, dysentery, and malaria. Eye disease affected many of the refugees, especially during the time when the cotton was in bloom. Like many of the women, I was asked to bury the dead, but I refused to do this job. Fifty bodies pushed into a mass grave had become a normal practice, but as horrible as things were, I could not do it.

Abram and I managed to buy a few kilograms of wheat by selling some of our personal items, my silver-plated brush and comb set that Adek gave me and a leather wallet. We went to have the wheat ground into flour in the hut of the Uzbek who owned the mill; there, in the middle of the room, lay a huge polished stone with a hole in the center. To the side was a small opening where the miller threw in handfuls of wheat to grind the seeds into flour. For each kilogram that he ground, he took a cup of flour for himself. The flour had to be put through a sieve to separate out the bran, but there was no sieve to be had. I went home quickly, made dough by adding water and shaped out *galuszki*, dumplings. I dropped them into boiling water and waited until they floated to the top, trying to forget about the bran inside the flour. In the end, we could not eat the dumplings; the bran was like thorns in our mouths.

Eva and her husband had brought pieces of fabric from the fabric store they once owned in Poland. From time to time, they sold this fabric to the Uzbeks, for almost any price that they asked. We learned about the local Uzbeks from Eva's trading with them. The Uzbeks spoke Turkic languages and were predominantly Muslim. The floors in their *kibitkas* were covered with beautiful red rugs, and they ate with their fingers from clay dishes. I never observed them use Western utensils. The women wore nose rings and braided black hair wrapped around their heads, and they covered their faces when they went out. Married women seldom left their homes or the surrounding property. They worked from dawn to evening taking care of the home and the children, laboring in the fields, growing everything from tea and barley, grapes and melons. The men had their heads wrapped in turbans like the Arabs of the Middle East. They socialized in teahouses, which were also off limits to women. The wealthier the Uzbek man was, the more wives he could acquire. They traveled on donkeys and camels. The Uzbeks mostly raised sheep, killing the young four- to six-week-old ones for astrakhan fur and paws. On the rare occasions we sold one of our precious possessions, and I would venture out to a nearby farm to buy half a liter of milk. Right in front of me, the cunning Uzbek would add water to the milk and there was nothing I could do. I was grateful to be able to buy milk.

* * *

Eva came down with typhus and she went to the hospital. Her husband Pawel stayed with us for a few days, until he, too, became sick with typhus. I walked with him to the hospital. He left all their belongings with us. The hospital provided only a thin, tasteless soup so we had agreed that I would come every day to see them. Pawel would give me money through a nurse and I would buy food for them. He made me promise that I would buy food for Abram and myself as well.

When all seems hopeless, a simple act of human kindness and decency will stay in your mind forever. I remember a specific day clearly. On one of my visits to the hospital, Pawel was unconscious. The head nurse told me that she had found a wallet under his pillow; she had waited for me to be her witness while she counted how much money there was. She then put the wallet in a locked, safe place so that the other patients would not steal his money. From then on, the nurse gave me money from the wallet and I brought food for Eva and Pawel. Eva still had no idea that her husband was sick and at the same hospital. They were both critically ill, and the male and female patients were in separate wards. One day, a nurse told me that my friend had a miscarriage; Eva had gotten pregnant before coming down with typhus.

* * *

We had arrived with the Polish army in Guzary at the end of March of 1942. A month later, we had to fend for ourselves. Demobilized and dismissed from the army, it was July when Abram finally found work as a mechanic at the Guzary train station. He was responsible for inspecting and assessing the track conditions. Repairing and maintaining anything that needed fixing on the trains or the tracks. His new job brought us hope and a place to live. He came home smelling of industrial grease.

By now, Eva and Pawel were getting better. I went to the hospital to find out what to do with all of our friends' belongings now that we were moving. They asked me to take their things with us wherever we went. We had paid a local Uzbek to take us to our new home, a room with no windows and a stone floor. We still slept on the floor, but Abram's new job entitled him to a card with which we could buy food rations. He received 800 grams of black, dense bread for himself and 400 grams for me. We could buy three days of bread rations at one time. The first time I bought the rations, I was so hungry that I ate my three days of bread all at once.

After three weeks in the hospital, Eva was released and I went to pick her up. She was weak and could barely walk. To cross the river, we had to walk on a low, narrow bridge made of wooden planks. There were no side railings, so we had only each other to hold on to. Somehow, we made our way across. Slowly, we made our way from the town to my room near the train station. A few days later, Pawel, was also released and came to stay with us.

After a short stay, Eva and Pawel decided to look for his brother who was living in the city of Almaty. They had heard that the earth was rich there, and that there were many factories. Before they left they gave me a little money, as a thank you for the three weeks that I had taken care of them. Then once again, Abram and I had to say good-bye to people who had become family. After they left, we realized quickly that a roof over our heads was not enough to sustain us.

Abram's boss decided to let us live across the road, in the bathhouse for the workers. It was a big room where a container for hot water was kept, but the stone floor provided no drainage for the water to run out. The windows were smeared with clay so that no one could look inside. We were ecstatic: It was big and we realized we could make a little money by secretly renting space to other refuges. There were still hundreds of people sleeping out in the field under the open sky.

To this day, I don't know how Abram's boss was able to just take this bathhouse and give it to us for living space. We felt incredibly lucky, but were also worried as to how long this good fortune would last.

The soldiers in Guzary were in training. By August of 1942, most had finished basic training. They were ready to travel from Russia to Iran, then on to Italy and even Palestine. Most people were doing business with the solders, selling them vodka and cigarettes, and there was good money to be made this way.

In the foothills of the Caucasus, there was a lifeline of English and American supplies for Allies troops: Uniforms, boots, blankets, belts, soap, and canned goods came through in vast amounts, and the soldiers sold some of those items to us. We in turn, sold those goods to the Uzbeks at a higher price. Although Abram's wages were low, he would not participate in the black market and trade with the soldiers. He only wanted to work; he believed in doing his job as best as he could. It was his upper middle-class background that made him think buying and selling on the black market as beneath him, whereas I was used to poverty, and knew that it was our best chance to survive.

We quickly found roommates: a single man and a married couple from Łódź. Once they moved in, life became tolerable again. I even managed to get a sieve to separate the bran from the flour so I was able to make dumplings that we could actually eat. We had money to buy milk, and on Sunday's we would buy *lepioszki*, the delicious local flat bread.

Once again, an order for soldiers to be transported to Iran was issued. Abram and I were on the train station, when the cargo trains arrived. We watched the soldiers go aboard. Suddenly a soldier came to us and said, "What are you staring at? Why are you standing, get on the train!"

I turned to Abram and said. "Let's go."

Abram said, "What's your hurry? We can go on another transport. We have possessions in our room and a little wheat."

I would not give up. "Abram, come, leave everything. We have this chance to get out of here." But I couldn't convince him and the train left without us.

After this transport, the Russian government realized that the civilian population was running away—either by leaving for Iran or going with the army. With the next transport, they started a tight control over the trains and civilians could not get on them. The opportunity to get out of Guzary with the soldiers had passed us by. As more and more soldiers departed, the situation in Guzary deteriorated. When soldiers were around, they traded, buying and selling things with the civilian population. As the last soldiers left Guzary, the black market slowly died.

We shared our living space with Haim and Irenka—a married couple—and the single man, Mr. Gradowski. He had a son in the army who was leaving with the last transport, and he had been hoping to be able to follow his son to Iran.

Haim was a clever businessman: He traveled around the region and often brought back vodka, which he sold to the soldiers. At first, he did this quietly outside our room. Soon, soldiers were coming to our room as if we were a store. The Russian government strictly prohibited this type of activity, and there were severe penalties if caught.

Since the room was registered in Abram's name, I was afraid that he was at risk. He worked long hours and he had no knowledge of what was going on. One evening, a drunken lieutenant came to our door and demanded to buy vodka. At the time, Haim was out. The drunken lieutenant banged on our door and would not take no for an answer. He was trying to break down the door, which was secured only by a small clasp. He threatened to use his gun if Haim didn't sell him his vodka. We jumped to our feet to support the door so that he would not succeed in breaking it down.

I started talking to him through the door in the hope of calming him; I kept reminding him that, as a lieutenant, he was drawing attention to himself, and that this was dangerous for him as well as for us. But the lieutenant continued yelling and banging for an hour before he finally gave up and walked away.

None of us slept that night. In the morning, Abram argued with Haim, telling him that he had no right to bring the vodka to our room. He was not willing to go to jail for Haim's black market business. But Haim continued bringing and selling the vodka from the room anyway. Abram was at work all day, but I saw what was going on. Abram and I decided that the next time Haim came home, I would stand in the doorway and block his path. When I tried to stop him, Haim threw himself at me and started to beat me. His wife Irenka could barely pull him away. Abram was still at work and they didn't want to face him, so they packed their belongings, paid me whatever rent money they owed us, and left. I later heard that they moved in with an Uzbek family not far from us.

When Abram came from work, we decided that although we had lost this income, our lives were safer without Haim. We still had the father who was waiting for his son to leave, but when the son's transport left soon after, the father followed his son. Now, the two of us were alone in the converted bathhouse room.

* * *

I remember when we realized that the room was infested with lice. They were everywhere. We did not sleep; we sat on top of our few belongings, waiting for the morning light. At daybreak, Abram and I found a few rags and kerosene, washed the stone floor again and again until finally, we won the war against the lice. All of our belongings had to be disinfected. I had to cut my hair very short.

At night, people who lived in the field during the day came to the settlement in search of a place to sleep. The entrance to our room had a little roof that was supported by two pillars, which created a kind of a niche. So many people slept there at night that we could not get through them to go out to relieve ourselves. We could not complain; these people were desperate, and they would have assaulted us if awakened in the middle of the night.

There were still some soldiers and army personnel left in Guzary waiting on final orders. The black market business was active, but on a smaller scale. One day on my way back from the train station, I ran into Hela, my roommate from Saratov. She told me that her husband and his sister had no jobs, but that she was able to buy food for the three of them and pay rent by participating in the black market, buying food from the Uzbeks and selling to the soldiers. Most groceries, especially fruits, vegetables, and kefir made a good profit. I told her that I was not working, and although Abram was working, that things were hard for us. Hela offered to take me with her and show me around.

The following day, she took me to the army camp where the battalion was getting ready to leave. We went inside the tents where the soldiers knew Hela. Among them was a corporal, a Jewish man. He introduced himself and we started a conversation. He suggested that I could sign my name as his wife so that I could leave Guzary. I was overwhelmed by this generous offer and I thanked him many times, but as desperate as I was to flee Guzary, leaving without Abram was not anything I was willing to consider.

There were fewer and fewer solders in the Guzary camps. I was alone the whole day. Even though the heat was unbearable, our room was big and cool. Jewish soldiers from Warsaw started coming over, and they brought me some of their own bread, soup, and any other provisions they could spare. Soon afterward, even the Polish soldiers started coming over, and they actually arranged for me to go to the army kitchen and occasionally get some coffee and soup. From time to time the soldiers sold army goods to Abram for a low price, so that he could sell it for a profit. Abram no longer argued with me about the black market. We were grateful for the help from the soldiers. On Sundays, Abram traveled to Gitapu, a two-hour train ride away. He would by a bucket of eggs or a sack of cucumbers, which I would then sell.

The final transports of soldiers were leaving Guzary, and three of my friends again offered to register me as their wives. Three times I thanked them and refused. I wanted desperately to flee Guzary, but I could not find it in my heart to leave Abram. Abram and I stayed behind and Guzary become a dead village.

Raised in Poland

I always lived with the strong belief that if I had been born in America, I would have grown up to be a different person. "In Europe historically, left-handers have been referred to as evil and left-handedness was for centuries considered to be in need of correction."[16]

My education took place in Communist Poland, grades 1–8. At this level, everything we learned was memorized. There was no opportunity for input or originality. The textbooks and teachers were gospel as we sat captive at our desks with our hands held on top where they could be visible. Our job was to memorize, recite, and give back to the teachers the same information we were given. In this atmosphere, there was no place for a creative child; we all had to conform to the same mold. I can only imagine the horror my mother must have felt when she realized I was left-handed. One year before I entered the first grade she started training me how to write with my right hand. Each and every time I picked up a pencil she took it from me and put it in my right hand. I could not get away from her. For her, the alternative was not an option. What I did not know was that in 1958, the teachers in Polish classrooms still tied the left hand of a child behind the back, forcing them to use the right hand. I still remember the boy in my class who had his left hand tied behind his back and the mockery he had to endure. "And I was brought up with the story that a generation ago, in the bad old days (and in the old country), foolish unenlightened people tried to force left-handed children to convert and use their right hands. My father said that my uncle, his older brother, had his left hand tied behind his back as a child." [17] By the late 1950s, in America, such practice had been long abandoned.

If raised in America, I would have never been made to give up being left-handed. But to spare me the torment, before entering the first grade at age seven, my mother forced me at age six to become right-handed. The cognitive activities involve the two hemispheres but not to the same degree; the left hemisphere plays a more important role in speech and in logical reasoning, whereas the right hemisphere is more dominant in processing special information. Some in the scientific community believe that our whole body is prearranged since birth and forcing to go against the natural development is to cause damage to that individual. I was ten years

[16] www.bing.com/search?q=Forcing+a+left-handed+to+be+right-handed+&pc=UP97&first=57&FORM=PERE3

[17] http://news.bbc.co.uk/2/hi/health/6923577.stm

old when my father died. It was then that I made up my mind to take revenge on the tyrannical school rules. Our school uniform was a black or navy dress, button down in the front with a sparkling clean, white collar. After the one week of sitting *Shiva* for Father was over, I took off the white collar from my black uniform and went back to school, declaring that I was in mourning for one year. My decree was accepted.

CHAPTER TWENTY

I cannot pinpoint the exact time we started feeling this way, but a number of events in Guzary brought us closer and closer to the depths of desperation. It was at this time that Abram and I started talking about ending our lives. We were alone, without family, vulnerable, and trapped. There was no one we could turn to for help. We were desperate. People around us either did not care or did not have the strength to help one another. Life became more and more hopeless. Subsisting on army rations was now a distant memory. We were constantly harassed and even arrested. All of our energy went into appeasing our greatest enemy, the nonstop hunger.

My arrest in the Guzary open market was certainly a step toward my growing feeling of helplessness. The English and Americans supplied newly formed battalions on Russian soil and the battalions moving on to Iran, Palestine, and Italy. Their goal was to establish a second front to attack the German army from behind. Some soldiers chose to shed their uniforms; they changed into civilian clothes and left their uniforms behind so that they could easily disappear into communities. This was one reason why surplus of army goods, like blankets, uniforms, and boots, came to be available for sale.

The Sunday market was where the Uzbeks sold foods: dry fruits, melons, vegetables, and *lepioszki,* the flat bread. They exchanged these items for blankets, pants, jackets, shoes, and belts. When the soldiers sold their extra supplies to us, we in turn sold those items to the Uzbeks. Abram and I had an army blanket we wanted to sell, but the penalty for selling army goods was arrest and jail. But everybody knew the officers did not make their rounds at the marketplace consistently.

The day I was arrested the marketplace was bustling. Everyone was selling something. Personal possessions were neatly displayed on the ground for passersby to see. Abram and I stood next to each other with the army blanket on the ground in front of us. Two men we knew ran over to us to warn us that the Russian police officers were inspecting the market. I wanted to take the blanket and leave, but Abram would not hear of it. He convinced me that the officers would not harass a woman, that they would not do anything to me. Two minutes later, as the officers walked toward us, Abram ran off as we had planned. The officers ordered me to pick up the blanket and to follow them.

At the army post, the police officers reported to their commander that I was selling an army blanket together with a man, but that the man had run away. They wrote up my arrest and gave an order to get my cell ready. The police signed off the arrest order, which meant writing their side of the incident. I was handed a blank sheet of paper and I was required to do the same. I quickly wrote that I was at the marketplace and that I was standing next to a man who I did not know, and that the army blanket belonged to him. The police officers mistakenly thought that the blanket belonged to me and arrested me. I emphasized the fact that this blanket was not mine. After holding me for a few hours, they realized they could not establish ownership of the blanket and they let me go, but of course, kept the blanket. At home, Abram and I rejoiced. If Abram had not run away, he would have been imprisoned. This incident however left us with a reminder of how powerless we were. Our senses were flooded with feelings of helplessness and hopelessness. Suddenly, I was fearful all the time and would look over my shoulder even when I was doing nothing. Having the blanket confiscated by the police was devastating; it would have earned enough money to buy food for a week.

The madness we were living with was all around us. A Jewish family was camping out in the open across the road from our room in the bathhouse. They had been deported from Minsk after Hitler's attack. The mother and father had an eighteen-year-old daughter and a twelve-year-old son. As their situation grew critical, the daughter told me she had decided to become a wife to a middle-aged Uzbek. She said she didn't even like the man, but she would marry him to save her family from starvation.

After the whole family moved into the Uzbek's hut, the mother brought me a piece of bread every day, and would tell me about their new life. She said the Uzbek worked at the wheat stockpiles and that, just like everyone else, he stole as much wheat as he could and sold it on the black market. That the family had enough food to eat and the Uzbek dressed her daughter, his new bride in nice clothes that he bought with the money he hid in the floor of their hut.

The mother also told me, with tears in her eyes, that there was a price to pay for this new life. The Uzbek controlled his family with an iron fist and they were expected to jump at his every command. She was probably too embarrassed to talk about the abuse that went on. It surfaced after her husband's sudden death, beaten to death by the Uzbek. The family stayed. I was not surprised. Having shelter and food was a matter of life or death, but the reality of this family's situation lay heavily on my heart, and wore down my spirit even further.

Every day, Abram went to work and I sat alone. From his earnings, we had enough money to pay for our food rations and our room. With the small amount left, we would buy a kilogram of wheat or an occasional liter of milk. To buy anything else, we had to trade on the black market, something I was scared to do after my arrest. I did go out for short trips to receive my daily ration of bread and soup, and I learned from those excursions that the Uzbek men were very attracted to white women. One of our Uzbek neighbors sent his wife and the rest of his family out in the mornings to work in the field before he would leave home to join them. It was during this time that he started coming to me for help with some simple chores. At first, I was pleased. This would be a wonderful way for me to make a little money. I tried to do all the family chores, folding their beautiful silk sheets and soft blankets outside of their hut. Compared to the other people in Guzary, this Uzbek's family lived in paradise. His wife dressed in expensive clothes from Tashkent, and they always had a surplus of food.

But I soon realized that the Uzbek had other things in mind than folding sheets. It was a struggle because he kept trying to get me inside. I was terribly scared, but afraid to say no. I knew once inside his house he would force himself on me, even rape me if I resisted. I realized I would have to stop doing chores for him. I had the good sense to leave my room and go for long walks early in the morning, so that I would not be home when the Uzbek came looking for me. Finally, he left me alone, but my despair stayed with me. I was grateful that I had found the will to resist his advances, but I was still hungry and felt that my body was slowly deteriorating. I was depressed and started to feel worse with each day. I found out I was running a high fever. It was at this time that Hela told me she had typhus. Typhus was an epidemic in the community. Thinking about it today, my getting sick in a sense saved us. I realized I wanted to live.

After Abram left for work, I summoned the strength to walk to the nearby clinic. The clinic operated with only one doctor and one nurse. There were already about fifteen people waiting, and no place to sit. But I did not stand there long. After a few minutes, everything went black and I fainted. When I opened my eyes, I was on the ground with the doctor and nurse kneeling over me. They were massaging my chest and my heart in an effort to resuscitate me. The doctor said that my heart had stopped. They helped me to a room where I got an injection and a bitter-tasting oral medication. There was no place for me to lie down. I sat in a chair and waited to regain my strength before going back to my room.

After about an hour, I saw a neighbor passing by and she helped me get home. Meanwhile Abram came at lunchtime to check on me and found only an empty room. He knew I had gone to the clinic and we met on the road where he had come looking for me. Abram helped me lay down on the stone floor. My entire body was shaking. My teeth chattered so much I could not speak.

It was not typhus. Instead, I had malaria. The regions close to the river were swarming with malaria-carrying mosquitoes. We had no way of protecting ourselves. I stopped menstruating, which was the least worrisome of the symptoms. I was frail, running a high fever and unable to do anything. For months, attacks left me more dead than alive. My fever raged and I could not stop shaking. I struggled to swallow the quinine pills. This vital medication was hard to get, but I was lucky—because we lived in an area plagued by malaria, quinine medication was available from the local clinic. My skin became yellow and my hair fell out by the handful, from the quinine. Although the quinine saved my life, it also left me with permanent kidney damage.

While I was still sick, Hela was released from the hospital and came to visit me. Hela looked dreadful; her hair was shaved to the scalp and she was wearing a hospital robe. Her story was even more depressing. She said that during her hospitalization, her husband and his sister never once came to visit her. She had no idea why, but she was alarmed, believing they, too, were ill. It soon became clear, as painful as it was to Hela, that while she was sick, her husband and his sister had taken all their possessions and left her to her destiny. What happened to Hela was not unusual. Many couples deserted each other in this terrible time of need. I thought of all the different men I could have married. I remained loyal to Abram.

Hela was unsteady and weak from typhus, and it was difficult to look at her. There in my room, she started to cry. I didn't think she would ever stop. I shared our soup and bread with her and she stayed with us for a few days. As soon as she regained some of her strength, she moved to kolkhoz, a communal farm, where she could live and work. As difficult as life was for us, Abram gave her a few rubles before she left.

While I was still ill, the couple that once lived with us—Haim, who sold vodka on the black market, and Irenka—needed us again. I was still haunted by the memory of Haim attacking me. Now, they were living with an Uzbek family, but Irenka was very sick. She sent the Uzbek woman to beg us to let them live with us again. She apologized for the way they behaved in the past, and said she wanted to die in my room. We decided to let them back in. We wanted to give them another chance. But in all honesty, we were mostly desperate to make a few extra rubles.

Irenka and Haim moved in with us right away. I did what I could between my malaria attacks. We put what had happened behind us, and lived in relative harmony for about a month. The money they gave us for the room made life more bearable. We were able to buy more food. Haim could not find a job. He sat in the room all day, growing more and more depressed. Irenka was nursed back to health and they decided it was time to pack up and leave for a bigger town.

We, too, decided to go. I was glad to finally be leaving Guzary, where for six months we struggled to stay alive. We carried our meager belongings on our backs as we walked to the town of Kamuszyn: a few pieces of clothing, two old tarnished metal plates, some utensils. At night, we slept on the ground in the train station. We were not alone. Many people came to sleep there, one next to the other, strangers but all glad to at least have the drinking water that every train station provided. We stayed in Kamuszyn from August 10 until September 5, 1942. There were no jobs in this town.

We heard rumors that the next town of Gitapu had a wine factory that might be hiring, so we moved on. Abram was lucky he got a factory job. His job varied from bottling the wine to corking, capping, and labeling to loading the bottles into trucks for distribution. The work was hard, but every day, he got to drink a glass of wine. The factory put us up in a small, dark windowless room which we had to share with a Russian man, a stranger. We protested, but it did not help. The boss, a Russian Jew, was cruel. Our new roommate was a sick man; he got up to urinate at least ten times a night. He would open the door and urinate right outside the door. The putrid smell of urine drifted back into our room and stayed there.

Though my malaria attacks left me unable to stand on my feet for weeks on end, the factory director taunted me by saying, "You're eating Russian bread and you're not working. Just wait until I go to the N.K.V.D. They will take your husband away to the army and you will have to work."

A few days later Abram was summoned to report to the army.

I will never forget the moment they took Abram away. I was alone and sick. I had only 400 grams of black bread, a little soup and water to survive on. The Russian government did not have the right to draft to the Russian army men from the part of Poland occupied by Germany. They held Abram for four days and then the NKVD released him. He came home and went back to work. Somehow, we succeeded in getting a different room to live in. This room had a window with bars on it; we still had to sleep on the floor.

The town of Gitapu was a regional center where the Russians trained the young and drafted Uzbek men for three months; there were hundreds of Uzbek recruits there. After their training was over, they were sent to the front lines. During World War II, over two and a half million Uzbek soldiers served in the Russian army. When a young Uzbek was called to the army, his entire family came with him. There was a lot of crying and lamenting. This enlistment was considered a great tragedy for family that stayed behind. Most young Uzbek men had never seen a laced boot, let alone a gun.

Near where we lived was a camp with hundreds of Uzbek men waiting to be mobilized. As I walked by, they would surround me on all sides. I tried to avoid the soldiers as best I could but some were polite. As I could not avoid them, sometimes I engaged in a dialogue with each of the young Uzbeks soldiers. After a few friendly conversations, they started to bring me *lepioszki*, black bread, and sugar. At first I did not want to accept the gifts, but the men were insistent and seemed genuine. Once I accepted the initial offer, the young soldiers brought more food. Abram knew about this and we decided that the young Uzbeks were good people who were only trying to help us.

Late one night, while Abram was still at work, some of these soldiers came to my door and demanded that I open it. They banged and pushed on the door; I was terrified they would break it down. When they saw they could not break the door down, they moved to the window and tried to pull off the bars. I warned them that if they did not go away I would start screaming for help. I told them my screams would alert the neighbors and they would be punished for leaving the barracks at night. That scared them off and they went away, but I was still shaking when Abram came home at midnight. We had been naïve, and we realized that their friendship and gifts of food had an ulterior motive. If they had succeeded in getting into my room, I would have been raped that night.

After this incident, Abram went to the director of the factory and told him that he could not work at night, because the soldiers were trying to break into our room to attack and rape his wife. The director gave him the day shift but with it came a new hardship; they moved us to a different, dirty hut, *kibitka*. The small, gloomy room had no windows.

Most of Uzbekistan's fertile flatlands of the rivers Amy Darya and Syr Darya were irrigated for growing of cotton. The cotton, harvested from summer until autumn was shipped to all parts of Russia. Stalin forced the people who lived here into farming during the second Revolution. After Stalin and Communism took control over Uzbekistan and the other countries of the Central Asia region, experts came from Russia to create collective farms, 'kolkhozes.' Stalin turned the small existing cotton fields into huge enterprises.

Gitapu was a fertile region. Cotton still grew there along with rice and wheat. On Sundays, at the big bazaar, the Uzbeks brought fresh produce to sell. We would always buy fresh fruit with the leftover money from Abram's wages. The huge grapes that grew there, harvested for wine, were the sweetest I'd ever tasted. All kinds of melons grew there too; the watermelons were as sweet as sugar.

One Sunday, Abram and I were at the market eating fresh cucumbers. Abram was peeling his with a small knife. We were a large group that day, all from Poland. Among us at the market was always a Polish man, a non-Jew who walked with a limp. He had a reddish nose and a small black mustache. We did not know him well but everyone thought of him to be a war veteran. He too was eating a cucumber. When he saw Abram's knife he asked to borrow it. The man peeled his cucumber and put the knife into his pocket. Abram asked the man to give him back the knife. The man began to strike Abram on the side of his face with all his strength. He then threw himself on Abram. We were all standing together and our Jewish friends had to pull the man away. We left the market place without the knife, in a state of shock. We did not dare try to get justice and call attention to ourselves. The night of the attack, Abram had awful pain on the side of his face and an earache. At the clinic, in the morning, they told him that there was an ear doctor in the town of Karsi, about two hours away.

The following day Abram left early, on the first train. It felt like the longest day of my life. I was sure it would never end. I went to the station every time the train came from Karsi to see if he was on it. Hela's husband and his sister had abandoned her, and thoughts of Abram abandoning me raced through my head. I needed him to survive. Finally, he came back on the last train of the day. The doctor gave him eardrops and told him he had to come back for checkups a few more times.

Abram said he liked the town of Karsi, and he talked of nothing else. He was especially impressed with the big, lively train station. He found out there was a factory there, and he thought constantly about getting a job there. But other times he said he didn't want to "throw away the dirty water since he didn't have the clean water yet."

CHAPTER TWENTY-ONE

Abram's ear healed, but he could not get Karsi out of his mind. As we fell asleep, he would describe repeatedly the city's beautiful train station. Finally, he got up enough courage to go back and look for work. I didn't want him to leave me alone. My malaria attacks were intolerable, but Abram insisted that moving was our only chance to get away from our depressing situation. After being gone for two days, Abram was back; he had found a job at a factory that manufactured tractors and farming equipment.

We purchased train tickets, full of hope that our luck would finally change. Our trip began on October 25, 1942. Since we lived far from the train station, we could not carry all our belongings. Our greatest wealth at that time was our fifty-kilogram bag of wheat; we could not leave it behind. The wheat I took to the mill to grind into flour, which I then made into *galuszki*, dumplings. We rationed out the wheat, making sure it would last as long as possible. As soon as Abram gave up his job at the wine factory in Gitapu, we had to vacate our room. We also had to give up the card for our food rations. We slept out in the open while we waited for all the papers to be finalized by the town's officials. Fortunately, it was October and the weather was still like summer.

After we were allowed to legally leave Gitapu, we hired an Uzbek for a few rubles to take us to the train station with his *furmanka*, a flat carriage pulled by a donkey. Our few possessions, blankets and clothes, two metal plates, cups, utensils, a small rusted metal bowl that we used for washing, were packed in small bundles. The *furmanka* was unsteady and it was difficult to balance our things and stay on it at the same time. The bag of wheat was our most valuable cargo, and we spent most of our energy protecting it. The carriage was made of wooden planks on top of two large wheels. It had no side railings, and as the donkey moved forward, the packages dispersed. Abram and I sat on either side with our legs hanging down to the ground. The back wheel kept hitting my leg, so without thinking I bent my legs and put them between the packages. I was wearing the only shoes I had, rubber boots. As I was bringing my legs up, one of my rubber boots slipped off without my realizing it. We were about halfway to the station when the Uzbek stopped at the river for a drink of water. As I got off the carriage to get a drink, I saw I was wearing only one boot. At first I thought that the boot was stuck in between the packages, but we looked and it was not there. We asked the Uzbek to wait while Abram went back to look along the road. Abram walked back a full kilometer, but he did not find my boot. I wore the one rubber boot for the rest of the trip.

Abram held all the money we had left in a small pouch under his shirt, strung on a cord around his neck. It was not safe to keep money in your pockets. At the same time, thieves knew where people hid money, and it was also risky to keep money around the neck. Thieves would surround a person from all sides and pretend to offer help, and while creating a diversion they stole whatever they could.

There were hundreds of homeless people at the train station, and every one of them was hungry. Many had been living out in the open. Some were just out of Stalin's Gulag, discharged from the army, without jobs and hungry, and they paced the train stations day and night. Stealing was the only way they could stay alive. They would chase after a piece of bread or a job.

Old memories returned: of Pola leaving her belongings in the field, ending up with only the clothes and shoes she was wearing. I also remembered when we were robbed in Saratov, left with an empty room. Now I kept my eyes open at all times, alert and vigilant. Abram and I agreed ahead of time that I would be the one guarding the packages while he carried them to the rail tracks. The Uzbek who brought us to the station waited until he got paid. The packages were positioned around me so I could watch them all. As Abram put down the heavy sack of wheat, the string that held the money purse around his neck broke. The purse fell out of his shirt. In that, moment a man reached over to snatch it. I screamed, "Abram, our money!" And I instantly I threw myself and covered the pouch with my body.

The train came at last, but we knew it would not stay long at the station. I don't know how, but we managed to get everything on board without anything getting stolen. As the train slowly left the station, I allowed myself the luxury of feeling happy and at peace, knowing we did not lose our money or the wheat.

The trip to Karsi took two and a half hours. Our train passed through meadows filled with cattle and crops. The windows were open, and I gulped deep breaths of fresh air. The warm air and the gentle breezes lulled me into thoughts of a better life. We had the few rubles we had saved up, we had the wheat and the promise of a new job for Abram. For the first time since we left the city of Saratov, we dared to be optimistic.

The train was packed with people carrying all kinds of goods from Gitapu to Karsi, presumably to sell on the black market. Russian government officials could take any passengers off the train, strip-search them, and take away anything they deemed illegal. Looking around me, I saw only tired and worn-out faces.

I knew that those who worked in the mills and warehouses where the wheat was kept usually stole wheat. Abram told me not to worry. He said that we would be fine, since his papers showed he had a job waiting for him at the factory manufacturing heavy equipment.

As our luck would have it, the police officers boarded as the train approached Karsi, and they began to check everyone's identification papers and personal belongings. When they reached us, they immediately focused in on the suspicious looking bag of wheat. They barked at us, accusing us of carrying too much wheat, of intending to sell it on the black market. Abram took out his papers and showed the officers he was on his way to a job in Karsi. The police officers ignored him and told us we were being detained at the next stop.

At the train station in Karsi, two menacing Russian officials met us. Abram had to carry the bag with the wheat. I dragged most of our other packages behind me; one of the officers carried two of the smaller ones. Fortunately, the police station was close by.

The police station consisted of a small house divided into several rooms. There were a few police officers keeping guard inside. The officials looked over our papers and asked us about our departure city and where we were going. Abram explained, showing the papers indicating that a job at a factory was waiting for him in Karsi. The officials then took the bag of wheat to weigh it. When they saw it weighed fifty kilograms, they said it would be confiscated. They measured out twenty kilograms, the legal amount and gave it back to us. I could not bring myself to make the smallest sound, not even a whisper.

Abram, on the other hand, broke out in a loud cry. This was the first time I had ever seen him cry. I always saw him as the strong one, the one who keep us alive. It broke my heart to see him like this. He kept repeating, "The wheat is ours, I worked hard for it, I am hauling it for us so that we can have a little flour, so we won't go hungry. We're not selling it." The police officers once more accused us of being involved in the black market. They said wheat was much less expensive in Gitapu than in Karsi and we were profiteers. They told us to take the twenty kilograms of wheat and go, or else they would put us in jail. We knew that the Russians had the power to do whatever they wanted.

Abram took our twenty kilograms of wheat and we left. It was getting dark, and we had no place to go. We hauled what was left of our possessions behind us, now thirty kilograms lighter. We moved slowly, as if in a daze. We did not know what direction to walk and we did not dare look at each other for the fear we each would start crying. Finally, we sat down under a tree and spent our first night in Karsi there. In the morning, we were dirty, thirsty, hungry, and sleep deprived.

We could not get bread or soup since we did not have a ration card. Abram made his way to his new job while I stayed with our belongings. He promised he would come back. I was exhausted and just sat there, too tired to worry if Abram was in fact going to come back for me. Two hours later, Abram drove up in a truck. It was a glorious sight.

The factory was not far, and in just a few minutes, we were there. Abram had told the factory director what happened to our wheat. The director promised to look into it, but of course, nothing ever came of it. Abram's new job came with a tiny room, which had one window and a stone floor. We no longer had to sleep on the ground. For the first time since we left Saratov, we had two beds. They were made up of wooden planks placed over old tractor parts, which functioned as legs.

Next to our room was a small market for factory workers. A kind woman named Nina ran it. Her husband was sent to the front, and she was caring for herself and her two small children. She sold bread and other groceries that made their way to the market from time to time. Workers had their rations reserved for them, and from our room, I was able to see when the bread was delivered. We no longer had to stand in long lines. Our lives became tolerable.

The factory had its own mess hall where we were also given soup twice a day. Abram and I began to believe that we had finally made it to a better life. The town of Karsi was very different from Gitapu; it was bigger, cleaner, and had a lot of greenery. Not far from where we lived, was a nice park with a small bazaar, where you could buy local fresh fruits and vegetables, and at good prices. We met more Russians here, who either had run away, or were evacuated when Germany attacked. The Russian people were in charge and held all the important jobs. There was a good hospital here but it was only open to the train employees and their families, and the workers supported the hospital.

By the time, we settled into our little room, we were completely worn out. Our legs could barely support us. Abram and I decided to put our lives in destiny's hands. I agreed with Abram when he said, "What has to be will be. We're staying here."

Abram's factory was a secure place. A clay wall surrounded the whole factory. At the end of a large yard was the tall factory building with armed guards at the two main gates. The factory also had a bathhouse for the workers. An enormous container kept water hot all day. Everyone was given a rusted bowl to pour the water over one's body. The supply was limited since the factory employed many workers, so you had to wash quickly. There was a clean bathroom—in actuality, an outhouse made of wooden planks. It was divided into two compartments, each with a door that could be locked on the inside with a little chain latch. Inside was a platform where you stood over a huge hole. You had to be very careful not to fall in.

Across the street from the factory were the worker's barracks. There were individual rooms, wooden floors, big Venetian windows, and a clay stove. There was also electricity. In the middle of the yard was a pump from which clean water was accessible. It was such a relief not to have to worry about having clean drinking water.

Leaving the factory through one of the gates you entered a vast empty meadow. The Uzbeks raised their cows there. The Russians didn't raise cows but they did keep chickens. From time to time, we heard someone complaining of a chicken that vanished, we all knew that on that night somebody who didn't raise chickens had a delicious chicken dinner.

Another factory gate opened to an old railway track. Unhooked train cars always stood there, as if resting. This was where coal was brought in and collected. A guard with a gun was posted here day and night.

Past the railway tracks, one entered a beautiful neighborhood with attractive homes. The factory and the office bosses lived there. I can still remember today how impressive it all was. I looked at the vegetation and the gorgeous flowers. While these streets were a feast for my eyes, it made me envious.

Abram received a working uniform and a pair of shoes with rubber soles that was supposed to last him a year. After losing my rubber boot, I still had no shoes and had to walk barefoot those first days.

October was still so hot you could not go out in the middle of the day. The clay ground burned like fire. Abram said he actually felt better in this climate but I was having a hard time. The Malaria attack returned and I became sick again, constantly shaking. My teeth chattered and my fever was extremely high. Abram took me to the hospital that belonged to the train employees. Even though I was very ill, they would not help me. We begged and pleaded but they kept saying the hospital was only open to the train workers. They suggested I go to the city hospital for help. I could no longer stand. I sat on the concrete floor but nothing moved the administration workers. We had to leave, but the city hospital was eight kilometers away and I was in no condition to walk there. Abram's factory director promised that the following day a car was going to the city and would take us to the hospital.

* * *

A covered truck carrying tractor parts to the city took us across a river. The river was not deep or wide but it had no bridge; in a track, we crossed it with no difficulty.

The city hospital admitted me, but they placed me in the ward where everyone had typhus. I was put in a small room that held four people. A mother with her two sick daughters occupied the other three beds. The hospital was crawling with lice. I was there to get better, but I was afraid instead of catching another disease.

Twice a day, we were given soup that tasted just like water. The hospital didn't have bread. Instead, it relied on each patient having a card for food rations at their work place. Abram took mine when he went back to work. He promised he would bring me my bread ration at the end of the week. The hospital was eight kilometers from the factory, so I knew how hard it was going to be for him to come and see me. The doctors and nurses did whatever they could for the sick, but there were too few of them and too many of us.

After a few days, Abram came to the hospital. He crossed the river on foot and he appeared at my bedside soaked to the knees, water dripping from him to the floor. He brought me my bread for the whole week. It was dark outside when he left.

Alone in my bed, I closed my eyes. The future looked bleak. Before he left to go back across the river, he had promised he would be back, but I started to think that maybe Abram would do what so many other men had done. He could take everything and leave, abandoning me alone in the hospital. What would I do? Where would I go? I was so sick that I started to think that I might never leave the hospital alive. Maybe death would just take me away.

Old memories came to torment me. What had happened to Pola? After I left Saratov, Pola was supposed to follow me to Guzary with the next transport. Instead, we lost contact with each other. I last saw her when she took me to the train station in Saratov, almost a year ago. For the first time in months, I allowed myself to think of Sevek. What had happened to my brother? Was he looking for me? I thought of my siblings back in Warsaw, of my five, young nieces and nephews. I tried to imagine their faces now, two years older. Would I recognize them? Would they recognize me?

I lay like this, overwhelmed with worry until I finally drifted off to sleep. During the night, my hunger was always at its worst. I sat up in my bed and thought of eating a piece of my bread to pacify my hunger. I felt my way around the chair where I left the whole week's ration of bread. My bread was gone.

I told the doctor and the nurses of what had happened, but there wasn't anything they could do. They advised me to keep the bread in my bed so that it was not visible to all the starving people around me. That whole week, I was without bread and the only food that kept me from starving was the hospital soup.

By what I call miraculous intervention, a Polish charitable organization came to my rescue. They heard about me from a hospital nurse. Every day throughout my stay in the hospital, they brought me a small amount of porridge, noodles, or flat bread. I was so grateful. The kindness they showed me, however small, seemed in my eyes to truly be an intervention from God. Meanwhile, the doctors performed all the tests and confirmed that I did, in fact, have malaria, and not typhus! I breathed a sigh of relief. I would be able to keep my hair.

A week later, Abram came and brought my weekly ration of bread. He looked so sad when I told him what had happened to last week's ration. The doctor prescribed quinine for the malaria. My body turned yellow from the pills and my hair started to fall out, but a week later I was released from the hospital.

Tears sprang into my eyes when I saw Abram drive up in a truck to get me. He somehow managed to get the factory's truck to take me home. He did not want me to get wet while crossing the shallow river. I felt so lucky to have him in my life.

My mind raced to the many times I had the opportunity to leave Abram and save myself by running off with a persuading soldier. Now, as he pulled up in the truck, it became suddenly clear: Abram was every bit as capable of the same devotion for me as I had for him. He would never abandon me.

Chapter Twenty-Two

After I came back from the hospital, the factory moved us to a different space in one of the barracks. This room had a large window. The floor was made of wood instead of stone, and we had electricity. Although there was no separate kitchen, we had a small, round iron stove with an exhaust pipe that went out the window. Cleaning the soot from the pipe was Abram's job, but as our living conditions had improved significantly, he did it without complaining.

Unbelievable as it seems, once in Uzbekistan, Pola and I lived close to each other but never knew it. Like Abram, Salek was discharged from the Polish army. Afterward, they moved from town to town in search of work and food. Almost a year passed before Pola found out my whereabouts. She wrote that she wanted to come and be with me. I was overjoyed, and I wrote that she should come immediately. She came, but without Salek. They did not get along, and Pola saw my invitation as a way to end their relationship.

Pola looked tired. She always managed best when she was close to home, in familiar surroundings. I remembered our earlier days in Warsaw when she would hardly ever venture from our tenement building. Sleeping out in the open, exposed to extreme heat and cold, these had taken their toll on her. Her youthful but worn-out face confirmed a life of chasing after the worst jobs and meager food rations.

The day Pola moved in, we shed many tears. We agreed that we would never be separated again, and that Pola could stay with Abram and me no matter what. We hugged and clung to each other. As miserable as our lives were, we were together again. Abram had no problem sharing our small rations with my sister while she looked for a job.

* * *

We lived about two hundred meters away from a wheat warehouse. Surrounded by a fence, it was guarded day and night by a security guard. The wheat was piled up high, to the first floor of the building. We passed it every day, and it was painful to look at the mountain of wheat.

In Karsi I ran into Hela. She was still living at the *kolkhoz*. So that we could be together, I suggested that the three of us should get jobs in the wheat warehouse, and we were temporarily successful. I remember the first day clearly. A full sack weighted about seventy kilograms. We were expected to carry it about fifty meters to the storage place. I was so hungry I could hardly stand. You had to hold a sack under the opening of the machine and caught the wheat seeds as they came out. I noticed that inside the empty sacks there were clumps of dried up flour. Without any thought, or shame, I stopped what I was doing, scraped the dry flour and ate it. Pola and Hela saw what I was doing and did the same.

That was our first day and also our last day. The factory supervisor watched quietly from the office overhead. At the end of the day, he didn't fire us, but he did not have to. We had started the day thinking how lucky we were to have found work. Now, at the end of the day we realized the job was too strenuous for us. None of us could manage the physical part of the job. We walked home exhausted and in tears.

Hela decided to go back to the collective farm. Pola tried to hide her interest, but in the end, she asked me to let her go with Hela. She said she was not happy being a burden to Abram and me, eating our food and sharing our small room. Pola was not the kind of person who would ask permission anyhow, it was just that we swore never to be apart again. However, Pola was right. At the farm she would get her own food rations in exchange for work, and she would have a roof over her head. I had to let Pola go.

The farm was not far away, and Pola and Hela came to see us every Sunday. Sometimes they brought us sheep livers. The farm bred baby sheep for their *karakuls*, the fur that the Russians loved. Karakuls are unique. They are usually black and the only sheep known to be covered by lustrous fur instead of wool.

Time passed slowly. I started adjusting to the climate, and my malaria attacks became less frequent. I was regaining my strength. Abram introduced me to his boss. Jobs were almost impossible to get, but the boss liked Abram and the fact that I was his wife made a difference. My first job was sitting next to an older woman and together we cleaned rusted machine parts with paraffin.

I received larger soup and bread rations, a few rubles every week, and even a little sugar or candy once a month. But I hated this work. At lunchtime, I had to eat with dirty hands, still saturated and smelling of paraffin, my piece of bread. I choked with every swallow, which was even worse for me than hunger.

After a while, Abram pulled some strings and got me a new job as a night guard for the factory, at one of the main gates. I had to carry a rifle, which terrified me. I tried my best to pay attention when they showed me how to use it but I knew I never would. I carried this burden in total darkness and silence. Everyone was asleep. It was boring and seemed senseless to be out there. The nights were long, never-ending. To make matters worse, there was no guard's hut. When my legs became so tired that I could no longer stand, I would curl up on the ground next to the wall. I tried, unsuccessfully, to be careful because the supervisor was a mean Uzbek. He lived in the barracks next to Abram and me. I knew his wife and two small sons. His wife always cried; she told me that her husband beat her and the children. She wanted nothing more than to take her two boys and run away.

Most nights, the supervisor of the guards caught me lying on the ground, asleep. He wanted to fire me, but the director of the factory liked Abram and he transferred me to the second gate where there was a hut with a bench and a window. There was even a stove. This job was the morning shift and it was my responsibility to open and close the huge gate. Life became tolerable.

The climate in Karsi was dry, but occasionally in April it would suddenly rain in a gushing torrent, for about an hour. I loved going outside after it stopped. On those occasions, I could breathe freely. The air was filled with a fragrance, as if someone spilled a thousand bottles of perfume. The peaceful quiet after the storm always gave me a renewed hope.

In this region, people grew grapes the size of pinkies, and melons that were sweet as honey. At first, we didn't have money to buy these fruits or any groceries. Eventually I made friends with Nina, the woman at the factory's market, and she was able to secretly sell me an extra few kilograms of bread. I took this bread to the open market early in the morning and sold it at a higher price. Abram and I decided it would be best for me to give up my factory job. I would be free to sell the bread more often. Abram couldn't give up his job because it was because of his work that we had a place to live.

Twice a day I took a loaf of bread to the market and sold it. Besides selling bread on the black market, occasionally I traveled with other groceries like tea or rice Nina sold to me on the sly, to the

Gitapu market where I sold them at a higher price. I would come back from Gitapu with walnuts, which I easily sold at a higher price in Karsi. I followed this routine for many months until the Gitapu police stopped me and confiscated my packages. After this incident, I stopped going to Gitapu. Selling on the black market was illegal and I was terrified of going to jail. Still, hunger was stronger than fear and I learned during my trading that when the soldiers traveled through Karsi, they sold a variety of items like, shoes, pants, jackets, and coats at cheap prices. People bought those items from the soldiers and then resold them to the Uzbeks. I made Abram go the station with me when a train was due.

We would walk up and down the train platform and try to buy something. This, too, was illegal; it was against the law to purchase anything from soldiers. It was also illegal for the soldiers to engage in selling, but when the police officers were at one end of the train station, selling and buying took place at the other end. At first, we bought one item then quickly sold it and made a small profit, but as time went on, we bought more items. On Sunday mornings, we walked eight kilometers to the city's largest bazaar to sell the whole collection of goods we had acquired during the week. We were then able to buy watermelons, grapes, a delicious yogurt drink, and even half a kilogram of mutton, sheep meat that now made its way into out diet for the first time since leaving Saratov.

* * *

Pola came back to us when work at the collective farm slowed down. It was during the winter season and it was impossible to stay warm. There was nothing for us to burn in the stove, so Abram brought unusable paraffin from the factory. We walked along the road and collected pieces of raw cotton that fell from the trucks to soak in the paraffin. We were able to burn this in our little stove, but the smell was appalling.

It rained nonstop throughout the three months of the rainy season. We could no longer go on foot into the city because of the mud. The open market was empty except for a few hearty people selling raisins, other dried fruits, and spices.

Abram was arrested in the winter of 1944; the rain had been falling nonstop. Just when it seemed we might enjoy some peace, the Russian government gave new orders: It called for refugees to become Russian citizens. At this point, we were a large group of Polish citizens living in Karsi. After the edict, rumors started flying. One of them was that whoever became a Russian citizen would have to stay in Russia forever. Panic started. People started running from town to town trying to avoid the new decree. It was becoming more difficult to dodge the police because they seemed to know all of us.

When we had first arrived in Karsi, Abram had said, "What has to be will be. We're staying here." Now, Abram and I were among the few who did not want to run. Abram had a job, we had a place to live, and our room had electricity. So we waited. Each day, however, brought new commotion and continued anguish. The latest rumor was that as soon as we accepted Russian citizenship the Soviets were going to send the men to the front lines. The rumors passed as quickly as they started; at the same time, the Soviet officials started arresting the men who wouldn't accept citizenship.

Abram was confident that the Russians would not touch him. He was a conscientious worker and the director of the factory loved him. It was a mistake for him to think like this. One afternoon when I was home with Pola, Abram entered the room with two police officers. They had taken him right from his job. His face was white, he whispered in a shaky voice, "I have been arrested. I came to take a blanket." The police officers explained that they were taking him away because he wouldn't accept Russian citizenship. I gave Abram a blanket and the bread that Pola and I were going to share for lunch. I was overwhelmed with despair. We had promised each other that we would find a way to make it back to Poland as soon as the war had ended. Now Abram was being detained at the city's police station. The officers informed me I had the right to bring him his daily rations. Besides water, he would not be receiving food from the jail. Pola and I sat as if frozen and did not utter a word. Abram was my link to the living. My reason for staying alive had just vanished. How were Pola and I going to survive?

Pola and I did not know what to do. The night seemed to last forever. I could not close my eyes. My mind was flooded with the horrors that awaited Abram and the agony that was my life without him. Abram was the one who had brought paraffin to burn in the small oven. The next day, when morning came, our room was as cold as if we were sleeping outside. We waited silently until we heard the bread transport come into our market. My only thought was to get Abram's bread ration to the jailhouse. Suddenly the door to our room burst open. The Uzbek supervisor of the guards entered, kicking and screaming. He accused us of being enemies of the people.

"You eat Russian bread but you don't become Russian citizens," he screamed. "Pack your things. You have no right to live here! Here live only factory workers!" He proceeded to throw our belongings out of the room, and chased us out into the courtyard. It was still raining. Pola and I gathered our wet things, but we had no place to go.

Not far from the factory was a little house where a Jewish woman, a child, and a brother lived. Lydia's husband had been sent to the front, and she hadn't heard from him since. Because her parents came from Poland, and because she was worried for her husband, I would spend time with her talking to her whenever I could. Lydia saw us with our belongings around us, in the middle of a field. She came to our rescue, letting us live in the small shed next to her house. Again, our most valuable possession was a bag of flour. Pola and I didn't want it to get wet; we were able to protect the flour bag with our blankets, managing to move it, along with our belongings, into our new home.

The shed had no doors, only an opening, so we had to bend low to get in. Once inside we could not stand up. We either sat on the ground or slept. For Pola's sake, I tried to be brave and not cry, but it was not easy. Abram was gone, the ground we lay on was cold, and we were wet and hungry beyond words. I felt like an animal. I think back now and see that things couldn't have gotten any worse than they were.

The bread supply was delivered at noon. I had to go through the courtyard of the factory to the market, petrified that the Uzbek monster would see me. I got the bread for Abram who was seven kilometers away in a police station. I will never forget that before leaving for the prison Lydia helped me to make *galuszki*, dumplings, for Abram, in her kitchen.

Pola and I walked to the jailhouse together. It was not easy to travel that far by foot. The clay earth had turned to slippery mud, making our trip twice as long. When we got to the checkpoint, I was filled with joy that at least I could bring Abram something to eat.

Suddenly two police officers walked over to us and asked us to follow them. I wasn't worried when they asked for the identification papers that we were required to carry at all times. This was a normal procedure. Everything after that happened very quickly. They slapped special documents on the table. Pola and I were expected to agree to become Russian citizens, right then and there. They handed us pens and demanded we sign.

Suzanna
Living with Fear

My father and mother would not join the Communist Party. When my mother was a teenager in Warsaw, she had her suspicions of Communism. She joined the Bund Movement and fought for Socialism instead. After personally experiencing the hypocrisy of Stalin's regime during the war, she never considered joining the party. This decision, however, had a great impact on our lives. My mother could not get a job, and my parents were forced to operate a small business to support us, selling used merchandise. In order to make ends meet they sold new items as well, on the black market, which of course was illegal.

After the war, businesses were nationalized. The few, remaining private enterprises were small and carefully monitored by the government. Owners lived in fear of arrest for breaking the strict laws. But in order to survive, my parents had no choice but to break the laws. The war was over, but we still lived in fear.

Our home was inspected often. The police came regularly, searching apartments for illegal merchandise. It is easy to recall the fear in my mother's eyes when those raids occurred. I was home once, sick with strep throat, when a surprise house check took place. A friend came running to warn my parents. My mother took new clothing and shoes for sale and hid them under my covers. I still remember the fear I felt that day. I watched two policemen go through our personal possessions from the large bed I shared with my sister, covered up by a thick comforter, blankets, pillows, and with all the 'illegal' merchandise. That day we were lucky. The police did not check my bed.

Another action taken by the Communists after the war was the so-called "nationalization" of private property. This was done under the ideology that the property was "Returned to People"; in reality this action confiscated property belonging to individuals without any compensation. A painful blow followed. I remember how this demoralized and depressed my father. He never recovered from such a humiliation, from the fact that he could do nothing, there was no protesting.

CHAPTER TWENTY-THREE

Pola and I were speechless. The officers kept repeating that if we didn't do as we were told, they had orders to arrest us.

I looked straight into the eyes of the officer in front of me. I asked him if I could at least take lunch to my husband who was hungry and was waiting for me. I even promised that we would do this together as a couple. After we pleaded and begged for an hour, they let us go. They threatened that if we did not return to sign the papers, they would find and arrest us.

Outside the checkpoint, I could not stop trembling. There would be no avoiding of signing those papers. We could run, but Abram was in jail. I was overwhelmed. All I could say, over and over, was, "I can never stay in Russia for the rest of my life."

I prayed I would not faint and scare Pola, but it was her voice that brought me back to my senses. Her voice sounded strong, though her eyes were filled with fear.

"Don't worry," she said, holding me tight. "We will think of something."

I wiped away the tears I could no longer control. "Abram is hungry; we must go to him and bring him food." I knew she was right. Before anything else, I had to get Abram out of jail.

It looked like it would start raining again any second, but luckily the day remained gray and gloomy. The police headquarters and the jail were located just outside the city center, but by the time we got to Abram it was late afternoon. We walked through a lightly populated area of farm homes, fields, and pastures. Pola caught me and pulled me up when I slipped on the ground, still wet from the night before. But not before my skirt got covered with mud.

Abram jumped off his cot when he saw us. "I am starving," he shouted, "and you take your time coming here? I can't believe you have forsaken me."

I knew he was famished—it had been twenty-four hours since he had eaten—but I was shocked by his angry voice and the look on his face. I couldn't comprehend that this was my Abram talking. He was filled with a rage I had never seen before.

When I told him of what happened to Pola and I, Abram shook his head in disbelief. He kept repeating, "We have to find a way out of this. Please don't sign any papers."

The Russian guards let us stay with Abram for just half an hour. While he ate the bread and the cold dumplings, Abram urged me to go and talk to his boss and beg him to intervene on our behalf. I nodded my head in agreement. I didn't have courage to tell him it was useless. I also didn't tell him that we were no longer living in our room, but a shed in a field instead.

Pola and I took the longest route back through the muddy fields to avoid the checkpoint. We arrived back at the hut late in the evening. It was cold inside and we were exhausted. We would need to wake up early the next morning to go back to the factory's market to get bread for Abram.

We curled up on the ground under our one thin blanket. Pola pressed against me to keep warm. "Roma, don't worry," she whispered in the dark. "I just know they will let Abram go. They can't keep him much longer. He really didn't do anything illegal."

I knew she was just saying these things to make me feel better. She didn't sound like she believed it herself. It took all my strength to hold me back from crying. "Tomorrow," I said. Maybe they will let him go tomorrow."

The next morning, again, we took the longest road possible through the fields. We were able to see the checkpoint in the distance and the two officers standing on the road. I saw them turning in all directions. I was sure they were looking for us. We were terrified but kept moving. If they captured us this time, they would not let us go free.

This time we got to Abram on time. I couldn't believe how tired and gaunt he looked since the last time we saw him, only a day earlier. I smiled as best I could to mask my fear.

"I wish I had another blanket." Abram's hands trembled. "It is so cold in here." I reached across the table and took his hands in mine. "I wish I'd thought of the blanket. I will bring one tomorrow. I promise." My mind was already racing with the realization that all of our possessions were wet. Abram did not know we were no longer living in our room. I tried to think of someone who might give us a blanket.

For the next seven days, Pola and I took the route through the fields to Abram. Miraculously we avoided detection. By the end of the week Abram was running a fever. It was no surprise. Held in a cold, wet cell, without food, he was exhausted and ill from deprivation and also humiliation. On the seventh day, Abram gave in "I need to stay alive, this way I have a chance to do something. I will even sign their papers just to get out of here."

Pola and I just stared at him. I didn't dare say a word. "It is better than dying here." There was nothing to discuss or debate. Pola and I accepted his decision. With his signature, Abram was released from jail.

Pola and I had no choice and did the same. The Russian guards put in front of us the same papers Abram had just signed. I whispered to Pola, "I will sign if I must to survive, but in my heart I will never become a Russian citizen."

Pola nodded and I knew she felt the same.

Not only was Abram's job waiting for him, but the room was, too. I forced him to stay in bed at least one day before he left the next morning for work. I marveled at myself as I went back to selling bread as though nothing had happened.

Pola, who had always been a bit of a loner, suddenly started making friends with people who worked at the wheat storehouse. Most of them were from Odessa. Before the war, Odessa had a large Jewish population, around 180,000, or 30% of the city's total population. The massacre of Odessa's Jews by Romanian troops and the German "Einsatzgruppe" refers to the 1941 and 1942 mass murder of Jews in the areas between the Dniester and Bug rivers. This mass murder claimed well over 100,000 Jews. The men in the families worked hard, carrying bags of wheat back and forth all day long and loading them onto trains. The storehouse operated in three shifts, but the night shift was the most profitable. Although the night watchman stood guard and watched carefully, the workers were able to pour the grains of wheat into their pant legs, tightly secured at the bottom so that the grain would not fall out. The guards were also paid off to look the other way. Pola was soon buying one or two kilograms of this wheat from the workers, several times a day. She went back and forth to the market where she then sold it at a higher price. She had to be careful. If caught, the police would confiscate the grain. She would not go to jail as long as she had less than three kilograms to sell, which is why she made so many trips each day. In actuality, a person could sell a small amount of wheat as long as with this money they purchased other provisions, including sugar or soap. Eventually, I started to sell wheat as well.

We even saved up a few rubles, which we hid in the wall. We locked the door to our room with a small padlock, although truthfully, it provided little security. You could open it with one hand. The real security came from the fact that people thought that there was nothing in our room to steal.

Not far from us was a repository for coal, where the night watchman sold a bucket of coal for 30 rubles. We were soon able to buy coal to avoid burning the noxious paraffin. Abram found yet another method to warm our room: He walked behind cows and collected their dung. After drying it in the sun, he mixed it with dry straw and the coal particles we found on the ground outside the coal repository. Mixing a bucket of coal with the dung and the particles gave us more fuel to warm the room for a longer period.

In this way, we made it through the winter, and then, spring. In the summer, we all did our cooking outside on top of two bricks. In the little makeshift fire pit, we burned the wood that the Uzbek men sold to us in bundles. We made dumplings and flat breads from flour and milk. Occasionally we were even able to buy meat.

* * *

As our involvement in the black market expanded, we met more people from Poland. Every one of them was involved in some form of illegal trade. But we still had to look behind our backs at all times, living in constant fear of arrest and jail and the knowledge that at any moment the Russian authorities could send all our men to the front lines. There was no relaxing. Nobody knew what the next hour might bring.

Pola came home one evening with a glow on her face that I hadn't seen before. She confided that she had become close friends with Lev, an older gentleman from Odessa. He had left behind a wife and two children. Lev assumed that they were dead, that they did not get out of Odessa.

The next morning, I met Lev and could see that he was indeed smitten with Pola. His job was weighing the wheat that the Uzbeks brought in from the fields. He had gray hair and his kind face had the beginning of some wrinkles. I knew that Pola always preferred older gentlemen. Maybe it had to do with her losing a father when she was ten years old. But at least she found someone who was gentle and smart—and who loved her the way she needed to be loved.

Lev was being well paid at the storehouse. They moved in together in a nice room not far from us. On Sundays, the four of us spent the day together. We went for long walks and talked about our return to Poland after the war. Lev was generally a happy person, but when the conversation turned to Odessa, his eyes filled with sadness. He would acknowledge his dead family but otherwise he never spoke of his former life.

A few months after Lev and Pola became a couple, Pola officially became Mrs. Rozen. There was no ceremony; a local city official signed a marriage certificate. Her face was relaxed and she had a ready smile. My sister Pola, in love and happy, was more than I had dared to dream. During each visit, she said, repeatedly, "I have been waiting for someone like Lev all this time."

Occasionally Abram took a day off from his job and traveled to Tashkent, the capital of Uzbekistan. He bought beautiful silk handkerchiefs that the Uzbeks loved. After every trip, he would always give one to the director of the factory for his wife. I would sell the rest. We made more money from the sale of these handkerchiefs than I expected.

Abram also brought me little presents from Tashkent, a blouse, a comb, a mirror: things he knew reminded me of a life in Warsaw. "I hope this brings you joy," he would say. "I know you miss having pretty things, you deserve to have them."

We were no longer hungry. For the first time since we left the city of Saratov, we allowed some pleasure to enter into our lives. On Sundays, we even went dancing. Abram was usually the best dancer and other women always wanted to dance with him. We were persistently interrupted, but I was not jealous. I always made my way back into Abram's arms. With hunger and my malaria attacks gone, Abram and I remembered what it was like to be intimate, to be human again. We rekindled the closeness we felt when we first met. As the depression lifted, we looked into each other's eyes with love.

I became pregnant. But I did not know what to do. It was 1945 and the war was not over. Although we were happy, we knew that at any moment the Soviets could give orders and mobilize our men. I had no one to go for advice. When I confided in Pola about my predicament, she had nothing helpful to say. Abram and I knew that we could not survive on just his factory wages. I made good money trading on the black market and a baby would bring a stop to that. We could not subsist on Abram's wages. Before long, we would be starving again. At that time, we were friends with another family who lived near us. The married sister, Natasha, was older than I was. I let her convince me to end my pregnancy.

Natasha's younger sister was a nurse at our factory. She managed to smuggle out a large quantity of quinine tablets. On her advice, I took a handful of quinine tablets, one after the other. Soon I started to hemorrhage and lost consciousness. I don't know how long I was on the floor when I came to. I was lying in a pool of my own blood. There was a mass mixed in with the blood that could have only been the newly formed fetus. I realized I had taken a life.

Grief overwhelmed me. A vision of my sister Sala appeared before me. I knew that this was her way of letting me know that she felt the same way when she had her abortion. My mind drifted back to that dimly lit doctor's office in Warsaw, how I sat there and promised myself that I would never do what Sala did.

At noontime, Abram came home for lunch. He had agreed that it was not a good thing to bring a child into the world with the war not over. Now he, too, was overwhelmed with emotion. We stayed in our room that whole day and we held each other as we cried. We promised, repeatedly, that we would never do this again.

I discovered a month later that Natasha was actually pregnant with her second child at the time she persuaded me to end my pregnancy. I realized later on that Natasha, who was Russian, harbored resentments toward me, a Polish refugee eating Russian bread. In her own struggle to survive, one more refugee eating her food was more than she wanted. That is how most of the Russians around us felt. We were looked upon as a burden. We were one and a half million, scattered throughout Russia. Although I know I could not have afforded to have a baby during a war, this incident convinced that there was no such thing as true friends.

The one thing none of us knew was that war was about to end.

It was three months after my abortion. The news spread quickly. The joy that Abram and I felt was tempered by our grief and guilt. If only we had waited a little while longer. If only I was not so frightened of being hungry. If only I had not followed Natasha's self-serving advice.

All our thoughts and discussions centered on going home. Everyone had heard a new rumor, new information. We heard that Germany had capitulated, and that America, England, and Russia had won. For the first time in a long while, I permitted myself to think about my brother and sisters waiting for me in Warsaw. Though our daily lives did not change, the air was filled with a renewed hope for the future.

* * *

When Germany surrendered in April of 1945, bringing with it the end of World War II, Poland was placed in the hands of its second enemy, Russia. Stalin's first order of business was to arrest and imprison Polish leaders of the prewar Polish government. In their place, he installed new leaders he handpicked. The free elections in Poland that Stalin promised England and America never materialized.

It took almost a year before Pola, Lev, Abram, and I were finally able to leave. While a Communist government was being established in Poland, a long bureaucratic wait was imposed on the refugees inside Russia. We were four people among the 86,500 Polish Jewish refugees who had survived throughout the Russian territories desperate to go home, but forced to wait.

We left Karsi, Russia on March 25, 1946. On April 30, after traveling west for a month through the vast Russian territory with our papers clutched in our hands, Pola, Lev, Abram, and I boarded freight trains for our return to Poland. After another six weeks of traveling, we arrived in Poland on June 14, 1946. As part of repatriation our transports were directed toward southwestern part of Poland, what had been Germany before the war. The destination was forty-two towns, including the city of Ziebice. There was such chaos, so much confusion, so many trains carrying refugees that Pola and I became separated. In the chaos that followed, some trains were diverted to the Displaced Persons camps that had been set up throughout Germany for survivors. Pola and Lev were on one of those trains. We would not find each other for ten years, only after Pola became an American citizen. We had promised each other that we would never be separated, and here we were apart once again.

In Uzbekistan, isolated from the rest of the world, we never knew about Hitler's Final Solution for Europe's Jewish population. What sustained us during the six year in exile was the notion that at the end of the war we would return to our homeland, to our families.

Abram took a train to Łódź to find his family. I went to Warsaw.

Home at last. I walked through the streets of my once beloved city. I was surrounded by nothing but rubble. Alone, overwhelmed, in a daze, I felt like I was drowning in a sea of pain and helplessness. I questioned my reason for living. Why had I fought so hard to stay alive? My family was gone. There was no one waiting for me. There were no neighborhoods, no streets, not even a single building I could recognize. Warsaw was gone. All was silent. I walked through the ruins, crying. We did not know what Hitler had done to our people. To discover now that they had all been murdered was more than I could grasp. I lost much of my sanity that day. I was twenty-seven and broken. I had lost everything. The war was over, but in my mind, the enemy had won.

There is no way to describe the devastation Abram and I experienced when we found out that our families had been murdered. We learned how the Łódź Ghetto was liquidated during the Nazi invasion. All off Abram's extended family was starved, killed, or worked to death—in either the ghetto or the gas chambers of Auschwitz. He was tormented, day and night, by his memories, with the knowledge that he had abandoned his mother, father, and two sisters, Sura-Blima, and Dwojra to their fate. We mourned the death of my family; I never was able to find out if they had perished in the Warsaw Ghetto or in the Treblinka death camp. At its height more than 400,000 people were trapped inside the Warsaw Ghetto. The death toll rose rapidly, 4,000–5,000 per month, from starvation, disease, and random killings. The extermination at Treblinka began in July 1942. By September 1942, 254,000 Jews from the Warsaw Ghetto had been murdered in Treblinka. I was haunted by my loved one's images on the day when I abandoned them to their fate.

We had spent six long years in Russia, always with the unshaken belief that we could come home to them, and instead we returned to a deafening silence.

We were unprepared for the shattering news, that all Polish Jews had been murdered. We did not know how to process this horrific information. The shock overwhelmed us. First came disbelief, denial came next. We grieved and mourned. Back in what had been our beloved Poland, we felt vulnerable, threatened, and fearful. We did not feel safe. The Jewish refugees stayed close together; any sense of security disappeared.

Refugees from the Russian territories returned to pick up the pieces of what were once our lives, but we were not allowed to return home. As part of repatriation, we were forced to settle in the southwest, a region that once belonged to Germany. Other Jewish survivors returning to Poland had to face a largely anti-Semitic population. Poles were now living in Jewish homes or on Jewish properties; they did not expect its rightful owners to be returning and were not willing to vacate when they did. We heard of pogroms that happened after the war against Jews on Polish soil: one of the deadliest took place a year after the war in the city of Kielce.[18] The local town people went on a rampage killing around forty Jews, all of them Holocaust survivors. This massacre was incited by the rumor of the kidnapping of a Christian boy.

A year after WWII had ended, the Kielce Pogrom started with a blood libel that Jews were kidnapping Christian children for ritual sacrifice. An 8-year-old Polish boy went missing and after he reappeared two days later, he told his family he had been held in a basement. The boy pointed at a man walking near a large corner building belonging to the Jewish Committee and home to some 180 Jews. Most of the Jews of Kielce were refugees who survived the horrors of the death camps that decimated over 90% of Polish Jews. The building did not have a basement. The mob amassed as the centuries-old "blood libel" spread. The police and military started the violence, although they were there to protect civilians and keep the peace. Instead they opened fire and began dragging Jews into the courtyard, where the people savagely attacked the Jewish survivors. A total of 42 Jews were killed, another 40 were injured. Miriam Guterman, one of the survivors of the pogrom, put it this way: "I couldn't believe that these were humans." To this day Poland refuses to hold individual Polish citizens accountable. Simon Wiesenthal's goal was to bring Nazis to justice. He believed that there is no such thing as collective guilt or collective innocence, but that individuals should be judged by their deeds.

At the missing persons' centers in Warsaw, I didn't find one member of my family who survived. Still, I waited for a miracle. Abram stopped talking. That year, surrounded by nothing but gloom, we were married in a civil ceremony.

---

[18]   http://www.jewishvirtuallibrary.org/jsource/Holocaust/Kielce.html

The newspapers, the Red Cross, and Jewish organizations set up records centers for missing persons. Once again, I permitted myself to hope. I started making inquiries about my family. I listed everyone and sent their names to every newspaper and every organization. I looked for my brother Sevek, cousin Isaac, his brother, and sisters in Russia. I stared at the door, always hopeful, never giving up that a loved one would enter, come back from the dead. I waited for miracles, but no one ever came or contacted me. Time passed, and my hopes died. By now, I knew about Auschwitz, about Treblinka, and the other extermination and concentration camps on Polish soil. I could not permit myself to visit the camps.

Before World War II, over 3 million Jews lived in Poland, making it the second largest Jewish population in the world. By the end of the war my mother came home to the world's largest Jewish cemetery. Barely eleven percent of Poland's Jews survived the war.

Born in Warsaw, educated in the public school, and indoctrinated into Bund's philosophy, my mother became a Polish patriot. After a hundred-year history of occupation and division by Russia, Prussia, and Austro-Hungarian Empire, Poland had become a deeply patriotic country. Studying, memorizing, and reciting the works of the great, patriotic Polish writers who wrote throughout those hundred years, was an important part of the school curriculum. At school, my mother's young mind was impressed with nationalistic spirit.

My mother and her siblings raised themselves and became productive, thriving members of society. Their generation broke away from the traditions of their parents and grandparents. They looked at the world through fresh eyes. They believed their world to be different than that of their parents. Women explored other options besides marriage and children. The Socialist Bund Movement brought awareness to the working classes and it empowered them. Unafraid, they embraced their plight, and worked tirelessly for social justice, to create a better world for all.

In Warsaw, many boys fell in love with my mother. A beautiful, young woman, dressed in stylish clothes. She had blond hair like wheat ready for harvest and blue eyes, clear like the Polish sky. My mother took pleasure from going to the theater, movies, and social events, not any different from the pleasures young people enjoy in life today.

But all this came to an abrupt end when Hitler attacked.

I often think of what my mother's life could have been.

In exile, in Russia, my twenty-two-year-old mother crossed paths with her cousin Isaac. An immediate attraction developed. They fell in love. For the next two years Isaac watched over her, doing everything he could to make sure she survived. The loss of Isaac was one more source of sadness for my mother. She talked about him often, with tears in her eyes. She would have given anything to know that he had survived. When I was older she revealed to me that she almost married Isaac. How she, too, might have not survived if she had chosen him.

* * *

My mother and her sister found each other through the Red Cross ten years after they became separated. Pola was already an American citizen. But it took ten more years before they would be reunited in America. It was not until after my father's death that my mother chose to leave Poland.

In America, Pola lived peacefully. She had married twice, each time to a loving and caring husband. The war, however, left Pola with physical scars. She never was able to have children. By the time Pola's and Lev's diverted train arrived at the Displaced Persons camp in Germany, she was critically ill. She was lucky to have survived. Once in New York, Lev became ill and died soon after. Some years later Pola met and married Morris.

Pola had a youthful looking face and fair skin. Her light hair was cut short exposing her high cheek bones. In the photographs Pola sent to us to Poland she looked glamorous, evoking the 1950's era of American cinema. I noticed that she had a fashion signature: a transparent, chiffon scarf that she liked wearing over her hair, draped down on her back. She looked attractive in her stylish clothes. The days of Warsaw and Russia were long gone.

I was lucky. I got to meet Pola and her husband Morris, visiting them in Florida. They were both so happy to see me. And just as my mother had said, Pola was a great cook. I always regretted that our tiny family didn't live near them. My daughters never had the chance to know Pola and Morris. They both died before my daughters were born.

As I translated my mother's pages, memories of my childhood in Poland flooded back. My experiences in 1950's and 1960's Poland were so different than hers. She grew up fatherless and motherless, reading the fairy tales of Maria Konopnicka, guided by the philosophies of Jozef Piłsudski and Bund, whereas I grew up in the shadows of the Holocaust aftermath. I had two traumatized parents, one who retreated behind a wall of silence and the other who could not separate from her daughters. My parents went on to raise a family, but in their minds the sorrowful wail of millions never stopped playing. Their hearts were forever broken from the enormity of their losses.

Growing up Jewish in Catholic, Communist Poland, most of my recollections are colored with fear. I remember having to constantly endure the popular belief that circulated in postwar Poland that Jews were responsible for killing Christ. This folklore had its origins in the Church, was accepted by Christian Poles, and passed from one generation to the next. In 1978, Pope John Paul II went on a mission to significantly improve the Catholic Church's relations with Judaism. But while I lived in Poland, I never knew that Jesus and his mother Mary were Jews from Galilee. Nor was I aware that it was the Roman Empire and Pontius Pilate who ruled Judea at the time when Jesus lived. And that it was under the Roman authority that Jesus was crucified. All I knew was that we, the Jewish people, got blamed for murdering Jesus.

* * *

After the war, my parents' life in Poland was a never ending struggle under the Communist government, inhospitable toward survivors like them who refused to join the party. We lived in a place where practicing ones religion was stifled. We suffered constant intimidation, the threat of going to jail, and random house inspections. We lived with uncertainty each and every day, with the anxiety that something terrible was going to happen at any moment.

Now, I can understand all those things that bewildered me as a child. Looking back at what I had to live through, I hold no regrets because it shaped me into the person I am today.

When I finally grasped the magnitude of the crimes Europe's Jews were made to suffer, I questioned why my parents thought it was essential to stay in Poland. With time, I accepted how important it was for them to restore their roots in the place where their ancestors had lived for almost a thousand years. How they needed to be among the ghosts of their murdered family, to keep their memory alive and insure that they did not perish in vain. My mother found courage and strength among the ashes of her family. Her generation was gone, but she was alive and she would have to make sense of what happened. She was compelled to give dignity to their senseless murder.

With her stories, my mother was able to bring her family back to life every time she took me to her prewar Warsaw. To me, staying in Poland symbolized my mother's courage to prevail over evil; her very existence represented hope for the future.

My mother always talked about her nieces and nephews. She mourned them the most, they were too young and innocent to be murdered, she lamented. I always wondered if Irena Sendler, the great Polish rescuer of Jewish children in Warsaw, saved any of them. Did my mother's sisters and brother have the courage to hand over their children to her, a Catholic woman, knocking on Jewish doors in the Warsaw Ghetto? In Sendler's own words, "I tried to talk the mothers out of their children." I often wonder, could Adek, Sala, and Anja be among those brave people to hand over their young children, my mother's nieces and nephews, to Irena, for safekeeping. Irena Sendler was born in Warsaw, Poland in 1910. She led the rescue of 2,500 Jewish children from the Warsaw Ghetto and those hiding in the Warsaw area during the Holocaust. The young children rescued by Sendler, in most cases, ended up being the sole survivors of their families, their true identity lost. In 1965, Sendler was recognized by Yad

Vashem as one of the Polish Righteous Among the Nations. In 1991, Sendler was made an honorary citizen of Israel. She was nominated for the Nobel Peace Prize in 2007 and again in 2008. Her legacy of good triumphing over evil will last forever. Irena Sendler died in 2008. She was 98 years old.

In the collective horrors of twentieth century, Nazism and Communism killed hundreds of millions of people. Territorial gains to the east and the Final Solution, the extermination of Europe's Jews, were the principal goals of Nazi Germany's ideology. Every country had collaborators and Poland was no exception. The Nazis might have won the war had they not diverted so many valuable resources to the wholesale murder of Europe's Jews. After the war the first victims of Stalin's Communism were the Jewish leaders of the wartime antifascist committee. The Jewish Anti-Nazi Committee (JAC) formed to mobilize Jewish resistance after Nazi Germany attacked Russia. The only reason for Stalin's post-war attack on the Jews was anti-Semitism. Stalin did not acknowledge the Holocaust, the genocide of the Jewish people. For him, it was the Russian people who were the true victims. To control people, deceitful ideologies promise the masses a vision of Utopia, an imagined place where everything is perfect. In reality Utopias do not exist. Just like when people vastly romanticize nature, yet they never think about that part of nature responsible for the suffering that my Mother's generation endured when surviving in a mosquito and malaria infested Uzbekistan or what it took to survive starvation in the frozen wastelands of Siberia.

After the war my mother no longer believed in God. Many survivors ended up seeing the world as she did. They could not fathom how a righteous and just GOD would allow for six million of their people to be murdered. I have spent a lot of time contemplating on this concept on Gods culpability when it comes to man's inhumanity to man.

God created the heavens and the earth in six days and rested on the seventh. He created Adam, the first man, and Eve, the first woman, and placed them in the Garden of Eden. He forbade them to eat from the tree of knowledge, "you must not eat from the tree of the knowledge of good and evil for when you eat from it you will certainly die." The command was simple: do not eat of that one particular tree. The consequence was equally clear: if you eat, you will die. The fruit was not poisonous, evidenced by the fact that Adam and Eve did not physically die after eating it. Eating the forbidden fruit demonstrates the choice of free will. The tree was not the problem, man was the problem. The tree simply provided an opportunity for man to obey or disobey. Man was explicitly commanded not to eat from the tree and he decided to do disobey. Adam and Eve's choice was to rebel against God's command. It is this act that banishes them from the Garden of Eden and it is this free will that was passed on to all of Adam and Eve's descendants.

The ancient Jews always blamed themselves and took responsibility for their own failures. The suffering is self-inflicted, suffering comes from our own faults, and therefore we can do something about it. If it's simply God's fault, we are doomed, and we cannot do anything about it. Abraham and his descendants, the Hebrew people, entered into a covenant with God. They organized into a society and later into an empire. Success brought pride, power, arrogance, and corruption. The agreement with God was forgotten. It took a prophet to arise and the people to repent and admit to their own failure to adhere to God's word and start over again. Things fall apart again and again because success makes people complacent. When we forget to follow the covenant with God corruption takes roots. This is not the fault of God, we have allowed our own faults and weaknesses to take over (the unchecked free will). When moral truths lose their value, Nihilism and Utopian ideas take over. In this aftermath, the great collective horrors of Fascism and Communism ascend. Dostoyevsky and Nietzsche predicted they would.

The collective evil we see throughout history, including the twentieth century in the form of Nazism and Communism, are the free choices made by men. Consequently choosing evil is part of human nature and suffering comes from men's evil actions.

Hitler is the most evil, single figure in history. Driven by a profound anti-Semitism, he killed six million Jews just for being who they were. With force and vigor, he repeatedly blamed the 0.75 percent of the German Jews for all Germany's problems. The Nazi Party ideology grew in strength and power in Germany, spread to every country occupied by the Third Reich.

Jews were left at the mercy of men's evil actions. In this framework they had to try to survive. They had a common enemy outside the Ghettos, the Nazis and all the Anti-Semites who cooperated with the Third Reich. Collective evil imposed a horrific chaos on their fellow humans. Using archives, historians like Richard J. Evans's three-volume history of Nazi Germany are able to shed light on things like "Ghetto Tourism" as a common occurrence. Swedish doctors toured the Warsaw Ghetto, witnessing 4 to 6 hundred Jews dying of hunger and disease, each and every day. Big tour buses organized by the Nazis brought German soldiers to the Warsaw Ghetto. The Jewish cemetery with stockpiles and cartloads of dead was a popular tour stop. Seeing dead Jews was for the German soldiers a sign of triumph. This endemic violence also explains how 1.5 million Eastern European Jews are still unaccounted for.

From 1939 until the end of the war the conditions for Jews were hopeless. They were left completely defenseless, in a mostly friendless Europe. Jews were trapped not by their own choices but by decisions made by others, decisions made by their oppressors. They were dispossessed of their citizenship, properties, homes, relatives, families, and their lives. They lived as condemned and traumatized people before they were murdered. Inside the Ghettos Jews had few choices, the Jewish policemen were engaged to do the dirty work, to get the daily quota, to carryout German orders in the deportations of their fellow Jews to their death. This only temporarily assured their survival. This is what dehumanizing does. Witnesses and survivals testimonies like that of Simon Wiesenthal's confirm that the Jewish policemen had no weapons but the Ukrainian and Polish Nazi collaborators did when engaging with Jews.

Nothing could have prepared survivors returning from the Soviet Territories to face the aftermath and the horrors of Nazism. The remarkable survival of my parents was overshadowed by grief of unimaginable proportions. The guilt of having survived while their families died overwhelmed them. Though I felt her pain, I sometimes saw my mother as both helpless and defeated. She was left to face the terrifying challenge of rebuilding a life after knowing that one man was capable to be so cruel to another and knowing she could never trust again.

* * *

Czesław Miłosz was a Polish poet and writer who fled Communist Poland in 1951. Embraced by America, Berkeley became his new home; he became a professor at the University. Miłosz spent World War II in Warsaw, under Nazi Germany's rule. During the Nazi occupation of Poland, Miłosz was active in the Pro-Independence Organization. While active with 'Wolność,' Miłosz gave aid to Warsaw Jews. For these efforts, Miłosz received the medal of the Righteous Among the Nations in Yad Vashem, Israel in 1989. Among his famous quotes is: "The living owe it to those who no longer can speak to tell their story for them."

Miłosz became an American citizen; but he remained a Polish patriot and he expressed his longing for his homeland in his work. His writings were banned in Poland by the Communist government, but when the Iron Curtain fell, Miłosz returned to Poland. He died at home in Poland in 2004. It is easy for me to identify with his longing for his mother country. I have always been overwhelmed with nostalgia for my Polish homeland.

Miłosz was born Catholic, whereas my roots although in Poland are forever connected to Judaism. The painful memories from my childhood, a Jew in a largely anti-Semitic country, get in the way of my nostalgia for Poland. I'm reminded of an antibullying campaign story:

> "The teacher gave each student a clean crisp sheet of paper. She then instructed the class to crumble up the piece of paper, toss it around, get angry

with it, and stomp on it. She then instructed the students to return to their seats (with their piece of paper), flatten it out and finally, apologize to the paper. When all the students had done their best to iron out the paper and apologize to it, the teacher picked up the paper on the first classmates desk, held it up so the entire class could see it, and said: If this piece of paper had been another person, and you had done all those things to him or her, by making them feel less than perfect (through your words or actions), these are the scars you would leave. That person would never be the same, no matter how many times you tell them you are sorry, no matter how many times you try to smooth things out ..." [19]

The above example is profound for me. Deep within me I carry my childhood scars, those I inherited from my traumatized parents, and those created by the fear from living under hostile conditions of the Catholic Church and Communist government. In spite of the turmoil I've experienced during my time in Poland, what remains impressed on my soul is the love my mother had for her country and the nostalgic memories I created by growing up in a beautiful, historical place.

I always knew I would return. Like my mother, I could not ignore the longing I felt for my ancestral home. To be a 'Memorial Candle' is to step into the past and connect it to the present, to give a voice to the generation that was made to vanish. Even after America became my new home, I stayed connected to Poland, foreseeing the day my children, the next generation, would need to know the place I once called home, a country where a vibrant Jewish culture flourished for a thousand years.

As the time passes, an urgent need is arising for future generations to take on the job of safeguarding and preserving a chapter in the history of the Jewish people. The responsibility of restoring our roots, connecting the past to the present, has to be carried out by the generations to come. I have raised my daughters to know about my Polish Jewish roots, but until now, only through art, music, movies, theater, and food. When they were young, I kept our family suffering hidden away from them, as if to protect them, the way I was not. It was during my daughters' high school years that I realized that they barely understood what the Holocaust represented to the Jewish people of Europe.

It was now my turn, to take responsibility and tell the story of a vibrant culture that my mother, their grandmother was part of. It was time to pass the torch to the third generation whose job it will be to safeguard our Jewish heritage, to uphold the history of Jewish people and of the entire Jewish population that was lost in Europe. It was vital to me that my daughters see their grandfather's vandalized Jewish cemetery, bear witness to what people are still capable of doing. I needed my daughter's to understand that racial and religious discrimination still exists and has to be

---

[19]   http://tomrimington.blogspot.com/2011/11/bullying-and-crumpled-paper-story-view.html

fought. A responsibility rests upon us—not just to preserve the memory of injustice, but also to prevent future injustice. As the descendants of Holocaust survivors, we have a unique obligation to preserve the legacy and history of the Jewish people. To tell the story of the 6 million Jews who were killed in Europe.

It was not until the fall of Communism, and especially in the last couple of decades, that we have started to unearth what happened to the Jews in Poland. Yad Vashem, Israel's World Center for Holocaust Research recognizes Righteous Gentiles for their heroism in saving Jewish lives. At the same time, it is critical that Poland's place in the Jewish narrative is identified. It must be fully understood and acknowledged by its citizens. Poland, as a nation, has to face its demons; truth has a force of its own, and it will not stay silent. Additionally, it's been twenty-five years since Communism fell in Poland and the subject of property restitution, real estate belonging to survivors and their descendants has been left unanswered.

Restoring the legacy of the vibrant Jewish culture before the Holocaust is important to combat religious ignorance and prejudice and to help fight the shocking rise of Holocaust denial and anti-Semitism throughout the world. When faced with social injustice, racial and religious discrimination, our conscience should never allow us to stay silent.

"Injustice anywhere is a threat to justice everywhere."
Dr. Martin Luther King, Jr., Letter from Birmingham Jail, April 16, 1963

Suzanna
Afterthought

My mother died in 2006. "Memory is Our Home" was published in 2015 in English and "Pamiec Jest Naszym Domem" in 2016 in Polish.

    My mother wanted for us to write this book together but in 2006, I set out alone on a mission to realize her dream. I became determined that our story about what happened to my mother's generation and about our endurance under Communism in Poland become part of remembrance. Giving up was not an option. Perseverance, passion, dedication and hard work payed off. "Memory is Our Home§ was first published in English and one year later the book was published Polish. For the book to be published in Polish, my mother's birth country, and that of her ancestors who lived there for centuries, is something that I am immeasurably grateful and proud of. Achieving a goal, which my mother started and I saw come to fruition, gave me an immense fulfilment.

    I would never have been able to work on "Memory is Our Home" without the complete support from my husband Barry Lederman and our daughters, Alex and Isabel. Their total acceptance of what I wanted to accomplish was my biggest motivation and a sign that I had to make my mother's wish come true. I knew my mother was watching over me, she was my biggest strength in moving me forward during the dark times when I could not see the light at the end of the tunnel. During the years when I was working on our book she often came to me in my dreams, arguing with me when needed and pushing me onward. She came to me especially during the times when I wavered and considered the possibility of quitting.

    From the very beginning, the driving force of getting "Memory is Our Home" visible was so that educators and students had access to a first-hand account. Stories told by real people in real voices are the most powerful and the future generations are the ones who will be our history keepers once survivors and their children are gone. I speak to adults and young people about my book and the history that led up to and culminated in what we call the Holocaust or Shoah. I post this information on my website, http://memoryisourhome.com/news/.

    Perseverance during the ten years did not come easy, the notion of failure, that success will not come, was real. However, overcoming obstacles and difficult situations was something I grew up with. Persistence is how I stayed focused in order to achieve my mother's dream. Looking back in time I see how my mother conveyed strength and perseverance, in everything she did. The hardships she lived through and those we experienced in Poland after the war trained her and me to be self-sufficient and free-thinkers. Survivors and second generation had to deal with the psychological trauma of the Holocaust which was not understood for decades. Life at home had an impact on the 2Gs, who had to cope with the trauma of the Holocaust aftermath and being different among their peers. At the same time, survivors and their children moved forward. We never adapted the victim mentality attitude. As hard as things were, we never complained. The sacrifices my mother made in the present were to insure that the future would be better and that my sister and I would live in a free world, able to accomplish anything we set our minds to. Those are the same lessons I have always conveyed to our two daughters, who when I started writing "Memory is Our Home" were in college and high school. Since that time I have watched our daughters complete graduate schools, find successes in their respective fields, and become productive members of society. They have learned not to give up their goals, to suffer through the hard work that it takes to achieve results, to be moral and ethical and contribute by example. I could not be more proud of them.

Suzanna Eibuszyc
March 2020, South Carolina

"Injustice anywhere is a threat to justice everywhere."
Dr. Martin Luther King, Jr., Letter from Birmingham Jail, April 16, 1963

OUR ROOTS IN WARSAW, POLAND
ON MY MOTHER'S FATHER'S SIDE

http://data.jewishgen.org/wconnect/wc.dll?jg~jgsys~jripllat2

Talasowich Gerszon (deceased by 1852)

Talasowich Mordka, 1812

Talasowich Gerszon, born on January 11, 1853

Talasowich Pinkus, born in 1882

Warsaw record #13: Talasowich Mordka, aged forty, married Herbain Rajzla, aged twenty-nine, on September 1, 1852

Mordka's father's name Gerszon (deceased), mother's name Hana

Mother's father's name Szyja (deceased)

Rajzla's father's name Josek, mother's name Baila, mother's father's name Mordka

Some of Talasowich Mordka and Herbain Rajzla's children are:

Record #78: Talasowich Gerszon, born on January 11, 1853 (Roma's grandfather, my great grandfather)

Record #79: Talasowich Abraham Izaak, born on May 17, 1854

Record #80: Talasowich Jachwet, born on January 25, 1857

Talasowich Gerszon

Talasowich Pinkus is the son who married Symengauz Bina in 1901 record #234 (Roma's mother and father)

Our Roots in Łódź, Poland
on My Father's Side

http://data.jewishgen.org/wconnect/wc.dll?jg~jgsys~jripllat2

Scattered bits of information about Ejbuszycs from Wloszczowa, they date back to the years 1858 and 1884, based on marriage records. The two family units were headed by Henoch Berek Ejbuszyc born in 1844 and married in 1863 to Sura Cieselska, daughter of Szya and Malka.

Henoch Berek Ejbuszyc was the son of Jakob and Kayla.

Janas Ejbuszyc born in 1847 in Zarki and married in 1867 to Szprynca Frayda Maltz, daughter of Jankel and Pessel. Janas Ejbuszyc was the son of Judka and Hana from the town of Zarki.

Jcyk Dawid Ejbuszyc's parents' branch of our Father's family, came from Jews of Wloszczowa settled there only in the last half of the nineteenth century.

Icyk Dawid Ejbuszyc, born on May 25, 1876, married Ita Mariem Grinszpancholc, born in 1883.

My father Abram is the son of Icyk Dawid and Ita Mariem Grinszpancholc.

Abram-Chil Ejbuszyc, born on March 22, 1911 in Wloszczowa, Poland. His two sisters and one brother are: sister Sura-Blima, born on October 25, 1904; brother Jakub Szya, born in 1908; sister Dwojra, born on December 10, 1909.

Maps and Calendar of Events

Warsaw

http://www.warszawa1939.pl/index_arch_main.php?r1=strony2/plan_ogo
lny.htm

http://fcit.usf.edu/Holocaust/MAPS/map007.HTM

http://warszawa.getto.pl/index.php?show=kalendarium&lang=en

Poland after WWI

http://freepages.genealogy.rootsweb.ancestry.com/~atpc/maps/poland-
1919.html

Poland Divided Between Germany and Russia WWII

http://freepages.genealogy.rootsweb.ancestry.com/~atpc/maps/poland-
1939.html

Poland Today

http://freepages.genealogy.rootsweb.ancestry.com/~atpc/maps/poland-
detailed-lg.html

Recommended Books

Adelson, Józef; Tomaszewski, Jerzy (red.): *W Polsce zwanej Ludową: Najnowsze dzieje Żydów w Polsce w zarysie (do 1950 roku)*. Wydawnictwo Naukowe PWN (1993).

Applebau, Anne: *Gulag: A History*. Anchor (2004).

Ascher, Abraham: *Russia: A Short History*. Oneworld (2009).

Berger, Alan L.; Berger, Naomi (eds.): *Second Generation Voices: Reflections, By Children of Holocaust Survivors and Perpetrators (Religion, Theology, and the Holocaust)*. Syracuse University Press (2001).

Bracken, Patrick J.; Petty, Celia (eds.): *Rethinking the Trauma of War*. Free Association Books (1998).

Davies, Norman: *Heart of Europe: The Past in Poland's Present*. Oxford University Press (1984).

Dawidowicz, Lucy S.: *The War Against the Jews: 1933-1945*. Bantam (1986).

Dubnow, Simon: *History of the Jews in Russia and Poland, from the Earliest Times Until the Present Day*, Vols. 1–3. Nabu Press (2010).

Eldad, Israel: *The Jewish Revolution: Jewish Statehood*. Gefen (2007).

Flannery, Edward: *The Anguish of the Jews*. Paulist Press (1985).

Freud, Sigmund: *On Murder, Mourning, and Melancholia*. Penguin Books, Limited (UK) (2007).

Friedlander, Saul: *Nazi Germany and the Jews, 1933-1945: abridged edition*. Harper Perennial (2009).

Gross, Jan Tomasz: *Neighbors: The Destruction of the Jewish Community in Jedwabne, Poland*. Penguin Books (2002).

Gross, Jan Tomasz: *Golden Harvest: Events at the Periphery of the Holocaust*. Oxford University Press (2012).

Grabowski, Jan: *Hunt for the Jews: Betrayal and Murder in German-Occupied Poland*. Indiana University Press (2013).

Hay, Malcolm: *Europe and the Jews: The Pressure of Christendom over 1900 Years*. Chicago Review Press (2005).

Herman, Judith: *Trauma and Recovery: The Aftermath of Violence—from Domestic Abuse to Political Terror*. Basic Books (1997).

Hoffman, Eva: *After Such Knowledge: Memory, History, and the Legacy of the Holocaust*. Public Affairs (2005).

Hoffman, Eva: *Shtetl*. Public Affairs (2007).

Karski, Jan: *The Great Powers and Poland: From Versailles to Yalta*. Rowman & Littlefield (2014).

Kirsch, Jonathan: *The Short, Strange Life of Herschel Grynszpan: A Boy Avenger, a Nazi Diplomat, and a Murder in Paris*. Liveright (2014).

Overy, Richard: *Russia's War: A History of the Soviet Effort: 1941-1945*. Penguin Books (1998).

Pinchuk, Ben-Cion: *Shtetl Jews Under Soviet Rule: Eastern Poland on the Eve of the Holocaust (Jewish Society and Culture)*. B. Blackwell (1991).

Polonsky, Antony: *The Jews in Poland and Russia: A Short History*. Litman (2013).

Rabbi Beliak: Telling the Story of Jewish Renewal in Poland: We're in the News. Father Wojciech Lemanski's Bialystok Visit. http://rabbibeliakblog.org/father-wojciech-lemanskis-bialystok-visit/ (Last accessed: 02.10.2014).

Shama, Simon: *The Story of the Jews*. Harper Collins (2014).

Snyder, Timothy: *Bloodlands: Europe Between Hitler and Stalin*. Basic Books (2011).

Solzhenitsyn, Alexander: *The Gulag Archipelago Abridged: An Experiment in Literary Investigation*. Harper Perennial Modern Classics (2007).

T'Homi, Abraham: *Between Darkness & Dawn: A Saga of the Hehalutz*. Bloch (1986).

Teunissen, Harrie: *Topography of Terror: Maps of the Warsaw Ghetto*. http://www.siger.org/warsawghettomaps/ (Last accessed: 22.09.2014).

Wasserstein, Bernard: *On the Eve: The Jews of Europe Before the Second World War*. Simon & Schuster (2012).

Wiesel, Elie: *The Accident*. Hill & Wang (1991).

Zamoyski, Adam: *Poland: A History*. Hippocrene Books (2012).

Acknowledgments

This book was meant to be written while my mother was alive; it was her wish that together we translated her pages from Polish to English. Twice we sat down to work on her pages but my own life got in the way and my mother's wish was never fulfilled. On the day of her death I knew what I had to do. It took time, but in the end my mother's memoir came to life. The first person I need to acknowledge is survivor and Prof. Elie Wiesel. It was in his classes at City College of New York in 1974, at the Department of Jewish Studies, that I first came to realize the importance of my parent's history and the consequences the Holocaust and its aftermath had on our family. I persuaded my mother to put down on paper her eye witness account of her tragic and triumphant life. When my mother died in 2006, it was Prof. Wiesel that I contacted first. He encouraged me to start translating her memoir and not be afraid of the journey ahead of me. Professor Wiesel and I corresponded by letters in 2007 and 2009; his encouragements gave me strength to keep going. "It is important for young people to learn about the Holocaust" he wrote. He was pleased that my mother recorded her memoires "of those dark times and clearly you are sensitive to the suffering she endured" he told me.

My mother's pages were very familiar to me, full of stories she repeatedly told to me as a child, triggering my own memories of how my family struggled to live in Communist Poland after the war to surface. With this book I hope to pay homage to the second generation who more often than not lived traumatized lives just like their surviving parents, not always grasping the effect the Holocaust aftermath had on them.

Christian Schön and the team at *ibidem* Press, thank you for bringing my book into the world. This rich, living document pays tribute to my parent's generation. Committing to memory what they had endured and connecting it to the present makes their experiences meaningful. Thanks to your keen-eyes and hard work, you have rewarded my long journey and made my vision a reality.

I am indebted to Dr. Matthew Feldman, Professor of Twentieth Century History, thank you for being the kind of scholar who acts on what he preaches, for watching over my book from across the pond. Thank you for your guidance and unyielding support. You are an inspiration and a great role model to all students.

I would like to thank Hadassah-Brandeis Institute and Dr. Joanna Michlic for recognizing my work: "Your mother's memoir will become an important source in the historical investigations of social history of Eastern European Jewish women and Eastern European Jewish family in the years

1918-1968." I am grateful for your support and the small grant you awarded me.

I have to acknowledge Cora Schwartz, Judy Weissenberg Cohen, and Rita B. Ross: they were the first women to offer me help and most of all moral support. They believed from the very beginning that this story needed to be told.

Thanks to Katarzyna Markusz, a journalist in Poland who was the first in bringing attention to my mother and me by writing about us in the Polish paper.

Thanks to the editors at Aish.com, Winnipeg Jewish Review, Poetica, Jewish Magazine, The Jewish Writing Project, Women in Judaism, Women in the Holocaust, California Writers Club, and Warsaw Stories for being the first to publish excerpts from my work in progress chapters.

Marcy Dermansky, thanks for your wisdom and the sound advice you gave me when looking over all my chapters.

There are numerous colleagues and friends I would like to thank: Victor W, Alexandra G, Ania P D at the Emanuel Ringelblum Jewish Historical Institute, Warsaw, Poland. Thanks for offering me your help. And thanks to all my Polish, Israeli, and American colleagues and friends: you know who you are, thank you for being there for me on this amazing journey.

I would like to thank my family, my husband, and two daughters. I know that for the last seven years I have been lost in my mother's world. You have accepted my journey, gave me all the space I needed, and encouraged me at every turn. Thank you for your patience and understanding. Bringing back to life my mother's decimated generation is my duty and it also is a labor of love. Isabel, thank you for working on my vision for the book cover, your input was invaluable. Alex and Isabel, because of our trip to Poland in 2008, you have a better understanding of who you are, not just with regard to the Holocaust but with regard to our one thousand years of Jewish legacy in Eastern Europe to which you are forever connected. I want this book to be a reminder for you and future generations that when faced with social injustice, racial and religious discrimination, you should never stay silent.

I dedicate this book to my sister, for whom reading my pages is still painful today, to Roma's and Abram's descendants, and to their generation that was decimated. And to my mother without whom this book would not have been written, who silently watched over me from above.

Suzanna Eibuszyc
Calabasas, CA
June 2014

Edition Noëma
Melchiorstr. 15
D-70439 Stuttgart

info@edition-noema.de
www.edition-noema.de
www.autorenbetreuung.de